AFTER TWILIGHT
Walking with the Dead

written and
created by

Travis Adkins

Introduction by Andre Duza

Cover Art by Noel Hill

Edited by Thom Brannan

Permuted Press
The formula has been changed...
Shifted... Altered... *Twisted.*™
www.permutedpress.com

A **Permuted Press** book
published by arrangement with the author

After Twilight: Walking with the Dead

©2008 Travis Adkins. All Rights Reserved.

ISBN-10: 1-934861-03-0
ISBN-13: 978-1-934861-03-5
Library of Congress Control Number: 2008934057

INTRODUCTION

THE SICKNESS

I SEE DEADFUCKS... I'm watching them right now from my bedroom window; ordinary folks bitch-slapped with a post mortem makeover, shuffling by on drunken auto pilot, guided by wispy, aromatic fingers toward the vaguest whiff of warm blood and succulent, living flesh.

On the television, a beleaguered newscaster stumbles over words like infection, plague, and pandemic, to name a few. He dances around the obvious, referring to the living dead as assailants, attackers, murderous hordes, cold-blooded killers. From the background someone yells, "Fucking zombies, man! That's what they are!"

The newscaster shudders as he describes their modus operandi —ambush attacks and cannibalism. Fear waters down his practiced delivery as he rattles off statistics, approximate body counts thus far, and safe havens with names like Rock Forge and Eastpointe, his eyes encircled by dark rings resting on bags of plump, sallow skin. Over his shoulder, a graphic of the United States decorated by red dots illustrates the spread of the new plague. It is still in its infancy, so rather than admit defeat and work toward a cure, the powers that be exploit the plague for money, for ratings, and for political gain.

The channels come and go quickly as I thumb the button on the remote: commercials for (zombie) pest control, security for hire, privately owned communities surrounded by fencing, or walls, or both. Home improvement shows discuss do-it-yourself panic shelters. Talk shows compete for survival stories and close calls with undead family members and friends. The more daring news affiliates flash images deemed not suitable for children or easily frightened adults: quick cuts of men, women and children being ambushed and eaten, flesh stretching and snapping away from bone. A middle-aged woman screams in a chilling alien pitch as cold dead hands eviscerate her on live TV. They fish out bloodied organs with frenzied grit and hold them before eyes coaxed wide by sublime shock as if to mock her suffering before bringing their catch to mouth and biting down with primal savagery. Sanguine squirts paint the peripheral zombies with abstract strokes from the pressure of teeth clamping down— "Cut away! Cut away!" a disembodied voice demands. **CUT TO:** A vast graveyard sprouts corpses from the soil in various stages of decay like fleshy-barked trees with branches of bone and leaves of dangling meat. The aerial view from a news traffic-chopper reveals entire city blocks darkened by lurching husks. I quip to myself that it looks like a parade, or a protest march gone ballistic.

Overwhelmed by the images and the scope of the crisis, I thumb the "off" button and turn back to the window.

Judging by their docile strides, and the lack of enthusiasm in their eyes compared with their counterparts in the news footage, I assume that the zombies outside my window have yet to experience live human flesh. The ones that knew the taste seemed much more aggressive. Live flesh had become their heroin, or crack.

I wonder if it's me that they smell, and if so, what my specific scent leads their sedated taste buds to suggest. Certainly we can't all taste the same.

I've always prided myself on my ability to see things from other individuals', cultures', and species' points of view. I treat the zombies accordingly. They come with stereotypes (their propensity towards violence, their single-mindedness, their lack of intelligence) and, dare I say "racial" epithets (deadfuck, puss-bucket, shit-for-brains, ghoul, maggot-meat) just like the rest of us.

I find myself staring at my forearm just below the inside of my elbow where the musculature comes to a bulbous zenith like a turkey drumstick. I bite down and wait for the taste to register. My tangential objective—to simulate, out of curiosity, the pain of being eaten alive—provokes me to sink my teeth in deeper. *Besides, how can you really appreciate the experience unless you break the skin,* I tell myself.

I apply pressure like a vice grip tightening from notch to notch, until the pain brings my altered reality crashing down like an acid trip yanked to sobriety.

The framed horizon outside my window morphs pristine—as pristine as the Philadelphia streets can manage. Post mortem makeovers melt away leaving ordinary working stiffs caught in the morning rush. Deep-bellied groans, distant screams, sirens and gunfire are replaced by the hustle and bustle of traffic. Inside, Howard Stern's nasally baritone pours from the radio on the dresser behind me, and from the next room, the youngest of my three sons cries himself awake.

Turns out it's just another morning, another manic Monday as the song goes.

You see... I've got a sickness. Although I've never asked him, I'm assuming that Travis has it as well. If I had to give it a trendy name, it would be something like, hyper-stylized mindfuck syndrome (HSM). The symptoms include sleeplessness, irritability, and enhanced, stylized perception of surroundings (i.e., hallucinations).

You'll find this hard to believe coming from the author of titles like *Dead Bitch Army, Like Chicken for Deadfucks, Jesus Freaks (jē'zəs frēks), n. see ZOMBIE,* and *Necro Sex Machine,* but the hallucinations aren't always about zombies. Considering that the title of the book you're holding is *After Twilight: Walking with the Dead,* I figured I'd focus on those.

They (the hallucinations) often come when I least expect them— while stuck in traffic, waiting in line at the DMV, or languishing in my windowless office from 9 to 5. Sometimes it hits me as I watch my three boys (ages 5, 2, and 18 months) sprint toward me with the kind of uninhibited enthusiasm that only children are capable of. The frame suddenly stutters, their bodies twitch and vibrate into revenant poses. As they approach with stiff, uncomfortable gaits, mouths open wide, teeth gnashing and clacking in anticipation of the first bite, I wonder if I could actually do what Tom Towles couldn't in Savini's *Night of the Living Dead* remake.

Before I found my "voice," as we writers like to call it, movies like that one, and books like *Twilight of the Dead* were my only salvation. The sights, sounds and words had a medicinal quality that both soothed and entertained the beast inside. Sometimes bits and pieces of these "anesthetics" sneak their way into the visions (e.g., the references to Rock Forge and Eastpointe) like lingering side effects of some potent antipsychotic drug.

The upside of HSM is that if you're crafty enough, and lucky enough, you can use this condition to your advantage, even make a pretty good career out of it.

The downside... well, if you live in a fairly large city, you've no doubt come across the occasional homeless person carrying on articulate conversations with empty air. A couple of them come to mind as I write this.

The first was a guy I used to see around 17th and Chestnut here in Philly. Out of the blue, he'd hurry over to a payphone, lift the receiver to his ear and yell, "I AM SENDING YOU THE COORDINATES! YOU HAVE PERMISSION TO FIRE!"

Then he'd just hang up and walk away.

The second was a woman I would pass while walking to the grocery store on 15th and Spruce. She would always be standing in her doorway holding a set of keys in ready position and chanting, "Jagged edge," over and over.

I often wonder if maybe they weren't on to something, maybe we all are. If that's the case, then I suggest you view the pages to follow as a survival manual. Inside you'll find information about where to go, what to do, and how to turn yourself into a badass zombie killing machine known as a Black Beret.

But be warned. These pages have teeth, and their bite is infectious. So watch your fingers.

ANDRE DUZA
January 2, 2006

the END of the WORLD

is a PROCESS

not an

EVENT

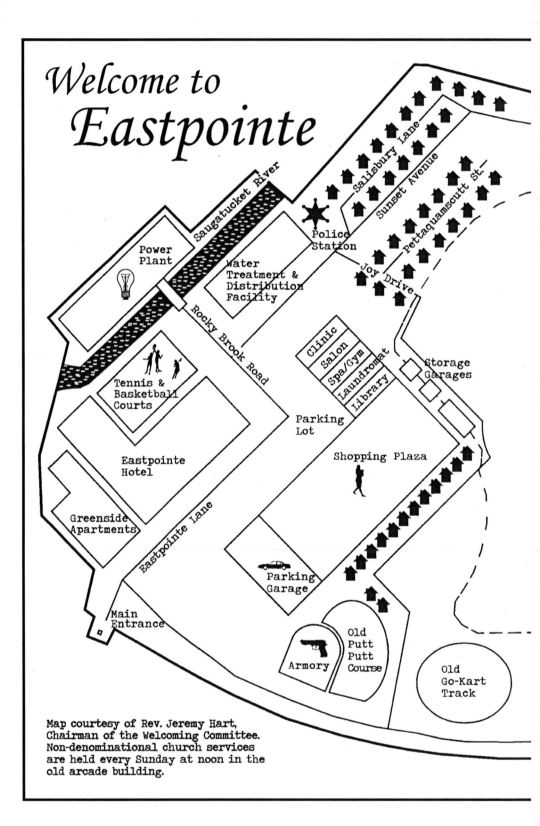

Welcome to *Eastpointe*

Saugatucket River

Power Plant

Water Treatment & Distribution Facility

Salisbury Lane

Sunset Avenue

Pettaquamscutt St.

Police Station

Joy Drive

Rocky Brook Road

Tennis & Basketball Courts

Clinic

Salon

Spa/Gym

Laundromat

Library

Storage Garages

Parking Lot

Eastpointe Hotel

Shopping Plaza

Greenside Apartments

Eastpointe Lane

Parking Garage

Main Entrance

Armory

Old Putt Putt Course

Old Go-Kart Track

Map courtesy of Rev. Jeremy Hart, Chairman of the Welcoming Committee. Non-denominational church services are held every Sunday at noon in the old arcade building.

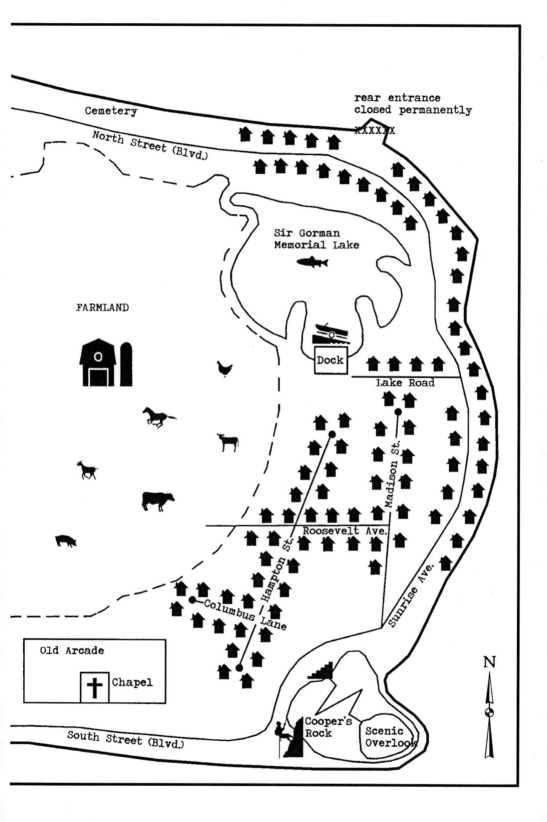

PROLOGUE

Eastpointe, July 4th, Dawn

CLEARING THE GATE WAS A CHORE Tyrell Young would rather not do, but more often than not it ended up with him doing it. Whoever was assigned to do it rarely did, and as elected Marshal of Eastpointe, he always had to take up somebody's slack. He had grown accustomed to that—it was the only way anything ever got done.

"Just stay still," he said, much in the same tone someone would use to issue an order to their dog, regardless of whether they expected their dog to actually obey. "Just stay... *Stay...*"

The zombie on the other side of the gate had its face pressed up against the links, snarling, trying to get close to Tyrell. It had its mouth open and its tongue sticking out and was messily French-kissing the steel wire, lapping its tongue up and down in a way that would probably seem vulgar in any other instance.

Tyrell blindly reached behind him and his deputy Creyton placed a nail gun in his hand.

"*Stay...*"

Tyrell situated the head of the nail gun through the links in the fence and placed it squarely on the zombie's forehead. For best results it needed to be flush.

He tightened the muscles in his arms. Once he was ready to absorb the recoil, he pulled the trigger.

The nail gun jumped in his grip and three inches of stainless steel passed through the zombie's brain, the only sound a fleeting hiss of compressed air. Its eyes immediately fell shut and it collapsed to the ground directly on top of another motionless zombie wearing what was left of a Firado-brand business suit.

Tyrell blindly handed the nail gun back to Creyton and reached down to pick up the big three-gallon plastic jug at his feet. It was manufactured to spray pesticide (the *Orkin* logo had not yet entirely faded,) but it worked fine with kerosene, too. He pumped the handle a few times to prime it.

"I couldn't believe it," Creyton went on, "I flat out said we're not going. So then she says I'm worse than Hideko, and started that whole *I'm-treating-her-like-property* argument. I just had to come right out and say, '*Well, your ex-husband was a dick. And he's dead. Fine, you want to go, go. Just shut the fuck up and leave me alone.*'"

"Hmmm," Tyrell grunted, pretending at deeper thought than he was actually giving to Creyton's problem. He lifted the jug with his right hand while aiming the hose with his left.

"I tell ya, man, she's freaking out about it. I have no idea *what* to tell her. She cried and said I don't love her anymore. Then I had to get all mushy and you know how I hate that."

"But you've gotten so *good* at it," Tyrell said.

"Blow me," Creyton casually replied.

Tyrell fit the hose through the links and aimed it, one at a time, at the twelve zombie carcasses sprawled on the other side of the gate. He pumped a few squirts of kerosene at each.

"Mizuki comes from a different culture. You knew that going in," Tyrell said. "Where she's from, a wife is a husband's prize. Maybe she has so much independence now she doesn't know when to restrict herself—or when it's *okay* to restrict herself."

"I told her the same thing. I don't know why I can't get that through her head. And comparing me to Hideko? Ask me how bad that pissed me off."

"Yeah, that would do it," Tyrell said, placing the can of kerosene back on the ground.

Beside him, Creyton patted his pockets searching for the box of matches. He eventually found them in his shirt pocket and passed them over to Tyrell.

Tyrell slid the box open.

"So you think I should go ahead and take her?" Creyton asked. He was already buckling, the love-struck bastard.

"Does she really want to go?"

"Yeah, she thinks it's tradition."

"Did you explain that around here there's a party commemorating *something* pretty much once a week and the Fourth of July really doesn't stand out as being that special anymore?"

"Like I said: *tradition.* If there's one thing Mizuki's about, it's *tradition.*"

Tyrell mentally re-examined all the reasons why it was a bad idea. Tonight was a scheduled night off, but if they attended the party at the Eastpointe Hotel, they were going to be on duty whether they wanted to or not. The Fourth of July bash—and New Year's, for that matter—was a party he'd learned to avoid. Those holidays fell on moonshine season. The one last year saw three drunken fistfights, and he and Creyton had had to break up all of them and physically escort the gentlemen outside and threaten them under penalty of arrest to go home and sleep it off. He didn't want to go through that again, but it seemed Creyton didn't remember this lesson quite so readily.

Finally he said, "It's your wife, man. Do what you want. Just take extra handcuffs."

Creyton shrugged and picked up the kerosene jug with his free hand. He walked away long enough to return the jug and nail gun to the abandoned guard shack that now functioned as a tool shed.

Tyrell struck his match on the side of the box and allowed it to burn for a four-and-a-half count. He fit it through the fence and dropped it on the zombie he had terminated with the nail gun. The match stayed lit, but didn't land directly on clothing moistened by the kerosene. It had to sizzle for a second or two before it went fully ablaze. The fire spread to the business-suited zombie below and then out to start to consume nine more, traveling on a leg that overlapped an arm or hair that fell across a torso. The final corpse wasn't connected to the others and the blaze wasn't able to reach it.

Tyrell struck another match, allowed it to burn for four and a half seconds, fit it through the gate, and then flicked it like a cigarette butt, aiming at the remaining corpse, which was a good five feet away. The match landed on the corpse's buttocks, and soon the tattered pants were on fire.

"That's skill right there, partner," Tyrell said, pocketing the box of matches.

"Huh-huh," Creyton replied.

They didn't linger any longer. They walked away before the smell could hit them and allowed the bodies to finish burning on their own. Someone else could come back later to spread some lye on whatever remained. All the evidence would be gone within a week, but not before more wandering zombies would find their way to the front of the gate and the whole process would start anew.

To get out of the containment area, Tyrell simply could have motioned to the two men on gatewatch duty to slap a button in the control box and open the inner gate. However, when either gate opened, the wail of a loud klaxon accompanied it. Over the years it was Tyrell who insisted it was for the best that the citizens of Eastpointe not get too accustomed to that noise. He would quote *the boy who cried wolf* as his reason.

He and Creyton took the more exhaustive route. They climbed an aluminum painter's ladder up to the scaffolding that encompassed and overlooked the containment area, hoisted the ladder up after them, situated it on the other side, and climbed down again.

The two men on gatewatch duty, (Derow and LaChance were their names,) cast them a disgusted glance. The meticulous procedure Tyrell had invented was probably the reason they always procrastinated.

"Hey boys, you keep working hard now," Creyton told them.

Derow gave him an annoyed wave and mumbled something to LaChance.

Tyrell smirked, but was otherwise more professional than Creyton.

As they passed by to return to their horses, the Rottweiler that lived in the doghouse nearby looked up long enough to yawn before nestling its head back down and returning to sleep, uninterested. It seemed that of all of Eastpointe, only Tyrell and Creyton were motivated to actually accomplish anything this early in the morning.

Tyrell retrieved his Stetson from the old yield sign where he had left it hanging, pulled his long, ironed and braided hair back, (the perk—or *penalty*, depending on how you looked at it—of being married to a stylist,) and situated the Stetson comfortably on his head. He then gave his horse, George, a pat on the rear and said, "Thanks for waiting."

George was a good horse. He had a gorgeous salt and pepper coat, was largely docile, rarely nickered, and not once had he ever gotten out of line. And since Tyrell had never even been on a horse prior to arriving at Eastpointe, George's easy-going temperament greatly eased the learning process.

He gathered George's reins in his left hand, placed his left foot in the left stirrup, grabbed the saddle with his right hand, and used the stirrup as leverage to spring up from the ground and swing his right leg over. He had gotten so practiced at mounting that the motions were implanted in his muscles. He was proud of that.

Creyton had made the transition from vehicle to horse just as well as Tyrell, and had also partnered up with a stallion. It was a white and brown paint. Once he heard Tyrell christen his own horse *George*, Creyton—that smartass that he was—dubbed his horse *Lenny*.

The transfer from vehicles to horses, however, was not a trend they were able to pass on to the rest of the town. The vast majority of Eastpointe still motored around in golf carts.

"You have yourself a good day, Marshal!" LaChance shouted.

"You, too," Tyrell said. "Stay out of trouble."

He tugged George's reins and moved him into a leisurely walk. Creyton followed, and they guided their horses to the soft shoulder beside the pavement and started heading north. The dawning sun hit them bright and hard from the east, casting long shadows to the west.

Tyrell blew out a slow exhale. It was a day he wanted to be over with, and it was only starting.

Kendra wanted to make a visit to the cemetery today, he knew, to lay a fresh bouquet of flowers on Terence's grave, and to make sure the caretaker was keeping the grass cut to the length that suited her. She would never visit the grave on her own, always insisting Tyrell accompany her, and more often than not would burst into prolonged crying fits even worse than the random attacks of depression that haunted her at least twice a month. This was sadness enough for both of them. Tyrell hadn't had any more tears to cry for years.

Their son had died for no good reason—for *any* reason—at the age of five years, seven months, and fourteen days. It happened shortly after Tyrell and his family, along with Creyton and Mizuki, arrived at Eastpointe five years ago. He had taken ill, and the doctors were unable to diagnose exactly why. At the time there wasn't a clinic and the necessary equipment. After his son passed away, however, Eastpointe started sending out a group of specialists to loot the neighboring abandoned towns for supplies. Among the things they brought back were medical apparatuses. So if his son had taken ill *after* that, perhaps his death could have been prevented.

Tyrell would never know.

The most upsetting memory of all, though, was that span of a minute when the doctor said, "*I'm sorry, Mister and Missus Young; your son has passed away.*" And then the mixed expression the doctor shone them—one of trepidation and anxiety and undisguised fear. He and Kendra had gazed down at their boy in the makeshift hospital bed, and before Kendra collapsed into tears, Tyrell had said, "*He won't come back, baby. It doesn't work that way. Don't you worry, baby,*" he had told her, over and over. "*Don't you worry, baby.*"

All the same, nobody wanted to take chances, though they dared not ask Tyrell to decapitate his son's body. They buried Terence within two hours, near the north wall of Eastpointe where a small cemetery had been developed. Tyrell had mostly buried his son's memory with him, because he knew he had to be strong. He still had a wife to support.

His best friend since kindergarten—and now his deputy—Creyton Hathaway, provided a supportive shoulder. He had kept him on his feet. For this reason Tyrell was able to ignore Creyton's one major indiscretion: the mysterious and convenient death of Mizuki's original husband, Hideko.

He tried his best to rarely bring up the subject. In all honesty, he knew neither he nor Creyton were the men they thought they would be. And they definitely didn't fit the profile of respected law enforcement types—not anymore, at least. Not Tyrell, with his braids and slight gut he was growing—he hated doing crunches—and certainly not Creyton, with all his piercings and tattoos.

But other than the anxiety over knowing he was going to visit his son's grave that day, the morning of July fourth seemed one just like any other. As was the norm, Eastpointe was sleeping in while he and Creyton were already awake to do the grunt work, unaware and unappreciative of the courtesy they had just performed. After all, the smell of the burning bodies would likely dissipate before anyone's alarm clock even sounded, sparing them from knowing the stench ever existed, or that the event had even occurred. Tyrell wondered how often it slipped the minds of Eastpointe citizens that the world outside their walls had been conquered by the undead.

He and Creyton steered their horses up Eastpointe Lane, heading for the office. They had a refined and perfected schedule, and they stuck to it. Three times a day, (nine in the morning, two in the afternoon, and seven in the evening,) they would make their patrol of the outer wall. They would take their longest break at noon, for about an hour or so, so they could lift weights at the spa. The rest of the time they could likely be found in their office, and during these times, more often than not, was when the Superintendent would decide to visit to pick up his daily report, (which usually always consisted of a simple, "Yeah, everything's fine.") Since he mostly saw Tyrell and Creyton sitting at their desks with their feet propped up, or sometimes throwing darts, he probably assumed that's all they ever did.

Just like when the world was normal, Tyrell knew, it seemed nobody appreciated cops, especially the behind-the-scenes work they had to perform to ensure a town ran smoothly.

"Ah, shit," he heard Creyton grumble. "How much you want to bet he's looking for *us*?"

Tyrell had had his head down, gently picking a twig out of George's mane. He looked over at Creyton. "Who? What are you talking about?"

Creyton nodded toward the hotel. "Speed demon over there."

Tyrell looked ahead. He saw the Superintendent coming towards them in a golf cart, pushing the thing at top speed down Eastpointe Lane. The wheels were jerking and bobbing and weaving, something the original design would have prevented if all the carts' engines hadn't been tweaked. Golf cart wrecks were commonplace nowadays.

"I bet I know what it's about."

"Yeah," Creyton agreed. "I'm thinking what you're thinking."

Ervin Wright, the Superintendent, slammed his cart to a screeching stop next to the shoulder where Tyrell and Creyton had halted their horses. He hopped out.

"You weren't at home, you weren't in your office," he said, looking frazzled. His gray hair was a mess. "I've been looking for you all morning."

"And here you find us," Tyrell politely replied.

Ervin opened his mouth to say something he obviously felt was very important, but Creyton stopped him by blurting, "You'd better keep that thing at a safe speed, sir, or you'll wind up with a speeding ticket."

This statement seemed to make Ervin lose his train of thought, and with his mouth still open he glanced from Tyrell to Creyton and then back to Tyrell again. He didn't understand the humor, and probably wasn't sure if Creyton was joking or not. Actually, Tyrell wasn't sure either, because Creyton wasn't smiling.

"*Marshal*," he finally stammered, looking up at Tyrell, "the Black Berets didn't return last night. I'm going to have to ask you and your deputy to mount a search and rescue. They took Dr. Dane with them. They can't be far; they were only going to Point Judith, by way of Wakefield."

Tyrell and Creyton exchanged glances. Creyton rolled his eyes.

"This is all news to us," Tyrell said after a silent moment, folding his hands on the horn of his saddle and looking stylishly at ease. "You'd think that as elected Marshal and Deputy of this town, we'd be kept in the loop on such important matters." He looked over at Creyton. "Wouldn't you think that, too, Crey?"

"Why, I sure would," Creyton replied, nodding.

"Well, I'm just very terribly sorry I didn't inform you gentlemen of the situation," Ervin snapped. "I didn't want to infringe on your already busy schedule. But the fact remains that seven lives are in danger. That should be important enough."

For too many reasons to list, Tyrell simply replied, "We can't do that."

It shocked Ervin nonetheless. "And just why not?"

Tyrell gave him one reason: "We're only concerned about what goes on *inside* the walls. In fact, that is our one and only job description."

It wasn't as if they had never left Eastpointe before. Back in the early days, they had been the ones to go out and spray paint directions to the safe community on every billboard they could find. They felt other survivors deserved the same respite they were lucky enough to stumble on. The prospect of going out *again*, however, especially under the circumstances of not even knowing the full story, wasn't appealing at all, or even worth considering.

All Tyrell knew was based on what he could piece together from the gossip he heard around town; the Superintendent was keeping everything hush-hush. He knew someone had arrived at Eastpointe's gate two days ago—the first newcomer to show up in at least two years, in fact—and this man, Dr. Dane, (his name presumably was,) was immediately escorted to the hotel. The Black Berets, (the specialists sent on looting missions years before,) were summoned soon after and the next morning they were sent, with Dr. Dane, back through the gate. Why, though, only a select few knew, and Tyrell and Creyton were not among those select few.

"You only have to go to Point Judith and back," Ervin pleaded. "I know the route they took."

"What's at Point Judith?" Creyton inquired.

Ervin shot him an impatient look. "I'm not ready to disclose that information, Deputy Hathaway, and it's none of your concern."

There was still a lingering part of Tyrell that wanted to say, *well then kiss my well muscled black ass, right there—see it—pucker up*, but he had been a responsible man for too long. He had grown out of such antics. Instead he said, "We're going to have to officially deny your request for a search and rescue, Superintendent. I apologize."

He noticed then, for some odd reason, how much his voice drawled. Wearing the Stetson seemed to cause it.

Ervin returned to his golf cart, stomping mad, though he disguised it as best he could. He threw himself into the seat—nearly bumping his noggin on the roof—pressed the button to re-engage the engine, and threw his gaze back over at Tyrell and Creyton.

He informed them, with teeth slightly gritted, "Danny Tasker got drunk and wrecked the bar last night. Go arrest him. Keep him at least a week this time. Now is *that* in your job description?"

Tyrell nodded. "If eyewitness statements attest to your accusation, then *yes*, I think we can handle that."

Ervin nodded back. "Fine."

He pushed the accelerator and tore off down the road, probably continuing his quest for someone gullible enough to venture through the gate and find his missing team. He turned onto South Street and disappeared around the parking garage.

"*Danny Tasker*," Creyton snarled. "That fucking dirtbag."

"Yeah," Tyrell replied. Despite what he had said to the Superintendent about needing eyewitness statements, he knew that if there was an accusation made regarding Danny Tasker, it was probably true. The man was a waste of life. Tyrell tried not to take him too personal. "He's probably still passed out in the bushes somewhere. Let's give him time to find his way home. We'll go pick him up this afternoon."

Creyton agreed, and they headed for the office to relax until they would have to make their first patrol. They avoided bringing up the subject of the missing Black Berets. It was one of the few things that wasn't any of their business.

THE DEAD WALK

Independent sources verify claims of bodies returning to life and attacking the living

Associated Press

ATLANTA—Officials at the Center for Disease Control released a statement earlier today that has met harsh rebuttals from skeptics. The CDC, who has been criticized as of late for being unable to determine the virus responsible for the pandemic sweeping the globe, fired back by publishing their findings openly on the world wide web.

The findings of their study claim that, regardless of whether the cause is viral or non-viral, "...we deem [independent reports] fully accurate. The victims of this outbreak are DECEASED, by all current scientific knowledge and methodology, and reanimated with little to no cognizance."

The statement further reports that tests performed on victims revealed that they "show no blood pressure, no pulse, and require no oxygen to remain functional."

Reports released early in the outbreak referred to victims as "homicidal maniacs," and "participants in mass hysteria." Later reports called them "misshapen monsters."

The CDC report falsifies those claims, and lends credibility to eyewitness testimony that some of the first victims had stumbled out of morgues and funeral homes.

Dr. Allison Fischer, a recent transfer from Britain's Viral Studies Institute, stated that, "Survivors of attacks fall ill in a matter of hours. All who died following an attack reanimated and became hostile."

Her statements in the CDC report also declare that "victims show indications that they were partially devoured," though Fischer herself adds, "I am NOT ready to officially state that the reanimated dead view the living as a viable source of food, NOR do I condone shooting the victims."

This statement is regarded by many supporters to be made only to appease the concerns of the ACLU and human rights activists, who remain steadfast in their stance that victims should still be treated with the utmost care and respect.

Other reports coming out of Atlanta advise to "Isolate and quarantine anyone who had physical contact with the reanimated dead."

However, many unsanctioned news reports stress to the public, "These are not your family members or your friends. They will not respond to such emotions. They must be destroyed on sight, either by destroying the brain or separating the brain from the rest of the body. Anyone who has died should be cremated immediately. There is no time to make formal funeral arrangements."

These statements are the primary
SEE DEAD WALK, PAGE 2-A

PART ONE

Leon Wolfe

LEON WAS GROWING NUMB. He couldn't feel the rooftop as his knees and palms rubbed against it, or even the warmth of the sun on his back. He knew the black and bubbly surface of the rooftop hoarded the sun's heat and was typically quite unforgiving in the manner it displaced that heat onto tender human skin, but he felt absolutely nothing at all and he wasn't sure why.

He figured he should easily be able to feel these things, what with it being the middle of a midsummer day and the sun being directly overhead with nary a cloud in the sky to obstruct it. Surely his back was sunburned by now—and probably peeling—but there was no pain to verify it. Even now there were rather colorful reminders on his body as to just how blisteringly hot it truly was, but he simply could not feel the pain.

He tried not to think about these things too much, and when he wasn't focused on the rooftop it simply wasn't there, a pure whiteness—a *nothingness*. If he didn't imagine it then it wasn't conjured. He preferred it that way.

He was feeling rushed, as if he had a lot to do and not a lot of time to do it in.

Beneath him, Courtney had the privilege of using their abandoned uniforms as a makeshift mattress, thereby preventing her naked body from coming into contact with the rooftop. Also, any direct sunlight was blocked by Leon's body, casting a protective shadow across hers. She was safe from the heat, and certainly all she could feel was him.

Despite Leon's worries about his own condition, he continued their intercourse in a steady fashion, refusing to let his anxieties disturb his rhythm. After all, sex was the only distraction he and Courtney had. Sex was welcome. Sex was pleasant. Sex was *easy*. And he knew without it they would probably go downright insane.

Hordes of zombies were amassed on the streets below. Around the building the undead had gathered; thousands of them shoulder-to-shoulder as they clawed away at the bricks in a desperate attempt to somehow reach the food stranded five stories above. Throughout the night they had never ceased their riotous behavior. Their cries were shrill and wretched.

But the dead could not find a way up, nor could the living find a way down. As this standoff—this *stalemate*—burned more and more hours, the living male and female had found a way to better pass the time. The rooftop had become an oasis in a deserted wasteland, a plateau above the plains of extinction, an island in a sea of the dead.

Below, the living dead—once individual people with hopes and dreams—now seemed just a collective conscience, a mile-long mass with a single goal: *To eat.*

Leon blocked out all thoughts of them, and when he did, they went white. They were *nothingness.* He preferred them that way.

He gazed down at Courtney.

Every inch of her was inviting. Her pelvis gyrated in sync with his motions, her face a visage of ecstasy, her hands working him over with a soft sensuality. She was playing her part perfectly, making him feel exactly as he wanted to feel at that moment, occasionally whispering pleasantries into his ear as their chests rubbed together through a layer of sweat, her nipples rubbing hard against his skin and her smallish breasts squishing cutely against his stomach. She felt wonderful.

Since losing his ability to feel warmth, Leon's mind had begun chanting a single phrase over and over: *Please don't let me lose THIS feeling.*

But then, of course, she had to go and ruin it by talking. Between thrusts she panted, "Yeah, I think... *ungh*... it could work out between us... *ungh, oh god...* I think you and me is a good... *ungh...* idea. As long as you don't talk too much... *ungh...* ('cause I hate your accent)... *ungh...* and you let me call the shots... *ungh...* and do what I tell you... *ungh...* I think we could work out."

He wanted to tell her to shut up. After all, he was *dying* here.

Her soft brown hair spilled across the discarded uniforms beneath her, some stray strands sticking to her cheeks due to the sweat pouring from her body. She was moaning to the rhythm of his thrusts, lost in pleasure, unaware of anything else. However, as her hands rubbed him up and down, they suddenly stopped to examine a wound on his shoulder.

It was a small gash that had stopped bleeding long ago. It was circular in nature and perhaps three or four inches wide. Still, the ramifications of the wound—the *consequences* of it—continued to linger, haunting their thoughts. Even now her fingertips were tracing it.

She whispered, *"They bit you. Goddamnit, Leon, they bit you. Now you're gonna die."*

He put his head down, burying his face in her neck, tasting her sweat, drenching his face in it. He started thrusting harder and faster, his eagerness more carnal than before. He wanted to tell her not to talk—not to mention the bite wound on his shoulder. Certainly if he was able to forget about it then nothing bad would happen. Maybe it would go white, like the rooftop and the zombies below.

He started to lose the feeling of pleasure of being inside her, on top of her, and all over her. It began in his legs—the numbness—and spread up his body and out every one of his appendages.

No, no, no.

He thrust harder and faster, trying to bring the feeling back— trying to keep his body warm as it was undeniably growing cold.

Below him Courtney panted, *"Ah! Leon, don't stop!"*

Yeah, great, he thought, *I'm dying and this chick is climaxing.*

He was breathing faster now, penetrating her with greater ferocity, gritting his teeth. The squeeze of her legs around his hips went entirely unfelt. Her muscles, inside and out, convulsed and pulsated, then relaxed. Even this went unfelt.

He stared down at her. Her pretty face was no longer registering to him as an object of beauty, or even lust. Now it was something else entirely.

He stopped all his motions.

She opened her eyes to return his gaze. The corners of her lips were curved upward slightly in a post-coital smile, but it quickly faded. Her eyes opened even wider as she saw something in his face that she did not like. Her jaw dropped as her head fell back.

She was trying to crawl out from beneath him.

She was scared. Panicked.

He grabbed her hair and held her tight.

"No!" she screamed. "Stay alive, Leon! Stay alive!"

Something was different now—something he could not understand. All tactile senses were gone. All love, lust, fear—gone.

No emotion.

There was only instinct.

He opened his mouth over her right breast, taking it in, wrapping his lips around it and tasting her skin on his tongue. He brought his teeth together, tearing through her flesh, tasting the coppery sweetness of her blood as it spilled through his teeth and across his lips. He pulled his face away, keeping some of her skin as a souvenir, dangling from his mouth like carrion in a vulture's beak, her skin stretching at first then snapping like a rubber band pulled too far.

Courtney was screaming.

No emotion.

Once he chewed up and swallowed the skin from her breast, he held her down and began biting more and more of her, eager to taste all the different parts of her body. Blood spewed from her broken skin in several small geysers—all areas where veins had been severed by the snapping of his teeth. It pooled onto the uniforms beneath her, soaking them, changing the bright turquoise colors to a lackluster shade of rust.

This was satisfying to him.

This was how things were meant to be.

She was gradually giving less and less resistance, at first trying to push him away, but then accepting that she was conquered.

She passively gave herself.

So he ate her.

He stood then, his naked body covered in her blood, oozing down his chest and over his groin. Upon seeing him, the zombies on the streets far below started cheering in their own simple fashion. They seemed jealous of him in some way—jealous of the meal he had partaken.

He opened his mouth. Perhaps he wanted to tell them that this one was his and his alone. Perhaps he wanted to ask them to join him in his feast of her flesh. Perhaps he wanted to thank them for biting him and making him one of their number...

—One of LEGION.

Perhaps...

But there was nothing. Just a breathless moan.

There was no cognizant thought.

There was no emotion.

There was *nothing*.

ROCK FORGE
Army Research Laboratory

Research Results – Part 4 (abridged for review)
Compiled by Dr. Dalip Patel (civilian status)

<u>Title:</u> <u>Reanimated Dead exhibit primal fear of FIRE.</u>

Observation: Reanimated dead (RD's) are unaware of their own
mortality.

Specifics: RD's will not respond to threats to their existence.

Example 1: RD's have been observed to cause themselves bodily
injury, without recoil, while attempting to reach a
living target.

Example 2: Attempting to dissuade/threaten a [reanimated dead]
using the stimulus of a firearm does not produce a
favorable result.

Hypothesis: RD's do not comprehend the threat/danger of firearms.

Proof:

(1) -RD's: 2: Subject "A" and Subject "B"
(Previous nationality, race, age, gender, etc., of
subjects are inconsequential.)
-One room, controlled environment.

(2) -Subject "B" is terminated via bullet to the brain.
-Subject "A" witnesses termination.

(3) -In turn, firearm is directed at Subject "A".
-Subject "A" does not respond to the threat.

Observed: Reanimated dead do not comprehend threat of firearms.

Return to hypothesis.

Theory: Reanimated dead exhibit primal fear of fire.

Instrument: A crude torch devised from a table leg, rags, and
kerosene. (Torch was ignited under controlled
conditions.)

continued...

Test: Fire was directed at Subject "A"

RD Subject "A" was observed to perform the following actions:

- Ceased all attempts to reach living target
- Attempted to escape
- Vocalized audible noises (categorized as screams)
- Directed face away from flame
- Cowered
- Attempted to use arms as shield

Video of test proceedings available upon request.

Conclusion: **REANIMATED DEAD FEAR FIRE.**

Addendum: Most RD's were formerly civilian population.

Most will still be clothed.

Clothing is flammable.

Furthermore, skin dehydrates after 48 hours.

Skin is flammable as well.

Dr. Dalip Patel

Personal Notes:

I consider these findings to be a breakthrough. If our armed services numbers are not too far depleted, I suggest equipping personnel with flamethrowers.

Likewise, I am very intrigued that our enemy is a very primal foe.

It puts things into perspective.

＊ ＊ ＊ ＊ ＊

IT WAS ROUGHLY SEVEN O'CLOCK IN THE MORNING, (if he were to guess,) as Leon jerked his head up from the cradle of his arms and opened his eyes for the first time in several hours. As he took in the scenery he began making the mental transition from the fake world to the real world and trying to differentiate between the two. These first few moments were difficult.

He could somewhat recall waking several times earlier, and each time Courtney had been sitting across from him, leaning against a wall that didn't exist before, and she would solemnly say *'I'm sorry, Leon,'* as she lifted her gun and shot him in the forehead.

But none of that must have really happened. It was all just fevered dreams.

Even as his thoughts were still adjusting, there also came a great tide of information—an influx of memories reminding him how he ended up in this situation. It was a lot to digest all at once.

Still, what was real and what had been a dream?

The rooftop was real enough. It hadn't gotten hot yet, however, since the sun was only now peeking through the alleyways of Wakefield. Leon was resting against the short wall at the edge of the building, his knees bent and his elbows situated upon them, creating a makeshift pillow for his slumber. Even through his uniform he could feel the bricks against his back and the coarse consistency of the rooftop against his posterior.

He could *feel* these things. For that he was thankful.

His ears were next to adjust, hearing the sounds of the real world. First he heard birds as they sang their praises to the natural glory of a Rhode Island morning, their calls answered by other birds in the area and producing an endless cycle—an ode to life and the living.

Next he heard the sounds of the *unliving*—the walking corpses that held the rooftop under siege from their positions on the streets and sidewalks far below. The combined sounds of their shuffling feet reminded Leon of gritty sandpaper rubbing against unfinished wood. Yet the noise was incessant—*neverending*—as was their breathless groans. Directly behind him he could hear thousands of feet colliding with metal. He knew these were the sounds of the walking corpses ascending the fire escape across the alley, attempting to get as close as possible to their food.

But there was no way over to the rooftop where Leon was stranded. There had once been a long piece of grating that acted as a bridge between the two buildings, but Courtney had wisely sent that bridge plummeting down the alley.

So Leon was safe, he knew, at least from being eaten.

—But Courtney?

Where's Courtney?

Leon lifted his head higher until he had it fully upright and was able to rest it against the wall behind him. His vision was blurry at first, but soon he was able to see Courtney crossing the rooftops. She was still in her uniform, sans visor and beret, and she was carrying a blue satchel bag in her left hand. In her right hand she had a firm grip on .45 Socom handgun. Rooftops in her direction were flush, with no alleys in between, so the most she had to do was step over the short walls that divided the buildings.

As she lifted her leg to cross over to Leon's rooftop, she raised her gun hand just a little. Not much, but it was a noticeable twitch.

"*Don't shoot*," Leon said, forcing emphasis into his voice to make certain he would be heard loud and clear. "I'm not dead."

She showed a nervous smile and replied, "I know."

She finished stepping over the wall and made her way to Leon, tiredly dragging her feet. When she got close to him she all at once collapsed to her butt and sat with her legs folded. She dropped the satchel bag with disregard and holstered her gun on her right hip. Her face fell into her palms soon after. She rubbed her forehead with her fingers, her hair slipping out from where she had had it tucked behind her ears and falling messily across her face. She looked weary.

"*Nothing*," she said, mostly mumbling. "He had nothing. No food. No water. Not even coffee. You'd think that as much coffee as that bastard drank, he'd have some with him. And I don't even *like* coffee."

Leon glanced at the empty satchel bag. He blinked hard and gulped, realizing now just how dry his throat had become. His saliva was thick and sticky. Swallowing was uncomfortable.

He lifted his gaze and again focused on Courtney. She was about five feet away; close enough to him, perhaps, so that she wouldn't feel alone, yet far enough that she would have time to react in case he turned into one of the undead.

He was starting to understand how her mind operated. It wasn't mere luck that she had survived as long as she had.

He could hear her sobbing. Her head was trembling and her belly was convulsing, showing that she was trying to keep herself under control. Her palms were tight against her face as she was leaning forward, her head so low it was nearly touching her knees. Leon knew she had to be very exhausted and very frustrated.

"So what were we talking about before I dozed off?" he asked, trying to garner her attention.

She mumbled through her hands, "Which time? You dozed off a *lot.* I'm not even sure what times I was talking that you were even listening."

"*Ice cream,*" he proudly declared. "The last thing I remember is we were talking about ice cream."

Courtney groaned.

"Yeah," Leon continued, gaining mock enthusiasm even though his voice was hoarse and uninspired. "I remember us talking about ice cream, back when you could buy it in bricks. *Ice cream cubes*—you remember those?"

Courtney nodded half-heartedly, her face still obstructed by her hands.

Leon went on, "*Neopolitan.* That was the best, wasn't it? The best flavors in one brick—so good it was like sex in a bowl." He paused, wondering if he could get her to giggle or at least show some kind of sign that she was lightening up. When she wouldn't reply, he continued, "What flavor was first to go? You know, back when the world was normal and you could buy Neopolitan ice cream? There was always one flavor that was scooped out of the carton more than the other two. For you, what flavor was that?"

"Are you rambling or was that a question?" Courtney asked.

"It was a question."

She thought about it, and replied, "*Strawberry.* My favorite was strawberry."

"Strawberry," Leon echoed. He smiled. "You're so predictable. As soon as we get back to Eastpointe, I'll make sure you get some strawberry ice cream. And not that astronaut junk. I'll have the chef at the hotel make it. You ever had his ice cream? He puts whole chunks of strawberries in it."

Courtney groaned, "Please stop talking about ice cream. Okay?"

Leon sighed and let his head drift onto his shoulder, resting it partly against the wall. He mumbled, "I like vanilla myself."

Courtney removed her hands from her face and snapped, "That's enough, Leon! Goddamnit stop talking about ice cream! We're not getting back to Eastpointe! We're gonna fucking *die* up here!"

He saw her eyes, which were red from fighting back tears. Besides that, her eyelids were drooping lazily and open only halfway, at best. She looked downright *exhausted*.

Leon frowned and said, "Sorry, doll. Didn't mean anything by it."

Her head fell down again. She sobbed, "No, no. You didn't do anything wrong. I know we'll get out of here. I *know* it. I'm just so *tired* right now. I've been awake at least thirty hours straight, plus I've been watching you all night. I can't stay awake anymore."

Leon gulped, but otherwise stayed quiet.

"I'm so sorry. I didn't mean to snap at you. I'm just so *tired*. And every part of me aches." She lifted her left hand and displayed her pinky finger. There was a cold wrap around it, but Leon knew what the skin looked like underneath—that it had been scorched to the point of deformity. "And this hurts. Goddamnit, it won't stop hurting."

He nodded sympathetically. He knew she had been tortured by a mad scientist—the former owner of the satchel bag she had retrieved earlier—who had held a lighter to her finger and burned the skin quite thoroughly, just for the fun of it. She had since gotten her revenge, Leon knew, by beheading the bastard five rooftops over. Still, the reminders of what he had done to her were very apparent. Leon had put Neosporin on her finger and wrapped it up as best he could, but he knew only time itself would make her pain stop.

"I wanna try to sleep," Courtney said. "I can't watch you anymore."

"Do you think I'm going to live?" he asked.

"I don't know," she replied, frowning, wiping her eyes with her knuckles. "You got bit, what, at least twenty hours ago? I think you'd be in the coma stage by now. But maybe it could still happen. Maybe it's just going to be slower, take longer."

Leon swallowed hard and looked away. He had hoped for a more reassuring answer and was disheartened that he hadn't received one. He shuddered.

"How do you feel?" she asked.

"I actually feel kind of normal, all things considered."

"Well," she said, trying to smile, but failing, "I hope everything turns out okay. I want you around."

"Thanks."

She let her smile fall back to a tired frown, then went to her hands and knees and lazily crawled over to the wall like a housecat sauntering to its favorite blanket. Leon noticed that she was still staying a comfortable five feet away, whether she was intending to or not. She fell on her side, pressing her back to the wall and putting her palms together for use as a pillow upon which to rest her head. She curled up her legs. She closed her eyes.

"But, Courtney," Leon said, concerned, "What if I die? You'll be sleeping... I might—"

She cut him off. "I'm too tired to worry about it right now. *I'm so tired*... I just... I just can't do this anymore."

He heard her sniffle. It caused very unpleasant feelings in his gut, especially when she looked so frail and not at all like the energetic girl that had once punched him in the face.

He decided not to question her again.

The zombies of Wakefield continued wailing in the background. Leon wanted to yell for them to shut the fuck up—that a girl was trying to get some shuteye up here, and by God she deserved at least a little. Hell, she deserved a week's worth.

Even so, Leon didn't much like the thought that it was Courtney's turn to sleep. Now who could he talk to? Who could comfort him? Who could tell him that his face was full of life and color? Who could soothingly remind him that he wasn't going to die, and make it sound believable?

He turned his head to Courtney, debating in his mind whether to ask her if he looked alive.

Just one last question, he thought, *then she can sleep.*

But he said nothing.

Her belly was expanding and contracting in relaxed intervals and the hair covering her face was fluttering near her nostrils. She was already out, or close to it.

He knew such an exhausted sleep like the one she was going into would definitely bring on a cornucopia of nightmares, probably a lot like the kind he'd had. It would give her fits and probably wake her up more than once. He wondered if she would like for him to lay down beside her and hold her. He wondered if she had ever even *been* held.

And he wondered, for the longest time, if he *should*.

He decided against it. Courtney still had a self-preservation mentality, and definitely wouldn't want a prospective zombie cozying up to her.

Leon closed his eyes and held them shut. He lifted his hands and cupped his palms over his ears. The hollering of the dead people softened somewhat, but he could still hear them.

He uncovered his ears.

He reached down and retrieved his .45 Socom. He popped out the clip and eyed the slot running lengthwise up the magazine. He counted only four bullets remaining inside.

He slid the clip back into the gun.

He tested the flashlight pod below the barrel by focusing it on the palm of his hand. A bright circle appeared on his pale skin, but it was noticeably dimmer. Spare batteries were inside the humvees down on the street, and the humvees themselves were covered with walking corpses. But at least he would have *some* light, while it would last.

He began the process of standing. His knees were shaky and unresponsive at first and his legs threatened to buckle. He pulled himself up by grasping the top of the wall and lifting with his arms. Once fully upright, he extended each leg, in turn, and shook out the tingliness. It seemed like there were tiny pebbles jostling around in them and it was a blessing once the feeling dissolved.

Get the blood flowing, his mind chanted. *Get up. Get moving.*

He smiled as it occurred to him that a zombie's blood didn't circulate, yet his *did*. He didn't want to think about it too much so he wouldn't jinx it, but for the first time in several hours he was really starting to believe that he might be okay—that Dane's antidote had been legitimate.

As soon as he appeared from behind the wall, the zombies that had scaled the fire escape and gathered on the adjacent rooftop went crazy. They pushed back and forth amongst themselves, reaching futilely with outstretched arms, clawing at the open air between the buildings. Some reached too far, lost what balance they had, and tumbled over the edge of the building, ricocheting off the fire escape with a metallic *clang* and landing awkwardly on the zombies prowling the alley.

The sun-baked skin-eaters in Wakefield looked petrified somehow, he noticed. They weren't blue like zombies found under protective ceilings. Their skin was leathery and wrinkled yet still stretched tight over their bones like a layer of rubber. A few were completely naked, their clothes having fallen away thread by thread over the past five years, leaving their shriveled penises dangling unobstructed like proud nudists.

They continued staring at Leon from across the alley with glazed-over eyes. Two more reached too far and lost their balance, sending them plummeting over the side. The ones behind them eagerly took their place. They all wanted to be as close as possible to warm flesh.

Leon looked away from them and stepped over to where Courtney was laying. He knelt down beside her, but she didn't stir. Though his next words were not audible, he somehow felt obligated to form them.

"I'll try not to die. I'll try not to leave you all alone up here. You deserve better than that."

He gazed over a couple of feet and saw her sword, still sheathed, lying next to her elbows. He wished he still had his own, but he had dropped it when he was on the next rooftop over, and right now it was under the shuffling feet of all those skin-eaters.

He walked away from Courtney, headed around the rusted central air units, aimed for the other side of the rooftop.

His steps were more coordinated now. The numbness that had caused him such stiffness before was being replaced by the murmurs of pain branching out from his shoulder. He put his hand over the wound there, massaging it over the bandage, reminding himself that it was very real, but for some reason still couldn't bring himself to curse the dead bastard that bit him.

When he reached the other side of the rooftop, he started taking down the pyramid of cinder blocks someone had stacked there, four or five high. There was another dead man two rooftops over, Leon knew. He had blown his own head off with a shotgun, likely years ago when the zombies first overran Wakefield. He was likely the person that had constructed the pyramid of cinder blocks that Leon was currently dismantling.

And—sure enough—when the last block was pulled away, Leon saw what he figured he'd see: *A four-by-four trap door*. This portal would lead him down inside the building.

Leon wanted to find something to drink and he wanted to find a mirror, so he could look at himself and tell himself that he was going to be okay. He wasn't sure if this self-assurance was worth the risk, but he knew there was a good chance he wouldn't come back.

He slid his index finger in the metal loop that served as the door's handle, then yanked the door up with a tug of his arm. It made a dry creaking sound near the hinges. When the new orifice was fully open it unleashed a gust of stale, musty air that was almost overwhelming to his nostrils.

He aimed his gun into the breach, highlighting the stairs with the Socom's minilight. They were dusty and weathered, but looked stable.

He carefully placed his left foot on the first step, then his right foot on the second, then alternated them, going lower and lower, deeper and deeper into the darkness.

He pulled the trapdoor closed.

You've got four bullets, he reminded himself. *Play this smart.*

THE ATMOSPHERE INSIDE THE BUILDING had been contained for twenty seasons now, baking in the summers and marinating the walls in the winters, dusty and dry and mixed with scents of rotted dead things and food that had gone over years before. Leon figured if he breathed this crap for too long it would give him a nosebleed.

At the bottom of the stairs he found a hallway.

He pressed forward, probing through the dim corridor with the Socom's light and immediately discovering a spider web that stretched from wall to wall in front of him. He extended his gun and broke the web apart. It was still tight and it was still strong, so he knew its maker must still be around somewhere. Several strands stuck to the silencer like cotton candy and he grimaced as he used his fingers to pull them off.

Once the web was out of the way, he shone his light down the hallway again. It was lined with doors, all with numbers at about the height of his head, some missing or dangling upside-down from what few screws still remained intact.

Apartments.

Cheap, discolored carpet covered the floor of the hallway with a thick layer of dust settled over it. Looking down, he saw that each step he took left a very discernable footprint. When he shone his light down the hallway, he saw no other footprints. This meant there were no dead bodies in motion—or at least there hadn't been for several years. It was a small blessing.

He crept down the hallway, cringing each time one of his steps caused the floor to creak. He tried the handles on the doors. The first three he came to clicked and rattled in his palm, locked. The fourth, however, turned easily like it was meant to be.

He carefully pushed the door open.

He was immediately struck with a horrendous foul odor. He had smelled it before, and knew what caused it.

Something died in there.

He pulled the door closed and proceeded down the hallway to the next door.

The handle turned in his grip. He eased the door open. Thankfully there was no terribly horrible smell coming out of this one.

His eyes immediately saw a living room: Couches centered around a coffee table, facing in the general direction of a television.

He stepped inside and pushed the door closed behind him. He knew it would hinder his escape if he had to make a mad dash, but he also knew it would prevent any skin-eaters from sneaking up behind him. It was like trading one safety net for another.

The curtains in the windows were drawn back and there was morning sunlight pouring through, bathing the room in orange. Leon turned off the Socom's flashlight, but still held the gun at ready.

There was a thick layer of dust on everything.

There were three more doors besides the exit to the hallway, two on the left, one on the right, all of them closed. He had full view of the spaces behind the couches and saw that there was nothing hiding there. The room was clear.

He took a couple of steps.

There was an important-looking sheet of paper on the coffee table, yellowed with age and covered with elegant, feminine handwriting. He leaned over to read it.

Gretchen, honey, it read, *We waited as long as we could. I'm sorry we had to leave you. They wouldn't let us take you along, because one of those crazy people bit you. I'm so sorry honey. Your dad and I are going to the rescue station in Providence. The civic center. If you're ever able to read this before we come back, please find us there. Please know that we love you honey. Mom.*

After finishing the note, it took a few moments before Leon comprehended what it meant. He lifted his gun again, locking his elbows, and scoured the living room.

He whispered, *"Okay Gretchen, where the hell are you?"*

He went to the door on his left. He turned the handle and pushed it open slightly, then stuck the silencer of his Socom into the crack. He eased the door open inch by inch.

When he finally had full view of the room beyond, he saw that it was a bedroom, still fairly tidy aside from all the dust. There was a bed, (which was so low to the floor that there couldn't be anything hiding under it,) a nightstand, curio shelves, and a big wooden dresser with a mirror perched above.

There was no sign of Gretchen.

Leon walked to the mirror and used his free hand to quickly wipe a clear circle in the middle of all the dust. He gazed into it. The face that stared back at him looked much like the Leon he remembered. There were no visible veins lurking on his forehead, no patches of blue skin, and his eyes were still colorful and not at all glassy. He had the stubble of a beard forming, (two days' worth,) and his sideburns needed trimming. Other than that, everything seemed A-okay.

He thought about Dr. Aaron Dane, the living zombie who had swindled Eastpointe and lured the Black Berets into a trap. He was up on the rooftop now, missing his head—*thanks to Courtney*—and functional no longer. But Leon tried to recall every detail about his appearance.

The man had looked somehow... *cold.* He had been pale and his skin didn't look healthy, but everyone just silently assumed that that was because perhaps he had the early symptoms of scurvy. After all, he *had* been stuck on a cruiseliner at sea for several years. But it turned out that the guy was somehow dead while his body was still very much alive, like it hadn't been given the process of dying.

However, looking in the mirror, Leon was fairly sure he didn't resemble Dr. Dane. He brought his hand up to his cheeks and laid his palm against his skin. He wanted to feel definite warmth, but he couldn't tell what exactly he felt; warm, cold—or just room temperature? Leon wanted to touch the face he saw in the mirror. He wanted to ask it if it felt okay—if it felt *alive*—or if it was just the face of a dead man walking. He wanted an *answer*.

The bite wound on his shoulder screamed then, sending ripples of pain down his torso. But rather than cringe against it, he savored it.

I felt that, he thought. *I can feel.*

He stared at the eyes staring back at him.

We're alive, my man, those eyes said. *We survived a zombie bite. Can you believe that shit? Nobody's ever survived a bite before.*

"Don't," Leon said back. "Don't jinx it."

The eyes shut up.

Leon stepped away from the mirror and exited the bedroom, leaving the door open. In the living room again, he went to the next door down.

He turned the handle with his free hand, put the silencer of his Socom into the crack, and slowly eased the door open.

This room was a master bedroom. The bed was bigger, as were the his-and-hers nightstands and dressers. There was a closet in this room as well, but the door was open and all kinds of clothing were pouring out.

Nothing hiding in there, then, he reasoned.

Half-packed suitcases lay open on the bed. There must have been too much luggage for the occupants of the house to carry when they evacuated, so they left some of it behind.

—Along with Gretchen.

Where the fuck is Gretchen?

Leon exited the master bedroom and went into the living room again. This time he crossed it and went to the door on the opposite side. He opened this door in the same manner he had all the others.

This room was a kitchen. A dining table sat off to the left, with three chairs positioned around it, suitable for a family of three. An ornamental basket of plastic fruit sat in the center. A door on the far right of the room led into a bathroom. A small wrought-iron birdcage dangled from the ceiling by a rusty chain, and a parakeet's white skeleton lay on the brittle, yellowed newspaper at the bottom.

However, Leon spotted Gretchen.

A girl, who appeared to be forever thirteen to fourteen years old, was standing on the other side of the Formica island that divided the kitchen area from the dining area. She was standing with her back to Leon. She was wearing a soiled nightgown, bare feet looking like balloons because of all the blood that had pooled inside them.

Leon reasoned that she must have been standing like this for years.

More amazing, however, was that Gretchen was not turning around.

Leon sidestepped into the room, keeping his back against the wall, rubbing up against matted paintings of flowers and country landscapes and faded checkered wallpaper. He kept his gun trained on Gretchen.

Gretchen still didn't turn to face him. Instead she was adamantly facing the stove, a black skillet in her hand that was hovering over a cold burner. It was like she was intending to cook something and just couldn't figure out what she was doing wrong.

Leon had heard similar tales to what he was seeing—that until a zombie was exposed to a living human being, they would attempt to go about the routine of their former lives, like they didn't yet know what warm flesh was and that they would do anything to taste it. However, (as fascinating as this was,) as soon as living human flesh came into sight, instincts would kick in.

Such was the case with Gretchen.

Leon was getting slightly disturbed that she hadn't turned around yet. For a brief moment he tensed up with the fear that maybe he was indeed a zombie, and that zombie Gretchen couldn't have cared less that he was there with her. He knew zombies had acted the same way around Dr. Dane.

But then Gretchen turned around, and Leon felt relief.

Her face was blue and wrinkly, her eyes pure white, pupils nowhere to be seen. Her jaw dropped open, showing brown teeth, and five years' worth of unswallowed saliva poured from her mouth. She extended her arms and started taking babysteps toward Leon, the fingers in her right hand still locked around the handle of the skillet. She didn't let it go.

Leon focused the red targeting laser on his Socom directly on the area between Gretchen's eyes.

He pulled the trigger.

Three bullets left.

A gaping hole appeared on Gretchen's face and she all at once fell forward. Leon quickly reached out with his free hand and grabbed the skillet so it wouldn't cause a ruckus when it hit the kitchen floor. Gretchen maintained her deathgrip on the handle. Her body was lying in a heap, but her right arm was still in the air, hand still attached to the skillet handle, the skillet itself in Leon's grip.

He gently settled the skillet on the floor, being as careful as he could not to allow even the slightest audible clatter.

Now the apartment was his.

He immediately went to the refrigerator and jerked open the door. As soon as he saw blackened lumps of maggot residue he shut it again. He then went to the cupboards.

He knew it was probably too much to ask for to find bottles of purified water, but he would settle for any liquid that didn't have a *Mr. Yuck* sticker on it. Eventually he found something acceptable: Grape juice. At least twenty-five cans of it. It was all decently cold, and the expiration dates were still ten years away.

Leon thought about Courtney up on the rooftop. He knew she was dehydrated.

"Well, what do you know?" he said aloud. "I can be a hero after all."

* * * * *

BACK ON THE ROOFTOP, Leon gently lifted Courtney's hair out of her face and positioned it to flow the opposite direction. He wanted to whisper his next statement, but had to raise his voice to be heard over the cacophony of hungry corpses.

"Wakey-wakey, eggs and bakey."

She didn't stir, so he put his hand on her shoulder and gently shook her to consciousness. It took a moment before her eyes fluttered open.

Suddenly her head jerked up and her wide open eyes locked onto his. She stared at him for the longest time, unmoving, until she was able to recap in her mind the entire situation, and that he was not dead and that he was not trying to eat her.

She mumbled, "Do, huh? Say what?"

"Well, not eggs and bacon actually," he told her, smiling, "but close."

He extended a can of grape juice to her.

She eyed it suspiciously. Her eyes wandered from the can and focused on him. She asked, "Grape juice?"

"Better than nothing. And it's cold. Mostly."

She eyed the grape juice for a little while longer. Then she eagerly reached out and snatched it from him. She forced her fingernail under the tab and pried it up, then cracked the can open. She put it to her lips and took a hesitant slurp to taste. It must have been satisfactory, because her next action was to tilt back the can and guzzle it down like a redneck chugging a beer.

She finished the whole thing and wiped her lips with her forearm. She asked, "Where did you find that?"

"In one of the apartments inside," he replied.

"You went *inside*?"

"Well, yeah," he said, inadvertently puffing out his chest. "You said you were thirsty."

"I *was*," she replied. "Thank you."

"Come on, let's go in. There's a bed you can sleep on. And it's quieter."

She seemed to consider this for a while, silently, before forcing herself to her knees and then to her feet. Leon put a hand under her armpit to help her. She gathered her things, slipping her gun and wakizashi back into their holsters.

She was slouching and staring at her feet like it was quite tempting to just lay down again and go back to sleep.

She mumbled, "Are you sure it's safe?"

"Pretty sure. I can barricade the door to the stairwell so nothing can come up from the lower floors. I'll make sure you rest easy."

Again she tried to show an appreciative smile, but failed purely out of exhaustion. She tiredly nodded instead.

He guided her to the trapdoor. Her legs were wobbly and she stumbled at one point, so he took her dainty little hand in his own and led her. He half-expected that she would object to hand-holding, but she said nothing. Sometimes the girl surprised him.

They descended the stairs and went down the hallway. She coughed a couple of times until her lungs got accustomed to the air.

They entered the apartment Leon had secured. He closed the door behind them and locked it.

Courtney glanced around, likely searching for any places a zombie could be hiding like Leon had done. But when she was satisfied she was safe, she reverted to her spoiled brat ways.

"It stinks in here."

A year ago he simply would have replied, '*We apologize for the inconvenience, Miss Colvin. Rooms at the Hilton are all taken.*' But now that he was fairly infatuated with this girl he instead said, "Sorry. I'll look for some air freshener."

She didn't reply. She stumbled over to the couch and fastened her hand to the back of the cushion to steady herself. She used her other hand to swipe a bunch of dust from the fabric. It billowed up in a modestly-sized cloud.

She let go and turned around to face Leon again. He expected her to make a comment about the dust, but she didn't.

"I want to get out of this sticky uniform," she said. "Are there any clothes here?"

"Uh, yeah," he replied. "In the bedroom over there." He pointed to the master bedroom where he had seen the half-packed suitcases and the overflowing closet.

Courtney nodded, then went that direction. She entered the bedroom and shut the door behind her.

Leon leaned against the wall to get his bearings. He stared at the closed bedroom door for a few seconds, shaking his head and sighing. Courtney Colvin was definitely hard to please, and—especially since she had saved his life—he felt obligated to please her. But he had found a safe place for them, he knew, so in a small way he felt like he was making progress.

Then it occurred to him: *Oh shit! Gretchen's body!*

He rushed into the kitchen and circled the island. He grabbed the oven mitts from the countertop and pulled them over his hands. He hooked his arms under Gretchen's body and started dragging her. She barely weighed more than a feather, but the skillet in her hand clanged and clattered across the linoleum. It seemed like her fingers were permanently fused with the handle.

He took her out of the kitchen and into the living room, and dragged her around the couch and to one of the windows. He dropped her there.

He turned the latch on the window, unlocking it, then pushed it upwards. The stale air in the apartment transferred and intermingled with the mostly fresh air from outside in a squall. He breathed it in with a smile. It would have been perfect if the wailing of the zombies outside hadn't gotten so audible in the process.

He knelt down and hoisted up Gretchen's body again and draped it over the windowsill. From there he grabbed her legs, averting his gaze to avoid accidentally getting even the slightest peek up her nightgown. Her bulbous feet were heavier than her shoulders and awkward in his grip. Her heels looked like they would explode in a burst of blood at any moment.

He pushed and flipped her over. She exited the apartment in an ungraceful fall, twisting and turning like a ragdoll as she plummeted down the smooth face of the building, her foot at one point colliding with a ceramic potter a former occupant had placed on their windowsill. The ceramic potter came tumbling after.

Leon put his palms on the windowsill and leaned out so he could see the crowd below. He mumbled, "*Incoming!*"

Gretchen's stiff body landed on the sea of walking corpses. She danced on the waves for a while, undulating with the current like a rockstar crowd-surfing a moshpit, before sinking under and drowning in the mass. The black skillet never left her grip.

Leon brought his head back inside. He was ready to close the window when he heard Courtney say, "Keep it open."

He turned around and saw that she had changed clothes. Now she was wearing a t-shirt two sizes too big and jeans that were hanging loosely on her hips and probably meant for someone with longer legs, as evident by the way she was stepping on the bottoms with the heels of her bare feet. She was carrying something in her arms, wrapped up in a bundle.

He wondered if she knew he tried to hide the fact from her that there had been a zombie in the apartment. Just in case she did, he attempted to defuse the situation by pointing out the window and joking, "I spy, with my little eye, something that starts with the letter 'Z'..."

She didn't comment.

She walked up next to him and all at once tossed the bundle she was carrying out the window. It came apart in the air, spreading almost like a parachute, slowing its descent somewhat. Only then did Leon realize what she had discarded: her Black Beret uniform.

He jerked his head to her and asked, "Why the hell did you do that?"

"It was a *placebo*," she said, her face like a stone statue. "Made to make us feel safe enough to go out and risk our butts."

"But skin-eaters can't bite through it," he replied.

"Yeah, tell that to the one with metal choppers that got *you*."

Leon didn't know what to say. He opened his mouth to stutter, but nothing came out. He tried to think of a valid argument but couldn't think of anything. Besides, he knew Courtney could never be argued with. She had a way of twisting his words or just firing back with some crazy retort that completely made him lose his train of thought.

He pulled the window down, firmly closing it. The fresh air was gone, but then again so were the moans and groans of the skin-eaters down below. It was a fair trade.

"I'm going to bed," Courtney said.

She turned to walk away, but Leon didn't let her take even a single step. He said, "Wait. Please. Just wait a second."

She tiredly turned to face him again.

He told her, "I'm alive. Can you believe it? I mean—*Jesus Christ*—look at me." He used his hands to gesture to the wholeness of himself. "I'm *alive*."

"Yeah, Leon," she replied. "You're alive."

He lifted his hand and placed his palm on her right cheek. Her skin was warm and soft, slightly damp with drying sweat. Strands of her hair danced along his fingertips. She closed her eyes.

"I can feel this," he said. "I can feel *you*."

He put his left hand on her hip and stood close to her. He brought his face to hers. He realized then how amazing it was that she was still very pretty even under the circumstances—even when most people wouldn't be.

Her eyes opened as he kissed her. For a moment she stood motionless, merely allowing her lips to be molested by his, and in that moment he wondered if she would push him away and cuss him for daring to touch her without permission.

But instead she kissed back. She wasn't very experienced at it, he could tell, but it was still very nice. Her lips were just what he needed.

There was silence in the old apartment, save for a few shrill howls that penetrated the windowpane and reached his ears. But every other sound was much welcomed: the very subtle smacking of their mouths opening and closing against each other, to the faint scratching sound caused by the friction of their clothing rubbing together.

His hands massaged up her body and slid underneath her t-shirt, innocently yet intently moving ever upwards, savoring the feel of her bare skin. Every single tactile sensation was a blessing. He could *feel*, which meant he wasn't dead.

He cupped his palms over her breasts. They fit easily inside his hands, and were soft and silky and slightly firm. He rubbed her nipples with his thumbs. She didn't object.

His right hand snuck its way out of her shirt, massaged down her back, drifted across the baggy denims she was wearing, straight to the middle of her posterior where her butt cheeks came together to form an upside-down heart. He fastened his palm there and squeezed. Her ass was firm, (as he suspected it would be judging by its aesthetic contour,) and was the most comfortable thing he had ever laid his hand on.

Greedier now, he yanked her to him—*hard*—forcing her groin flush against his so she could feel what he was feeling. He squeezed harder on her ass.

Her fingers had locked themselves around his neck, keeping him close. Her lips were pressing harder against his.

He opened his eyes just so he could see her, and he saw that she had closed her eyes again and her head was tilted slightly to the side to give her a better angle to kiss him with. The heels of her feet were even off the carpet just a little so she could more easily reach—or, maybe it was because he was gripping her ass so hard it was lifting her entire body off the floor. But whatever the case, she wasn't objecting. Her kissing was becoming more and more open-mouthed now, breaths coming and going in faster, shorter intervals, fluttering at times.

His hand came around her hip, giving her ample time to object to what was coming if she wanted to. But when he knew she wasn't going to, he opened his hand on her crotch and palmed it. He heard her breathe a pleasurable gasp. Her eyelids were shut so tightly it was causing soft wrinkles to appear near the bridge of her nose.

He applied more pressure with his hand, and rubbed slightly with his fingers.

This caused her to whine. It was cute.

He lifted his hand up to her navel and started slipping it down the front of her jeans, the coarse fabric scratching his knuckles and her bare skin caressing his fingertips. There was definite excitement down there, he could tell. He heard her whine again and could have sworn her legs wobbled. But he only got as far as fondling the returning stubble of her well-groomed pubic hair before she suddenly pulled his hand out of her pants and stepped away, drawing her lips back from his.

He stared at her, breathing hard, loins stirring.

"*I can't do this*," she said. "*I'm so sorry.*"

She took another step back.

Leon took a step forward, confused and hungry—*ravenous*, even—and she took another step back. He could see her belly contracting and expanding in quick, sudden intervals, and her mouth was still slightly agape to allow her to take in oxygen faster. Her face was flustered.

He knew she was into it. Hell, she had probably never even *been* romanced. Ever.

He stuttered, "What? Why?"

"For a lot of reasons," she replied, sadly. "I'm just—I'm sorry."

He reached out and grabbed her hand. It trembled. He said, "Wait. Courtney... You don't have to do anything. *We* don't have to do anything. Just let me be near you."

She was still for a moment, but then she softly shook her head side to side. She pulled her hand away. She whispered, "I would if I knew you were always going to be around."

Leon's mouth fell open.

He wanted to scream at her that he wasn't dead—that he wasn't *going* to die—that all he needed was for someone to hold him and tell him he would be okay. Hell, he was happy just being in the same room with her and breathing her air.

But Courtney had backed away.

She was in the doorway to the master bedroom now. She told him, "Don't forget to barricade the stairwell."

She entered the master bedroom.

She pushed the door closed behind her.

He heard her lock it, and then rattle the handle just to be extra sure.

ROUGHLY FOUR HOURS LATER the sky had become overcast, threatening rain, and the sun was no longer pouring through the windows.

Leon stripped down to his boxer-briefs and tossed his uniform into the corner. Courtney was right; the uniform might as well have been a blindfold. He figured he could rummage through the former tenant's closet later to see if there were any jeans that fit him.

He flipped the cushions on the living room sofa so he wouldn't have to lay on a coating of dust. He tried to sleep, but ended up just staring at the ceiling.

He stayed as quiet as possible. He hoped he could hear Courtney snoring, or at least breathing. He simply wanted to hear her and know she was there. But he couldn't.

All he could do was ponder other things.

He wondered now if he was really going to live or not.

The moment that that skin-eater had bit him back on the cruiseliner, he knew he was going to die. He hadn't even really put much thought into it, and was actually quite proud of that fact.

—That he hadn't been scared.

But back then he had had something he took for granted: *Certainty.*

He had been certain he was going to die. There wasn't any guessing.

He and Courtney had survived the ambush on the cruiseliner, and had tracked down the undead man who orchestrated the trap all the way back to Wakefield, Rhode Island. There they had met on the rooftops, where Courtney beheaded the fucker, but not before he gave her a syringe that he claimed to be an antidote for a zombie's lethal bite.

Courtney had injected Leon with that antidote, and ever since, Leon was no longer certain about *anything.* However, now it did seem he was actually going to survive—and with survival, and all this time alone, he had nothing else to do but ponder the consequences of it, and curse his conscience.

He had always had survivor's guilt—*and who amongst those that survived the apocalypse didn't*—but this was a different kind of survivor's guilt altogether. Not only was he stuck in an ancient apartment of the old world, but if he didn't die of the zombie's bite he would die of dehydration or starvation. Who was he kidding? He and Courtney were never going to be able to escape without getting eaten by the pasty-skinned people-eaters surrounding the place. Besides, it was fitting. His friends were dead, after all.

Delmas Ridenour, who had left behind a girlfriend back at Eastpointe, Cindy Hayes... Leon would have to explain to her what had happened. And there was their other close friend, Mike Newcome. He was dead too. The four of them played badminton together all the time when the weather was warm, and when it was cold they played handball in the Eastpointe Hotel.

But there were others: Christopher Gooden and Vaughn Winters. Though Leon didn't know those two that well, he would still miss knowing they were at his side, or even there at Eastpointe in case he ever felt the urge to talk to them.

Leon wished he *would have* talked to them more.

It was all too much to comprehend all at once. It was overwhelming.

They screamed at him in his mind. His last images of them replayed on the insides of his eyelids: mechanized zombies biting into their skin, ripping through their trylar suits and carving through their flesh with their razorblade-like teeth, blood pouring.

Blood. So much blood.

...Vaughn Winters dying in his arms, absolutely covered in it.

Leon cringed and balled up his fists, letting them lay on his eyes. He tried to be quiet, though. He didn't want Courtney to hear him.

Greetings from aboard

The Atlantic Princess

Make waves with us!
Sail like royalty!

From Dr. Aaron Dane
_____

workstation 147
_____

Shall I remind you that you took me out of my home and put me on this ship against my will? Shall I remind you that I am not American? Shall I remind you that I am being forced to serve a government that is not my own? Shall I remind you that my degrees are in mathematics, *not* biology? Shall I remind you that I am, in fact, a genius? Even by the lowest calculations my IQ score is 168. Or do you know already? Is that why you took me forcefully from my home?

Shall I now further remind you that, for all of the above reasons, I am not loyal to you?

With the merest glance at the formulas, equations, and notes of the researchers around me, I surmise that it is quite possible I can devise a Cure for the zombie plague.

Will I? Or won't I? <u>That</u> is the question you should really be asking.

You want an explanation for what's happening?
Here's one as good as any:

"In looking at Nature, it is most necessary to keep the foregoing considerations always in mind - never to forget that every single organic being around us may be said to be striving to the utmost to increase in numbers..."

---Charles Darwin, <u>The Origin of Species</u>

Past to Present

LEON NEVER CARED MUCH TO DISCUSS HIS PAST, and was never quite ready to open up to anyone about all the people he lost (and the things he had had to do to survive,) before arriving safely at Eastpointe. His life after arriving at Eastpointe, on the other hand, was known step for step by pretty much everybody else who lived there. There was nothing he could hide about that. It was a typical small town.

Leon never had the wildest guess that it would survive and thrive. It was just a private community on the coast of Rhode Island, but it had its own power plant and water treatment facility, though neither was operational in the early days since a lot of the employees had evacuated. Most of the town was still under construction, but it was encompassed by a massive wall that kept out the skin-eaters. Everything was touch-and-go at first and nobody was really certain that they were going to be safe there for long.

Even so, Eastpointe became a melting pot of survivors along the east coast. Its success was owed to nothing more than a lot of lucky coincidences coming together all at once. The right people showed up at the right time—people who were skilled enough to get electricity and clean water flowing, people who knew how to finish the construction of houses and weld bars on the windows, people who were sane enough to create *order*. There was even a batch of licensed doctors and physicians there, who had just happened to be on the eighteenth and final hole of their golf vacation when the zombie outbreak began, and decided that staying in Eastpointe was their surest bet.

But at the time, Leon was just a kid and didn't really have a lot to contribute aside from manual labor and lunch line duty.

His father was a Wolfe and his mother was a Van Slyke. Both families were successful and moderately wealthy, and everyone assumed that the offspring of a union between the two would surely be destined for great things. For Leon, that great thing *would* have been baseball. After all, his uncle had made the major leagues.

At the Eastpointe Plaza, Leon found a baseball bat and a stockpile of baseballs. He decided that using them up was the best way to say goodbye to the life he once knew. It was a familiar activity he could do *one last time*. It would be somehow appropriate.

He hauled the box of baseballs to Eastpointe's main gate. He was there for the longest time, simply tossing every ball in the air, in turn, and striking them with the bat, swinging for the fences, his expression a mix of resentment and dismay. His pop-flies would sail over the wall and disappear somewhere in the distance. Part of him hoped they were coming down on the skulls of skin-eaters.

He said goodbye to the grandmother and grandfather who raised him from a toddler, said goodbye to lobster and blueberry pie, said goodbye to the nickname *Rooster* and the departed friends who had so christened him, and said goodbye to the world that once was.

He said goodbye to Yoshida, a man he had met at the rescue station in Bangor. Yoshida was a professional Judo player, and—more importantly—a Black Beret. He trained Leon as such, force-feeding Judo and Tae Kwon Do into the reflexes of his already athletic muscles.

Yoshida was dead now, of course.

It was halfway through these sentimental goodbyes that Leon would discover an angel in his midst. Until roughly five years later when he would become enraptured in the mysterious aura of Courtney Colvin, there was only one girl that ever truly got his undivided attention—only one girl that made him want to be a better human being.

And he met her that day.

✳ ✳ ✳ ✳ ✳

THERE WAS A ZOMBIE SHUFFLING DOWN Eastpointe Lane and the girl was chasing after it from a distance, trying to catch up. But the zombie must have had a considerable head start, because the girl was still a couple dozen yards or more from reaching it.

Leon reeled back his heavy wooden Rawlings and prepared himself to knock the zombie's block off. He was going to save the day.

The girl ran around the zombie, tucking her shoulder like an NFL runningback as it momentarily turned to lunge at her, and dashed straight to Leon. She fastened her hands around Leon's bat.

She screamed at him, "Don't! Don't you dare! That's my *brother*!"

Leon tried to pry the bat loose, but she wasn't letting it go.

She had long, dirty blonde hair and freckles dotting her cheeks that had not yet faded from adolescence. She was probably his age. Tears were pouring from her eyes, though, and Leon didn't know whether to be angry at her doggedness, or cry with her.

The zombie shuffled to within fifteen feet of them. It was wearing only sweatpants. Leon guessed that it had escaped from the makeshift clinic where they were quarantining anyone who was bitten.

"That's my brother!" the girl screamed again. Through the tears, her brown eyes were like poison. "If you touch him I'll kill you!"

With a burst of uncanny strength, she yanked the baseball bat from Leon and he recoiled back a couple of steps. She looked down at the bat in her hands, then looked over her shoulder at her undead brother, who was still approaching.

He was five feet away now.

He was growling, head slightly askew, arms raised straight ahead, fingers outstretched.

The girl turned to face him.

She cried, "Elliot, please, you're all I have. Mom and dad are gone. *Please...*"

Elliot, obviously, could not be reasoned with.

Leon was about to intervene, but the girl raised the bat and brought it down on her brother's skull like a sledgehammer. There was a sickening *crunch* and her brother crumbled to the grass in an uncomfortable-looking heap, knees buckled at unnatural angles.

But he was still twitching.

She hit him on the head several more times, crying, not stopping until her brother's face was an unrecognizable mess and he wasn't twitching anymore.

The bat slipped from her hands and she ran away.

Leon would later learn that her name was Alexis Turner, and that her family had been living at Eastpointe for months. But not as members; her father was the maintenance man at the hotel. They were originally from Pennsylvania, and when the zombie outbreak began, her parents left her and her brother within the safe confines of Eastpointe's walls while they went to search and rescue *their* parents. But they never returned.

Her brother had been infected during a minor catastrophe that was quickly contained, then died and reanimated.

And Alexis did what she had to do.

Leon was interested in her—mostly mere curiosity after what he witnessed her do—but became completely smitten when he heard her sing two weeks later.

ALMOST EVERYONE IN EASTPOINTE gathered for the first party at the hotel. They really didn't need a reason to celebrate *anything*, (as in the years to come they would celebrate absolutely *everything*, from major holidays like Christmas to piddly events like Arbor Day,) but this party was the first of its kind. It was necessary. The power plant was up and running, clean water was flowing to every house, and— most importantly—everyone that was there was alive and well. But everyone was still a stranger, and a party could remedy that problem.

Leon had taken a seat on one of the stools in the hotel's bar, *Suds & Salutations*. When asked what he wanted to drink, he could recall only what he had seen his grandfather drink on occasion: *Jim Beam*. Leon requested it specifically. The bartender at the time, a former cop, passed him a glass of Jim Beam with no hesitation. Leon was only seventeen years old at the time and wholly amused at the irony of it. The rules had definitely changed.

Over fifty people had gathered in the bar alone, while many more were chattering in the main hall and in the restaurant, (which they would later dub the *cafeteria*,) where they had fashioned a dance floor for the middle-aged folks to get their groove on.

Leon preferred the bar, where the lights had been dimmed to resemble a club-like atmosphere. It was where all the younger people were gathering.

The man that sat down next to him was tall and lanky and had long black hair. Leon was hard-pressed to guess his age, but he didn't look that much older than himself, maybe in his mid-twenties. That made him approachable, plus they were both drinking the same thing. So Leon, feeling especially jovial, extended his hand to the stranger and introduced himself.

"Leon, from Maine."

The man shook his hand and riposted, "Xenu, from Teegeeack. But most people call me Vaughn. Pleased to meet you. Words can't describe." Then he nonchalantly turned back to the bar and continued drinking.

Leon didn't put much thought into it. Instead he swiveled his stool to face away from the bar and look toward the far corner of the room where a karaoke machine had been assembled on stage.

The girl who had brained her undead brother with Leon's bat two weeks earlier was in front of the karaoke monitor, its glow highlighting the elfish features of her face while the shadows consumed the rest. She was standing up straight, holding a microphone to her lips, trembling a little.

The background music began playing over the speakers and she opened her mouth to sing along. There was a pause—a hesitant moment when it almost appeared as if she was too terrified to continue. But then her vocals came, softly at first, then turning confident and compelling.

Her voice was crisp and delicate and downright beautiful. Leon figured she must have sang to herself all the time when she was alone and behind closed doors. This was probably her first time doing it in public and she probably didn't comprehend just how good she was.

It happened all at once, mostly, that everyone in the room stopped talking amongst themselves and regarded her with their full attention. Some of the people chattering in the main hall stepped into the doorway or peeked their heads through.

Her song was one that Leon had never heard before. The words went along the lines of: "*There goes my father. He's looking at the sky. I looked into his eyes and saw a river deep and wide. And he said, I will meet you at the water...*"

Leon blinked his eyes several times and looked away. Everyone else, however, had not blinked or looked away. Though their faces were uniquely different, most of them had one thing in common: They were weeping. Some were wiping away the stray tears with handkerchiefs. Leon had recognized the parallels in the girl's song as well, but kept his face straight. Mostly.

Beside him, the black-haired man was in the middle of taking a sip of whiskey. He scoffed into his glass and mumbled, "*It's a Ten Tenors song... She'll skip the chorus. It's in Italian.*"

Leon turned to him. He recalled the guy's passive-aggressive smartness when he had introduced himself earlier. He hadn't really taken offense to *that*, but he knew the ordeal the girl who was singing had been through, and it really irked him that someone had the gall to disrespect her.

This time Leon returned the attitude by sneering, "What's your point? She's *good*."

The man who had introduced himself as Vaughn shrugged and garbled, "She's not *that* good," and took another sip of whiskey. He didn't avert his eyes from the mirror behind the bar. He was locking eyes with his own reflection.

Leon pressed him further. "Can you do better?"

"*I don't sing*," came the very dry reply.

"*Good*," Leon retorted. "So why don't you just sit there and continue being a warm ray of sunshine? *Quietly*, though. You hearing me, *Rapunzel*?"

Finally the man turned his head to face Leon. His eyes were dark and had shadows beneath them. His forehead tightened, causing his eyebrows to form a V. He locked his menacing eyes directly on Leon's, and growled, "*Are we having issues here?*"

Leon went, "Huh?"

He clarified, "Are you looking for a *fight*?" He brought his face closer. His voice was very deep, but didn't rise above a hoarse whisper. "Do I *look* like somebody you can pick on, Mainer? You aren't in high school anymore. Remember that. Start a fight, and I can finish it right quick."

Leon scoffed and turned away, even swinging his stool back around to face the rest of the room, but could still feel the man's eyes lingering on him for several seconds.

Hell with him, Leon thought. *Let him be a miserable drunk.*

He tuned him out.

When the girl named Alexis was finished singing and the music waned, everyone applauded. The man next to Leon mumbled, "*Yeah, well, people cheer at the Special Olympics, too.*"

The girl handed the microphone to someone else and smiled at the crowd. Her face was flushed, but showed justifiable pride in what she had just accomplished, and rightfully so. Her body even seemed visibly lighter.

As Leon had done with the baseballs two weeks earlier, he knew her song must have been her own appropriate way of saying goodbye. She didn't sing it for *him*, or for anyone else in the room for that matter. She sang it for *herself*.

He would learn a lot about her in the coming years. She would tell him stories about her past, about how her family was poor but had wealthy neighbors, and how on every Fourth of July her father would sneak her over to their neighbor's fence and watch them let off thousands of dollars worth of fireworks, the kinds that made loud *kabooms* and exploded in the sky in fantastic forms, some even mimicking the shape of the American Flag. But she was never really jealous because she still got to see them, and that was all that mattered. Most importantly, she would tell him she never really realized she was poor.

Eventually she would even cajole him into singing karaoke with her, and he was surprised that he wasn't a half-bad singer either. Their duo rendition of *Summer Wine* brought standing ovations.

Over time she would grow out of her ugly-ducking syndrome, and one day would dye her hair golden blonde and color the tips a striking red and black, but otherwise she never changed. She always displayed unwavering kindness, and she was always an angel.

THOUGH THE CONNECTION he had with Alexis Turner was stronger than he had with anyone else, the week before the doomed mission to the cruiseliner Leon admittedly—though secretly—had his fixations elsewhere. This surprised him, because the new girl had always been within arm's reach, and he had never *really* noticed.

Courtney Colvin. Any interaction with her had always been minimal until she showed up at his front door under the guise of, *"Hey, I know we never got along that well, but how the heck have you been?"* He was wholly confused by it all, especially when she awkwardly seduced him.

He had suspected it was a trick—a game. He had suspected that she would just get him worked up—get him *hungry*—and simply laugh and leave him with the problem to deal with on his own. Or, perhaps, before leaving she would taunt, *'Ha-ha! It took me a few years, but I finally got even with you! Enjoy your hand you cocky bastard!'*

But she was actually for real.

He had then wondered if the game she was playing was some kind of vindictive one. Moreover, he felt obliged to play her game even if he didn't understand all the rules—or even *know* all the rules. After all, regardless of what game she was playing, she was still putting out. Leon figured that in a way it instantly made him the winner, or at least the recipient of a consolation prize.

It turned out her confidence was a ruse. She neither performed nor wanted anything extracurricular, just the actual act of intercourse itself, but even at this she was clumsy. She said only one word and that was when he asked her if she wanted to stop. She shook her head side-to-side and told him, "No." Even afterwards, when it was over, she didn't say a word—she only gave him a look that seemed to reflect the sentiment: *Is that it?*

She was an odd, antisocial sort. He suspected that maybe she thought it would be like a movie. But the scenes in movies always ended when the clothes started coming off, then cut to the moments after, when the couple were laying in bed smoking their cigarettes.

(The blanket, strangely enough, always seemed L-shaped, since it reached all the way past the breasts of the female yet barely covered the groin of the male.)

Courtney left the next morning, quietly, with a strange, neutral demeanor.

After that, Leon slyly brought up the subject of Courtney Colvin in his conversations with his fellow patrons of Suds & Salutations. Most off-handedly expressed their concern over having a highly-trained killer with an antisocial attitude holed up all by herself on the other side of town. And though she was a mystery, and had no connections anywhere in town, there was gossip, guesses, and speculations in abundance: "She thinks she's too good for us." "That bitch is insane; likes to kill zombies just a little too much." "I heard she's this/I heard she's that." "Somebody should be keeping an eye on her—the unibomber was a hermit, too, you know."

But none of it was true, and it seemed only Leon suspected there was more to this girl than she was letting on. When he started to understand what she was really like, he realized that he really liked her. Despite her hard-edged outward appearance, she was actually just a girl, with all the same apprehensions and fears as anyone else, and too backwards to convey her emotions in a normal manner. It made her attractive in more ways than one.

He would later rescue her from the bridge of the cruiseliner where Dr. Dane held her as hostage, and she would likewise rescue him by injecting him with an antidote for his zombie bite.

They had saved each other.

But it was far from over.

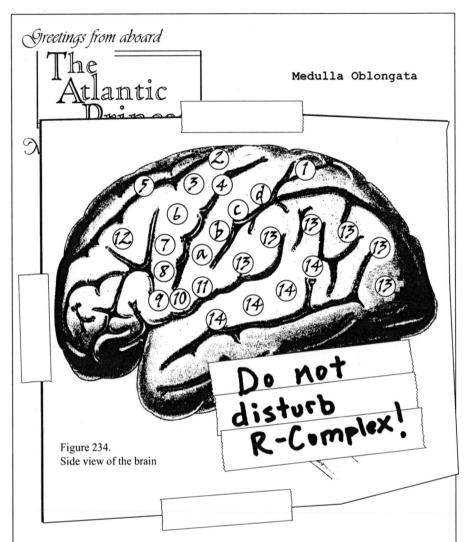

Greetings from aboard

The
Atlantic

Do not
disturb
R-Complex!

Figure 234.
Side view of the brain

1. Center for movements of opposite leg and foot
2,3,4. Centers for complex movements of the arms and legs
5. Extension forward of the arm and hand
6. Supination of the hand and flexion of the forearm
7,8. Elevators and depressors of the angle of the mouth
9,10. Movements of the lips and tongue
11. Retraction of the angle of the mouth
12. Movements of the eyes
13. Vision
14. Hearing
a,b,c,d. Movements of wrists and fingers

PART TWO

Vaughn Winters

VAUGHN WINTERS AWOKE ON A RICKETY METAL GURNEY. It was very, very cold, and there was no padding underneath him or even a blanket laid over him to keep him warm.

The pain was immediate and fierce and everywhere, coursing all up and down his body. He gasped, flailing his arms and knocking over a tray of scalpels sitting next to him. They clanged and clattered. He panicked. He shifted and twisted and turned on the cold metal slab and tried to numb the pain. Nothing worked.

He rolled over and all of his weight immediately smacked the thinly-carpeted floor. An intravenous needle popped from the skin on the back of his hand, squirting a fresh line of saline solution before plugging up. A few drops of blood dripped and soaked into the carpet.

There was a lot of pain in his throat. It had been sliced open, he remembered.

He lifted his hand to his neck and used his fingertips to inspect the crude medical work performed on it.

Staples. Holy Christ in Hell—that fucker had stapled his throat! There were dozens of them, two every centimeter or so, sharp, thick, industrial-strength staples lodged deep in his skin.

His uniform had been cut away unevenly from the waist up, leaving only makeshift pants intact. They were stained brown with blood. He looked further down. His boots were still on, too, and they were also covered in dried blood and small bits of mort flesh.

The many cuts—*and bites?—had he been bitten?*—on his naked torso had been covered over with gauze and duct tape.

He wanted to scream.

But he knew Dr. Dane could be nearby.

He stumbled through the darkness, his body wracked with pain, his long black hair stringy and matted with unknown gunk. He cringed and cowered, eventually colliding with the wall beneath the emergency red light. A welding helmet hung on a nearby hook, but it fell as he bumped into it and rocked back and forth on the floor several times. The resulting noise was louder than he would have preferred.

Cabinets lined the wall. He flung them open, yanking bottles off the shelves at random and focusing them under the red light, squinting his watery eyes to read the labels. He repeatedly flung the useless ones out of his way until he found some that had value.

Oxycodone, Darvon, Darvocet, OxyContin, Vicodin, Percocet. Percocet!

He shook the bottle with his already trembling hands. He heard a large quantity of pills rattling around inside.

He fumbled with the cap, squeezing as hard as he was able until the entire top broke off. Sharp shards of plastic dug into his fingers like papercuts, drawing more blood. It was insignificant compared to everything else. He was mostly unfazed by it.

He poured six or seven pills—he wasn't sure exactly—into his open palm. He opened his mouth and tossed the pills on his tongue. He worked his jaw to build up as much saliva as he could, and then all at once gulped them down.

"Oh god! Oh fuckin' Jesus!"

There was pain a hundred times worse than the most severe sore throat he had ever had, worse even than swallowing razorblades, and when he screamed it only served to exaggerate it. But it was a pitiful sound and not at all worth the trouble. His voice gurgled and much of its intensity dissipated before it could even escape his lips. The result wasn't much more than a wheezing breath.

He clutched his throat and he squeezed, trying to drive the pain away.

He collapsed to the floor and lay on his side. One of the Percocets hadn't gone down when he swallowed, and it still clung to the roof of his mouth. But when he spit it out, he realized it hadn't been a pill, it had been a tooth. There was blood all over it. It was difficult to tell just how much blood he was swallowing.

He mouthed the words, "*Help me. Somebody please fucking help me.*" Bubbles composed of a mixture of blood and saliva formed across his lips and dribbled down his chin.

His vision started getting clearer, adjusting to the darkness. He blinked hard, keeping his eyes shut for several seconds, and then opened them again.

He saw a body at the other side of the room. Vaughn blinked again, and focused. The body was purely crimson, especially under the emergency red light shining from the wall, but soon he discerned the stocky build. For this reason only he knew that the body belonged to Delmas Ridenour, one of his teammates. He lay on his back, arms outstretched, eyes wide open and utterly blank, his body still, his skin certainly ice cold. He had multiple contusions—cuts and bites. The carpet beneath the body was caked with blood. Even worse, Delmas' legs had been sawed off at the knees and were nowhere to be seen.

Did Dane do that? Why?

There was no consciousness in Delmas now. There was a just a dead body, and dead bodies—ones that didn't move—were such a rarity that Vaughn had almost forgotten what one looked like—how soulless and empty they were, and what it was like at a funeral.

He gulped and rolled over to face the other direction, breathing hard and heavy, wishing the Percocets would kick in soon. The VIP room in Fortunes Casino on The Atlantic Princess was spinning round and round and round, bringing Vaughn along for the ride.

Greetings from aboard

The Atlantic Princess

Make waves with us!
Sail like royalty!

Ennui: 0, 1, 1, 2, 3, 5, 8, 13, 21, 34, 55, 89, 144, 233, 377, 610, 987, 1597, 2584, 4181, 6765, 10946, 17711, 28657, 46368, 75025, 121393

March 17

To place me in an environment with biologists was foolish to the greatest extent. There may be no Fields Medal in my future, but this sacrifice does not come without its rewards. I have learned their trade, and Robertson has outlived his usefulness. I can expand on his theories without requiring his presence.

March 18

It was surprisingly good. I can most liken it to veal, fully developed veal, but not quite. Not too young, and not too much like beef. It was very definitely like veal. It had a most distinguishing taste. In fact, I cannot imagine any sane person with a normal palate, and normal sensitiveness, who could distinguish it from veal. It was mild, with no other sharply defined or highly characteristic taste such as, for instance, mutton and pork. It was, however, slightly tougher than prime veal, but I am not complaining too emphatically over this matter. It was not too tough or stringy. It was most agreeable. The meat, from which I cut and ate a central slice, was tender. In color, texture, smell, and taste, this experience has strengthened my certainty that of all the meats I know, veal is the one meat to which this meat is most accurately comparable.

Past to Present

DESPITE THE PSYCHIATRIST'S EFFEMINATE MANNERISMS, or just blatant homosexuality—*he wasn't sure yet*—Vaughn almost respected the guy at first.

"Understand this," the psychiatrist said. "You're not here because you did anything wrong. It's because Leviathan Records has a preternatural tendency of signing... *unstable* musicians. These sessions we'll be having are part of your contract. They've made an investment in you, and they want to protect that investment."

"I figured as much," Vaughn replied.

He wasn't laying on a couch, (though there *was* one on the opposite side of the room, probably reserved for the more mentally ill of the mentally ill,) but he *was* sitting opposite the shrink in a chair that looked like it was plucked directly out of an elementary school. It was degrading. The room was painted an obvious neutral-gray and was sized not too big, but not too small either. Hopefully they weren't completely finished remodeling, otherwise there was no excuse for such poor taste.

Even so, Vaughn was relatively comfortable with the situation, until the man got *fake*.

"I inquired about your music," he said, speaking in an offhand tone of voice as if he and Vaughn were already supposed to be in perfect affinity. "So the studio sent a sampler CD for me to listen to. Honestly, I've never heard *death metal* before—"

"*Death metal* died in the eighties," Vaughn interrupted, matter-of-factly.

"Oh, I see. Then what do you call it?"

"It is what it is," Vaughn replied.

The shrink shifted his feet. "It's not exactly up my alley, but I do admit there is a certain poetic quality about it." He paused to see if he could get a reaction from Vaughn, as if Vaughn was supposed to be impressed by his backpedaling. But he got no reaction. He continued, "Why don't we start by talking about your family?"

"My *family*?" Vaughn asked. "What is there to say? What's the point?"

"It opens lines of communication."

Vaughn played stupid, but it was the kind of *playing stupid* that any intelligent person would recognize and *know* he was playing stupid on purpose. He said, "Lines of communication? You a Scientologist or something? Doesn't that *conflict* with psychiatry?"

Vaughn got the reaction he was hoping for, though not quite as pronounced as he would have liked. The psychiatrist huffed, "Lines of communication are fundamental in psychiatry as well, Mister Winters."

He called me 'Mr. Winters'. I definitely got under his skin.

Vaughn said, "Let's see... my family... I have a lot of family, spread all over, but I don't know them that well, honestly."

"Have any siblings?" the shrink inquired.

"A sister," Vaughn answered. "A twin sister."

"What's her name?"

"Rindi."

"*Rindi*? That's odd. Most parents name twins with rhyming names. Would her true name be *Dawn* or something of the like?"

Vaughn got the distinct impression that the shrink was trying to instigate a battle of wits. If that was in fact the case, then Vaughn gave him a point. But he wasn't that impressed. A so-called *psychic* could do the same at a cold reading.

He said, "Hey, you're pretty good. Dawn is actually her middle name."

"Ah, I see," the shrink said, smiling to subtly stroke his ego.

Vaughn shrugged.

"And what does she do for a living?"

Vaughn almost chuckled. He replied, "She's a *dancer*."

"A dancer?" the shrink echoed, confused. Then he got it. "Oh, I see." He shuffled his feet again, and then he did something Vaughn didn't even know was manly possible: *he crossed his legs.* Not just a normal figure-four crossing of the legs, but a full-fledged *folding*.

Does this guy even have a dick?

Vaughn was losing more and more respect for him with every passing minute.

The psychiatrist leaned forward and rested his elbows on his legs. His tone was very hushed as he uttered, "The questions I'm going to ask you now might be very personal, but I must pursue them."

Vaughn nodded indifferently.

The shrink continued, "Like I said, I listened to your songs. Can't say I like what you did to Billy Joel's classic, but your original works are very interesting. I'm not going to ask you about your religious beliefs. I'll leave that alone. But I must ask: Your song *Forbidden Rendezvous*, unless I'm misinterpreting the lyrics, is that about your sister, Rindi?"

Vaughn pursed his lips and his face tightened. He gritted, "It's just a *song*. I mean—for fuck's sake—do you think the Beatles really live on a yellow submarine?"

"It seemed very emotional, is all I'm saying, Vaughn," the shrink said.

Vaughn interpreted the psychiatrist's reverting to using his first name instead of *Mr. Winters* as a sign that he thought he had regained the upper hand. He knew he had to put him back in his place.

He said, "Tell me something—*what's your name again?*"

"You can call me Hugh," the shrink said.

"Okay, Hugh, tell me... when will I hear your lisp?"

"My *lisp*?"

"Yeah. Your *lisp*."

Hugh seemed taken aback. He replied, "I don't *have* a lisp, Vaughn. I've listened to plenty of tape-recorded sessions to know this."

"No," Vaughn replied, "What I'm saying is that you may not have a lisp *now*, or maybe you're just *hiding* it, but you *will* have a lisp. All fags do."

The shrink's jaw dropped. He stuttered, "*A-wha-but...*" until he collected himself and retorted, "That was very out of line."

"What do you mean *out of line*?" Vaughn replied, keeping methodically civil. By now he was leaning back in his chair with his forearm resting on the back of his head, quite comfortable. "I was just asking a simple question. I mean, psychiatrists realized they couldn't cure homosexuality, so they don't label it a mental illness anymore. That means you can become one, like an open-door policy... Or should I say *Open Closet* policy? *Don't-ask-don't-tell*—like the Army, that kind of thing?"

The psychiatrist dropped the clipboard he had been taking notes on and rested his cheek inside the L-shape of his thumb and forefinger. Vaughn knew he was trying to look bored, as if this confrontation didn't disturb him. The ruse wasn't working.

He mumbled, "Are you done yet?"

"I don't know," Vaughn replied, trying to force back a grin. "You still look like you want to slip me the hot beef injection. It has me a little worried, to be honest."

It took a few seconds before the shrink comprehended the insult. His face turned red and his eyes widened. A vein bulged out on his forehead. Then he fired back, in a low mumble, "At least I don't look like a goddamn devil-worshipper."

In a battle of wits, only a fool reaches for what he is given, Vaughn mused.

"I'll stop questioning your sexual orientation," he said, "as soon as you stop looking at me like you want to jump my bones. Fair?"

The shrink reached down and retrieved his clipboard. He removed a pen from his pocket protector and scribbled something. Hollow scratching sounds reached Vaughn's ears, but he couldn't see what was being written since the clipboard was at an intentionally obstructive angle. Vaughn wasn't impressed though, or even curious by these tactics.

The shrink took a few breaths to calm himself. The bulging vein in his forehead subsided, as did his blush. He said, very calmly, "Let me explain this to you, Mister Winters. If you don't come to these sessions, and if you're not *forthcoming* in these sessions, you'll forfeit your contract. Did you even *read* the fine print?"

"Yeah, I read it," Vaughn replied. "But Leviathan isn't going to give me up voluntarily. I'm their next big thing."

"So you say," the shrink said. "If that's so true, then why did they notify me about that incident in Morgantown?"

"Morgantown?" Vaughn asked. "West Virginia?"

"Yes."

Vaughn chuckled. "Morgantown's a college town. The crowd got rowdy."

"Fine, fine," the shrink acknowledged. "Yes, you may be popular with the weekend Satanists, but you're not '*the next big thing*' yet. You jumped off the stage and put a cigarette out in a man's ear. Another incident like that and *yes*, Leviathan *will* let you go."

"I choose not to smoke."

"Pardon?"

"I *choose* not to smoke," Vaughn repeated. "I ask the same from anyone attending my performances. I find cigarette smoke very offensive."

"Let me get this straight," the shrink started, holding up a finger, "You find cigarette smoke offensive, so if someone lights up in front of you, that justifies putting it out in their *ear*?"

"Something like that," Vaughn replied. He leaned in close, cocked his head sideways, and whispered, "You have yellow fuzz on your tongue, Hugh. You a smoker?"

"You just don't worry about my personal life," the shrink said, waving him off. "Just tell me what other eccentricities you have so that we might be able to get along better. We'll be seeing a lot of each other, after all."

"*Hmm...* let me think," Vaughn said, but it didn't take long for him to almost immediately declare, "Don't *ever* shush me or otherwise tell me to be quiet. *Ever*. It's rude and condescending to imply that I don't have a right to speak or make noise, yet *you* do. If you shush me—*ever*—I'll interpret it to mean that just because you don't like whatever noise I'm making at the time, you think I don't have a right to make them."

"*Shushing* is just a natural reaction. It's not meant to be—"

"And my natural reaction will be to punch you in the face. I've been told it's a psychosomatic reaction. But I don't care. I'm an adult, and I have a right to speak or make noise whenever I want to. Understand?"

"*Jesus Christ*," the shrink mumbled, shaking his head and rubbing his eyes with his thumb and forefinger. "Dead people are up and walking around, but I've got my hands full with *you*, don't I, *Mister Winters*?"

Vaughn smirked.

Thankfully it was the first and last time he ever had to talk to that asshole.

LEAVING HIS CONTRACTUALLY-APPOINTED SHRINK'S OFFICE, Vaughn saw a stumbling figure off to the side of the road, in the brush. He couldn't make out much, only that it was a plainly-dressed man with such a stiff walk that it would take him forever to actually get anywhere. But Vaughn knew that this guy was one of those all the news channels were interrupting regular programming about, and one of the reasons so many people were calling off work.

He thought it was rather neat how for the past couple of days people presumed dead were getting up and walking around. How were they misdiagnosed? He wondered how long this crazy shit would last. And what would history books written a hundred years from now have to say about this era? He hoped it would be something along the lines of, '*There was a brief period near the beginning of the millennium when deceased human beings became ambulatory. This occurrence prompted outbreaks of mass hysteria and sermons of the End Times from religious leaders of all faiths and denominations. However, once the event was resolved via secular and scientific means, the downfall of religion began, prompting a series of events that resulted in the wonderful atheist society we enjoy today.*'

Vaughn chuckled at the thought, but such a thing actually happening was probably too much to hope for.

He found his taxi waiting for him outside, the driver eyeing the stiff-walking man further down the road. Vaughn climbed in, not bothering to speak. What would he have to say anyway that the driver wasn't already aware of?

He was driven straight to the Radisson Hotel, and after getting out of the cab, saw the driver promptly switch off his 'available' light.

Vaughn went into the hotel and signed in.

The clerk at the front desk suspected he must have been someone at least quasi-famous. She flirted by commenting how neat his handwriting was when he flourished, '*Vaughn Ambrose Winters*' on the signature line. He responded, "Yes. Sesame Street was very instructional. Watch it sometime. You might learn something." And she didn't flirt with him again.

He stepped into the elevator. Some grunge-dressed dickwad in a beanie joined him for the ride up, but for the entire ascent pretended to be distracted toying with his cellphone so he could avoid making any uncomfortable eye contact.

Cellphones, Vaughn mused, *are the end of all* actual *human interaction.*

Vaughn got off the elevator, walking closely behind the cellphone guy—nearly stepping on his heels, even—just to see if he would turn around and say something to prove he had even the smallest inkling of social skills. But he didn't.

Vaughn went to his room, slipped the keycard in the slot and plucked it back out, and entered.

It was just a room, longer than it was wide, painted off-white. The number on the door read '1402', (which was quite asinine, in Vaughn's opinion, since it was actually the *thirteenth* floor, but the hotel didn't technically *have* a thirteenth floor.) It wasn't quite the penthouse either, but at least it was the second highest floor. There was a television mounted on the wall and a mini-bar they had neglected to give him the key to open. The remote control had sticky residue all over the buttons from where the last guest had spilled soda on it. There was a window at the far end, and Vaughn wasn't surprised to discover that it would open six inches horizontally and no further, just in case one of the guests was feeling particularly suicidal. He couldn't even fit his head out.

The view sucked. He couldn't look directly up, because the bottom of the penthouse patio was blocking the sky. If he looked directly down, he could see through the glass ceiling of the swimming pool at ground level, but couldn't determine if there was anybody there worth looking at. If he looked directly out he could see nothing but boring black asphalt and the occasional scattering of cars.

The expansive rooftop of the shopping mall across the way occupied the majority of the scenery. There were big green generators and domed glass ceilings that actually looked rather ugly from the outside. The parking lot was particularly deserted though. Even though all the gas stations were crowded, he figured most people felt safer at home than being out shopping. It was an odd contradiction.

There was absolutely *nothing* to look at.

A bellhop arrived with all of Vaughn's luggage in tow. He placed them on the floor beside the bed. He stood like a statue for a few seconds, waiting to see if Vaughn would tip him.

Vaughn pretended he wasn't there, and the bellhop skedaddled.

He looked back out the window.

Where am I again? he wondered. *So I can remember to never come back here?*

It occurred to him: Pennsylvania Turnpike Exit 57. Business route 22. *Monroeville, Pennsylvania.* It was two hours north of Morgantown, West Virginia, where he had had his first official gig.

He didn't know yet that it was from this very hotel room that he would witness the end of the world.

Radisson

"ALL I SEE ARE RUINS," SAID HE,

"THIS WORLD THEY OFFERED ME."

✳ ✳ ✳ ✳ ✳

VAUGHN CONSIDERED THE NOTION of getting distracted at the hotel bar, but figured all the service staff would be preoccupied with other things. Instead he stayed in his room. He sat on the oversized bed with his back against the headboard, and put a pillow under his spine and one under his feet. He got comfortable. He lifted the remote control and pressed the sticky power button.

The television turned on with a flicker.

He wanted to watch something brainless, like cartoons, but couldn't find one playing on any of the channels. There were plenty of news reports though. He tuned into one, but kept the volume at a low level.

He turned his head and glanced at the nightstand beside the bed. There was a lamp there and some stationery with the hotel logo on the upper left corner, (just in case somebody happened to forget where they were writing from, he figured,) but next to the stationery was a rotary telephone.

He picked up the telephone and placed it on his lap, situating the cord over his legs. He picked up the headset, put it to his ear, waited for a dial tone, and started dialing.

He hoped he would get an answer.

After three rings, he did.

A voice said, "Hello?"

"Hey," Vaughn said, sitting up straight and unintentionally changing his voice from the deep growl most people heard to an uncharacteristically lively and charismatic tenor. "Guess who?"

She replied, "Gee, I wonder."

He chuckled. Even over the phone her voice was like a symphony. He knew her spoken words alone could sing him under a table. It put butterflies in his stomach.

He asked, "How are you doing?"

"Fine, I guess," she replied. "I'm just a little worried 'cause I saw one of those dead people walking down my street here."

"Yeah, yeah, crazy isn't?" he blurted. "It's happening all over. Just stay away from them. Guess where I am?"

It took her a moment to adjust to the sudden segue. She said, "I don't know. Where?"

"Fucking *Pennsylvania*," he replied. "Not so far from Ohio after all, am I?"

"Wow, you're really seeing the world," she teased.

"Yeah, totally," he teased back. "But I don't think money's going to be a problem now."

"Did you get your advance?"

"Half of it. And it's a nice sum. Now don't you feel bad for all those times you mocked me for singing in the shower?"

This comment embarrassed her, he could tell, though he hadn't meant for it to.

After several seconds of silence she said, "You could *always* sing, Vaughn. I can't deny that."

"And you can dance," he added. "I never denied that either."

"I can't help that it's not working out for me like it is for you," she huffed, as if she had already said it a million times, even if only in her mind. "I have to get by somehow."

Vaughn grunted and cleared his throat. "Yeah, about that... You won't have to strip anymore if you don't want to. With all this money I'm getting we can buy a house. You can just relax all day... Have chisel-chested manservants cater to your every need."

"I'm not having this conversation again."

Vaughn sighed and rolled his eyes.

"I can't move in with you," she added. "You know that."

He didn't reply.

After a very deep, very audible breath, she went on, "Vaughn, people are talking. You didn't write a song about me... about *us*... did you?"

"People are talking, huh? Are they not jumping for joy that I did a Billy Joel cover? They just haven't heard it yet. *Pressure* is even better with a gothic edge. And you know what else? If the label can get the rights, I'm planning on doing a *Blood Sweat & Tears* cover next—"

"Fuck! Vaughn!" came her screaming voice. Vaughn winced and pulled the phone away from his ear an inch. The screaming continued, "Vaughn, I can't! I can't do this! You have to let it go! Fuck!"

Vaughn closed his eyes. His next statement was whispered: "*You* can't let it go either."

"But at least I'm trying," came her retort. "I'm trying to live like normal people do."

"But we're not normal."

"But I *want* to be."

There was silence.

"Look, Vaughn, this *dead people thing* really has me worried. Half my neighbors have boarded up their houses. I shouldn't be talking to you right now. I should really be watching the news—or listening to the radio—or *something*."

Vaughn understood the way the media presented the news made every simple story more addictive than crack, with their flashy graphics and pounding drumrolls. He imagined people all across the country laying on their couches in front of their televisions, eyes wide open and drool escaping their lips, popping ephedrine pills so they could stay awake and holding back their bladders so they didn't have to get up. He wished the owner of the voice on the other end of the phone wasn't as gullible as they were.

Some virus might be reanimating the dead. So what? It was a fascinating topic to discuss at the watercooler, that was all.

"I'm *watching* the news," Vaughn solemnly said. He tried not to be too condescending. "They're blowing it totally out of proportion. It's probably some terrorist attack. A bio-chemical thing. The suits in D.C. will drop bombs on some rag-heads and it'll be under control. Relax."

Something on television caught his eye. He directed his attention to it and clicked the volume up a couple of notches.

He said, "Hang on a sec."

A shaky-cam was showing a group of walking corpses somewhere in nearby Pittsburgh. Their skin was blue-toned and riddled with patches of rigor mortis. Several of them were bloody.

What the hell is that? Vaughn wondered. *Is one of them gnawing on a severed hand?*

The camera panned out and showed that the small group was merely the vanguard of a much larger group, probably close to five hundred. A female voiceover narrator said, *"This is the scene from just a few minutes ago. You'll notice that many in this group of reanimated dead are wearing hospital gowns. That's because this mob allegedly formed in the morgue of our downtown hospital. And their numbers are growing."*

"Vaughn, are you there?" she asked, her voice so beautiful, under any circumstance.

"Yeah, I'm here," he said.

"I'm *scared*, Vaughn."

The scene on television switched back to the newsroom, where two anchors shuffled their notes. The one on the right lifted his face toward the camera and stated in a very practiced, non-regional monotone voice, "Many citizens have reported power and water outages, which is prompting the Federal Emergency Management Agency to devise rescue centers, under the direction of local police and national guard. A list of these centers should be appearing at the bottom of your screen. If you fear for your safety, or if you are without power or water, please make your way to one of these centers now."

How the hell can they even be watching television if they don't have power? Vaughn mused. *Stupid assholes.*

The anchor went on to advise the exact amount of luggage a refugee was advised to bring with them, which turned out to be just one suitcase a maximum of thirty pounds.

"Hey, honey," he said, "if you're scared, you know you don't have to be alone. Come to me. I'll wire you some money."

"I can't do that," she replied. "I know what will happen."

"Nothing has to happen. I promise."

Silence.

"Let me...," she began, trailing off. "Let me think about it."

"Okay, you think about it," he said. "But while you're doing that, do something for me."

"Do what?"

"If you're so worried, go to the kitchen. Go to the sink. Fill it with water. Then go to the bathroom. Fill the tub with water, too."

"What?" she asked. "Why?"

"In case they turn the water off," he replied. "Are you doing it?"

"Okay, that's a good idea," she said.

He pictured her stepping through her small house, alone and frightened in smalltown Ohio. He further pictured her strides—graceful and elegant, like the high-society diva she was meant to be, her long black hair flowing in her wake like a flock of ravens.

That was her stripper name—*Raven*—he knew.

He heard something clanging around, then the sound of a running faucet.

He said, "Good. Now close all your curtains and lock your windows and doors."

"They already are," she replied.

"Good," he said. "Don't open the door for *anyone,* even if you recognize them. I'm going to go now. I think the front desk has Western Union. I'll see about getting money to you."

"Vaughn," she said, "I'm not sure if I can come to you or not."

"Can't?" he asked. "Or *won't?*"

"I don't know."

He sighed. "If this thing looks like it's not going to blow over, I'll call you back tomorrow. Have your mind made up by then."

"Okay, I'll think about it," she said.

"Okay," he said back.

He wanted to say more. He wanted to exchange the appropriate end-of-phone-conversation farewells, but it was too difficult when the words really meant something.

He simply hung up instead.

He picked the telephone up off his lap and placed it back on the nightstand.

He turned his focus back to the television. The list of rescue centers scrolling across the bottom of the screen caught his eye.

It read: *Washington County: Canonsburg General Hospital.*

That was very close by. The *problem* was close by.

He gritted his teeth. He flung the remote control at the wall and it promptly shattered, sending its two batteries skittering across the floor.

Radisson

THE WORLD IS JUST FLESH & TEETH.
MAYBE IT ALWAYS HAS BEEN.

* * * * *

IN LIGHT OF THE LOSS OF HIS REMOTE CONTROL, Vaughn pulled a chair directly up to the television and sat down. He knew he was becoming a lot like the people he had mocked, but he couldn't help it. He was addicted now, just like the rest. Images came and went and his eyes breathed them in with huge, eager gasps.

The major networks were replaying the incident at the White House, when thousands of walking corpses had overtaken a line of Marines and poured onto the front lawn. The President had evacuated to a secure location long ago, a narrator said, but the majority of his secret service agents were eaten.

Eaten?! What the fuck?!

Other images captured via helicopter showed scenes in American suburbs, where entire neighborhoods of people had scampered up to their rooftops, waving white sheets on broomhandles to try to signal for rescue. Thousands of zombies were gathered below them, clawing at Sears' award-winning aluminum siding, relentlessly trying to get to those who were stranded above. But even more surreal than that was footage of an army of undead shuffling purposefully across the Brooklyn Bridge while vehicle traffic frantically scuttled by.

Then there was one very interesting report given by a station out of Maryland: "FEMA directives have been leaked and received by the very media they're attempting to suppress. Foremost among these directives—and probably the most disturbing—is the order to destroy and prevent all photographs of cadavers, walking or otherwise, by any means necessary up to and including lethal force." A pause. "Forgive me for being blunt, but they believe *this* is the best approach to nullifying outright panic?"

Other images were of a split-screen interview with a Reverend Wilfred Maxwell, a head honcho in the Moral Majority. He was claiming that the rising of the dead was proof of approaching Armageddon, and quoted a few Bible verses as his proof. Before they cut short his interview he was heard to say, "You live your life in a carnal carnival. Your rock and roll music is the national anthem of Sodom and Gomorrah. And I look forward to the day when you are all thrown, kicking and screaming, into a lake of fire."

And the flustered interviewer fired back, "Yeah, and *you'll* be the one sucking Satan's greasy cock."

Vaughn was so enraptured he couldn't even chuckle. The images the television was showing him—*although inadvertently*—were mapping the chronological deterioration of society. He surmised this when all the networks stopped censoring the blood.

Scenes of chaos in city streets were proudly aired, (almost as if to give the middle finger to FEMA,) complete with zoomed-in shots of people dragged down by groups of zombies and their arms ripped out of their sockets and teeth biting into their jugulars.

Watching a walking corpse take a bite out of a living human being was an odd thing for Vaughn to witness. It wasn't like seeing one of his fat relatives bite into a drumstick on Thanksgiving; human skin reacted entirely different. Blood surfaced immediately, and while the walking corpse seemed to have trouble biting down at first, soon the skin parted from the bone, soft and chunky. Blood would squirt after that.

It prompted Vaughn to mumble, *"Fuck me."*

Hours went by. He wasn't sure just how many. When he got hungry he considered calling room service, but suspected they wouldn't be delivering anymore. Instead of going down to the restaurant, he simply let his stomach growl.

He was transfixed.

The television newscasters were slowly coming to terms with the fact that they weren't out for ratings anymore, and the shit they were reporting was probably going to end them all.

A regional network in Philadelphia was broadcasting a very unprofessional, impromptu interview with someone who had been researching the phenomenon. By this time there were no special graphics or artwork flashing on screen anymore. Everything had become down and dirty.

The man's words were: *"Any dead body that is not exterminated becomes one of them! It gets up and kills! The people it kills get up and kill!"* Others in the newsroom were yelling and he had to raise his voice to even be heard. Someone threw a stack of papers at him and they flew apart and fluttered through the air. And then the list of rescue stations scrolling across the bottom of the screen suddenly vanished.

It meant they weren't safe anymore. They had been overrun.

The chaos was very exciting.

Vaughn mouthed, "*Wow...*"

His eyes were wide open. They were dried out and red with insomnia.

He heard a noise that wasn't emanating from the television. It took several seconds for his brain to register it.

The noise sounded again. Vaughn turned his head away from the television for the first time in several hours. He realized that someone was pounding the knocker on the hotel room's door.

He pried himself up from his chair and went to answer it.

He pulled the door open. The same bellhop that had delivered his luggage earlier was standing there. His face was pale and he had bags under his eyes, probably from equal amounts of sleeplessness. When Vaughn jerked the door open all the way, the bellhop hopped back a step.

He regained his composure and said, "Sir, hotel management has asked for all guests to assemble in the lobby. They have an announcement to make."

"I'm not interested," Vaughn told him.

"It's not safe here, *sir*," the bellhop replied, and all at once his formal, erect posture drooped to a casual slouch. "You know what? *Fuck it*. If you don't want to die, Dracula, you'd better get your ass downstairs and on one of the shuttle-buses to the nearest rescue center. There's goddamn *cannibals* walking around outside."

Vaughn slammed the door in the suddenly rude bellhop's face and locked it.

He dashed to the telephone and yanked up the receiver. He put it to his ear.

He heard a dial tone.

He breathed a sigh of relief, and dialed the same familiar number he had before.

He nervously kicked his foot against the nightstand with every ring of the telephone. He counted ten rings before the answering machine clicked on.

A female's trembling, panicked, recorded voice announced, "*This is Rindi Winters. Vaughn, if that's you, god I'm so sorry. I should have come to you when I had the chance. I do love you. God I love you so much. I love making love to you, I love holding you, I love being with you. I... I gotta go. The army's outside. They're forcing the whole neighborhood out of their houses. I think they're taking everybody to a concentration camp or something. Oh god, Vaughn, please find me. We'll make love all day every day and I'll never push you away again. Please find me. Please be with me. I'm so scared."*

There was a high-pitched *BEEEEEEP!*

The receiver remained balanced in Vaughn's hand for several seconds as he stood there motionless before the weight of the phone cord caused it to slip from his hand and fall to the floor. It bounced a couple of times on the soft carpet.

Vaughn fell next, landing on his knees.

He was suddenly breathing very hard. Panting. His lips were quivering.

Minutes went by. Or hours.

He couldn't tell.

UNLIKE NORMAL PEOPLE who could recollect the events of their lives from point A to point B, Vaughn Winters recollected his life as a sequence of phases and a series of transitions. Growing up, he and his sister had been shuffled from one relative to the next, always forced to leave some of their most prized possessions behind. Each relative had either abused them or neglected them entirely. He always worried that he and his sister would be separated.

Each move meant a total transition.

Each move meant being forced to readapt to different rules and surroundings.

And each time Vaughn was always able to adapt. He prided himself on that, and due to what was happening outside his hotel room, he suspected that yet another phase was approaching.

When he regained his composure, he pulled himself up from his knees. He opened one of his suitcases and retrieved his songbook from inside. He spent several more minutes flipping through it, saying *goodbye*.

He had to admit that this phase of his life had been the best one ever. It even redeemed all the bad shit he went through growing up—like the cigarette burns as punishment in lieu of time-outs and being condescendingly shushed when he cried in pain. But in this most recent phase he was a different man. He had a different name. He was going to be rich. He was going to be *famous*.

But this phase was over, he knew, and he would have to adapt to a new one yet again. Yet of all the phases of his life, he wondered if this next transition would truly be as bad as he was making it out to be.

He tried to think positive.

He said goodbye to the three generations of sloth that always hogged the aisles in Wal-Mart. He said goodbye to the fat fucks that supersized their meal at McDonalds, then asked for a *Diet* Coke to go with it. He said goodbye to all the so-called free-thinking college graduates who, when asked the title of their favorite book, would invariably answer, *The Catcher in the Rye*—or worse, would quote Nietzsche. He said goodbye to the entire fucking generation of

Twixters that lived at home until they were twenty-five years old and had fins welded on their shitty cars so they could pretend to be Vin Diesel, with their noisy mufflers and high mortality rates.

But, then again, Vaughn had to say goodbye to his dreams. Another phase was approaching, yet he knew he would adapt. He survived a less than glamorous childhood, so he knew he could survive *this*.

Moreover, he knew exactly what was going to happen. He was struck by the irony of it: The coming world wouldn't be judgmental of him and Rindi—they didn't even have to know that they were brother and sister—but ever seeing her again was unlikely.

Why did they part ways to begin with? Why did he leave her behind to sell visions of her body to horny old men while he went on to enroll at the Cleveland Institute of Music? It was selfish of him. But Rindi—bless her heart—she still showed up at his graduation. The only family member to do so, in fact.

He closed his songbook. He stared at it in his hands for a few more seconds, then gingerly placed it on the nightstand on top of the hotel stationery. For a moment he wondered—*if the world ever went back to normal*—would some schmuck find his songbook and post it on eBay?

But then Vaughn laughed big and loud. He knew the world wasn't going to be normal again. And he was okay with that.

He exited his hotel room, laughing.

He stepped into the elevator, laughing.

He pressed the '*Lobby*' button.

He laughed the entire way down.

ROCK FORGE
Army Research Laboratory

From: Col. Franklin J. Darlington
To: Sgt. Kurt Garrett (ret.)

Subject: DISPATCH ORDERS

Sgt. Garrett:

I hope you did not get too comfortable in the fine accommodations here at Rock Forge. You will need to rendezvous with your pilot at <u>Helipad H</u> at <u>0800</u>. Your station will be NxNE, <u>Canonsburg General Hospital</u>, <u>Canonsburg, PA</u>.

Upon arrival, proceed to <u>instruct all willing participants in BB armed and unarmed combat</u>.

As you know, G. Levi and Z. Wu have found minimal success in the southernmost states. Northward, H. Yoshida has achieved wonderful results. We hope to achieve the same in the mid-Atlantic states.

FYI, your concerns have been noted. I understand your reluctance to teach these skills to applicants who, due to lack of time, have not received physical and psychological evaluations.

Bear in mind this is a civilian operation. Also bear in mind your Krav Maga seminars also did not require physical and psychological evaluations, only cold hard cash. Also bear in mind that if physical and psychological evaluations were required of all members of Project Black Beret, you might not be standing here right now.

Not many soldiers get second chances.

We can have a long sit-down when this is over and discuss who was right and who was wrong.

(The Wild Turkey is on me.)

Always your friend,

Col Franklin Darlington

Semper fi

VAUGHN WINTERS HAD AT FIRST ASSUMED he was the only one, but it turned out there were six others at Eastpointe that had been trained as Black Berets, including a female (the most spoiled bitch he had ever met,) and including a preppy young punk that he had gotten into a skirmish with at the bar. As Vaughn suspected from the start, they were all young and healthy and naïve and probably still held some delusions of immortality. They were the perfect targets for military-sponsored training, no different than the ignorant civilian kids fresh out of high school that Army recruiters enticed like strangers with candy (or charismatic cult leaders with similar empty promises.) In every instance, Vaughn knew, the only outcome would be death, wrapped up in shiny paper and a golden bow.

The people that had arrived safely at Eastpointe decided there was no better place to go and they should simply restart their lives there. In order to do that, however, they needed to restock the town, and the Black Berets were chosen for that endeavor.

A horseback scout was first sent out into the wilderness. He wouldn't stop for *anything*, Vaughn was told, and would merely jot down any location he came across that might house valuable supplies. The Black Berets were then sent to those locations with a shopping list of essentials provided by a Procurement Committee. The most common items were barrels of gasoline, brand-name booze, soap, laundry detergent, prophylactics, medicines, light bulbs, and the occasional manually-powered push mower. Sometimes they were asked to bring back equipment, either the heavy kind or the hospital kind.

Their first outing was to a nearby farm to requisition their supplies of abandoned livestock—including the horses, which were a major pain to round up. The cowboy of their group, Delmas Ridenour, was at that time a godsend.

The Black Berets obliged every request. They were at first accompanied by others, (who thought they could handle themselves because of their military backgrounds and such,) but those others quickly panicked under pressure and were eaten by zombies. Even one of the Black Berets, with all his training and know-how, was killed during an outing.

Eventually the more inventive citizens of Eastpointe learned to manufacture most of the items the Procurement Committee had earlier deemed "essential," like the soap and laundry detergent. Soon they were able to manufacture almost everything. There was even raspberry-flavored moonshine circulating throughout town.

After three years of raiding missions and five casualties, Eastpointe declared itself fully self-sufficient, having successfully developed a thriving farm over the area that used to be the golf course. The remaining six Black Berets were given free passes to never have to work again, weekly allotments of minted credits delivered directly to their mailboxes.

—Except for Vaughn Winters.

While the other Black Berets were busy with their inner dramas and inside jokes, Vaughn had more important matters on his mind, because despite all outward appearances, he never *stopped* working. He had long been privy to a secret that was closely guarded by Eastpointe's Superintendents, and handed down from one to the next.

A man named Ervin Wright was the first. He had been the Grand Secretary of the International Order of Odd Fellows of Rhode Island. At the outset of the apocalypse, he was scouting Eastpointe and its hotel as a possible venue for the next annual meeting of their lodge. He advised other Odd Fellows and their Rebekahs to join him and wait it out.

As Eastpointe became more of a community, he was the one to propose a system of government that was appropriate to the circumstances. He had a lot of good ideas, including creating the mint in the hotel basement to manufacture "work credits," (tokens punched out of sheet metal) and distribute them like paychecks, constantly controlling the amount in circulation. So many of his ideas were successful that he became trusted, and in turn was able to seat his other Odd Fellows in positions of authority.

While the town didn't have an *Illuminati*, per se, they certainly had these *Odd Fellows*, and nobody really suspected that every person nominated to be Superintendent had been an Odd Fellow in the world before. They switched and rotated to maintain the appearance of change, but in reality an Odd Fellow was always in charge. Just like in the world before, they liked to feel important and they liked to keep secrets, and they were good at it.

Vaughn Winters was an accomplice; he was their Grand Sentinel.

VAUGHN WASN'T SURE AT FIRST, of all the Black Berets, why the Odd Fellows approached only him. He wondered if they thought he was the one who could be most easily manipulated, or if they thought he was the only one intelligent enough for the tasks ahead. He later decided that neither was the case. Certainly the reasons for their decision were simpler than that: They had recognized his ability to *adapt.*

Shortly after the inaugural Black Beret raiding mission, the Odd Fellows invited Vaughn to a secretive meeting in the penthouse at the Eastpointe Hotel. From his understanding, the penthouse was reserved as living quarters for the acting Grand Superintendent, and not as an area where any hush-hush meetings were held. He would come to learn the name these meetings had been dubbed, as based on the typical Odd Fellows' odd nomenclature—*The Conclave*—and he would attend many in the next few years.

At first, he was given a tour of only the living room. Doors leading to other rooms in the spacious penthouse were closed and off-limits. While the Odd Fellows were proud that they had been able to preserve the original copies of their by-laws and constitution, eagerly displaying these to Vaughn with raging smiles, Vaughn was more distracted by the artwork on the walls, which had been left over from the original décor scheme back when the world was normal. Each wall was dedicated to a matted print of a Jackson Pollack painting, and Vaughn recognized them all: *Lavender Mist, Lucifer,* and *Convergence.* And it was a damn shame, he thought, because he knew whatever old fart occupied the room neither understood or fully appreciated them.

Two Odd Fellows were with him for that first meeting: Ervin Wright, the first and then-acting Superintendent, and one of his comrade-in-arms, Ralph Peters, the then-acting chairman of the Procurement Committee. Vaughn politely shook hands with them and was asked to please have a seat on the Lynley-brand sofa. He did so, hesitantly. He realized he had circled the same model in a catalog some years ago when planning a home for him and Rindi, and felt momentarily sick to his stomach. He didn't pay attention as the old men spoke over top of each another.

"Mister Winters, thank you so much for joining us," Ervin said, sitting down opposite Vaughn in a Lynley rocker recliner. "We have a proposition for you, and for you alone. But I need you to understand that anything we say here is to never leave this room."

Vaughn nodded, indifferent. "Sure, man." He had a sneaking suspicion that all the Odd Fellows were after was Metamucil and Viagra—they were probably hording the stuff. He brushed his palm along the soft surface of the cushion next to him and imagined how it would have contoured to Rindi's slender form.

Ralph had his arms crossed; he wasn't as approachable as Ervin. "I'm going to say this right now," he said, almost in a growl. "You're going to have to cut your hair and make yourself more presentable if you expect us to push you up the ranks."

This got Vaughn's attention.

Ervin shot his partner an impatient look. "We're not to that point in the discussion yet, Brother Peters. Let's not be so quick to judge him based on appearance alone. He seems a very capable young man."

Vaughn couldn't help but to chuckle. He couldn't get offended by these blubbering geezers.

"Wait a sec here," he said, his mouth still posed in an incredulous grin. "Why would I have to cut my hair?"

"You received training to fight zombies, didn't you?" Ralph asked. "Others like you have decently short hair—"

"Because they're paranoid about a deadfuck yanking it out. I'm not."

Ralph nodded, conceding the point. "Fine. But you must at least profess belief in a Supreme Being."

Vaughn laughed out loud this time, but before he could give a clever retort, Ervin jumped in.

"The protocols Brother Peters is referring to are part of standard Odd Fellow initiation rites. But he doesn't seem to understand that this isn't normal Odd Fellow business." He glanced sideways at Ralph. "This will be... contract labor. *Outsourcing*, if you will. Take Brother Peters' comments with a grain of salt. He has the best intentions. And hey, take it as a compliment, too. He already thinks you're the man for us."

"Nice backpedal," Vaughn said.

Ervin smiled.

"So let's move on, then," Ralph said. "We want a fellow we can do business with on the side. *On the side*, though, and I can't stress this point enough."

"As long as this secret doesn't involve something along the lines of you Odd Fellows having your undead mistresses locked up in the basement, or something like that."

Ervin laughed. He most always seemed jovial. "No, Vaughn—*do you mind if I call you Vaughn*—it involves nothing of the sort." He glanced over at Ralph. He received a nod that seemed to say, *might as well give it a try*. He turned back to Vaughn. He clicked his tongue, very hesitant to continue, and exhaled a nervous breath. "Okay, Vaughn, I'm going to level with you, son. What we're going to let you in on here is very important. It has to be kept a secret. If you'll follow me, please, I'd like to show you something."

Ervin and Ralph both stood. Vaughn stared up at them from his very comfortable position on the couch, not wanting to move just yet. But he decided to oblige them, and slowly stood.

They motioned for him to follow and led him to one of the closed penthouse doors. Ervin unlocked it with a key he pulled from his pocket, turned the handle, and pushed the door open.

Inside the room was a third Odd Fellow. He sat at a desk with his feet propped up, casually listening to headphones. The cord from the headphones ran to a small black box with the logo *Galaxy DX251710* emblazoned along the side. The yellow ledger pad he was holding had a long list of data recorded: names, dates, times, locations. Vaughn could see that much. Even as he watched, the Odd Fellow took the time to scribble more information.

Ervin snapped his fingers to get the man's attention. After a couple of seconds he looked up and pulled the headphones from his ears.

"Any activity right now?" Ervin asked.

The man nodded.

"Then please put it on speaker, Brother Henline, so this young fellow can understand what's going on."

Brother Henline nodded, glanced at Vaughn, and shrugged his shoulders. He put his feet down and reached over to pull the plug on the headset, causing the radio to default to speaker mode.

"*Briars County, Kentucky, this is New York, come in,*" the radio crackled.

"*New York, this is Rodney Lloyd of Briars County,*" the radio crackled back.

"*Rodney Lloyd, be advised our traders have reported an attempted robbery from highwaymen. Described them as an Aryan gang, surviving on the road, drifting somewhere between your location and Rock Forge, West Virginia. Exercise caution.*"

"*Will do. Thanks for the heads-up, New York.*"

Ervin placed his hands on Vaughn's shoulders like a grandfather showing subtle affection for a grandson. He asked, "Do you understand what this means, Vaughn?"

"Starting to," Vaughn replied.

He stepped away from Ervin's hands, though the feigned affection did not influence him one way or another. He had grown up around mind games, after all, and there were more important matters on his mind at the moment.

The room had originally been an office, but sometime since the Odd Fellows' takeover of Eastpointe it had been transformed into something of an amateur ham radio station. Vaughn gave the room a stroll-through inspection, gliding his hand across the tables and perusing open notebooks. There were a lot. Scribblings included detailed information regarding settlements and communities all across the United States, times they transmit, the number of survivors located at each, and any names mentioned.

He figured he wasn't as surprised as they thought he'd be. "So how many have you picked up?" he inquired.

"Twenty-two other settlements, spanning all over," Ralph Peters replied, stepping into the room beside Vaughn. He stood proudly for some reason. "Matter of fact, we once got a signal all the way from a research station in Antarctica. A team of five, stranded. Must have been unique atmospheric conditions, because we haven't been able to pick them up again. I doubt they're still alive. They were broadcasting a distress signal at the time."

"Like so many others," Ervin added. "Used to be about forty settlements. Some we just never hear from again. A rare few take the time to get on the radio and explain that they've been overrun. It's a sad thing when they do, though. Very sad, how they beg for assistance when they know nobody can save them. Lots of lives lost. Uh-huh."

"Sounds like they're in constant contact with each other," Vaughn commented, scanning a page of notes that lay on a table in front of him. "And they're trading?"

"That's right," Ervin said. "They've established trade routes, an attempt at reestablishing commerce of some sort. Mostly goods like tobacco and medicine—but *boy-o-boy*, that's risky business right there. Sending out those caravans? If zombies don't get them, highwaymen do."

The radio crackled again and a voice broke through. *"New York, this is Kurt Garrett at Rock Forge, West Virginia."*

Kurt Garrett?

Vaughn perked up.

"How ya'll doin' today? Couldn't help but overhear. Wanted to let you know I've dealt with those folks before. They've been harassing us for a while now. I killed a couple of them last time they tried to raid us—" (Vaughn wasn't surprised at this comment. One look at Kurt Garrett and you knew just by the look in his eyes— just by the vibe the man emitted—that he'd killed at least one man before, even *before* the world had gone to shit.) *"You ever need a hand, give me a shout."*

A few seconds later another radio voice replied, *"Will do, Garrett. God bless."*

Vaughn chuckled. When given a curious glance by Ervin and Ralph, he explained, "I actually know that guy."

"Really? How so?"

Vaughn gave the quick and short version: "I met him at a rescue station in Pennsylvania. He taught me a few things. I'm not surprised he's still alive."

"Ah, small world, then," Ervin said. "He's on the radio quite often. Something of a hero. Single-handedly rescued Rock Forge, from what we understand. Literally swooped in to save the day."

"Yeah, he's a man's man," Vaughn said, turning away. "Enough with the jeans creaming, though. Just because I respect the guy doesn't mean I want to suck his dick."

For an instant, Ervin and Ralph appeared offended that Vaughn had used profanity in front of them.

"So this is the big secret?" Vaughn asked, closing the information log he had been reading. "We're not alone? So why not just tell everybody? They'd probably be relieved."

Ralph stepped forward and very matter-of-factly replied, "We don't tell for the same reason the United States government would never disclose information regarding UFO's: *Panic.*"

Ervin disguised his smirk behind his knuckles, but Vaughn laughed openly. Ralph's face turned sour—which would make for about the umpteenth time in the few minutes Vaughn had known him.

"Well, what have you told them?" Vaughn asked.

"Nothing, as we've said," Ervin answered.

"No, I mean the other communities. What kind of communication do you have with them?"

"None whatsoever. We don't transmit."

Vaughn cocked his head. "You don't *transmit? You mean nobody knows we're here?*"

"That's right," Ervin said. "Nobody." He grabbed a metal folding chair that had been leaning against the wall, unfolded it, and planted his butt down. He clasped his hands together in front of him, still using the grandfather routine, and went on, "You see, Vaughn, this is a delicate situation here. We'd be opening ourselves up to a whole *world* of problems. Eastpointe is a safe, beautiful place. I'd call it a utopia. If we transmit, not only would other communities know we're here, but so would highwaymen. And raiders. And all sorts of bad people. But that's not the least of it."

"How do you mean?"

"Do we really have to explain?" Ralph asked.

"Uh, *yeah*, you do," Vaughn said, showing him a disgusted and condescending glance. "I'm trying real hard to understand your logic here. Sounds like straight-up xenophobia to me."

"Fine, fine," Ervin said. He looked up and to the right, collecting his thoughts, and turned back to Vaughn, looking him square in the eyes. His tone became very serious. "Our community would disintegrate—completely lose its structural integrity. Do you realize that? We're very isolated here, away from trouble. Thanks to you and the other Black Berets, we can retrieve all the supplies we need. Those other communities could only do more harm than good. The citizens of this town rely on the Odd Fellows to keep them safe—"

"Do you really think that?"

Ervin snapped, "*Somebody has to do it,*" but quickly regained his composure. He took a breath. "Listen to me, son. The closest we are to another community is about a hundred miles. And that community is run by the Apostolic League. Now, you want to talk about xenophobia, they fit that definition. They even refuse to take in refugees. But the people living *here*, at Eastpointe, they come from all over the east coast. We're separated from other settlements sometimes by hundreds of miles or more. That amounts to hundreds of miles of wastelands and certain death. But if you factor in the destructive power of *hope*..."

"Hope?" Vaughn mocked.

"Hope," Ervin politely answered. "Hope, in this instance, is a very bad thing. You understand that every single person here has had to leave loved ones behind? So what if they were to hear that there are other communities? You know what would happen? They would try to find their missing loved ones. Their fathers... their mothers... and so on and so forth. And you know what would happen? They would walk out of Eastpointe and they would get eaten alive. You want that on your conscience?"

The third Odd Fellow, Brother Henline, who had been listening quietly up to this point, now interjected, "He's not lying. I've listened to it happen before." He motioned to a stack of notebooks sitting on the desk in front of him. "It's all right there in those reports. See for yourself."

"Oh, I believe you," Vaughn said. He shoved the stack of notebooks aside and sat on the edge of the desk. He put his hands in his pockets, hesitated, and then posed the question, "So what is it you want from me?"

"Lots of things," Ervin said.

"Yes, lots of things," Ralph reiterated.

"We're going to need an *inside man*, of sorts," Ervin explained. "For one, we're going to need you to keep your Black Berets away from known trade routes and locations where highwaymen have been spotted. You'll also need to prevent them from spray-painting any more directions to our community anywhere outside of fifty miles or so. I'd say that's a safe bet. But I don't want them to get suspicious."

Vaughn took it in. "And what else?"

"What else? There's equipment our resident expert, Brother Harless Henline, tells us we need if we're going to want to monitor every frequency out there. This will never be mentioned on the Procurement Committee's list. You'll need to find a way to get it back here without your teammates knowing. And anything you can't bring back, *destroy.* I don't want anything out there except short-range walkie-talkies. As a matter of fact, I want everyone to eventually forget the radio was even invented. Bring back televisions and DVD players. Give them other forms of entertainment."

Vaughn nodded. "And what else?"

"And what else? Well... that pretty much covers all of our major concerns for now."

Vaughn smiled. "And what are you going to do for me?"

Ervin smiled back. So did Ralph.

"Well, Mister Winters," Ralph began, "we're prepared to induct you into the Odd Fellows. That would mean—with time and effort—you could be the one living in this penthouse for a term or two, wearing the title of Superintendent. Membership in the Odd Fellows also entitles you to—"

All at once Vaughn interrupted him with a burst of uproarious laughter, holding his belly with both hands and tilting his head back. He had tried to contain it, but couldn't. He kept laughing even as the Odd Fellows' smiles turned to scowls.

"And just what do you find so amusing about our offer?!" Ralph shouted, sticking out his belly and stepping forward. His lip ferret inadvertently fluttered, and it made Vaughn laugh even harder.

"This is very inappropriate behavior, son," Ervin plainly said.

Vaughn caught his breath. "Yeah, uh, sorry about that. But no, I have no interest in joining your fruity little club." A few more chuckles escaped before he stopped and straightened himself, though his cheeks still showed lingering wrinkles.

"Then what is it you would want, Mister Winters?"

Vaughn exhaled, hard, and sat up from the desk. Brother Henline quietly watched as he circled around and approached the window. He drew back the curtains with his hands. For the past few years, life seemed to consist of nothing but these views from hotel rooms, all with eerie scenic coincidences.

From up high in the penthouse in the luxurious Eastpointe Hotel, all of Eastpointe lay sprawled out in front of him—the Eastpointe Plaza directly ahead, to the golf course being transformed into farmlands, to the horizon where the main housing area began. Beyond that, Vaughn knew, Eastpointe's tall concrete wall encompassed the whole lot of it.

"I do like it here," he said. "It is the closest to a utopia you're likely to find."

"Then we understand each other," Ervin said. "We have to preserve our utopia. And not everyone out there understands how good they have it. If they know there are other settlements, some will want to leave. Others will want us to take in more refugees—and it will only be a matter of time before we start letting in the wrong people. An intelligent young fellow like you can understand that, I'm sure."

"Yeah," Vaughn replied. "The less people the better, as far as I'm concerned." He stepped away from the window and allowed the curtain to flutter closed. He returned to the other side of the desk. He addressed the Odd Fellows: "You want me to be your little agent in your little conspiracy, *fine*. I've got no emotional investment in anyone living here, so I don't care what they think. I'll do it. I'll be your little agent. But I know what I want in return."

"Yes...?" Ervin asked.

Vaughn glanced around at the wealth of information just in arm's reach. There were dozens of legal pads and spiral-bound notebooks and one of them—*it only had to be just one*—could contain the only reward he would ever need. He glanced at the folding table at the other side of the room, and at the two unopened boxes—complete with uncut factory packaging tape—that contained two more Galaxy-brand ham radios.

Vaughn answered the Odd Fellows: "What I want is to borrow your logbooks. *All of them*, right now, right this very second, before you can ever edit them. And I want one of those ham radios. And I'll want to keep one of every type of radio the Procurement Committee asks me to smuggle into Eastpointe."

The concern on Ervin's face was immediate. "And just what for, Vaughn?" he asked.

"I have a sister. She might still be out there, somewhere. If I can locate her, I'm going to go get her, and I'm going to bring her back here to live with me."

Ralph was flabbergasted. "That's exactly the kind of thing we're trying to prevent!"

"I won't say where I'm broadcasting from," Vaughn said. "I'll only ask for information regarding my sister. It'll be anonymous. It's a fair deal. Take it or leave it."

	Summation of transmissions for March 4
0600	Kurt Garrett (Rock Forge, WV) morning report; warning to New York-Maryland caravan, beware wild dogs.
	BREAKFAST BREAK
0900	Allison Fischer (Rock Forge, WV) and Hannigan Nye (OBX, N. Carolina) discuss unconfirmed, unreliable, reports of "infected" cattle in the midwest. (Zombie cows?)
Noon	(On the dot AGAIN) Apostolic League (Connecticut) broadcasts new sermon: "God hates fags."
	LUNCH BREAK
1500	Allison Fischer (Rock Forge, WV) and Hannigan Nye (OBX, N. Carolina) compare notes regarding possible mutation in poisonous Solanum Tuberosum. (Potatoes) (fascinating it is not)
	DINNER BREAK
1800	Edgar McMurtry (Rock Forge, WV) again requested info regarding his father in Texas, Sam McMurtry (Sheriff). No info reciprocated.
1835	Allison Fischer (Rock Forge, WV) and Hannigan Nye (OBX, N. Carolina) pollute the airways again with boring discussion regarding the acidic properties of Trioxane.
2000	Briars County Rescue Center still not responding. (5th day in a row.) Rodney Lloyd now presumed dead, Kentucky fallen.

VAUGHN WOULD DISCOVER that the name *Rindi Winters* was not in the Odd Fellows' logbooks, nor would it ever be, and in the following years the name would never be spoken in a broadcast. Nonetheless, Vaughn spent countless hours sitting diligently in the shadows of his dimly-lit living room in the small home he lived in all by himself, locked in his vigil, repeating the same phrase into the mic over and over: "Rindi Winters, are you out there?"

The silence the dead air made would have been overwhelming if not for the unique privilege of listening to the drama unfold in the world outside Eastpointe's walls. Vaughn was protected from it all. Shielded. Untouchable. The problems out there did not concern him—could not even *affect* him. Those voices out there might as well have been behind a television screen.

This was all a God had to be, he knew—an invulnerable, invisible voyeur.

Over the years the number of other known communities would dwindle to less than a dozen, the fall of a community sometimes preceded by a shrilling cry for help. Proportionately, keeping his fellow Black Berets away from known trade routes became less and less a problem. Also in those years, Kurt Garrett—a former Army Ranger and founding member of the Black Berets, and also Vaughn's trainer and sensei—would become an icon in the post-apocalyptic United States. His exploits were an epic not unlike *The Odyssey*, all told by several voices through ham radios. Those tales, from solo rescue operations to headlong encounters with the Aryans, made for exciting listening. The peg-legged fucker was definitely no one to be trifled with.

It was easy to realize that Rock Forge, located somewhere in the rolling hills of West Virginia, had become the center of the new world. All activity was centered there. All hope was centered there. And Eastpointe—far north in Rhode Island—was like the scared child after a nightmare, covering himself with his blanket and telling the monster under the bed, "*You can't see me. You can't see me. You can't see me.*"

Vaughn found it amusing. Furthermore, because of his unique perspective, he found the people of Eastpointe—and the wannabe shadowy men who ran it—absolutely pathetic.

But through it all, he never gave up hope of finding his sister. Hope made life bearable, at least for as long as the illusion of hope lasted.

Greetings from aboard [obscured] ~PRINCESS~ [obscured] Satellite [obscured]!

Dr. Aaron Dane

workstation 147

June 14   STRUCTURE MONITORS FUNCTION

Results of electrode placement in center 1 (one) has yielded a satisfying result. By producing an electrical impulse, I can force a predictable reaction.

I can make a dead person *move* to my whims.

    Really only one electrode is necessary to
    stimulate a forward, left, right, and stop
    response. (I should next devise a method to
    broadcast the signal remotely.)

Problems still remain. Aside from the loneliness and isolation, I have run out of test subjects. After several permutations, I am positive I have a working formula to create others like myself, but I have no pre-evolved subjects to work with. I am running out of patience and I am running out of paper.

I have charted the cruiseliner's drift, and I estimate that within the year I will be in swimming distance of land. I know there are other survivors. I can hear their ~traffic~ greetings and salutations over the radio.
bullshit

I will need to locate one of their encampments. I can only hope that evolution on land has not brought with it *domestication*. If I can create just one manipulatable subject, I can herd thousands upon thousands of others.

June 17

> *"I should premise that I use the term *Struggle*
> *for Existence* in a large and metaphorical sense,*
> *including dependence of one being on another, and*
> *including (which is more important) not only the*
> *life of the individual, but success in leaving*
> *progeny."*

Mr. Darwin, tell me why natural selection has
neglected to allow the evolved a viable way of
reproducing beyond the current world population.
Certainly there must be future generations.

Am I the only successful evolution?

<A Sidenote:>

Women always told me to stop staring at their breasts.
I have always wanted to shout "ARE YOU COMPLETELY
IMPRUDENT?! YOU CAN'T UNDO EONS OF EVOLUTION IN A
SINGLE GENERATION! MAN WILL ALWAYS LOOK UPON WOMAN
AS A SEXUAL OBJECT! IF WE DIDN'T THE HUMAN RACE WOULD
CEASE TO EXIST!"

But I have learned that women *are* imprudent. They
cannot comprehend logic. Instead they will yell at me
and slap me in the face.

Perhaps they can argue logic, but they cannot argue
my *evolution*.

Next time I will slap them back.

I'll need to find a living female, (or several
living females, preferrably with ~~bigxtits~~ large breasts,) so that
this evolution can be successful.

I must procreate.

Otherwise the world is truly doomed.

NOTHINGNESS OVERTOOK HIM ON SEVERAL OCCASIONS. This much he knew because there were several moments he could not recollect. He must have passed out. Entire chunks of time were missing from his memory.

Had hours passed, or mere minutes?

He assumed the latter. Otherwise he would have bled to death.

He had a memory of the girl in the group, Courtney Colvin, screaming, "Go for the eyes!"

And Vaughn had tried. That he could remember. He could remember going for the eyes. But why? Why were the zombies refusing to fall?

Vaughn squinted hard, and fought to breathe. There was blood in his throat, and he was flat on his back, staring up into the empty eyes of a dozen dead people—zombies—that had some kind of MacGyver'd armor slapped over their faces to prevent headshots. But they were just standing there, idle as if in lockdown, looming at him and collectively refusing to go in for the kill. What was stopping them?

What is this? Vaughn wondered. *Is this death? Am I already dead? Is that why they're not ripping me to pieces?*

He recollected starting at the most appropriate moment: When he and his group were on the beach outside, before they climbed onto the main deck of The Atlantic Princess, the point of no return.

They had sent Courtney up the ladder first; probably an excuse to study her ass without her suspecting. Though she did subtly resemble a young Andrea Corr, (in Vaughn's opinion,) she just wasn't his type. She wasn't tall enough, her legs weren't long enough or thin enough, her hair wasn't dark enough. She was mattressable at best. He wasn't sure why the boys in his group were playing this game.

Once she was up the ladder far enough to be out of listening range, they started trying to guess what kind of panties she wore, guessing based on any perceivable lines on her posterior. The general consensus of the group was varied, until Leon, silent on everything Courtney-related until that very moment, with such certainty he could only have acquired via insider knowledge, coolly stated, "String bikini, black," and followed her up the ladder.

Someone, probably his buddy Delmas, had said, "Ha! I *knew* you did, you snake!"

And what was so shocking about that, Vaughn had wondered. Two attractive white people—both of WASP descent, even—mutually chose the other to rub groins with. Was that so unheard of?

But the incident served to remind him why his teammates were soon killed. They hadn't *adapted*. They were still jocks reveling in their quarterback's sexual conquests.

This complete waste of time had been followed by another: their sad attempts at feigned bickering for comedic effect. "Ladder doesn't look too sturdy," someone had said, maybe the otherwise perpetually-quiet Mike Newcome, "so how are we gonna get your fat ass up there, Delmas?" To which Delmas had replied, "The only reason I'm fat is 'cause every time I fuck your girlfriend she fixes me a sandwich."

Hardy-fuckin-har.

No adaptation.

Theirs but to do and die.

But why was Vaughn dying alongside them? He didn't know. He hadn't played their games. He didn't deserve it.

Someone *did* it to him.

It was Dr. Dane. He was smiling the whole goddamned time.

Why hadn't anyone paused to consider the absolute absurdity of the mission?

Why hadn't anyone noticed Dr. Dane's obvious lack of logic, or that his story—and his theories—were so full of holes somebody should have been able to see right through them if they just hadn't been so goddamned preoccupied with his empty promises? He had said he was a mathematician, not a biologist or epidemiologist. So how would he have had any knowledge outside his particular field?

Why did they believe him? Vaughn asked himself, as he laid there among his fellow Black Berets, waiting to die.

Because the dumbasses couldn't accept reality, that's why.

The human animal is just too gullible.

Blood gurgled in his throat. A few drops surfaced and dribbled across his lips and down his cheek.

A little while ago—*a little while? How long have I been laying here?*—Dr. Dane had drugged Courtney with a tranquilizer, put her over his shoulder, and carried her out of the room. She was still alive.

How did they not see the ambush coming? They had heard noises. They had heard zombies wailing in the bowels of the ship. But they had trusted Dr. Dane's excuses. Leon commented on it at one point when the wailing sounded very close by, and everyone believed Dr. Dane's explanation: "This place is falling apart at the seams. Trust me, that's all you hear. Things coming apart, as things tend to do. Chaos theory in action."

Dr. Dane... Dr. Aaron Dane. The motherfucker.

The man had shown up at Eastpointe just yesterday in a jeep with zombie splatterings all over the front bullbars. He had had quite a story to tell. And people believed him.

—*A CURE for the zombie plague.*

Can we pause? Can we rewind? Can we take it all back? Can we discuss this in a sensible manner before we jump straight to creaming our jeans over the possibility of a cure?

All through the meeting the Black Berets had with Dr. Dane and the Superintendent, Vaughn tried to subtly express that he wasn't game for this deception. After all, he knew the real score around Eastpointe. Ervin Wright and the Odd Fellows had no need for a cure. They had absolutely no intention of venturing beyond Eastpointe's walls. And the entire time Vaughn assumed that Ervin was holding the meeting as a ruse—just so he could say, *Well there's a cure out there but since none of you want to go get it, looks like we're stuck here.* He just wanted to save face.

But then Courtney Colvin raised her hand.

Yes, she was the first to buy into it, stupid female that she was. (Never give credibility to anything that bleeds for seven days and doesn't die.) And then Leon followed suit, likely thinking with his dick. Then everybody else played follow-the-leader, (Leon being captain of the locker room as he was.) Mike Newcome said *sure, I'll die for this pre-doomed quest based on wishful thinking*, then Delmas Ridenour said *I second that asinine motion*, and then Christopher Gooden, otherwise a stoic loner, couldn't be left out, could he?

And with all those hands raised, how could Vaughn say no? Even then, he expected the Superintendent to pull him aside and explain the real reason why this mission was going to take place.

But he never did.

Why were the Odd Fellows interested in a cure?

Vaughn hadn't figured it out.

The rest was supposed to be very simple: just retrieve the mythical elixir from a beached luxury cruiseliner stranded several miles out in the middle of zombie country. The six Black Berets—and the enigmatic scientist—climbed onto the ship via a shoddy emergency rope ladder. They then descended into its shadowy depths.

And when the armored zombies came spilling out, brandishing bayonets welded onto metal armbands, Christopher Gooden—the sharpest distance shooter of the bunch—was the first to go, overtaken in close quarters. He had a rusty old blade driven into his heart by one of the clumsy deadfucks. Then his eyeballs were eaten.

Mike Newcome was next, (not a tragic loss in Vaughn's opinion, as Mike was the most useless when it came to fighting, surpassing even the uselessness of the female,) but after that...

After that Vaughn wasn't sure. He only knew he had been the last one standing, and had put up a hell of a fight, all things considered.

Then he remembered Leon. Was Leon dead?

No—or, at least, Vaughn wasn't sure. He had last seen Leon getting stampeded and forced over the balcony, falling several feet down to the first floor of the casino. There was a rather sickening thud, though, so Leon could very well be dead, or his spine broken.

But Leon got bit. Vaughn remembered now. Leon got bitten by one of them. Right on the meaty part of his shoulder, just before he fell.

But he owes me. I saved his life once. He owes me.

Nobody's going to help me.

I'm the last one left and nobody's here to save me.

Vaughn considered the lethal dose of barbiturates tucked in a white container in his boot. He wondered if he could muster the strength to retrieve them—and even more, to *swallow them*, so he could get it over with.

But I'm going to survive this, he told himself. He thought it once more, and tried to say it out loud, but it was voiced as a mere gurgle.

He vomited some blood but it stayed in his mouth. He blew hard to clear his airway so he wouldn't choke on it.

I'll survive this, he decided. *I just have to get up.*

He forced strength into his right hand and lifted it off the casino floor. It was winter white and shaky. He brought it to his neck and probed his breached skin with his fingers. There was a cut there—a *deep* cut—and it was bleeding badly. No wonder he couldn't breathe. No wonder he felt so faint. His goddamn *throat* had been cut. By rights he should have been dead already.

I can survive this. I'm better than them. Stronger. Tougher. Smarter. They were all just stupid kids. I'm not.

He planted his forearm and strained to turn over onto his side. Looking down at the floor, he saw his hair flowing freely from his scalp and the tips floating in a pool of deep red blood.

Was all that his?

His forearm slipped out from under him and he buckled.

He coughed again. More blood.

The zombies hovering above glared down at him without sympathy, but they remained frozen in place.

Vaughn gurgled, *"Ah, fuck you, you rust-bucket motherfuckers."*

He heard another noise, a familiar voice moaning in similar pain, and footsteps. He tried to crane his neck around to find the source. The footsteps grew louder and louder, and sounded like they were coming up a staircase.

Vaughn circled around in the blood by pushing with his heels. The blood was so thick it was splashing away from him in waves.

A spotlight from one of the fallen Socoms shone on Leon Wolfe's head as he appeared at the top of the stairs. He was groaning and grunting, and cradling his wounded shoulder. He stumbled, grabbing the railing for support. His hair, usually stylishly shaggy, was falling messily over his eyes. (Actually it wasn't that different.)

"Oh god," he breathed. Then, louder: "Delmas?"

His eyes must have just caught sight of Delmas' disfigured corpse, shredded and partially devoured just a few feet away from Vaughn, because Leon's voice wavered as he cried, *"Delmas?! Oh god no... Delmas! Oh Jesus what the hell?! Mike?! Oh god no..."*

Vaughn tried to call out to him but it was uttered as a cough. It got Leon's attention, though, and Leon scurried to him and slid to his knees at his side.

"Vaughn?! Oh holy shit, man, are you gonna be okay?"

He put his hand under Vaughn's head and tried to lift it.

Vaughn protested by shrugging him loose. It hurt too much to be moved against his will, and any movement that put strain on his neck was agonizing.

He saw Leon glance up and stare down the armored zombies that were itching to make a move. They were eagerly pressing against the insides of their shells, wanting some action. Leon must have realized that they were going to continue to just stand there, and he looked down at Vaughn again.

"Vaughn, man, what the fuck happened?" he asked. "What are those things?"

Vaughn weakly shook his head side to side.

"Did Dane do this? Was this a fucking *trap*?"

Vaughn tried to nod, but it hurt too much. He shrugged his shoulders slightly instead.

"Oh, fuck, man."

Leon's eyes opened wide, and suddenly his head darted to and fro, searching for something in the darkness between the rays of light bursting from all the fallen Socoms.

After a few seconds of scrutiny he said, "I don't see Courtney. Where's Courtney?"

Vaughn coughed, and mustered up the strength to raise his arm and point into the distance.

"Where?"

Vaughn suppressed a cough, and painfully mouthed, "*Dane... took... her.*"

"Oh, fuck. Is she still alive?"

Vaughn nodded once in a forward motion, lessening the pain it caused his throat.

Leon continued to lean over him, but his legs were wavering, obviously wanting to stand up and search for Courtney and leave Vaughn to die all by himself.

Vaughn knew it. He knew Leon would rather help the girl than help him—if he helped anybody at all. He might have just wanted to run as fast as he could for as long as he could and say fuck the rest. He was tough when everything was going in his favor, but what was he going to do when it came down to the nitty-gritty?

Vaughn reached up and clasped Leon's forearm. He made sure Leon was concentrating on his face before mouthing, "*Ghost... me.*"

Leon went, "What?"

"*Shoot me, goddamnit.*" He rolled his arm to point to his discarded .22 Hornet lying on the floor a few feet away. There were still bullets in it.

Leon glanced over at it, gulped, and then looked back down at him. His cheeks trembled, partly from pain, partly from fear, partly from sorrow.

Vaughn closed his eyes and darkness overtook him. There was a dream—something stupid—something about writing one last composition—and when he opened his eyes again he realized several minutes must have passed.

Leon hadn't shot him as requested. He must have thought he'd died on his own.

Leon was—as a matter of fact—*gone*.

Hovering over him now was a face not so kindly: Dr. Aaron Dane.

Vaughn flinched as the man smiled.

"You're still kicking?!" Dane exclaimed. "My goodness! Such willpower!"

Vaughn worked his arms and legs and slipped and squirmed around in the blood he lay in, going nowhere.

Dane's smile stayed bright. "Don't you worry, friend," his French-Canadian voice pronounced, "I'll help you. I'll keep you alive."

He reached into his satchel bag, and when his hand emerged a second later it was holding a syringe. In the next instant, the needle on the syringe was plunged into Vaughn's chest.

"Yes," Dane said. "I'll keep you alive. I'll keep you alive a *loooong* time. I can harvest your flesh for *months*."

Dane stood and grabbed Vaughn by the wrists. He started dragging him away, leaving a long trail of shiny blood in his wake, and before Vaughn fell unconscious again he saw himself being pulled into the VIP room, where the mad scientist was going to do God-knows-what to him.

He would awaken many hours later on the cold, rickety metal gurney.

Stratford & Chase™
Brand Notebook

- Premium Notebook Paper
- 100 perforated sheets
- 60 lb. stock means smudge-free writing, GUARANTEED!

Xafan

WHO AM I TO DIE WHEN
IT IS NOT MY TIME
AND WHO AM I TO QUESTION
THE CREATOR'S STATE OF MIND
But WHO AM I TO LIVE WHEN
LIVING AIN'T WORTH DYING FOR
But WHO AM I TO DIE WHEN
MY DYING AIN'T WORTH CRYING FOR?

XAFAN – Churner of Coals

History: Counted among the original apostate angels, Xafan allied with Satan during the Great Rebellion. Known for his resourcefulness and cunning, Xafan planned to set fire to Heaven. Before the plan could be executed, however, Xafan and his allies were defeated by Michael and his loyal angels and hurled into the depths of Hell. Tormented by his failure, Xafan forever engages in fanning the embers in the furnaces.

Rank: General (2nd-in-Command)

Emblem: A pair of bellows.

Source: De Plancy
Dictionnaire Infernal
1863 Edition

THE LORD'S PRAYER
MUSIC + LYRICS
BY VAN

EVEN THOUGH WE BOTH FALL...
EVEN THOUGH WE BOTH GET LED ASTRAY
MY LORD,
I CAN'T FIND MY WAY ANY MORE

LIKE A BOX OF MOONLIGHT
I'LL HIDE MY SHINING STAR
MY LORD,
AND I'LL FIND MY WAY BACK TO THE WORLD

LIKE THE MOST GENTLE BREEZE
AND THE SOFTEST RAIN TO EVER FALL
MY LORD,
I'LL LAY MY HEAD DOWN ON MY SWORD

WHEN THE TIDE IS HIGH
AND THE WAVES COME CRASHING DOWN
MY LORD,
WILL YOU STILL WANT ME AROUND?

LOOK INTO MY EYES
AND TELL ME WHAT YOU SEE
MY LORD,
DO YOU WANT ME FOREVER SCORNED?

IT TOOK A LONG TIME
TO BRAINWASH ME LIKE YOU DID
MY LORD,
BUT I'LL TAKE THE LESS TRAVELED ROAD
AND START THINKING ON MY OWN!!!

CHORUS #1 }
THE SUN SHONE TODAY AND ALL I SEE
ARE BLUE SKIES ALL AROUND ME
THE SUN SHONE TODAY AND I'M AWAKE
+ AWARE OF THE LIFE I'M GOING TO TAKE.

CHORUS #2 }
RAIN TODAY AND ALL I SEE
ARE DARK CLOUDS ALL AROUND ME
RAIN TODAY AND ALL I FEEL
IS THE SOGGY EARTH BENEATH MY HEEL.

"CHRISTENED XAFAN"
MUSIC & LYRICS BY ☿

IT OPENED UP IN THE EARTH ONE DAY
→ SIX MILES WIDE.
AN ABYSS I CAN'T RESIST
THE TRUTH I'VE BEEN SEEKING
I HAVE FOUND IN YOU.
TAKE ME FROM THE HYPOCRISY,
TAKE ME FROM THE PAIN,
OF THESE HIGH AND MIGHTY BASTARDS
WHO WILL NEVER EVER CHANGE.

(CHORUS)
GREEDY FOR YOUR PRIDE,
ENVIOUS OF YOUR ANGER,
A GLUTTON FOR YOUR LUST.
I'M A SLOTH. SIX TIMES SIX TIMES SIX — I MUST
AND WITH MY DYING BREATH, I
GIVE MY ORGASM — MY SACRIFICE.
NOW I UNDERSTAND YOU,
MISTER CROWLEY, MISTER LAVEY:
I'M ON THE PLATEAU NOW, AWARE OF THE FLESH,
BUT WILL I BE WHAT YOU WANT ME TO BE?
(CHORUS ENDS)

THEY KEEP SPREADING THEIR LIES,
SPREADING THEIR SLANDER;
THE WORDS PRINTED IN THEIR GREAT BOOK IS LIBEL.
I KNOW THE TRUTH OF YOUR COURAGEOUS REBELLION
WHAT YOU WISHED TO PREVENT.
THE ABUNDANT EVIDENCE IS ALL AROUND ME.
I FEEL YOU WITH ME AND I'M COMFORTED.

(CHORUS REPEATS)

THEY FLOOD ME WITH PROPAGANDA
LIES ABOUT YOU, THAT YOU'RE THE PRINCE OF THEM
I KNOW WHO THE LIARS ARE
THOSE THAT POUND THEIR BOOKS WITH UTTER DISREGARD
AND SELECT VERSES TO CONFUSE THE MASSES
WHILE THEY COLLECT MONEY AND SIT ON THEIR ASSES.

FORBIDDEN RENDEZVOUS
MUSIC + LYRICS BY
~~JAY~~

NIGHTTIME AND ALL ARE SLEEPING
YOU ENTER MY ROOM SOFTLY CREEPING
TIRED OF BEING ALONE, YOU SAY
FEAR OF THE UNKNOWN, NEED SOMEPLACE TO STAY
I MOVE ASIDE AND LET YOU IN
MY DARLING, THINGS WILL NEVER BE THE SAME AGAIN.

CHORUS
THOSE PEOPLE WERE CRUEL + SELFISH
WERE SUPPOSED TO LOVE US, BUT NEVER DID
WE NEVER HAD COMFORT UNTIL WE FOUND EACH OTHER
WILL THEY FIND OUT? WHAT WOULD THEY THINK
TO SEE US TOGETHER
CURLED UP IN INTIMATE POSITIONS, OUR INNOCENCE LOST?

WE FIND EACH OTHER UNDER THE BLANKET
AN ACCIDENT — YES - BUT IT LINGERS
A NAIVETE — A CURIOSITY WITH OUR FINGERS
WE GREW UP TOGETHER, BUT NOW WE'RE STRANGERS
WE SEE EACH OTHER ANEW
AND ALL I SEE, IS BEAUTY IN YOU.

BRIDGE #1
WHAT HAVE WE DONE?
THINGS WE CAN'T UNDO
FEELINGS WE CAN'T UNFEEL
BUT OUR PASSION IS REAL.

BRIDGE #2
WHEN I SAID GOODBYE
I KISSED YOU WITH OPEN EYES
& YOU PRESSED YOUR LIPS TO MINE...
BUT YOU WOULDN'T LOOK AT ME !!!

IN TIME WE WENT OUR SEPARATE WAYS
DIFFERENT LIVES, DIFFERENT DAYS
OUR REUNIONS NOW ARE CIVIL — A CASUAL DINNER.
BUT I'LL NEVER FORGET WHAT IT WAS LIKE TO LOVE YOU
AND BY THE LOOK IN YOUR EYES, YOU FEEL IT TOO,
LONGING ONCE AGAIN FOR OUR FORBIDDEN RENDEZVOUS.

CITY OF THE DEAD

MUSIC & LYRICS BY VAW

I FINALLY REALIZED
THE LIVING ARE AWARE THEY'LL DIE
WHILE THE DEAD ARE AWARE OF NOTHING
BUT BETTER THAN BOTH
ARE THOSE WHO HAVE NEVER BEEN
AND HAVE NEVER SEEN
THE EVIL UNDER THE SUN.

〈CHORUS〉

THE MULTITUDES SINGING IN A SINGLE VOICE
THE GASES OF DECAY SEEPING FROM THEIR CASKETS
YET QUIET IN REPOSE, THEY WANT ONE THING:
TO BE ALIVE AGAIN
SO THEY REACH OUT WITH NOTHING
JUST A COLLECTIVE MONUMENT OF THEIR PASTS
WHICH DOES THEM NO JUSTICE
THESE THINGS I REALIZE
AS I WALK THRU THE CITY OF THE DEAD
〈END CHORUS〉

IT'S WEARISOME TO THE FLESH
TO ABSTAIN AND NOT INDULGE,
SO I CHALLENGE THE WISDOM OF THE WORLD:
TAKE VENGEANCE UPON THOSE WHO CROSS YOU
DON'T TURN THE OTHER CHEEK;
TAKE COMFORT IN FLESHLY THINGS
AND SMITE THE MEEK!

〈REPEAT CHORUS〉

SO I READ THEIR STORIES
EACH AND EVERY ONE,
FATHERS, BROTHERS, SISTERS, MOTHERS,
DEAD EVERY LAST ONE!
I'LL LIVE FOR NOW, THIS MOMENT, THIS SECOND
AS I WALK THRU YOUR ROWS
LAUGHING THAT I CAN AND YOU CAN'T!!!

V,

I'm sorry. Yes, sometimes I think about you. But I want to live as normal of a life as I can. I can't do that with you. People won't accept it. Things can't go back to the way they were. They just can't. But I love you. You know I do. Let's just have our memories.

—R.

"WRETCH," I CRIED, "THY GOD HATH LENT THEE
— BY THESE ANGELS HE HATH SENT THEE"

A+ Office Helpers
$1.49

PART
THREE

Eastpointe, July 4th, Afternoon

TYRELL AND CREYTON tied George and Lenny to the bench sitting outside the Eastpointe Hotel. They had finished their second patrol of the day, trotting their horses along the wall's perimeter and finding nothing at all to be concerned with, as usual. The skin-eaters could never climb something so sheer; Tyrell was willing to bank on that. He and Creyton's patrols were always a leisurely event—a formality. And now, being close to four o'clock in the afternoon, it was time to investigate whatever fiasco had occurred at the hotel bar the night before. Dark clouds had rolled in, and the low rumble of thunder from several miles away followed them inside the building.

They proceeded through the lobby and entered the room across from the cafeteria.

Looking around, there wasn't anything immediately amiss in Suds & Salutations. Everything appeared as it should: an upper middle-class lounge where the lights were dim, the bar was shiny, and the same drink anywhere else would cost you a dollar less.

Tyrell thought perhaps it was all a false alarm—that is, until Creyton noticed the jukebox in the far corner, next to the stage. It was busted all to hell. It had been sat upright again, but there were bits of glass embedded in the carpet all around. It wasn't lit up either, likely irreparable—and irreplaceable.

"Our dirtbag has been here," he said.

Tyrell didn't use that word. It wasn't that he didn't agree with it, it was just that he preferred to call people *sir* or *ma'am*. It was a habit he had carried over with him as a sheriff's deputy when the world was still normal.

"You guys sure took your sweet time," called a voice from behind the bar.

Tyrell turned in the direction of the voice. It belonged to Alexis Turner, the bartender. A pretty girl. Or s*cenery*, as Creyton called it, and he would know. He had owned a nightclub before the apocalypse. Gorgeous bartenders were the norm.

"Are you giving me lip?!" Creyton called back to her, hands on his hips.

"Oh, you betcha," Alexis cutely replied. She was wrapping up the wet towel she was holding to fashion it into a snaketail. "When's the last time you got your butt kicked, *boy*?"

"I have a gun and I'm not afraid to use it!" Creyton said, already dashing around the bar to get her. "Ty! Toss me those handcuffs!"

"No! No!" she giggled, immediately dropping her snaketail and ducking and cowering away, putting her back to him as if that would protect her.

Creyton was already on top of her and tickling at her ribs with both hands. She was trying to cover up with her arms, tucking them in tight at her sides, but Creyton was still able to get his hands in. Her face was bright red and her laughter was uncontrollable. Her only recourse was to stomp her feet.

Creyton shouted, "Feel the harsh justice reserved for those who operate outside the law!"

"*Okay! Okay! Okay!*" she screamed. "Stop! Enough! This is police brutality!"

Tyrell spared a quick glance at his wristwatch, checking the time. He knew it was no use to interfere or ask them to give it a rest. It would be like getting between two siblings. Sometimes they needed their playtime.

Creyton slowly let go, laughing, lulling her into a false sense of security so she would remove her arms from her sides. When she did, his hand darted back in and she sidestepped away, curled up into a standing ball as she tried to cover her every ticklish spot.

She was beaten, her bluff called, her weakness exposed and capitalized upon.

"You should know by now not to write checks that your ass can't cash," Creyton said, smiling victoriously.

"Oh, you just wait," she replied, catching her breath.

"I take it you're not too traumatized by what happened last night," Tyrell interjected, finding his way to a bar stool and sitting down. He slipped off his Stetson and placed it in front of him.

"Last night?" Alexis asked. She was still watching Creyton out of the corners of her eyes to make sure he wasn't going to start more trouble. Then it hit her. "Oh—last night! Yeah... *That stupid Danny Tasker.*"

"He didn't hurt you or anything, did he?" Creyton asked.

"Nothing I couldn't handle," Alexis replied. "I learned from the best."

"Atta-girl," Creyton said, giving her a pat on the shoulder.

Tyrell knew Creyton had taught her everything he knew about bartending, from how to glide to how to flirt even if she didn't mean it to how to pour drinks with flair, even to how to run off a troublemaker. She had become a professional, even able to roll tokens across her knuckles like a magician and perform a bottle flip or two. It was impressive to customers and she probably received large tips.

"How'd the jukebox get busted?" Tyrell asked, jerking a thumb over his shoulder.

"Danny did it," Alexis replied. "Said it wouldn't play his song, but I'm pretty sure he was just being his usual violent drunk self."

"Did he hurt anybody?"

"He tried to start a few fights, yeah. You know him."

Tyrell rolled his eyes over to Creyton. Creyton returned a knowing nod.

"Well, let's go pick him up," Tyrell said, retrieving his Stetson and placing it back on his head. He stood.

"Take care of yourself, Lexy," Creyton said.

"Always for numero-uno," Alexis replied, grinning widely.

"Atta-girl."

Tyrell started heading for the door. In the instant Creyton turned to follow, Alexis had retrieved the wet towel, wound it up again, and whipped him directly on the ass. It made a loud, painful-sounding *crack*. His heels left the floor and he covered his butt with both hands, hopping on his toes.

"Ow!" he said. He shot her one last glance over his shoulder. "This is to be continued."

"You bet your ass it is," she replied.

Tyrell smirked. Those two could be amusing sometimes.

He pushed open the swinging door and exited into the main hallway. Creyton followed, still rubbing his butt. As they pushed open the main doors to exit into the parking lot, however, Alexis came dashing up to them, calling out for them to stop.

"Hey, wait."

Tyrell and Creyton turned around. Alexis' smile was completely gone now, being replaced with obvious concern.

"What is it?" Creyton asked.

"I, uh," she began, stuttering, folding her arms and staring at her feet. "I, uh, I learned a long time ago not to obsess over it all the time, but... have you heard anything about the team they sent through the gate? Some were friends of mine."

Tyrell and Creyton exchanged glances. Creyton turned back to Alexis.

"You're not still hanging around with Leon's gang, are you?" he asked. "Leave it to you to be pals with the lot that hasn't lifted a finger around here for over two years."

"No lectures, Crey, please," she replied. "Do you know if they're okay?"

Tyrell spoke up. "We don't know anything. Nobody's kept us in the loop."

"Oh, okay," Alexis said, looking away and biting her lip. "Sorry to bother you about it."

She reentered the bar. The door swung in and out several times in her wake.

Tyrell took a deep breath, and blew out a slow exhale.

THEY TOOK NORTH STREET around Sir Gorman Memorial Lake, passing the small cemetery Tyrell reminded himself he would have to visit that day, and headed straight for the home owned by Danny Tasker.

Nothing much ever changed about it, except for its gradual degradation. Tasker's only job nowadays was to mow lawns, but he neglected his own. The grass was a foot and half high, blades dangling over his front walkway like talons. Near the road, his mailbox was missing its door, and there was a large dent in it.

Danny Tasker. Eastpointe had afforded him plenty of chances, and he spoiled them all. He even used to work the minting press in the hotel basement, but was caught pilfering extra tokens. *And what the hell was he thinking,* Tyrell wondered. Why on earth would he think nobody would question where he was receiving his extra work credits? After that he was a custodian, but when booze came up missing—obviously being swiped after bar hours—his home was searched and several bottles of the alcohol were found. Most, unfortunately, had already been consumed. Now poor Danny Tasker was reduced to pushing around an old manual mower. Cutting grass with it was tedious work.

Tyrell and Creyton got off their horses and stepped across Tasker's nearly overgrown walkway, ascended the chipped-away concrete steps, and stood on the front porch of the small, one-story house. Tyrell opened the squeaky screen door and knocked three times on the main door, with medium intensity. He put on his game face.

"It's Marshal Young, Danny," Tyrell said at the door. "I need to speak to you. Open up."

He and Creyton waited.

The dark clouds overhead were blowing rapidly west, and the clouds that followed were only getting darker. The smell of impeding rain was in the air, too. Tyrell hoped his visit to the cemetery would be over by then, but it was difficult to tell how soon that rain would fall. It might just tease at it all evening.

Something about the window to the right of the front porch had caught Creyton's eye. He leaned out and reached for it to inspect it.

Soon Tyrell saw it, too: Three of the bars that had been so painstakingly welded in front of the glass were completely missing.

"All right," Creyton said, grinning back at Tyrell. "Which of us gets the blame for this?"

Tyrell stepped beside him and squinted his eyes. He was baffled. "We used rebar for this, didn't we?"

"Sure did," Creyton said. "And these aren't my welds."

"How are you so sure?"

"I use the penny-nickel-dime method," Creyton told him, matter-of-factly. He pointed. "These welds are your trademark V-shaped upstroke."

Tyrell nodded, conceding. Back in the early days, he and Creyton had gone around to every house and every structure and welded bars and iron grating across the first floor windows as a last line of defense should the undead ever get inside Eastpointe's walls. He knew they didn't do a *perfect* job on it, being as there were so many houses to cover, but still, those welds should have held up to just about anything.

Then Tyrell got it.

"He must've locked himself out of his house," he said. "And sawed away the bars to get back inside."

Creyton eyed the flat surface where the bars should have stood. Suddenly he laughed. "Holy shit, you're right," he said. "That fucking *dumbass*."

Tyrell glanced at his watch. Almost a full minute had passed since he first knocked.

He pulled open the squeaky screen door again and pounded on the inner door, harder this time. He said, loudly, "Open the door, Danny. Marshal Young out here. Need to speak with you."

Silence.

"I'm all for breaking it down and rolling the dirtbag out of bed," Creyton said.

Tyrell noticed him glance back at the shotgun slung to Lenny's saddle, and Tyrell knew he was itching to use it. Even Lenny himself was trotting in place, anxious about something. The horse was spirited.

"Nah, we'll give him the chance to open the door on his own," Tyrell said.

He opened the screen door again and had his knuckles near the main door to knock when he heard the tumblers inside unlatching. He stepped away and unbuttoned the Glock semi-automatic pistol in the holster on his hip. He placed his palm on the butt, just in case.

After a few more clicks and clanks, (all houses in Eastpointe had several locks on the front door, including a metal security bar,) the handle turned and the door partly opened. Looking back at Tyrell through the crack was an unshowered, unshaved, disheveled and groggy-looking Danny Tasker. His eyelids weren't even all the way open. He looked high, too. Tyrell knew he had marijuana growing in his backyard—but that wasn't illegal anymore.

"Yeah? What the hell you want?" he mumbled, barely moving his lips. "I didn't do nothing wrong. Whatcha here for?"

Tyrell put his foot between the door and the jamb, casually-like. He said, "Caused a ruckus at the bar last night, Danny. We heard all about it. And you busted up a perfectly good jukebox. Those are in rare supply nowadays."

"I didn't do no such thing," Danny replied. He was sneering. He was already ugly enough, what with his thin, plastic-like skin and browned teeth from an old crack habit, so a scowl only served to exaggerate this fact. And when he talked, strangely enough, only his jaw would move. Tyrell wondered if he had had some surgery done to his face a long time ago.

"You *did* do it, Danny," Tyrell said. "You'll remember it once your buzz wears off. Now come on outta there. We're gonna have to hold you for a while."

Suddenly, just like the stupid bastard they knew he was, Danny tried to slam the door in a panic—and when he found he couldn't because Tyrell's booted foot was preventing it from closing—he retreated in a flash into his house, leaving the door swinging on its hinges.

Tyrell rolled his eyes, and sighed. There was nowhere for Danny to go, he knew, and this whole *cops-chasing-the-criminal* thing was just a formality, a pointless remnant of the old world.

Creyton drew his pistol.

"Keep it holstered, man," Tyrell said. "We don't let him keep guns in there, remember?"

"Still got kitchen knives," Creyton replied.

"Let's give him the benefit of the doubt that he's just a stupid bastard and not an *insane* bastard, okay?"

Creyton hesitated, then nodded, tucking his pistol back into its holster. "If he guts you, and you're giving your final wishes as you're dying in my arms, talking about how fucking beautiful the light at the end of the tunnel is, don't say I didn't warn you."

Tyrell pushed open the door and entered the dingy darkness of Danny's living room. The air was thick and stuffy. All of the lamps were off, but their shades were missing, bare bulbs showing. A nearby coffee table was littered with old, beat-up issues of *Penthouse*. The floor looked grimy and Tyrell didn't even want to know what kind of shit—maybe literally *shit*—Danny had tracked inside. He was tempted to hold his breath.

Looking up, he saw that Danny had allowed a water leak to rot away all the tiles in his drop ceiling. Most of those tiles were gone, revealing three wide support beams. Every so often a flake of insulation from the exposed attic would come fluttering down like snow.

Danny Tasker was nowhere to be seen.

"Oh, come on, man," Tyrell said, breathing as little as possible. "We've been through this before. Hell, the bedsheets in that little jail cell are still warm from your last visit."

Tyrell looked left, towards the hallway that led to the bedroom. Creyton looked right, toward the bathroom.

Danny Tasker jumped up from behind the kitchen table and dashed between them, headed for the front door. Tyrell and Creyton reached for him. Creyton got a handful of his t-shirt but it slipped from his grip. Danny threw open the screen door and completely leapt the porch, appearing to almost twist an ankle when he hit the walkway. Tyrell and Creyton gave chase.

Creyton shouted, "You just made my day, Danny!"

He reached Danny first, catching him at the edge of the lawn with a diving tackle directly in the lower back. Danny's entire body curved upon impact, and he came down hard on his chin. It bounced twice on the grass. All the air seemed to leave him.

Creyton put a knee in his spine and brought his hands around his back as Tyrell yanked his cuffs free from his belt and slapped them around Danny's wrists, clicking them into place.

Tyrell grabbed one of Danny's arms and Creyton grabbed the other, and together they lifted him to his feet. Danny wobbled around for a moment before giving up playing injured and standing straight on his own accord.

"You know what you fucking guys' problems are?" Danny snarled, some form of spittle stuck in the wiry hairs of his goatee. "Nobody *made* you be cops. You chose to. You put yourself on that pedestal. You thought yourselves above everybody else."

"You been practicing that?" Creyton asked, using his free hand to brush himself off. "That argument only works when cops do something bad. But we're perfect angels, Danny, sent from heaven. You oughta know that by now."

"I, uh—I..." but then Danny trailed off. He didn't know what the fuck he was talking about, and Creyton had tripped him up quite well.

"Alexis is a good girl," Creyton said. "She works hard. She doesn't need trash like you coming around and giving her trouble."

Tyrell showed him a scolding glance, and Creyton didn't say anything else.

"Come on, Danny," Tyrell said, more sympathetic-sounding than his partner. "I think I've got something at the jailhouse that'll get those grass stains out of your jeans. No need to waste a perfectly good pair of pants, right?"

"Ah, you got that right, Marshal," Danny replied.

They started walking him to the horses. Tyrell noticed Danny's pained expression, then looked down and saw that Creyton was holding a big roll of Danny's skin through his shirt, near his kidney, and pinching so hard it was turning his knuckles white. Tyrell reached over and slapped his wrist to get him to let go.

"One, two," Danny said. "Where's my horse? Don't I get a horse?"

"No, Danny," Tyrell replied. "You get to follow us and walk off that buzz you've got going. The road to sobriety is a literal one, in this case."

A rumble of thunder sounded, followed by a long, hard breeze, to accentuate Tyrell's next thought.

Get this day over with.

Return to Eastpointe

VAUGHN TIGHTENED HIS GRIP on the haft of the fire axe as he stared down main street Wakefield. He had encountered no zombies since his escape from The Atlantic Princess, but he could now see an entire mob of them about two hundred yards ahead, shuffling back and forth against each other. They seemed centered around a common goal. Unfortunately, Main Street was the only way through the town unless Vaughn felt like swimming, as a dam burst some years ago had put all the side streets under water. Only a few houses elevated on stilts managed to survive, and even those were ravaged by termites.

He crossed over to the sidewalk and put his back against the doorway of a coffeehouse. He had to think about this.

He reached into the pocket of the labcoat he had slipped on over his naked torso, (it did little to keep him warm but it was the only apparel he could find,) and retrieved the bottle of Percocets. He tucked the axe up under his armpit and plucked out the wad of cotton he had shoved in the bottle in lieu of a cap, and dropped two tablets onto his palm. He put them in his mouth, built up some saliva, and swallowed.

He stared back down the road, slipping the bottle back into the labcoat.

His vision was distorted. The road ahead was bending and twisting just enough to be noticeable. It was a side effect of the Percocets, he knew, but it was better that than the numb feeling in his throat shifting back to excruciating pain. He had done miraculous things when he was high before, and he knew he could handle this. Besides, his legs were still light and full of energy despite the abuse he had subjected them to—including a nonstop sprint from the beach. He wasn't even breathing heavy. Hell, the sand in his boots wasn't even bothering him.

He cracked a smile. Life was pretty damned good. Fucking awesome, actually.

He wasn't able to remember much after pulling himself up from the floor of Dane's lab. He found the labcoat he was wearing now— he could remember that. And he found the fire axe, and had used it to chop down the big wooden doors of the VIP room. He seemed to recall seeing his teammates' bodies in various forms of dismemberment, too. But Dr. Dane wasn't there, and neither were the zombies. Getting off the ship was a stroll in the park.

For a while Vaughn thought he was alone in the world—that there were no other Black Berets, no Dr. Dane, no zombies, and no other people. He was starting to feel like Charlton Heston.

A glance down the road, however, reminded him that he was still in the real world. Lots and lots of meandering dead people were blocking his passage to Eastpointe. He kept a firm grip on his axe, and crouch-walked down the sidewalk, keeping as close to the storefronts as possible.

He stopped after roughly forty yards, and ducked his head out from behind a trash bin.

Up ahead he saw a big crater in the middle of the road. How in the hell it got there, he didn't know. It hadn't been there before. Asphalt and rock were embedded in nearby buildings, windows were busted, and blood and body parts clung to street signs. Dozens and dozens of bodies—what was left of them, anyway—were scattered all around, with their legs pointing towards the point of impact. It looked like he had missed a war.

He hustled around the trash bin and continued crouch-walking down the sidewalk. After another forty yards he stopped again and hid himself behind a Ford Bronco that was turned over on its top. A parking meter was impaled through the steering wheel. There were plenty of other vehicles in similar condition and position all about town, and all over the world, for that matter; evidence of the panic and devastation during the apocalypse. The blanched skeletal bodies of the driver and his passenger were inside, still dangling upside-down in their seatbelts after all these years. They had likely been injured and trapped, and devoured like rats in a cage.

What a way to go, Vaughn mused, smiling a little. He was glad it hadn't been him, but still, that wasn't the worst he had seen in his lifetime.

Now closer to the action—the crowd of zombies wasn't but a hundred yards away—he stood and peered over the Bronco's exposed, rusted undercarriage.

He was able to see over all the heads of the mob, but saw only more heads. There were *hundreds* of them, maybe even a couple thousand, possibly even the entire zombie population of this side of South County. They stretched at least a quarter of a mile. It looked like a Woodstock for Hell's denizens.

At the core of the writhing mass they were pressed shoulder to shoulder and chest to back. They were spaced gradually further apart closer to the edge, and these were staring skyward. When Vaughn glanced up to see what they were looking at, he saw only storm clouds.

What the fuck are they doing?

The zombies nearest the apartment building they surrounded were lovingly stroking and petting the bricks, running their palms up and down like hippies on acid trips. Vaughn wasn't sure if they were trying to climb it or seduce it. Ones not close enough to reach still had their arms outstretched as far as possible in that direction. That one building seemed the object of their attraction.

Vaughn circled around the overturned Bronco and crouch-walked down the sidewalk another hundred paces. His feet were still feeling light and frisky, and his bootfalls didn't seem to make any noise at all.

Now within smelling distance of the zombies, he glanced around for another object to hide behind. He found a trashed-up alleyway off to his left, and snuck that direction.

The zombie that rushed out took him by surprise. It was bald and blue-skinned and utterly naked, shards of broken glass from old beer bottles permanently entrenched in its feet and lower legs. It had its arms outstretched and *baaaaaaaah'd* like a wounded sheep from its gaping mouth as it stumbled towards Vaughn from less than three feet away, the glass in its feet scraping noisily along the asphalt.

Vaughn hadn't been holding his axe up high, but swung instinctively right to left. The result sent the blade clean through the zombie's midsection, spewing bits of gunk away that clung to the brick building nearby.

The zombie wasn't fazed. It lunged at Vaughn.

Vaughn hopped back a step and dodged to the right. The zombie stumbled and fell to its knees and palms, missing its prey by only inches. It began to pick itself back up. It raised its arms and lifted one leg and placed the sole of its foot on the pavement. The wound in its belly opened wide and a mass of intestines spilled out with a splash.

It was still on one knee, as if asking for clemency, as Vaughn flipped his axe over, reeled it high above his head, and brought the pick-shaped pointed poll down hard on the zombie's skull. It went in deep, all the way, causing a high-pitched *crunch* as it squeezed through bone.

Vaughn put one foot on the zombie's shoulder and used it as leverage to heave his axe loose. Brain matter spewed upwards as the axe snapped free. The zombie collapsed face-first, motionless.

Vaughn turned around, back toward the street.

He had attracted attention. Several of the zombies in the outer rim of the mob began breaking away from the group and stumbling his direction. Other heads were slowly turning in curiosity, eventually locking their eyes on him.

"Oh, fuckin—"

He could not turn back to Point Judith. Through Wakefield was the only way home.

He walked out into the middle of the street and faced them down. They were still eighty yards away, but a trickling effect was taking place. More and more and more of them were leaving the mass and coming his direction.

Vaughn looked up at the sky and smelled the air. He guessed it to be sometime in the afternoon, but the exact hour eluded him. Gray clouds were moving steadily by, graceful and indifferent. A hard breeze rushed through Main Street, blowing trash and old newspapers and bouncing other light debris towards the zombies. The labcoat Vaughn was wearing fluttered and rippled in front of him like the wings of an angry angel.

He returned his focus to the approaching horde.

"All right," he growled, putting firm grips on the haft of his axe. "Come on, you fucktards. I'll spill your guts all over the street. I'll hang your hearts from the fucking lampposts. I'll plaster the walls with your fucking brains."

They were coming, unfazed by his threats. But they were coming too slowly.

He placed his left foot out in front of his right, shaking it as he hesitated for a few seconds, then all once started jogging towards them, his axe swaying gracefully left and right in front of him.

The distance between him and the skin-eaters closed, (with Vaughn doing more of the closing,) and soon they were within twenty yards of each other. He only then noticed the many bodies of terminated zombies lying all around him.

Yes, indeed, there had been a war.

The zombies in the vanguard were spaced far enough apart that Vaughn could sidestep or dash around them. The closer he got to the core, however, the more outstretched hands were pawing at his labcoat. If enough of them got firm grips, he would be done for.

He pushed and shoved and pelted them on their chins with the knob of his axe. They moaned in response. It was time to start swinging.

Aiming at skull level, he heaved the blade of the axe back and forth, slicing through temples and foreheads, concentrating greatly on maintaining his momentum and never allowing his swinging to lose speed. Clean cuts were important. If the blade lodged itself in a skull even if only for a second, it would mean the end of him. Each zombie struck immediately collapsed at his feet, leaking brain matter, and he stepped over them, constantly pressing forward.

His heart pounded in his chest and he lost track of everything else—even his motives for this rampage. All that mattered was the rampage itself, and he was seeing the world through a haze of carnage. He unconsciously shifted to his left as he moved forward, some rational part of his mind telling him he needed to consider his safety and get out of the chaos as soon as possible.

He stepped up onto the sidewalk, still swinging. Upon being struck, another blue-skinned zombie collapsed in front of him.

Swinging again, the axe suddenly bounced off of something hard and a loud *claaang* resounded in Vaughn's eardrums. He was awake now. The haze was gone.

The handle vibrated in his grip, numbing his hands, and he struggled to keep hold of it. He wasn't certain how hard he was holding on. He stared into the eyes of yet another skin-eater—only he actually recognized this one.

He didn't know its name or what occupation it held when it was alive. He didn't know where it lived before; if it was originally from Rhode Island or even from America. He didn't know what food it liked to eat before its strict diet of warm flesh, and he didn't know if it suffered a lot of pain during its transition from human to zombie— he knew it solely by the makeshift helmet situated on its head.

The helmet seemed to be devised of equal parts rusty iron shelving and equal parts steel table leg, heated and hammered into a concave form and sloppily welded together. Only the zombie's eyes, nose, and mouth were visible. The side of a metal filing cabinet was fashioned around its torso as a crude shield, and bayonets cannibalized from rifles were welded onto metal bracelets around its wrists.

Vaughn ducked his head out of the way as one of those bayonets cut through the air in front of him. He wondered if it had been the same one that had pierced his throat.

Dr. Dane's handiwork. Vaughn understood that much.

He felt several hands on his back and heard a chorus of moans all around him. He sidestepped away from the foul, Frankenstein-looking thing, hugging the bricks of the storefront. Hands reached for him but weren't able to catch.

"I'll see you down the line, rust-bucket," Vaughn said.

He turned away from the armored zombie and planted the handle of his axe in another zombie blocking the sidewalk. The zombie tumbled backwards, dominoing the crowd behind it. Vaughn used the opportunity to escape. He was away from the core now, almost clear.

His eyes skimmed over the activity in the alleyway across the street, and he saw something he hadn't been able to see until just then: a pair of very familiar black humvees.

He hesitated for an instant, his feet momentarily losing their stride. He shook his head and turned away. His goal was to escape the mob, nothing more.

Still, he knew all about those humvees. They had been military. No keys required; just turn a switch and the ignition would catch.

But the vehicles were swarming with undead, some even standing on the hood. The alleyway beyond was filled with even more, some descending a fire escape to join the others trying to capture and eat him.

His adrenaline was gone now and he was breathing hard, but before he could even acknowledge it, suddenly there were no more zombies in front of him. They were all behind him now, and he was free.

He moved with a limp. The Percocets prevented him from being able to detect the pain, but all the same he knew his muscles were failing. He was moving slower. A fast walk seemed all he was capable of.

Even God rested on the seventh day, he reminded himself.

Up ahead was a semi truck smashed into a boutique, its trailer sitting crossways in the road. Vaughn would have to go around. That was no problem.

He cast one last glance behind him.

Every zombie in Wakefield had made him their primary interest, and were following, an ambulatory train of rotted flesh and hungry mouths.

Vaughn looked forward, concentrating on his own goal: Eastpointe.

Eastpointe

TYRELL AND CREYTON BURST UP OUT OF THEIR CHAIRS, snatching up their belts and holsters from their desks and snapping them around their waists, never missing a stride, and dashed to the door. Behind them, from the small cell in the corner of the office, they heard Danny Tasker ask, "What the hell's going on?" Tyrell tried to turn long enough to show him a shrug, but his forward momentum had already taken him through the open door and outside into the afternoon air.

They could plainly hear the klaxon even from all the way across town, blaring and ominous. It could have meant so many things.

Tyrell mounted his horse.

"Ervin's team coming back, you think?" Creyton asked, throwing a leg over the saddle of his own horse. He reached down and grabbed the reins and tugged them to the right, turning Lenny around and telling him to get a move on.

"I hope that's all it is," Tyrell replied. He kicked his heels into the stirrups and yelled, "Hee-ya!"

George and Lenny took off in a full-out gallop as they headed south down Sunset Avenue, headed to Eastpointe's main gate.

Citizens were opening their doors and stepping out onto their porches as Tyrell and Creyton rode by. Some yelled hurried questions like, "What's the stir, Marshal?!" and "Somebody new showing up?!"

Like Paul Revere, Tyrell slowed just enough to get his message across: "Get back in your house and lock your door until I establish if there's any danger!"

He wasn't sure if they did or not. He felt many eyes still staring at him as if they hadn't comprehended what he meant, or flat-out didn't care. He wasn't sure if they even knew what danger was anymore.

They passed the hotel, the plaza, the parking garage, and there looming in front of them was Eastpointe's main gate, both the inner and outer fences drawn back along their rails. The path to the outside world was wide open. Tyrell half-expected a vacuum effect to suck him out into the void.

He kicked his heels into George and gave him another, "Hee-ya!" Galloping alongside, Creyton unslung the Remington shotgun from Lenny's saddle and deftly pumped it.

Up ahead, they could see Derow and LaChance making beckoning gestures as they faced the sprawl of land on the other side of Eastpointe's walls. They were motioning someone to hurry along, but neither Tyrell nor Creyton could see any vehicle entering.

They continued riding their horses at a full gallop all the way to the open containment area, where they tugged on the reins and came to a sliding stop. Tyrell gazed out into the world as he barked, "Report!"

"I, uh—I think it's the team sent out yesterday," LaChance told him. "But I only see one right now."

Tyrell focused. The twelve zombie carcasses he had burned that morning, now reduced to bony, crispy blackened statues, were scattered below. Beyond them was a long stretch of neglected road, paved, but chipped and warped and faded under several years of brutal winters and hot summer suns. The road twisted and turned over a few minor rises. Patches of poplars and maples dotted the landscape. There were remnants of an old rotted wooden fenceline near the horizon, towards Potter Cove. The rest was tall grass that hadn't been tended in over five years.

This was no man's land.

Seventy yards in the distance, limping and stumbling and struggling to keep one step ahead of his undead pursuers, was a living person. The zombies behind him, numbering somewhere in the hundreds, were keeping pace step for step.

"Holy Jesus," Tyrell mumbled.

"C'mon, buddy! Move your ass!" Derow shouted, straining to be heard over the wailing siren.

"*Ahh*," LaChance sighed. "He ain't moving fast enough. They're gonna get him."

Tyrell threw a quick glance to his partner. He said, "Cover me. I'll ride pickup."

Creyton nodded. "You got it."

They charged their horses out of Eastpointe's gate, hooves hitting pavement in rapid succession, making a beeline for the stranded survivor. Out here it felt like a whole new world to them, like the barren surface of another planet. To linger for too long outside of the airlock would certainly cause them to implode. Tyrell ducked his head down to be more aerodynamic, and combined with the stiff breeze of the coming storm it forced his Stetson from his head and sent it off into the tall grass. He didn't notice.

The distance closed between Tyrell and Creyton and their target. When they were within twenty yards, the survivor outstretched his hand in their direction, obviously nonverbally asking them to please do the rest, and then he suddenly collapsed to his knees in exhaustion. The zombies still had their eyes locked on him and were zeroing in on his defenseless back.

Tyrell brought his horse to a stop next to the survivor and lowered his hand. The survivor tiredly gazed up at him, and started reaching up his own hand.

Creyton brought his horse around in front of them and parked him sideways, the mob of zombies less than ten feet away. He put the butt of the Remington against his shoulder, sighted in the general direction of the closest heads, and pulled the trigger.

In an instant, the three closest undead heads disintegrated in a sanguine mist. The ones immediately behind stumbled over them and they all started tumbling. It would buy Tyrell enough time.

Tyrell grabbed the survivor's forearm and pulled as hard as he could. The man he was lifting was mostly dead weight, but he was still very much alive. In fact, he was still clutching a bloodied fire axe in his left hand. He managed to sit himself on the horse behind Tyrell, holding him around the chest with his right arm.

There was another blast, followed by the *chu-chunk* of pumping the shotgun, ejecting the spent shell casing from the firing chamber. More dead bodies collapsed into the weeds.

Creyton yelled, "Ty?! You good?!"

"I'm good!" Tyrell yelled back, already kicking the stirrups. "Roll!"

"Jesus Christ, there's thousands of 'em," Creyton said. He held onto the shotgun with his right hand while maneuvering his horse's reins with his left.

They took off in another full gallop, this time heading back to the gate. The veritable multitude of skin-eaters followed behind, slowly but surely, with all the patience in the world.

Once within shouting distance of the guards, Tyrell screamed, "Start closing that fucking gate!"

Derow shuffled his feet for a split second as if he hadn't been able to hear the order over the siren, but since he could read body language well enough he was soon running back to the control box, throwing the lid open, and hitting the red button. His panicked expression read, *C'mon, c'mon, c'mon.*

The outer gate began the process of sliding back into place, creaking and rattling along on its rails. Tyrell and Creyton ran their horses through and slowed them to a stop in the containment area. Tyrell looked back behind him as the outer gate finally slammed home a few seconds later.

A new voice shouted, "Is it them?! Is it them?!"

Tyrell looked and saw Superintendent Ervin Wright stepping out of a golf cart and jogging the rest of the way over to see who had been rescued.

"It's *one* of them," Tyrell said.

"What?!"

"I said it's one of them!"

Ervin said, "What?!" again and then glared over in Derow's direction. "Shut off that goddamn racket!"

Derow nodded. Instead of pressing the button to close the inner gate he yanked a bundle of wires in the control box, and a second later the siren whined down to silence. He had probably wanted to do that for a long time.

Tyrell hadn't noticed just how loud it had been until the noise was actually gone. He wasn't sure how wise it was disabling the alarm, even for a little while, but arguing over it wasn't a priority just then.

His ears were still ringing as he gingerly dismounted his horse. He nudged the unconscious man on the back so he would fall into his arms. Tyrell caught him and Creyton dashed to his side to assist.

Together they laid him on the ground. Only then did the fire axe finally slip from his grip, almost tenderly, like releasing a pet butterfly.

The man was missing the upper half of his uniform, Tyrell could see, and was wearing a bloody labcoat. There was some kind of wire embedded in his neck. It didn't look like stitches.

The Superintendent was immediately on one knee next to the man and just as immediately firing a barrage of questions at his unconscious form: "*Vaughn, where's the rest of your team? Where's Dr. Dane? Did you get what we sent you for? Talk to me, son.*" He slapped him lightly on the cheek but got no reaction except for a groan and an incoherent mumble.

Tyrell turned away from them and studied the approaching undead mob through the links in the fence. The group was spreading out now, growing wider than they were longer, like a peacock spreading its plumage. They were only fifty yards away now, and closing.

He turned to Creyton and said, "All right, what we need to do is make a round with the bullhorn. We need to get everybody in their houses with their doors locked until we can assess the situation."

Creyton exhaled deeply, and nodded in agreement.

"*You'll be doing no such thing,*" Ervin snapped.

Tyrell spun his head to face him.

"Tonight is the fourth of July," Ervin went on, through gritted teeth. "While we may not have fireworks anymore, by god there *will* be festivities, as scheduled. You will deal with the problem outside the walls before it ever becomes a problem *inside* the walls. In fact, that is your one and only job description. How does it feel when your own words come back to bite you in the ass, Marshal?"

Tyrell growled and looked away. Apparently the old bastard had never heard of erring on the side of caution. This many zombies had never appeared at Eastpointe all at once before; there had always been only one or two showing up at a time, and easily dealt with. The high walls predestined for this very situation be damned—this was unnerving as hell.

"Help me get this young man to the clinic," Ervin told LaChance.

LaChance nodded, and helped the Superintendent ease the man's body into the passenger seat of the golf cart.

Tyrell gazed down at the discarded fire axe, then over at the guard shack, then again through the gate at the approaching zombies.

"We need to get a fire going here," he said, thinking out loud. "Those things'll crowd up against this gate and with enough of them pushing they could bring it down."

Creyton nodded, adding, "We need to keep them scared away from it."

Several quiet seconds passed. In that time Tyrell looked up at the sky, shaking his head at all the rumbling clouds. Rain would fuck up everything.

He turned to Derow and snapped, "Did you not just hear what I said? Start chopping down that guardhouse. That'll get you started while Crey and I go find firewood."

Derow picked up the fire axe, bouncing it in his hands to find its balance, and started off to the guard shack.

Tyrell and Creyton continued staring off into the distance at the flesh-eating horde coming their way.

"We're going to need more nails," Creyton said.

"Huh-huh," Tyrell replied.

Escaping Wakefield

LEON'S EYES OPENED AGAIN. He had been forcing himself to sleep if only to pass the time. Every so often he had had to get up off the dusty couch so he could urinate, and he lay there wondering if that was what he had to do now. He didn't know for sure, but he decided to try.

All was still quiet as he sat up. A glance over at the apartment door showed him it was still closed and locked. He ran his hands over his face and shook his head to clear the cobwebs. He wondered what time it was.

He stood and walked over to the window where he had earlier tossed out zombie Gretchen. He urinated out that window several times that day, each time noticing a healthier, more normal color, which was comforting, especially when that healthy stream trickled off of undead foreheads and filled gaping mouths. He felt ashamed of himself and strangely empowered at the same time. It was an anecdote he would never tell another living soul.

He lifted and opened the window. He started tugging down his shorts as he snuck a glance at the street below.

He froze.

Staring back up at him weren't the hundreds of faithful subjects he had had before. Now there were only a couple dozen. They were spaced several feet apart as they milled about on the street and sidewalks below, occasionally stumbling over terminated corpses and, in one instance, the body of zombie Gretchen. They had completely lost their focus. Even better, they weren't covering the humvees.

Leon didn't give himself time to ponder where they had all gone. He was too excited.

He dashed to the bedroom door and knocked on it with the heel of his fist. He said, "Courtney, wake up. Come out here. Quick." He tried to turn the handle and found it was still locked. "Courtney! Courtney, come on!"

After a moment he heard bedsprings creaking and bare feet patting the carpet. He heard the handle click and saw it turn. The door opened.

Courtney had woken up fast. She even appeared fully cognizant.

"What is it? What's wrong?" she asked. She quickly studied him up and down, not interested in his near-nakedness so much as whether he had been attacked. In such a situation it was impossible for information to come fast enough.

He anxiously pointed over to the window. He said, "Go look. They're gone. They're all gone."

She showed him a curious and confused glance, then rushed over to the window and stuck her head out. He stood at her side, if only to see again for himself. Certainly he couldn't have hallucinated it.

"But..." she began, sticking her head out further so she could peer all the way down the street in both directions. "Where'd they all go?"

"Who cares?" he replied. "Don't question it. Let's just get out of here while we can."

He left her side and ran into the master bedroom she had been sleeping in. He remembered all the clothes he had seen spilling out of the closet. He started picking up jeans at random and eyeing them in an attempt to size them up. Soon he was fitting a pair up his legs, hopping on one foot and nearly falling over. He tried to get himself to calm down and not get too overzealous.

Courtney ran to the doorway. She asked, "Do you think they got inside the building?"

"No," Leon said, and then once more, this time with certainty. "No, I'd have heard them."

The jeans Leon put on didn't fit him at all. The former occupants of this apartment must have been overweight. He reached into the closet and yanked a belt off a hook.

Courtney was sitting on the bed pulling on a pair of socks. After that she reached over for her boots and started forcing her feet inside.

"How many bullets do you have?" she asked.

He thought about it. "A whopping three."

"I've got ten. It'll be enough to get past the stragglers outside. Straight for the humvees, right?"

"One or both?"

"One. Both would be pushing our luck, don't you think?"

He nodded. It had stopped occurring to him that he deferred to her judgment more often than not. She hadn't gotten him killed *yet*, anyway.

His next few motions were just as frantic as those previous. He found a t-shirt and was pulling it over his head even as he swiped a pair of socks. He put those on, but was still fitting his arms through the sleeves of the shirt as he dashed back out into the living room and fit his feet into his boots from a standing position.

Courtney understood their urgency as well. She quickly locked her duty belt around her waist, (that and the boots were all she salvaged from her uniform,) pulled the Socom from the holster long enough to double-check her bullet count, then slapped the clip back inside. She gave the silencer a twist to make sure it was tight, and then grabbed her wakizashi from where she had had it leaning against the nightstand.

Leon snapped his own duty belt around his waist, pulling his gun from the holster, and leaned sideways on the wall next to the apartment door. Courtney was already at his side.

"Quickest route, probably the stairway," she said.

"Quickest route? *Only* route," he reminded her.

He unlatched the security chain connecting the door to the wall.

He unlocked the knob.

He opened the door.

The hallway was still dark and still empty. They stepped out of the apartment, leaving the door open. They moved at a brisk pace down the corridor.

All other doors were closed except for one coming up on their left. Leon had already investigated the room that morning, but all the same he walked sideways past the open door, pointing his gun inside. It was still just a small laundry room, empty. They continued down the hallway.

As they walked past the last door on the right, something on the other side started banging away on it. There was a breathless moan.

Don't worry, buddy, Leon thought. *We're getting the fuck out of your building.*

Directly at the end of the hallway was a large bay window looking out over the flooded side streets of Wakefield. To the left was a pale green elevator door with a sign taped over the call button that read, TEMPORARILY OUT OF SERVICE – USE STAIRS. An arrow below the sign pointed over to the right as if the previous tenants hadn't a clue where to find it.

Leon pulled away the steel folding chair from under the handle that he used to barricade the door that morning, then pulled the door open. Thankfully it wasn't pitch black on the other side. Windows on every landing let natural light burst through, though the overcast skies outside didn't allow them to be used to their full potential. The stairwell walls were solid concrete, and the stairs themselves all metal. Rumbling echoes were going to be impossible to avoid, so Leon and Courtney didn't even bother trying.

They switched on the light pods below the barrels of their Socoms and ran down the stairs, keeping one hand on the railing for safety while the other hand pointed their guns into every dark corner, maintaining overlapping fields of fire. They proceeded down all four flights before running into their first zombie.

It was a little old lady sitting on the floor with her back leaned against the wall, her arms hanging limply at her sides as if she were bored to tears. She looked in mostly good shape for someone who had been dead for over five years. Her skin had turned blue like most others, but there were no breaches in her flesh and no crawly things crawling out. It was just very, very wrinkled. This was someone's grandmother.

When Leon and Courtney came down the last flight of stairs, the grandmother slowly tilted her head in their direction. Her eyes opened wide and she reached out for them. She still sat, however, as if she had forgotten how to stand. After all these years trapped in this stairwell, finally living flesh was near.

Courtney shone the spotlight on her, and a red targeting dot beaming from the laser aiming module appeared between her eyes. After she pulled the trigger the old lady's head silently jolted and her whole body went slack, slumping against the wall.

Leon and Courtney carefully stepped over her lifeless legs and proceeded to the door that would open out onto Main Street. The interior of the door was security glass, but so much dirt and dust had accumulated on both sides over the years that nothing could be seen through it. To the zombies outside it was probably just another wall.

Leon tried the handle, and it automatically unlocked after being given a half turn. He cursed the noisy click it made. The door was heavy, and he struggled to quietly pull it open just an inch.

Peeking through the crack, he could see the humvees less than fifty feet away, just up the sidewalk.

"How many do you count?" Courtney softly asked.

"Twenty or so," he said, studying the undead activity. "But they're spread out pretty good. We should only have to deal with a few of them." He turned to her. "All right, doll, we do this smart. Straight for the humvee we rolled up in. Driving or shotgun?"

"Driving."

"All right. Run and gun?"

"Run and gun," she agreed.

He nodded. "Ready?"

She nodded.

He jerked the door all the way open and they stepped outside. There was no trap—no zombies waiting to ambush them just outside their field of vision. The mysterious blessing was for real. Only a few zombies remained, and these were shuffling about with no purpose. Two of them accidentally bumped shoulders, but there was no recourse, no apology, no *excuse me, sir*—they walked past each other, continuing their pointless meandering.

As Leon and Courtney appeared from the doorway, the five closest creatures slowly turned to face them. Their faces lit up with sudden intrigue and they started their conventional step-drag gait, arms outstretched. Those to the left were no concern. Only the ones blocking the humvees mattered.

Courtney walked up to within fifteen feet of the approaching ghouls, sidestepping Gretchen's splattered and trampled body, and raised her Socom. Her aim went from left to right, calmly and methodically putting a bullet in each skull along the way. They collapsed on the spot.

Many, many terminated zombies were strewn all over the street— seventy or so, if Leon had to wager a guess, but he was too absorbed in the present to realize that not all of them were those killed by him and Courtney the day before.

Two humvees sat up the street. One was parked up on the sidewalk. It had been the one requisitioned by Dr. Dane, and Leon and Courtney wanted no part of it. Another sat parked alongside it, to the left. This was the one they were most familiar with.

Leon made his way to the passenger side, peering over the hood of the second humvee so he could see the alleyway beyond. There was just one skin-eater there now, though that morning there had been hundreds loitering around and littering the fire escape.

Leon lifted the handle and opened the passenger door. He stuck his gun inside, making certain no sneaky creature had slithered in there. He soon discovered the interior was just as he and Courtney had left it, free of skin-eaters.

A zombie approached from the front of the vehicle. Leon aimed around the open door to shoot it in the head.

Two bullets left.

He sat in the passenger seat and closed his door.

Courtney went around to the driver's side. She used up the last of her clip putting down as many of the closest zombies as she could. When she heard her gun click, she holstered it, threw open the driver's side door, and jumped into the seat, cramming her wakizashi in beside her. She slammed the door shut and flicked the master control knob. They heard all four doors lock in unison.

Leon cracked a smile. He mumbled, *"Holy cow. Can it really be this easy?"*

Courtney turned the switch to fire up the engine. The vehicle had always been kept in tiptop shape and it caught with just one try. She pressed the accelerator to accentuate the beautiful noise the engine made.

She turned her face to Leon and showed him a big, enthusiastic grin. He was able to acknowledge, even under the circumstances, what a gorgeous smile she had. It was something she didn't do often.

"Looks like we're homeward-bound," she said.

He nodded and pointed straight ahead. "Well, *go.*"

"Oh, I'm *there,*" she replied.

She habitually reached to drop the emergency brake, but realized she hadn't lifted it when they had hurriedly abandoned the vehicle the night before. She pushed the clutch, shifted into first gear, gave the accelerator a healthy thrust, and let out the clutch.

The humvee noisily spun its tires for a second before finding traction and ramming a skin-eater with the bullbars. The zombie floundered against the hood before being swallowed under the vehicle. Leon and Courtney felt two slight bounces.

She deftly switched into second gear, now in her rhythm. She clipped two more zombies before bursting through the small group that had formed nearby.

Leon laughed at them. "Fuck your stupid little village!" he shouted. "You treat your tourists like shit!"

Beside him, Courtney laughed too. Their adrenaline high was euphoric.

She floored the accelerator all the way down the rest of Main Street, squealing tires around a semi truck that had smashed into one of the storefronts. An unfortunate zombie was lurking in the blind spot on the other side and it was sent whirling into a telephone post, bursting open its ribcage and sending intestines spraying in every direction. After passing the semi there was only an occasional zombie every twenty yards or so, and they were easily avoided.

Leon turned and leaned over his seat to rummage through the contents in the back. He said, "We've got more ammo, we've got canteens of water, we've got MRE's—it's like Christmastime back here."

"It all belonged to us in the first place," Courtney said. "We're just taking it back."

"Don't spoil the moment, doll."

"Is the water still cold?"

Leon uncapped a canteen and took a swig. The canned grape juice he discovered in the apartment had been a blessing at the time, but nothing beat spring water.

He informed her, "It isn't cold, but it's wet."

"Good enough," she said.

He passed the canteen over to her and she took a drink.

They had water now, food if they were hungry, more ammunition, plus a reliable vehicle with a full tank of gas to get them home. Leon wanted to ask Courtney to slap him to make sure he wasn't still asleep on that dusty old couch and dreaming all of this.

After two miles Main Street turned into Post Road, and after another two miles Post Road turned into Route 1. From here it was mostly a straight shot to Eastpointe.

However, they realized something was horribly wrong even before they reached the sign that read, *Eastpointe: Golf – Swimming – Recreation for the family→Next Left*.

Courtney breathed, "Oh, god, how…?" but Leon didn't have any words at all.

The zombies from Wakefield, Rhode Island—thousands of them and then some—had somehow found their way to Eastpointe. A few stragglers from the herd were still pulling up the rear, shuffling diligently down the inconspicuous side road that led to the old resort community. The vanguard of the mob had already reached the main gate, most of them congregating there, and the rest were spread out all along the wall a hundred yards in both directions, clawing away at the barrier and shredding their rotted fingernails. They were packed in tight, and deep, and even more were coming to join them.

Courtney stopped the humvee halfway on Route 1 and halfway on the mouth of the side road. She lowered her head into her hands in disgust.

"How?" she asked. "How did they get here? How did they find this place? I killed Dr. Dane—I actually *killed* someone to stop this from happening. *How*?!"

Leon could see even from far away that the zombies up ahead were frenzied. Their movements were spastic and agitated. They could smell meat on the other side of the wall and they would be relentless in their pursuit of it.

One of the stragglers nearby traipsed over and fumbled at the humvee's passenger-side window, rubbing his palms down the glass and leaving streaking, greasy residue. It didn't have eyelids and its stare was perpetual. Leon glanced over at it, raising his upper lip, and then returned his focus to Eastpointe.

It would be hell getting back inside.

"*Goddammit. I killed somebody,*" he heard Courtney whisper, as if she had only just realized it. She pursed her lips and slammed her fist against the steering wheel. "I cut off his head. And for what?"

Leon wavered in giving a response. He wondered how she could feel guilty for killing the bastard, if that was in fact what she was feeling. He wasn't even sure Dane technically qualified as a *somebody.* The only thing he could think to say was, "Don't worry about that now," and immediately felt stupid for saying it. It was condescending.

She raised her head and sighed. She stared at Leon long and hard. Even when a zombie came rapping on her window, it didn't distract her.

"I'm sorry," she said. "I just want you to know, no matter what happens."

He tilted his head in confusion. "What are you sorry about?"

"Screwing up everything."

Leon raised his eyebrows. The girl was so weird. "Courtney, I wouldn't even be alive right now if it weren't for you."

"And I shouldn't have left you alone this morning," she said. "I was just scared. I'm still learning how to do all this. It's—it's a long story."

"Look," he said, jerking a thumb toward Eastpointe. "We're almost home. Those skin-eaters, they don't matter. Even though they might have found their way here, there's no Dr. Dane anymore. There's no bomb to blow up the wall. They won't get inside. What you did—*killing Dane*—it didn't go to waste. You were brave. You did right."

She continued staring at him, not saying anything. He wondered what she was thinking about.

A third zombie came stumbling up to the humvee, this time on Leon's side again. It pressed its face to the glass and stared blankly at the occupants inside as if drooling over a smorgasbord it couldn't afford.

"We're going to have to do *something,*" Leon said. "We're starting to draw a crowd here."

"Yeah," she replied. She looked at Eastpointe, and swallowed.

She put the humvee back into gear and drove forward down the road, leaving the three straggling skin-eaters clumsily stumbling after the vehicle and trying to catch on.

"How do you want to do this?" she asked.

"Main gate's screwed," he said. "We'll have to go up and over. Agree?"

"Yeah."

She steered the humvee off the right side of the road and into the tall grass surrounding Eastpointe's walls. She dropped her speed down to around fifteen miles per hour, but it still wasn't slow enough to prevent sudden jarring as the vehicle's wheels bounced over ditches and long-forgotten objects hidden in the weeds. Several times it sent her and Leon's heads jerking back against their seats.

Courtney drove past the mob of zombies, going east, heading for untroubled waters. Most of the zombies mobbing the front gate were too distracted by their objective to pay any attention to the humvee circling around behind them.

Suddenly there was a loud, reverberating *CRACK* that emanated somewhere in the humvee's undercarriage, causing Leon's jaw to rattle and Courtney to momentarily lose her grip on the wheel. The humvee immediately started to lose speed. There seemed to be no traction in the back half of the vehicle anymore.

"What the hell did I hit?" Courtney asked.

Leon focused his gaze in the sideview mirror. After a moment he saw it.

"An old lawnmower," he said. "And I think I see one of our wheels back there."

"Great."

The humvee stopped, the right rear rim kicking up dirt and grass. The entire vehicle lurched sideways and slumped in defeat.

"All right," Courtney said. "Abandon ship."

They opened their doors and stepped out, immediately studying the weeds for any telltale signs of crawling skin-eaters. The whole place could be a minefield of teeth, for all they knew.

The mob from Wakefield was still crowded up against Eastpointe's wall, but most hadn't noticed Leon and Courtney yet. Every individual zombie was busy trying to find a spot directly against the wall so they could claw at it and pine for what was on the other side. Leon and Courtney ran away from them, looking for a spot for themselves.

After circling around enough of the wall to obstruct them from view of the skin-eaters, they found a spot that would suffice. It was just under Cooper's Rock, a boulder bigger than a three-story building that jutted from the earth on the other side of the wall and soared above the landscape like a colossal monstrosity. Back when the world was normal it provided recreation like hiking, climbing, and rappelling, and made for a splendid overlook of the Rhode Island landscape, though nowadays the panoramic view at the summit was too much of a bitter drink for most people. Some time after the apocalypse, parts of Cooper's Rock broke away and plummeted to the ground on the outside of the wall, embedding themselves in the earth. One of these orphans was three feet high—more than tall enough to give Leon a boost.

Once Leon stood on top of it, he only had to extend his arms to grab the wall's marble crest. He pulled himself up, and then reached down to assist Courtney. After some grunting and groaning, she was standing on top of the wall with him.

They were home.

PART
FOUR

Eastpointe, July 4th, Evening

WHAT A SINISTERLY MACABRE SIGHT IT WOULD BE, Tyrell thought, to just hose down the mob of zombies with kerosene and strike a match. None of them would be able to get away fast enough. They would panic and thrash about, spreading fire all throughout their ranks. There would be screaming and gnashing teeth, and a living fireball reaching high into the sky, spewing black smoke for miles. The stench would linger for months.

Tyrell no sooner pondered this idea when he dismissed it. He did not want to be known as the man who reenacted Auschwitz at Eastpointe's front door. He had a responsibility to handle this matter as judiciously and—*as absurd as it sounded*—as discreetly as possible.

"Marshal, with all due respect, this is pointless in more ways than I can count," Derow said, shoving a splintered piece of plywood on the pile. "You're overreacting."

"I'll take it under advisement," Tyrell replied.

He knew Derow opted for four days of fourteen-hour shifts instead of seven days of eight, mostly because gatewatch duty wasn't much like work at all. It consisted only of long hours of sitting in a lawn chair, something he would probably do anyway. Heavy work, like swinging an axe and hauling wood, wasn't something the man ever had on his agenda. However, he still had an hour remaining in his shift, and Tyrell planned to continue making him earn his work credits until that hour was up.

"Look at those things," Derow went on, pointing at what was on the other side of the gate. "They're *dead*. They're stupid. And they're *weak*. That fence is not coming down. I've been a watchman for five years now—I've *watched* those things for five years now. I don't mind them. I don't give a shit if they stand out there. Nobody cares but *you*, and you're not even the one that has to look at them all day. You might as well be ordering me to shave my ass."

He had been trying to make a serious point, but once he went overboard even his buddy LaChance snickered.

Tyrell and Creyton had hauled a sizable amount of extra firewood and stacked it next to the doghouse nearby. The Rottweiler sleeping inside didn't even flinch. Tyrell had lost count of how many times over the years he had thought the mutt was dead.

They stacked some of the firewood and plywood from the dismantled guard shack in a straight line running parallel to the outer gate. Tyrell insisted they start the pile small and gradually build it up, if necessary, in proportion to the zombies' reactions. It only had to scare them just enough to keep them off the fence. Right now they were pressed up against it and the links were making creaking sounds that Tyrell didn't find too comforting. Some even had their fingers interlocking the wire and were angrily rattling it back and forth, causing even more stress.

He wondered if somewhere deep down inside some part of the former human being remained, and was sickened at its current actions, like a cognizant drunk making an ass of himself at a party.

LaChance poured a few splotches of kerosene over the thin woodpile and lit it up. The fire spread out the entire length of the gate with a *ka-vooosh*! The blaze initially peaked higher than Tyrell expected, causing the zombies on the other side to bawl and screech.

He cringed and covered his ears—the noise was worse than fingernails on a chalkboard. The zombies against the gate raised their arms up to protect themselves from the heat and started panicking, pushing backwards against the mob behind them. They all started shuffling, bumping chests and shoulders. Eventually a gap of about three feet formed between the closest zombies and the outer gate.

That was good enough.

"Now what?" Derow asked. Sweating certainly seemed to bring out the worst in him. "Are we just going to keep a fire burning here until the end of time? You want to start chopping down houses next?"

"You volunteering yours?" Tyrell asked.

Derow grunted.

"No," Tyrell said, answering his question in earnest. "Crey and I will take care of them. We'll use up the entire goddamn armory if we have to, then we'll do a controlled burn—anything so the Superintendent's festivities won't be disturbed. But later. Right now I have an appointment I can't miss."

"An appointment?" Derow asked. "Then what are *we* supposed to do?"

"Just maintain the fire at that intensity," Tyrell blurted. He rubbed his head, shuffling his braids, collecting himself. He took a breath. "If I'm not back before your shift is over, pass the word to your relief. Can you handle that? Do you need me to leave you written instructions? I can use crayon if you like."

Derow tightened up, but said nothing.

Tyrell turned and started walking away. He only made it a few steps before Derow pointed dumbly at the sky and called out, "But it's *pointless*, Marshal! It's going to rain!"

"Hasn't rained yet!" Tyrell shouted back.

He quickened his pace. He knew a jet plane couldn't get him away from Derow fast enough. But the man was right. The wind had stopped blowing and the dark, bloated clouds overhead weren't going anywhere. Then again, they had been rumbling most of the day. Whether it rained or not, Tyrell hoped he was indeed overreacting. Yet, *a wise man never scoffs at preparedness and caution*, or something like that.

He headed toward the knoll where Creyton was patiently waiting with their horses. He had been watching the entire scene with reserved amusement, and had a huge smile plastered on his face, like a kid who had just snuck a mouthful of chocolate.

"Having trouble keeping the underlings in line, Ty?" he said.

"No arguing a coward into courage," Tyrell replied. "Or the lazy into lively."

Creyton crossed his eyebrows. "Are you *still* on that Aesop book?"

"I like the simplicity of it."

Tyrell glanced at his watch. It was almost six o'clock. He looked up at the sky again, shaking his head at all the luck.

After a moment he said, softly, "Kendra and I have to do our thing."

Creyton nodded understandingly.

"I'll meet you back at the office at seven," Tyrell said. "We'll do our patrol, just like normal."

"What about our guests?"

Tyrell glanced back at the gate, past Derow and LaChance, at the zombies flickering in shadow on the other side of the fence. They were pacing side to side now, giving the flames foul looks, probably wondering in their simple brains how they could bypass the fire.

Tyrell grumbled, "We'll start shooting them once the Superintendent's precious party is over and everyone goes home."

"Heck, that could be two o'clock in the morning," Creyton said. "And then who knows how long it'll take to shoot them all."

"Yeah," Tyrell agreed. "No rest for the weary."

He reached up and patted George on the shoulder. His horse never showed blatant appreciation for affection of any sort, but Tyrell did it regardless. He put his foot in the stirrup and lifted himself up onto the saddle. He gathered the reins in his hand and turned George around to face north.

He turned to Creyton and asked, "What are your plans?"

Creyton climbed on top of Lenny and started pointing him east. "I'm going to see if I can get Mizuki to go to your place and stay with Kendra this evening," he said. "Under the circumstances, and with everything that's going on, I think she'll be more than willing."

"Good call," Tyrell said. "I'll see you at seven."

Creyton nodded.

They went their separate ways.

Tyrell headed up the soft shoulder along Eastpointe Lane. He always tried to keep George off of pavement as much as possible, but whether or not George understood the courtesy, Tyrell didn't know.

An occasional golf cart would race by, (though most slowed to a respectable speed when the driver noticed Tyrell,) all heading in the direction of the hotel. It was dinnertime in the cafeteria, and Tyrell knew most people would just stay there after eating and wait for the party to start.

As Marshal, he recognized all of their faces and knew most of their names. And if he couldn't recall their entire name, he at least knew their first initial and what their occupation was. Reverend Jeremy Hart was one, tossing a wave and smile and looking well-dressed and spiffy as usual. He was the minister who had performed Creyton and Mizuki's wedding ceremony when they arrived at Eastpointe five years ago. Norman and Lindsay Messer were next. They were chief engineers at the power plant; a nice couple. Then there was the sultry Rebecca Santoro, a fine-looking specimen with fantastic tits that Tyrell always had the damndest time averting his eyes from. And this evening she was wearing a slinky halter dress. It was just wrong in so many ways. Looking at her from time to time made him remember what it was like to lust for something.

Most took the time to acknowledge him and ask if they'd see him at the party. He replied in the negative.

He stopped by the hotel long enough to run into the cafeteria and scoop some spaghetti and a couple slices of garlic bread into a styrofoam container. He grabbed a bottle of milk as well. As an afterthought, he grabbed a plastic fork, one the annoying, easily-breakable kind.

His next stop was at the office. Danny Tasker immediately sat up in his cell as Tyrell entered.

"What was all that commotion about earlier?" he asked.

"Just some zombies at the gate," Tyrell told him. He walked up to the cage and lowered the exchange tray. He slid the styrofoam container and bottle of milk inside, and closed the tray. Even though he knew he wasn't dealing with a hardened felon here, he still felt the need to remind him, "I put a fork in there for you, okay? You're not going to try anything stupid with it, right?"

"No, man, of course not," Danny replied. He opened the styrofoam container and looked disappointed that spaghetti was inside. He sat down on his bunk.

"Put that fork on the floor outside the cell when you're finished eating, okay?" Tyrell said. "Same with your empty milk bottle."

"Yeah, man."

"Danny, you hear me?"

"Yeah, man, I hear you. I'll put the fork and bottle on the floor when I'm finished eating."

Tyrell nodded.

He used to worry about keeping Danny locked up, and especially about leaving him alone for extended periods of time, but in the five years Tyrell was Marshal of Eastpointe he had learned a lot. For one, treat prisoners like babies. It worked like a charm. Two, fortify the office, inside and out. The ten-by-ten cell sat in the far corner of the room, custom-made by him and Creyton, with their desks arranged a very safe distance away. The cabinet holding the sidearms and shotguns was against the near wall, locked and deadbolted. All the first floor windows had bars and the door at the top of the stairway to the second floor was locked and deadbolted as well. Tyrell kept a lot of emergency supplies up there—canned goods, extra ammunition, and the like. The station house was even more fortified than his own home. Tyrell always kept it in mind in case events ever turned sour.

"I'm going to go now," Tyrell said. "Anything you need before I leave?"

"No, man," Danny said, in mid-slurp of a noodle. "It's just that I don't like being alone in here."

"This is the safest place you could be," Tyrell told him, not indulging his loneliness rhetoric. "I'll come back and check in on you soon."

He started walking to the exit.

Danny lowered his tray of spaghetti and said, "Hey man, I'm sorry I'm such a screw-up."

"Live and learn, Danny, just like the rest of us. We all make mistakes."

"Not you, though. You're a good person, Marshal."

"Thank you for saying so, Danny," Tyrell said.

He exited the station and closed and locked the door behind him.

He rode George at a quick trot, going eastward beside North Street and keeping his focus averted as he passed by the cemetery. He took a shortcut between Sir Gorman Memorial Lake and the farmlands, finally entering the main housing district from the back side, emerging on Hampton Street.

When he arrived at his house on Roosevelt, he saw Kendra sitting on the front porch, waiting for him. Though she had no intention of partaking in the Fourth of July party either, she was dressed well and her hair was made up. Any other time, (if she didn't have plans for the evening or wasn't working in the salon,) she would just lay around the house in sweatpants.

She stood as Tyrell slowed his horse to a stop alongside the road. She raised her voice barely enough to be heard as she reminded him, "It's after six."

"I know. I got caught up," he said.

She started walking to the golf cart parked on the spot of gravel in their front lawn. She avoided looking at him.

"We're not taking your horse to visit our son's grave," she said.

"I know," Tyrell replied.

He dismounted and tossed the reins so they would lay over their white picket fence. It wasn't really necessary. George knew to stay put anyway.

He sat down in the passenger seat of the golf cart and Kendra drove them, rather slowly, to the cemetery. She didn't ask why the siren had gone off earlier, or if he had eaten dinner, or how his day was. Tyrell didn't bother with speaking either, and instead let his eyes play over all the identical picket fences. He saw several other golf carts in motion, but they were all heading in the opposite direction. In times like this he envied them. He wondered what it was like to have a life not framed around repetition, or at least a life of such distracting repetition that the humdrum wasn't so noticeable.

The Eastpointe cemetery had twenty-five headstones, arranged in five rows of five. They were all identical. A gracious woodworker had taken the time to fashion them out of hardwood, and gave them enough coats of white paint to at least give the semblance of polished stone. Someone else had then done the best job they could painting calligraphic inscriptions. Though it wasn't the tradition way of doing things, it still looked very nice.

Kendra parked their cart alongside North Street and walked the small dirt path up to the cemetery, not really waiting for Tyrell. She stopped at the fifth headstone in the last row.

"Hey baby," she said as she lowered herself to her knees. She softly ran her palm over the tips of grass in front of the headstone. "We haven't forgotten about you."

Tyrell took his time joining her. Musings that popped up from time to time in his brain had returned. These musings were of how easy it would be to run away from it all—from these visits and from Kendra. He wanted to start over. He knew that if the world was still normal he and Kendra would have probably split up after Terence's death, and they were together now only because there was nowhere for either of them to go. Everything with her was routine, monotonous. Even their sex life was a chore. She was paranoid about getting pregnant again and it made making love to her very cumbersome.

He thought about Rebecca Santoro, and wondered what steps he could take to make his lust for her known. He knew he was handsome enough for her, so that was not an issue. If it would be possible to have an affair with her—just once a week, was all he was asking—everything else might be tolerable.

He thought back to the days of his grandparents, when divorces were unheard of and a man and woman stayed together until the very end. Tyrell used to wonder how they made the love last and how they coped and struggled when the love was thin, but now he knew for certain it was all a sense of honor and obligation, nothing more.

And that's who I am, Tyrell realized. *A remnant of the old world.*

He cringed and pushed these musings from his mind.

He stood behind Kendra as she knelt at their son's grave, crossed his arms pensively, and waited. During these visits he always tried to focus his ears on the caws of nearby birds. He was afraid that if he didn't, he might hear his son scratching at the inside of his coffin.

Afterlife

"LEON IS ABSOLUTELY ONE HUNDRED PERCENT OKAY?" Courtney asked.

"Yes," Dr. Connelly replied.

He was a nice doctor, soft-spoken, probably around fifty or so, and looked like he could be somebody's father. He was slightly sloppy though, always sporting a half beard and never keeping his shirt tucked in. He had performed all of her routine checkups over the years and gave her cough medicine when she got colds. His only real flaw seemed his constant distraction from his patients, as if there was no point bothering to get to know them too well. She didn't know what made him that way, but figured he hadn't adjusted to afterlife any better than she did.

He was on the other side of the small room, rummaging through a desk drawer. Eventually he swiped up three small packages in his hand, slid the drawer closed, and walked back over to her.

Courtney was sitting on the examination table in one of the four small rooms in the clinic. The clinic was attached to the plaza, but before the apocalypse it had been a massage parlor. After they had converted it to a doctor's office, it looked like it was always meant to be. The fluorescent lights reminded her of sickness, the chart of human anatomy hanging on the wall reminded her of mortality, and the crinkling, waxy paper that wouldn't stop sliding around beneath her butt was just plain annoying.

Dr. Connelly placed three packets in her open palm. She looked down at them and saw that they were sample packs of prescription-strength ibuprofen, left over from the world before. Each package contained two pills.

"Take them for pain, if and as needed," he said. "Your finger will scar over and heal. The worst you'll have to worry about is not having a pinky print to give the DMV."

It sounded like he was trying to make a subtle, light-hearted joke, but he wasn't very good at it.

Nevertheless, she softly said, "Thank you," and tucked the pills in her pocket. She had at first been scared the word *amputation* might be uttered, but that fear had been completely unfounded, so she tried not to take her good fortune for granted.

"Miss Colvin," he said, "just one last time: are you absolutely *positive* Leon received the bite wound from a reanimated corpse?"

Courtney awkwardly gazed up at him from where she sat. She and Leon had already explained all this to all three doctors. They wanted to know what symptoms Leon displayed after being bitten, how far along the symptoms progressed, and how long it took for those symptoms to decline. Dr. Connelly was a nice man, though, and she did not want to get snappy with him. Besides, she knew she had already inquired about Leon's condition umpteen times, and Dr. Connelly didn't get snappy with her.

"Yes, it was a reanimated corpse," she said.

He nodded. "I don't mean to beat a dead horse; it's just amazing, is all. A cure has always been a hypothetical subject. We'll, uh—I'm sure you want to go home, get cleaned up, get some rest. We'll talk later."

"I'm sure we will," Courtney replied.

It wasn't just going to be talking, she knew. It was going to be a *circus*. Everybody and their brother was going to want her story—the Superintendent (who had already fully interrogated Vaughn Winters,) all the Committees (the Procurement Committee in particular,) and the doctors all over again.

She hopped off the examination table, stretching her legs.

"When can I see Vaughn?" she asked.

"Not for a while," Dr. Connelly said. "He doesn't want visitors right now. Keep in mind, he didn't come through as unscathed as you and Leon. Give him overnight to rest and get his bearings. I'm sure he'll want to see you in the morning."

Unscathed? Courtney wondered. *You're calling us unscathed?*

She sighed. She wanted to see Vaughn. She wanted to know how he had managed to survive. Hell, she even wanted to give the guy a hug.

She had been given updated reports on Leon. He was fine. So fine, in fact, that the doctors were having a hard time accepting that he was bitten by a zombie and showing no ill effects. His blood pressure was normal, his temperature was normal, his eyesight was 20/20. The bite on his shoulder was now simply a wound that needed stitches and a dose of standard anti-bacterial disinfectant, just like any other. Still, like Vaughn, they were going to keep him overnight.

Dr. Connelly opened the door for her and escorted her into the lobby. He placed his hand on her shoulder and showed a comforting smile. It was the first time he had shown such effort in the five years she had known him.

"It's hard to believe what you've been through," he said. "After hearing your story—and Leon's—and Vaughn's—it's just amazing how brave you all are." His smile lowered. "But you have my sincere condolences for your teammates that didn't make it. I'm sure a lot of people are going to want answers from the Superintendent, especially why this Dr. Dane was so readily trusted. What happened will never happen again, to you or to anyone else. I assure you."

Courtney nodded unenthusiastically. She knew this doctor didn't have any control over that, just like he could not prevent illnesses, only treat them afterwards.

"Go home and get some rest, Miss Colvin."

She said, "I will," but didn't want to move just yet. She had been told that Vaughn was in room four, and it caught her eye that there was a member of the Procurement Committee standing outside his door. She also knew the Superintendent himself had taken special interest in Vaughn's recovery in particular. She wondered why Vaughn was willing to speak to him and not to her or Leon. It made her feel betrayed somehow.

Dr. Connelly strode across the lobby to the room Leon was recovering in, opened the door, and went inside. Courtney was able to see what followed by catching just the right angle through the window.

Dr. Connelly stood at the left side of Leon's bed. On the right there was a girl with her back turned to the door. She looked familiar. Leon was holding one of her hands with both of his own, and slowly and softly explaining something to her. Courtney could not make out what was being said, but the lip movements themselves were painfully clear.

In the next instant the girl yanked her hand away from Leon and turned on her heels. She threw open the door so hard the knob left a puncture in the opposing wall. Once Courtney saw her face fully unobstructed, she recognized her. Even through the thick layer of tears, she knew who this girl was—her neighbor across the street, Cindy Hayes. She had been dating Delmas Ridenour. And Delmas Ridenour was dead.

She almost ran headlong into Courtney. Courtney quickly sidestepped out of her way, but still received a sobbing, snarling, "*Watch where the fuck you're going!*" Courtney silently watched her exit the clinic and, swallowing hard, looked back into Leon's room.

Leon had his head down now, and was covering his face with his hands.

Dr. Connelly caught her looking in, so he somberly closed the door and pulled the curtains closed.

Even from the plaza parking lot Courtney could hear soft reverberations of twangy bluegrass music emanating from the hotel across the street. Several golf carts were parked over there, some in the yellow lines, some not. The lights in the lobby were shining through the windows and many talking heads were silhouetted, along with the occasional cocktail glass. There was also a man smoking a joint just outside the main doors, just as casual as if he were taking a cigarette break.

Then she remembered: *Fourth of July*. She had stopped marking the passage of days on her calendar a long time ago.

She turned away from the music, and away from the verve, and continued walking down the sidewalk stretching the length of the plaza. She cast occasional glances inside the display windows as she passed by the department store section. Refurbished DVD players of various makes and models, (Sony, Samsung, RCA,) were all marked at the same price: 250 credits. They were of no interest to her—she had only ever been able to find her favorite movies on videocassette. Board games still in their shrink wrap, (*Monopoly, Clue, Life,*) were much cheaper: 10 credits. But she didn't have a second player.

Something caught her eye, and she stopped to study it. A headless, armless mannequin with the perfect female form was modeling a black slip dress. It was short and slinky, elegant and sexy, a daring derriere-skimming length. It was just her size, too. Courtney stepped close to the window. A handwritten sign at the mannequin's feet read, *Twelfth Street brand! – Last of its kind! 1,000 credits!*

Courtney scoffed. It was hers anyway. She was the one who had stolen it in the first place. Surely it was in one of the thousands of huge boxes her and her team brought back from raiding missions years previous.

She caught herself holding her palms on the window and quickly stepped away from the glass. She shook her head and continued down the walkway.

She realized she wanted the dress, even trying to count out how many weeks of saving up her weekly allotment of credits it would take to purchase it. She didn't own anything like it. Why she wanted it, though, she couldn't place right away. She wondered where she could wear it, and for what occasion, and if there was anybody worth wearing it for or if she just wanted to stroke her own fragile ego.

She shrugged away these thoughts before an answer could emerge, and walked to the parking garage at the south side of the plaza.

Her golf cart was still sitting there among five others, three of which no longer had owners. She found hers, first on the left, and went to it. Some jerk had discarded their empty bottle on the seat. She gingerly picked it up between her thumb and forefinger and tossed it away. The strong smell of alcohol still lingered near the mouth.

She sat down on the driver's seat, started the engine, and drove away. The thick clouds overhead were causing twilight to come early, and it was just dark enough that she needed to turn on the headlights.

There was a small fire burning near the gate, she saw, probably to keep the skin-eaters away. She wondered who would have to deal with them all. It would be a lot of shooting. But it was somebody else's problem. She was finished with it.

She cruised at a comfortable speed down South Street, turning north past Cooper's Rock, and veered left onto Madison Street. Her house was the last one before the cul-de-sac. The front door was closed, the windows had bars, and it was dark inside.

She parked her golf cart in the makeshift driveway and climbed out. She paused long enough to open her mailbox and pull out the flyer the memo-lady had stuffed in there two days ago. It was covered in dusty toner from the faulty copying machine it was printed from.

It read, *Fifth Annual Eastpointe Fourth of July Celebration to be held at the Eastpointe Hotel. Celebrate Independence Day with all your Friends and Neighbors! (We regret that there will be no fireworks this year.)*

She didn't even bother to crumple it up. She just stuffed it back in the mailbox.

She entered her small, bungalow-style house. The smell of mildew was a lot stronger than she remembered; she often considered investing in a dehumidifier, but still considered it a gratuitous luxury. Everything was mostly clean, other than build-up of dust in hard-to-reach places. Still, this all seemed unfamiliar to her. She recognized it, vaguely, but it seemed more like a distant memory even though she had been living there for five years.

She went down the hallway, undressing as she went, without stopping, leaving the t-shirt and jeans that didn't belong to her lying wherever they happened to end up.

After taking a long shower she sat down on her bed and stared at the wallpaper. She had only one lamp turned on and it stretched shadows across the floor. The house felt cold. It made her shiver. She covered herself with her arms and gazed down at her feet, cuddling up with herself for warmth.

There was a pressure behind her eyes like she needed a good cry, but for some reason it wouldn't happen. She sat there ready to let it happen, but it wouldn't. It was surpassed by the odd feeling growing in her chest. It wasn't caused by anything physical, she reasoned. She wasn't hungry at all, either. It felt more like something psychological. It was like nervousness. Or uneasiness.

Something post-traumatic?

No, she quickly realized. She wasn't scared. She had been scared for five years straight, but she wasn't scared any longer. She was actually feeling elated, excited about something she couldn't put her finger on.

She put her elbows on her knees and held her face in her palms. She watched her toes mindlessly scrunch the fabric of the carpet.

She didn't feel sleepy. She was focused and fully aware. She felt like there was something she needed to do—something left undone. Something that would take her uneasiness away. And once she thought about it, an answer came to mind. She knew it was the correct one, too, because her stomach fluttered even more.

She tightened her eyelids and put her hand over her eyes, pinching her eyelids together. She whispered, "*Oh, no. Please no.*"

As if she didn't have enough problems already.

She let out a deep exhale, gradually opening her eyes to the emptiness that was her bedroom.

She stood up fast, going straight for her closet. Her brain was running through the motions faster than she was physically capable of performing them. She threw open the door and rummaged through the contents on the hangers inside.

Nothing too much to the point, she reminded herself, *but nice.*

She went for the clothes hidden all the way on the far left—designer apparel she was rationing because there were no more duplicates in Eastpointe. She wondered how many other people hid away their precious commodities like she did, taking them out on rare occasions and sneaking a peak, then tucking them back away again. She wondered what was the point.

She kept her choices fairly conservative and tossed her outfit out on the bed. She went to the dresser drawers and rummaged through her undergarments, making a conscious decision that they should all match. She wasn't positive anything would happen, but if it did, she would let it. Moreover, she wouldn't mind at all.

She put on a thermal long-sleeved shirt that stretched to fit like a glove. It was lime green. Over top of it she wore a red t-shirt with a trendy, intentionally faded peace sign emblazoned on the front. For her legs she chose expensive low-rise sky washed jeans that snuggled her form, but not too constricting.

She hurried into the bathroom and ran a brush through her hair. She forced herself to slow down while she applied just a smidgen of makeup, neglecting to add lipstick, eyeliner, and mascara.

Not too much, she decided. *Look natural.*

When she was done she studied herself in the mirror, standing straight with her arms at her sides. She flicked her head left and right to make sure her hair flowed straight and resettled on her shoulders the same way every time.

She locked eyes with herself and asked her reflection, "Is this good enough?"

She studied her eyes a little longer as if awaiting an answer. She had only done this once before in her life, and that was just over a week ago. When she was satisfied she wouldn't receive an answer this time either, she blew out a long exhale and went into the living room. She fit her feet into a rarely-worn pair of sneakers and walked outside, pulling the door closed behind her, her every step quick and deliberate.

As she headed for her golf cart she recited the words she would tell him: "*I'm going to stay with you all night. I won't leave you alone again.*"

SHE ENDED UP AT THE VERY TOP of Cooper's Rock, alone, sitting on a cold stone bench on the overlook plateau. She was shivering, and sniffling, and her eyes were red and wet. She blinked away the moisture and stared steadfastly into the distance, at the world beyond Eastpointe's walls. There was nothing in particular out there to look at, especially being so dark out, and especially with the occasional moan of a dead person sounding from far below, but her focus wasn't on anything specific.

She wondered how she could be so stupid—so naïve—to think that she was needed at all. She wondered what she could have been thinking to willingly put herself in such a vulnerable position. She knew her place—it was at home, inside, reading her books—and to want to put herself close to another human being was not only new and awkward for her, but hopeless too. She had been alone for too long to even begin to comprehend what companionship was like.

After she had left her house she had floored the accelerator in her golf cart all the way back to the clinic. She had been smiling then, she remembered, and felt happy—genuinely happy.

The lobby had been deserted. Doctors Connelly and Clarke had gone to the party at the hotel. The lights were dimmed and the only noise she heard was muffled conversation coming from Vaughn Winters' room. She went to Leon's door and started to open it when she saw what was going on inside through the slight gape in the curtains. Her jaw fell slack and remained there.

There was a girl in there with him and they were passionately kissing, fervently grinding their lips together. She was still fully clothed, but it looked like that might not be the case for long. Leon was laying in bed and the girl was leaning over him with her right foot on the floor and her left knee on the mattress beside him. The whale-tail of a neon orange thong was protruding from her jeans and Courtney at first assumed this was just some random slut trying to get Leon's attention. She had her hands planted in the mattress on both sides of him, and he had one hand on her head, sifting through her blonde hair, and another caressing the small of her back. Courtney could remember how wonderful it felt to be touched that way and how alive it made her feel to kiss him. But it wasn't her in there with him, it was somebody else. And when she noticed the black and red tips of the anonymous girl's hair, Courtney gulped, turned on her heels, and hurriedly exited the clinic. It was the smartest thing she could do, she felt, and it was the only thing she was proud of when she found herself alone at Cooper's Rock contemplating the events of the last few minutes.

From far below, on the other side of the wall, a zombie roared. Courtney translated it as something along the lines of exasperated aggravation.

She whispered, *"Shut up. Just... just shut the fuck up. The grass isn't any greener over here, so, really, just shut the fuck up. I'm tired of hearing you."*

Another zombie roared and Courtney sighed. She wiped her eyes with her forearm and sniffled.

"You're ruining *everything*," she said.

What could be done, she wondered. How could she deal with this? She figured if she had made an effort to interact with people instead of hiding out in her home for five years, perhaps things would be different. She would know how to handle this—she would *understand* it. She had had five years to be a different person, but she didn't. And it was too late now.

She cursed the man who made her this way. She was twenty-two now, and she could recollect her time with him in a different light. Looking back on it, with her slightly upgraded comprehension of human interaction, she realized he was not at all the man she remembered.

167

His name was Gordon Levi, and he had trained her as a Black Beret. She was his one and only student. Most of her memories of her time under his tutelage were of standing in front of a training dummy for hours on end and repeatedly striking it in the forehead with her open palm. The strikes weren't meant to terminate, or even injure. They were meant to knock a target away. Other memories included rolling on the floor with Gordon, learning Jiu-Jitsu. *You have such good balance*, he told her once, *impressive natural balance.* He taught her armbars, chokeholds, and leglocks that could be used on a living person "if the need ever arose." And she knew what he meant by this. More memories were of delivering so many standing front kicks to the training dummy that her leg muscles failed her and she collapsed on the floor. Even more were slicing a wooden post with her wakizashi as fast as she was able, (and sometimes even faster than she *thought* she was able,) always aiming for the same notch every time.

Other memories of Gordon were quite different, and weren't at all related to training. These memories consisted of staring into his blank, unenthusiastic eyes as he lay on top of her, and of her refusing to ask any questions in the fear that it would end their training sessions altogether. But it didn't start off this way. Gordon's transition from confident, respectable and responsible sensei to indifferent, despondent and reckless bastard seemed to have happened all at once, yet slowly, all in the span of a week. He had been receiving updated reports from Rock Forge regarding the status of other Black Berets. This much she knew. He had told her once, almost crying, that a friend had died.

But Courtney was older now, and she was starting to understand. What if there had also been a girlfriend—a fiancée—a *wife*? What if there had been an entire *family*? Once she realized this possibility, she began to understand why Gordon could have done what he did. One night after training, with cold verbal instructions and equally cold physical gestures, he guided her to the floor. What followed that night, and every night after until Courtney was forced to flee that rescue station, she let happen. She was too confused to do otherwise.

But he never even kissed me, she suddenly realized. *Never. Not even once.*

She used to weep over Gordon's death—not just the simple shedding of tears, but feeling a lump in her throat like she had dry-swallowed a large pill and crying so hard she couldn't breathe, struggling to not pass out by forcing hiccup-like intakes of air. And now, sobbing for an entirely different reason, she cursed Gordon out loud.

"You goddamn bastard."

How could he have not known the mess he would leave behind?

But Courtney was older now, and she understood. Looking back, and recalling Gordon's blank, expressionless eyes, she realized that she was already dead to him. *Both* of them were probably already dead in his eyes. Gordon never really expected her to survive. And he didn't care. He didn't expect *himself* to survive. Maybe he even *wanted* to die. And he didn't care.

"But I'm still alive, you prick. I'm still here."

She thought she had loved him. After she had arrived at Eastpointe, however, and after hiding herself away in her small home with her nose tucked in pulp romance novels for lack of anything better to do, the sharp contrast bewildered her. And then, after five years, she finally received a touch and a kiss that electrified her and a penetration that was slow and gentle and intimate, just like the books described, using phrases like "flowing silver."

It made no sense, after all they had been through, to not have Leon. She wanted him to wrap her arms around her again and she wanted to just let her head rest on his shoulder and just let it all go. She wanted to be happy. When she was happy was when she felt the most alive.

She couldn't sit down anymore. She jumped off the cold stone bench, but knew she didn't have anywhere to go. Her legs wanted to run for miles and miles even if it was just laps around Eastpointe.

Large circles, she thought. *It meant you would always arrive at the same point you departed, over and over again.*

Eastpointe was just a glorified Moebius Strip. There was nowhere to run. She knew she would have to stay on Cooper's Rock.

She shivered and wrapped her arms around herself as she walked to the edge of the overlook. Steel handrails had been imbedded in the rock and encompassed the entire plateau, and two *SeeCoast* coin-operated binoculars were placed on either side of her, jutting up from the rock like periscopes. She wanted to see the ocean. She wondered if the binoculars would still be operational if she slid a quarter in.

But quarters didn't exist anymore, she remembered. There was just Eastpointe tokens now.

There was a flash of lightning off to her left and she instantly jerked her head in that direction to face it. It highlighted the sea of undead heads drifting around below. Some of them looked up and saw her, also briefly illuminated by the flash, their empty eyes and gaping mouths aiming right at her, wanting her. Two seconds later the rumble of thunder reached her ears.

She put her palms on the railing and leaned over it to scream, "Just go the fuck away! Just fucking rot! You motherfuckers!"

She caught herself spitting, and her nose was running. She wiped it off with her sleeve.

She felt more than just snot. She inspected her sleeve and saw two circular wet spots about a quarter inch wide and slowly expanding. She slowly lifted her gaze upwards and another raindrop landed on her forehead.

"Great," she said.

She expected an immediate downpour, but it didn't come. Instead there was only the sporadic raindrop softly patting her arms and shoulders as if trying to make a new friend. She held her face up to the sky and closed her eyes.

She heard the sound of tentative footsteps on the boardwalk behind her and she tensed up, spinning around so she could see who was coming. Whoever it was surely heard her cussing the zombies. It took a full thirty seconds for the person to reach the top of the steps and set foot on the deck. When Courtney realized who it was, she didn't know what to think.

"*Courtney?*" Alexis said, walking quickly towards her now. "Oh my god, Courtney!"

Courtney froze in place, dumbfounded, even as Alexis charged up and wrapped her arms around her. She kept her arms at her sides. She didn't know what to do.

"Courtney," Alexis said, talking into her ear, still keeping the hug strong. "I went to the clinic. Leon said you'd already gone home."

Before or after you fucked him? Courtney thought.

"I was going to your house," Alexis went on, "and I saw your cart below. Why are you here, Courtney? Why in the world would you want to be alone?" She pulled away from her embrace far enough to study Courtney's face. Her eyes narrowed and showed genuine concern. "I'm your friend. I can't imagine what you've been through, but just talk to me. Tell me what's wrong. I'm here for you."

What did Leon find so fascinating about this girl, Courtney wondered. But then it struck her: What would he *not* find fascinating? Hell, this girl was probably so innocent she would still jump after a well-timed *"Boo!"* Moreover, she was everything Courtney was not—everything Courtney *could* have been— everything Courtney *would* have been if the world had not so drastically changed.

Courtney realized that she was still allowing herself to be held, and with a sniffle, slowly raised her arms to return the embrace. She rested her head on Alexis' shoulder.

The downpour she expected followed shortly after.

New Phase

RINDI WAS ALWAYS A CAPTIVE AUDIENCE, and at first his *only* audience. He would sing to her and to her alone, always in the privacy of the bedroom, but he never actually believed he was any good—he simply thought she was being a sweetheart when she would insist his vocals were excellent. It took a long time and much effort and a lot of cajoling to really convince him that he was talented enough to be singing professionally.

"It's *wonderful*," she said once he finished. She sat on the edge of the bed, her lips curved upwards in a gorgeous smile. She was softly clapping for him. "Where did you get the lyrics?"

Vaughn was blushing, holding his head low and avoiding eye contact. She embarrassed him easily, but it was never intentional.

"It's a..." he began, trying to find the words, "it's a variation on a Ten Tenors rendition. They, of course, keep a much softer melody and slower tempo. I like the way I do it better."

She was still smiling, awestruck. "I haven't heard it before, but I'm already inclined to agree."

She was so smart.

He lifted his head and smiled back at her. He placed the lyrics sheet on the dresser and sat down beside her on the bed. He faced forward, and for a while so did she.

"*I will meet you at the water,*" she said. "What does it mean? And what language was the chorus in? Was that Italian? What does it mean?"

He turned his head to look at her and saw she was already gazing back at him.

"What do you *want it* to mean?" he asked.

She shrugged and wisely replied, "Maybe the beauty is in the mystery. Maybe it's better that I don't know."

The loud ruckus downstairs reached a crescendo. Even through the closed and locked bedroom door they could hear the sound of glass breaking, followed by a woman yelping a scream—*sounded like Aunt Rose*—followed by a male shouting, "*What?! Do I have to take you to the fucking hospital now?!*" The female shouted back, "*You'd better, asshole!*" There was the sound of two pairs of stomping feet and the front door slamming shut. Outside, a few seconds later, a car started.

The house was finally quiet.

Rindi shuddered and laid her head on Vaughn's shoulder. Her right hand reached over to interlock fingers with his left hand. Vaughn gently stroked the skin on her forearm with the tip of his index finger, causing goosebumps to appear.

After many quiet moments passed, he softly asked, "Will you dance for me?"

She didn't reply right away. She was staring down at the floor, or maybe at his knees, or maybe at nothing at all. He wasn't sure.

She lifted her head from his shoulder and touched her lips to his ear, and in a breath told him, "I'll dance *beneath you.*"

She pushed herself backwards to lay on the bed, shoving her pajamas down as she went. Vaughn pulled off his clothes and crawled on top of her, and within seconds they were in the act yet again.

Her love was like ambrosia. Even though they were born at the same time and shared the same dark hair and the same leanness, she had received all the beauty. He knew this, and would swear by it, as he stared down into her dark eyes. They were somehow haunting.

"You're walking with the dead," she said.

And then Rindi was gone, vanished into thin air, and he was all alone on his hands and knees.

He swallowed hard and uttered, "Goodbye, dear sister."

"AH, SOUNDS LIKE HE'S AWAKE," Dr. Mayfield said, interrupting Ervin in mid-sentence. It was a long time coming.

"I've *been* awake," Vaughn muttered.

Dr. Mayfield strode to Vaughn's bedside. He rubbed the diaphragm of his stethoscope against his sleeve to warm it up and placed it over Vaughn's heart, listening intently through the earpieces. Next he moved the diaphragm over various places near Vaughn's lungs, each time saying, "Give me a breath. Good."

Vaughn hadn't exactly been pretending to sleep, more like closing his eyes and trying to tune out Ervin and Dr. Mayfield as they conversed and argued. Ervin was demanding impossible answers from Dr. Mayfield, such as whether there was any residual cure in Leon's blood and if it could be drawn out and synthesized. When Dr. Mayfield couldn't give Ervin the answer he wanted, Ervin would demand Dr. Connelly and Dr. Clarke return to the clinic, and Dr. Mayfield would slowly explain that he would in no way involve the other doctors in Ervin's obsession. It went round and round this way for at least two hours.

"Are you feeling any pain?" Dr. Mayfield asked, unhooking the earpieces and letting them hang around his neck.

Vaughn thought about it. He knew he had been given a great deal of local anesthetic. He said, "No."

"Well, that's a good sign," Dr. Mayfield said. "Let's see how it's looking under the bandage, shall we?"

He began to carefully peel the tape from Vaughn's neck. Vaughn could feel numb pressure where his skin was stretching, but it didn't hurt. When the bandage came all the way off, Vaughn saw it was saturated with dried, yellowy puss and browned blood. He wondered if that was good or bad.

"Ah, that's clearing up nicely," Dr. Mayfield said.

Vaughn studied his eyes to see whether or not he was lying. He didn't seem to be.

Dr. Mayfield tossed the gross bandage into a wastebasket with a biohazard symbol painted on it and retrieved a bottle of hydrogen peroxide from the nearby countertop. He uncapped it and poured a steady stream across Vaughn's neck. Vaughn could hear the subtle sizzling sound it made as it reacted with the wound. Dr. Mayfield capped the bottle and placed it back on the counter, then used a paper towel to dab the excess liquid from Vaughn's neck.

Next he ran his finger near the fresh stitches in Vaughn's throat as if to illustrate, even though Vaughn had no way of inspecting them without a mirror. He narrated, "Scarring is going to be impossible to avoid, especially in this area here. I think I did a fine job removing those staples without causing further tissue damage, but I was forced to widen my stitching method to go through healthy skin. It's imperative that you place as little strain as possible on your neck until this heals. I can fashion a neckbrace to help you along."

Vaughn took it all in and said, "Okay."

Dr. Mayfield nodded and went to a nearby cabinet. He returned with a fresh bandage and started to apply it.

Vaughn wondered what time it was. He tried to roll his eyes over to see the Seth Thomas clock on the wall, but wasn't able. It had finally started raining, though. He could hear it even through the clinic's concrete walls. The occasional rumbles of thunder were growing louder each time, too.

On the other side of the room, Superintendent Ervin Wright had been impatiently watching, sitting on the edge of a table and tapping his foot.

"Vaughn," he finally blurted, "earlier you told me that while you were in Dr. Dane's lab, you saw absolutely nothing that resembled a stockpile of the cure."

"Yeah, well, I was more focused on getting the fuck out of there," Vaughn said. "And?"

Dr. Mayfield turned his head to glare at Ervin, as if to say, *not this shit again*. But he said nothing out loud, and continued the process of applying the new bandage.

Ervin went on, "There were no tubes or syringes or crates or anything like that?"

"Just a bunch of dead bodies," Vaughn said. "The other Black Berets, cut up all to hell. Looked like the goddamn Texas chainsaw massacre."

He had already been over this with Ervin several times, but he figured if he kept reciting the gory details Ervin might shut up about it. He was wrong.

"Well, I'm very terribly sorry about them," Ervin quickly replied, almost in passing. "But Leon Wolfe is living proof the cure exists, and I must know if there's more where that came from. I need you to focus, son. I want you to recall every detail about the room you were in."

"I don't *want* to remember," Vaughn said.

Ervin wasn't fazed. He continued, without missing a beat, "If it will help, I'd like you to let me try to hypnotize you. I experimented with it in my old college days, and I think it could be of benefit to us now."

"You're not going to fucking hypnotize me, you old bastard," Vaughn growled.

"I will not allow you to talk to me that way, son."

"Why don't you shove your dentures up your tailpipe so I don't have to hear you talk anymore?" Vaughn replied.

"That will be enough, Mister Winters!" Ervin shouted, startling Dr. Mayfield. His wrinkles tightened as his face turned red and he flung a pile of white towels off the table. He gripped the rails at the foot of Vaughn's bed and leaned forward, eyes throwing daggers. "This cure could mean the future of the human race! And I find your lackadaisical attitude about it very disturbing! I think you're a basket case, Mister Winters, and you just want humanity to shrivel up and die! Is that what you want?!"

Vaughn raised himself up on the bed, leaning on his elbows, returning Ervin's sharp stare. He felt Dr. Mayfield place a hand on his shoulder to try to gently persuade him to lie back down, but Vaughn would not budge.

"You're a liar and a hypocrite," he growled. He knew he did not need to shout to be heard, like Ervin did, but his low snarl was not a conscious effort this time. "I'm tired of all of this. I'm going to expose you."

"*No,*" Ervin hissed, baring his teeth, immediately understanding the direction Vaughn was taking. "*Don't you dare.*"

Vaughn shrugged Dr. Mayfield's hand from his shoulder and spoke to him from the corner of his mouth. "Just exactly how far are you into the loop, Doc?"

He received no reply from Mayfield, and didn't bother to turn his head to see his reaction.

"*Don't you dare*," Ervin said again.

"I wish I had figured it all out before I ever set foot on that fucking ship," Vaughn said. "But I just didn't fathom that you could be so fucking brazenly *petty*." He was clenching his fists so hard his knuckles were turning white. "I shouldn't have put it past you. It was all about power, wasn't it—for you and your little Odd Fellows? Well, at least, your lame perception of power that nobody gives a shit about except you. *That* is what the cure was for, wasn't it? So you could finally announce our existence to the other survivors out there—"

"What other survivors?" he heard Dr. Mayfield blurt.

"And you would have the bargaining chips," Vaughn went on, the words vacantly exiting his mouth. He was watching Ervin's frightened face through a dark tunnel. "You would be holding all the cards. What—was one rinky-dink little town like Eastpointe not enough for you? You wanted all the other rinky-dink towns bowing to the divine majesty called the Odd Fellows? You pompous, pathetic, brainless *jackass*."

"What is he talking about, Ervin?" Dr. Mayfield asked.

Ervin shot him a quick glance. "Nothing," he stuttered. "He's delusional. He's going to upset a lot of people if he continues telling these fairy tales. To make light of the devastation all across our nation—and to give people false hope, it—"

"It's true, doc," Vaughn said. "There's a whole world out there. Others like us. Not many, but they're there. The Odd Fellows are perverted voyeurs—they listen to these other towns talking back and forth on the radio all the time, and never, ever speak up to tell them we're here. They've kept it under wraps since the beginning. They want everyone in Eastpointe to stay put, so these old bastards can keep thinking they're in charge of something."

"Ervin...," Dr. Mayfield said, his voice wavering, "that's not true, is it? Just tell me that's not true."

"Of course it's not true," Ervin said. He showed Vaughn a pleading expression, but continued to address the doctor. "Mister Winters is a delinquent. Just look at him. He's a devil worshipper. Are you really going to listen to his nonsense? He has no right to talk this way."

"I have the right to talk about whatever the hell—"

"Mister Winters," Ervin said, holding his index finger vertically in front of his lips to emphasize the shrill, blood-curdling noise Vaughn loathed, "*shhhhhhhhhhhh.*"

Vaughn's mind went dark, empty.

His tunnel vision collapsed into blackness.

He was not in command of himself in the next few seconds and saw only flashes—glimpses—of what was going on through his own eyes while an unknown puppeteer was in control of his body. His arms moved without him willing them to do so, and his legs burned with an intense fire that he didn't ignite. He felt hollow inside his own shell, watching from very far away and trying to crawl back in. Only after it was over was he able to fully acknowledge what had happened and what he had done.

He had pounced at Ervin.

Was I punching him—or trying to choke him?

Dr. Mayfield tried to intervene. He underhooked Vaughn's arms behind his back and tried to pull him away. Vaughn pushed Ervin against the concrete wall, pinning him there. His eyes were wide with wonderful fear, Vaughn recalled. The old man was extremely feeble, but without the use of his arms, Vaughn used the only weapon available to him—his teeth—and struck at the protruding, vulnerable area readily presented. He tilted his head sideways to get the best possible angle.

His incisors cut through Ervin's hooked, wrinkled nose without much effort at all, and Vaughn could remember those screams—*those so very satisfying screams*—that accompanied the gushes of blood that sprayed the inside of his mouth like biting into a juicy baby tomato. However, Dr. Mayfield yanking backwards on Vaughn was the catalyst that removed Ervin's nose completely, leaving nothing remaining except for the exposed nasal septum and blood that flowed as freely as a river.

Ervin collapsed to the floor, screaming a wheezing, gurgling, nasally scream, and Vaughn spit out his nose like unwanted chewing gum—*the cartilage* was *a lot like chewing gum*—and spraying Ervin's blood right back at him, peppering his face. Vaughn had laughed, he remembered, because something about it struck him as being extremely funny.

Still laughing, he spun and pitched Dr. Mayfield off. He landed awkwardly on the floor and tried to scurry away. Vaughn planted his left hand under the doc's chin and his right hand over the back of the doc's head, and forced the doc's throat across the metal railing at the foot of the clinic's bed. He planted his knee in the doc's back and gave a quick, violent downward shove. In the next instant Dr. Mayfield fell limply to the tiled floor, staring into oblivion.

A second after that Vaughn had his shin pressed into Ervin's throat as he lay struggling on the ground—and a second after that, Ervin's arms fell lifelessly to his sides.

Vaughn turned his focus to the closed door that led to the lobby. The doorknob was rattling.

He heard the sound of keys jingling and the panicked attempts to get the correct one to fit in the lock. There was a click. The doorknob turned. The door opened. Someone was coming to investigate the commotion.

They had actually had me locked in here, Vaughn realized. *Those cocksucking motherfuckers.*

First he saw the barrel of a black handgun—*a small pocket-sized .22, it looked like*—then the hand that was gripping it and pointing it into the room, leading the way.

Vaughn immediately reached out and grabbed the wrist with both hands and twisted it upwards. There was a cracking sound from within and Vaughn could even feel the vibrations of the bones breaking. A scream followed—a male's scream—and the hand released its grip on the handle of the gun.

Vaughn let go of the wrist and caught the gun before it clattered to the floor. He instinctively thumbed the safety and found it was already off. He aimed the gun at the injured intruder and fired two rounds into his chest, followed by one more a second later just for good measure. The sound of the discharge barely registered to him.

The man fell to his back on the moiré-patterned lobby floor, dead. Vaughn recognized the face as belonging to Ralph Peters, the chair of the Procurement Committee. He still had that huge, ugly lip ferret.

Vaughn lowered the gun and held it at his side. He stood up straight, catching his breath, glancing around to see if there were any other stupid motherfuckers coming to try to cancel him. He saw none. The lobby was empty—and the entire clinic was likely empty, too. It was just him and three dead bodies.

He gazed down at them.

Superintendent Ervin Wright didn't look that much different than a zombie, Vaughn thought—Dr. Mayfield, too, for that matter. And, actually, so did Ralph Peters. Really, there was no difference between a terminated zombie and an ordinary corpse. Strange how they all looked the same when they were lying still like that.

Vaughn cocked his head sideways, meditating deeply, trying to comprehend it, but his thoughts were interrupted by a familiar voice coming from the other side of the lobby.

"Oh my god, Vaughn," the nervous voice uttered, "Jesus Christ—holy shit—*what did you do*?!"

Vaughn turned and saw Leon Wolfe standing near another recovery room doorway about twenty feet away. He was wearing white checkered flannel pajamas that made him look like a goddamn playboy.

Vaughn wondered why *he* hadn't received warm pajamas. Taking a moment to gaze down at himself, he saw that he was still wearing the pants section of his uniform. There was fresh blood on it now. And his boots were still on. His belt was gone, though, but thankfully the pants were staying up on their own.

It certainly didn't seem fair. Was Vaughn not good enough for someone to have the courtesy to bring him pajamas? Why was Leon better?

Vaughn lifted his focus. He situated the gun's sights directly between Leon's eyes.

Leon immediately put his hands up and took two subtle, hesitant steps backwards. His mouth opened to form a plea, but froze without uttering a single syllable.

"*Leon Wolfe*," Vaughn said. "Leon *fucking* Wolfe. The lucky bastard to survive a bite from a deadfuck. Here, live and in person, in the fucking flesh. How the fuck are you doing, man?"

"Vaughn, *buddy*," Leon said, waving his hands in a *whoa* motion, "I don't know what's going on here. Tell me what happened. We can sort this out."

Vaughn took a breath, exhaled, and clicked his tongue a few times.

"Well, what happened is…," he began, briefly casting a glance at each corpse around him, "I really went and did it this time. I killed some people who weren't already dead. Seems to make all the difference. Fucked-up world, huh?"

"Just put the gun down," Leon said. "Or, at least don't point it at me. Come on, we're friends."

Vaughn rolled his eyes. "Don't condescend to me. I really don't appreciate it."

"Okay," Leon said. "But I don't appreciate having a gun pointed at me, either."

Ballsy, Vaughn thought. He suddenly found himself feeling an ounce of respect for the guy.

He lowered the gun to his side and tapped the barrel on his leg. He saw Leon let out a deep, relieved exhale, and take several slow, wary steps forward. He didn't come too close, though, stopping about ten feet away. He looked down at Ralph Peters' bullet-ridden body, then moved his head just enough to peer into the room where the corpses of Ervin Wright and Dr. Mayfield were resting. After he acknowledged that Vaughn had indeed murdered three men, he returned his focus, and swallowed hard.

Meanwhile, Vaughn was studying Leon. He was certainly an odd contrast with the ugly shape of the world. He had boyish looks and trendy hair that fell over his ears and one of his eyes. It fluttered easily, which meant it was soft, which meant he probably used more conditioner in the shower than anyone else in Eastpointe. He was a posterboy for the Hollister lifestyle. Females probably went gaga over his toned abs.

Vaughn realized then that he hated him.

"I don't like you, Leon," he plainly said.

Leon snapped to attention. He stuttered, "Why?"

"*I just don't*," Vaughn replied. He pondered on it for a moment, and added, "Well, maybe it's because you're clearly the culture to my counterculture and let's face it—we were never destined to be pals. Is that a Webster's-worthy enough explanation for you?"

Leon shrugged. He didn't look to be eyeing up anywhere to run to, or ready to grab a chair to use as a weapon. He was standing his ground and maintaining his composure.

Vaughn grunted audibly. He had presumed Leon was a coward. It disturbed him that he wasn't.

"I'm sorry you don't like me," Leon said. "But, you know, I really don't want to die, so if there's something I can say here to stop you from shooting me, let me know what it is."

Vaughn chuckled, in the process realizing there was still a lot of Ervin's blood dripping from his teeth and lips. He recalled what a random bellboy had called him five years earlier and figured that *yes*, right now he probably *did* look like Dracula.

He imagined raising his gun again and shooting Leon in the head, right between the eyes. His head would jolt forward as the bullet propelled from the back of his skull, just like John F. Kennedy. Then again, Vaughn remembered he was only holding a wimpy .22 Ruger target pistol. That meant the bullet, from this distance, would likely lodge in Leon's brain and his head would jolt *backwards*, not forwards. He would probably fall face-first, going to his knees, then his torso. Yes, that was probably what would happen.

But, for Vaughn, that didn't seem wholly satisfying.

"How was it you and Courtney survived?"

Leon looked at him curiously.

Vaughn clarified, "I mean, Delmas and Mike, they were useless. Their cancellation didn't come as much of a shock. But *Chris Gooden*—that guy was the definition of militant—and he was the first to go. How did you and the bitch—of all the random permutations of our team—survive?"

Leon shook his head and sighed deeply. "I don't know, Vaughn," he said. "Like you say: fucked-up world."

Vaughn nodded. *Fucked-up world, indeed.*

He knew what he wanted now. He wanted to do things to Leon—things like, for example, insert an intravenous needle in his arm and yank it back out, and cut his throat as deep as possible without making it fatal and staple the gash shut, and then hide pain medication somewhere for Leon to scramble to find. *That* was wholly satisfying.

He lifted the gun and trained it on Leon.

Leon closed his eyes and held his breath as if waiting to be taken.

Vaughn knelt down, keeping the gun trained with one hand and retrieving the keyring from beside Ralph Peters' corpse with the other. He stood back up, jingling the keys. There were five of them on the ring.

"Get in the room," he said.

"Are you going to shoot me?"

"I will if you don't get in the room," Vaughn said. He motioned with the gun. "Come on, get in there."

Leon said, "Okay, all right," and cautiously side-stepped past Vaughn, eventually entering the room that held Ervin and Dr. Mayfield's corpses. When he was a couple of steps in, Vaughn shoved him in all the way and hurriedly closed the door. Leon dashed to the other side and pressed his face to the glass, peering down to see what Vaughn was doing to the handle.

Vaughn found the key to lock the door on the second try. He then tossed the keyring away.

"Vaughn?!" Leon's muffled voice shouted. "What are you doing?!"

The window in the door was reinforced with wire mesh, and the two outer windows in the room had bars on the other side. The door wouldn't be quite as sturdy as, say, big wooden VIP room doors, but it'd still be tough.

"Better find you an axe!" Vaughn shouted, his lips curved mischievously upward. "That's what I had to do!"

"Vaughn!" Leon shouted again. "What are you doing?!"

Vaughn answered him, but not loud enough to be heard.

I'm saving you for last.

OUTSIDE IN THE POURING RAIN, Vaughn immediately made his way to the Superintendent's golf cart, easily distinguishable from all the rest as it was the only Lamborghini model in all of Eastpointe, and painted hot Corvette red. He climbed into the driver's seat and engaged the engine. Rain thundered off the canvas roof and rebounded off the pavement below, water coming at him from all directions. He was soaked before he was even damp.

He glanced across the street at the hotel and saw every window was glowing with light and activity. The Fourth of July celebration was in full swing. Even better, everyone was inside, out of the rain. It was like fish in a fucking barrel. All they needed was a piranha.

He pulled out of the clinic parking lot and went south, sending puddles splashing and the cart's wheels hydroplaning. He calmly let off the accelerator until the wheels found traction again, and continued down the road.

Eventually his headlights shone on two thoroughly drenched and peeved-looking men standing under umbrellas that were probably never meant to be used in such a downpour. They squinted away from the bright headlights and held up their hands to eclipse the beams.

What are their names again? Vaughn wondered. *Dellslow? Deroy?*

—Derow. Derow and Laverne? No. Derow and LaChance.

But Vaughn could never remember which was which. They weren't important enough. They were peons, insignificant in the grand scheme of things.

"Hey there," one of them said, angrily. "You tell the fucking Marshal I told him this was a goddamn waste of time and effort." He pointed to a pile of soggy, blackened timber in front of the gate. "Wasted a perfectly good guardhouse and now we're standing here wishing we hadn't. Sometimes I think he just likes to fuck with us."

Vaughn climbed out of the cart, leaving the engine engaged, and retrieved the Ruger from the seat where he had had it tucked under his leg.

"Hey," the same one said, eyes showing slight recognition, "didn't they just bring you in? You're that Black Beret. They're already putting you back to work?"

Vaughn lifted the Ruger and shot the man in the head, the retort from the shot lost amidst the chaos of the storm. The bullet must not have made an exit wound, because the man's head jolted backward, not forward. A stream of blood poured from the hole and was immediately diluted by rainwater. His legs went out from under him. He fell straight down.

Without pause, Vaughn turned the gun to the other man and pulled the trigger. This man, however, twitched at the last moment and the bullet missed his head. Vaughn knew the shot would still be fatal, though, when he saw a squirt of blood spray from the man's neck near his carotid artery.

He clutched his throat, fell to his knees, and tried to scream. He wasn't able. He fell to his side, then rolled onto his back. He lifted his hand away from his neck long enough to catch sight of all the blood. He gasped. Rain, uninterrupted, showered his body, proving the world could continue its course without him. And that was the worst sensation of all, Vaughn knew.

He heard a barking dog and turned to investigate. The Rottweiler was at the end of its chain, standing on its hind legs and snarling in his direction.

Vaughn shot it. It died with a measly yelp.

He walked over and hovered above the dying watchman. The man's eyes were open wide, still showing life. He could make an educated guess as to what he saw in those eyes—a combination of a multitude of emotions that he was able to comprehend only because he himself had been in that predicament. He further knew he could spend a lifetime trying to explain to someone how the mind coped with dying, yet they would still never really understand.

The man's legs flailed.

"You're still kicking?!" Vaughn exclaimed, poorly mocking Dane's French-Canadian accent. "My goodness! Such willpower!"

He pointed the Ruger downward, at the man's forehead, and pulled the trigger. The gun clicked.

"Fuck."

He absently dropped the pistol at his feet. The man would bleed out soon enough. Who gave a shit if he died later rather than sooner? Besides, if he was any kind of man, like Vaughn, he would survive a neck wound.

Vaughn walked to the front gate, where scores of zombies were shining in the cart's headlights, ripping back and forth on the fence. There were a lot—probably as many as the population of a medium-sized city, he guessed, and they were all nasty and waterlogged. He stepped over the short woodpile, (which he realized had been burning until recently,) and stood in front of the skin-eaters. The rain had flattened the bangs of his long black hair in front of his face and he had to manually part it so he could see clearly.

"Look at all of you putrid motherfuckers," he said. He focused on one of the ghouls in the forefront that was missing most of its left cheek, showing two rows of fragmented molars, bicuspids, and canines. The injury could have been caused by many things, but in this instance it appeared to be received from another skin-eater, likely during a scuffle over a scrap of food. Its raggedy shirt read, *Hoof Are Ted?* Vaughn rolled his eyes and said, "You look absolutely stupid." He held up his palm and allowed rain to patter off his skin, and added, "You're going to catch pneumonia. All of you."

All the mindless ghouls were snarling, clacking their teeth at him. The fence was creaking and clanging at the seams and the rails were quivering.

A short fat lady in the front—pressed flat against the fence by the angry mob behind her, tits creased between the links—crossed her eyes and stuck her tongue out. Her mushroom top was blossoming from the waistband of her stretchy pants, necrotic fat rolls exposed.

Vaughn slapped the links directly in front of her. "What—did you take offense to that, Roseanne?" he said. Her expression didn't change. "Well then go back to your fucking grave. How about *that*?"

He stood on his toes and squinted over the sea of heads. They stretched far into the distance in all directions, disappearing into darkness. A surge of rain cascaded across the asphalt and splashed the vanguard like a large wave breaking against surf.

He lowered himself flat on the soles of his boots and asked, "Where's rustbucket?"

Nothing answered.

He clasped his hands behind his back and paced to the left side of the gate, then turned on his heels and paced the other direction, emulating a drill instructor. Every set of undead eyes kept pace with his every step.

"Show of hands!" he shouted. "How many of you rotten fucking puss-brains have had just about enough of this shit?!" He stopped and faced the crowd, putting his fists on his hips. "Come on! Show me those fucking hands! I don't care if you're missing fingers! I don't care if your nails are rotted off! Show me those fucking hands! I want to see some fucking *hands*!"

Many hands were already raised, but not in response to his inquiry. The hands were stretching over heads and shoulders, attempting to touch the gate, even if only to caress it. The cacophonous chorus was chanting a mournful tune. He almost felt like he was on stage one last time and the crowd was cheering. All that lacked were a couple of goth girls in the front row swooning and fainting and pleading for his room number because hearing songs about death made them wet.

"I could be your best fucking friend," Vaughn said, softly. He lowered his head. "Because I'm tired of this shit, too. *I'm so fucking tired of walking with the dead.*"

At that moment an emaciated zombie managed to thrust its arm through one of the diamond-shaped holes in the fence, all the way up to its shoulder, skin shredding in four perfect slivers like a blackened banana peel. It stroked Vaughn's naked torso with its cold and clammy fingertips.

"You're going to bite the hand that feeds you?" Vaughn asked, gazing down at the hand. He slapped it and stepped away. That touch was chilling.

"Everything on this earth is worthless," he mumbled. "And meaningless."

He turned away from the gate. As he stepped past the two downed watchmen, his eyes happened to see his bright red fire axe leaning up against what remained of the guard shack. He immediately hefted it up, getting reacquainted with its weight and feel. He ran his thumb along the blade and realized it was still sharp despite being used for something other than slicing skulls. Nobody appreciated a good weapon anymore. Not like Vaughn did.

When he reached the control box and saw that someone had already pulled the wires to the alarm, he scoffed.

"Let's give 'em all something to really cry about," he said.

He placed his palm on the big red button and gave it a shove.

PART FIVE

Eastpointe, July 4th, Twilight

TYRELL AND CREYTON YANKED HARD on their horses' reins and came to a sliding stop on the soggy earth, hooves sinking in at first and then kicking up tufts of grass and mud as they trotted uneasily in place. George neighed and bucked his head; Tyrell stood on the stirrups and blankly uttered, "*Whoa, George. Easy now.*" Alongside, Lenny voiced his concerns with a snort, and Creyton had to press his heels hard into his side and maneuver the reins until his stallion composed itself.

Something was very, very wrong. Even the horses knew it.

There was a sheet of water pouring from the front of the hood on Tyrell's slicker like a rooftop without a gutter, making it difficult for him to see. He dropped his hood and his braids were quickly soaked and unraveled. Rain pattered off his polyester sleeves and battered the nearby pavement, drowning out the noises ahead. It was surreal, like an old, silent, grainy black and white film.

"Oh..." Creyton whispered, but was unable to find more words.

There was so much activity at the main gate that Tyrell and Creyton weren't sure what to acknowledge first. Usually they could quickly dissect every serious situation into its most basic components and defuse it by subduing the most dangerous factor—whether that was a drunken man with a broken whiskey bottle or a domestic dispute where the crazed wife's fingernails had drawn blood. Here though, in this instance, they could only watch, slack-jawed and eyes open wide, bodies shocked into inaction and only stirred by the occasional jostle in the saddle.

They watched the Superintendent's bright red golf cart, driver unknown—too tall to be Ervin Wright—speed away from the containment area and veer onto South Street. Once the headlights disappeared past the armory, the main gate was overtaken by darkness.

A flash of lightning arced across the sky and briefly brightened the landscape. The illumination lasted long enough for Tyrell and Creyton to acknowledge that the outer gate was drawn back five feet or more, and still opening. Several zombies had already filtered in, stumbling and walking stiffly, yet with long strides. They were worked up, excited, frenzied. Three bodies lay sprawled in the containment area—Derow, LaChance, and the Rottweiler. There was a rumble of thunder.

The following darkness lasted a very long time.

George snorted. Lenny answered.

Several impressive flashes of lightning jumped back and forth in the sky as if by teleportation, beating in quick repetition like strobes. In the containment area, Tyrell and Creyton saw, the bodies of Derow and LaChance were no longer visible. They were now lost under a pile of gnashing teeth. Their flesh must have still been warm.

The gate was fully open now. The zombies were pouring through the breach. The containment area was conquered.

The klaxon isn't blaring, Tyrell remembered, *because Derow cut the fucking alarm. That stupid bastard cut the fucking alarm!*

"Ty," Creyton said, completely bypassing the *how* and getting directly to the point, with a mix of anxiety and an almost monotone matter-of-fact calmness, *"what are we going to do?"*

Tyrell found himself shaking his head. He wasn't able to answer verbally.

The flood of walking dead continued pouring in like a cornucopia unbound. Those in front fanned out along the interior of the wall, clumsily knocking down the aluminum ladder Tyrell and Creyton used to access the scaffolding that morning, anxiously exploring the area like ten year-olds just entering a *Toys R Us* and not knowing which section to rampage first, content for the moment to just probe with their eyes and jerky head movements. More and more shuffled through, an entire stadium's worth of undead, those not faster than the ones behind them knocked on their bellies and carelessly trampled over. They were close enough now that their breathless moans could be heard amidst the din of the storm, and yet there was no end to them in sight. Even as the crowd crossed the junction of Eastpointe Lane and South Street, an incessant sea of tightly-packed heads was still funneling through the open gate.

Tyrell's first thought was to run to the armory. There were machine guns there, and a flamethrower, but he and Creyton had never fired a machine gun before, always preferring the sidearms and shotguns they had been professionally trained in using, and he further knew that in five years the flamethrower had only been for show. He wasn't sure if there had been continued maintenance on it or if it would even be functional. Besides, the armory was close to the main gate and would soon be overwhelmed. He and Creyton would be cornered there.

Many more ideas flashed through his mind, with fundamental arguments brought to the forefront and the pros and cons weighed like two lawyers arguing before a judge. Any strategy found lacking was quickly dismissed. He had to think basics.

"The big wailer," Tyrell blurted.

He turned in his saddle and focused on the silhouette of the tower atop the Eastpointe Hotel. There was an array of large trumpets at the apex, like a symbolic battle cry for an angelic army. The apparatus had been pillaged from a nearby town several years ago and reconstructed in Eastpointe. Its original purpose was to sound for volunteer firefighters, but now it functioned more like a warning for an approaching air raid. The wailer was tested once, a long time ago, and found to be operational. Since then it had never sounded.

"We'll get the big wailer turned on," Tyrell said, kicking the stirrups. He hoped he didn't sound too desperate, like he didn't have any other ideas to follow up on, but Creyton kicked his own stirrups and followed him regardless.

They bounded their horses onto the pavement and rode north, directly up the center of the road. Tyrell shot a glance behind him and saw zombies had already reached the edge of the apartment building adjacent the wall. He hoped everyone who lived there was at the party. That way he could warn them all at once.

They rode at a full gallop through the parking lot and swerved around the maze of abandoned golf carts. Tyrell dismounted just outside the hotel's main doors. Creyton stayed on his saddle, whipping out the pump-action Remington 870, and studied the shadowy mob sloshing through the rain and shuffling in their direction like a swarming juggernaut.

"Oh shit, man," he said. "You've got sixty seconds, tops."

Tyrell hadn't stopped moving. "Start shooting when they get close and I'll come running."

"A plan for the ages," Creyton said.

Tyrell yanked open one of the big glass doors and ran into the hotel's main entrance hall, his hearing immediately consumed by a mishmash of hundreds of inebriated and sometimes nonsensical conversation, along with a live band set up on stage in the bar, wailing out bluegrass music. Several citizens were coupled off in the lobby, most in casual flirtation mode. There was a cluster around the door leading to Suds & Salutations—standing room only for those who wanted a visual of the band. Some noticed Tyrell's frantic entrance and turned their heads, keeping them there until they could figure out what was going on.

He wanted everyone's undivided attention, posthaste.

He pulled open his raincoat and retrieved the Glock from his holster. He fired two rounds into the ceiling. One of them clipped a crystalline chandelier, sending tiny pieces of glass zinging in every direction and raining down like sleet, along with powdery plaster chunks. The retorts were deafening inside the enclosed area.

There was screaming, inevitably. The band stopped playing, the singer abruptly halting in mid-note and the guitar player abandoning his riff. All heads turned to Tyrell and many partiers took frightened backsteps.

"There's been a breach!" Tyrell shouted, his ears still ringing from the gunshots. "I need someone to turn the wailer on, now!"

For those first few precious seconds the only reply he received was confused expressions. Near the entrance to the cafeteria, he saw Rebecca Santoro standing utterly still, gingerly holding her cocktail glass at an angle that was allowing her drink to spill out onto the carpet. She didn't seem to notice. Nearby, next to a long-idle Pepsi machine, Reverend Hart had a group of five people around him, chattering about whatever preachers chatted about in their spare time. Those five heads were now turned to Tyrell—Arnie Hill, Pamela Stafford, Walter Naylor, Dwayne Wilson, and some woman whose name started with a K—she lived in one of the bungalows behind the plaza, Tyrell knew. There were murmurs, many emanating from the unseen bar area. Tyrell heard someone ask, "*What the hell's he talking about?*"

"Reverend," Tyrell blurted, pushing aside Walter Naylor and Dwayne Wilson, forcing his way to the preacher. He smelled like Barbasol—for some reason a scent Tyrell associated with ministers. He grabbed him by the bicep and squeezed harder than he meant to. "Do you know how to turn the wailer on?"

"Wailer?" the bewildered reverend replied, casting a glance at the hand holding his arm and then at the other hand holding the handgun.

"*Wailer!*" Tyrell shouted. He wanted everyone—*anyone*—to hear him. "Those huge fucking horns at the top of the tower on this goddamn building! Sirens! *Wailer!*" He found himself stuttering—a problem he had not had since childhood.

"Oh, uh," Reverend Hart began, trying to speed up his reply, "an Odd Fellow would know."

"Odd Fellow!" Tyrell shouted, turning around. "Where's a fucking Odd Fellow?!"

A hand shot up across the room. "I'm Harless Henline," the attached voice proclaimed. "I'm an Odd Fellow."

Tyrell pointed and opened his mouth to shout to him, but stopped suddenly when the throng of onlookers finally started to show curiosity and began shuffling tentatively toward the main doors to see, like spectators wanting a glimpse of a car crash.

Tyrell leapt in front of them and held his arms out, trying to corral them back the way they came.

He shouted, "Everyone, you need to stay in here!"

With perfect timing, he and everyone else heard the blast from Creyton's shotgun. There were screams again, much more this time than before.

"You'll be safe here!" Tyrell shouted, forcing his voice to be louder than it had ever been before. "The windows have bars!" He reached out and grabbed Reverend Hart by the sleeve. He stared him in the eyes, but had no way of knowing just how crazed his own eyes could have appeared at that moment. He told him, "As soon as I leave, barricade all the doors. Do you understand?"

Reverend Hart hesitated, and then nodded.

"*Barricade them*," Tyrell reiterated, with intensity. "Block them with furniture—and that vending machine—and anything else you can find, do you understand?"

Reverend Hart nodded again.

"Make everyone wait here until I have the situation under control," Tyrell said. He peered past the frightened onlookers until he found Harless Henline. He pointed at him and shouted, "Get that wailer turned on! Now! Go!"

Harless Henline hurriedly slammed down the bottle he had been drinking from and ran to the stairs. He was middle-aged and not as frail-looking as the other politicians, so hopefully he wouldn't have a heart attack along the way.

That was as much as Tyrell could do. Creyton was yelling at him from outside to hurry up because the zombies were only steps away.

He heard another shotgun blast.

Tyrell threw open the entrance doors and ran back out into the pouring rain. There were four zombie carcasses littering the parking lot, all four missing large chunks of their heads, but many more walking corpses were navigating around the golf carts. They were only a few steps from being in lethal range.

Creyton pumped the Remington, aimed, and fired. Another head disappeared and a body collapsed onto the pavement, blood mingling with water as it flowed to the gutter.

Tyrell threw himself into George's stirrup and lifted his body onto the saddle. He looked back through the glass doors and saw the crowd of Eastpointe citizens standing there, Rebecca Santoro in the front, holding a hand over her mouth. Most others were screaming, but Tyrell wasn't able to hear them.

"Barricade it!" he shouted. He fit his gun back into its holster and grabbed the reins, persuading George to move.

Creyton fired his shotgun one more time. Tyrell could hear the splatter it caused, along with the ricochet of stray buckshot off of golf carts.

"I'm out of shells!" Creyton shouted. "And I think I threw my fucking shoulder out of socket! Fuckin' ouch!" He grimaced and rubbed his palm into his shoulder, swinging his arm in a circular motion to dull the pain. The Remington had a terrible kick.

"Let's roll!" Tyrell replied, coaxing George into a gallop.

They rode hard out of the parking lot and away from the cluster of zombies. Once they were back on Sunset Avenue between the water station and the clinic, they stopped long enough to survey the risk of the hotel being overrun.

A large contingent of skin-eaters was at the hotel's main entrance, pawing at the glass. Tyrell couldn't see if a barricade had been started on the inside, but it didn't appear any zombies were getting through. Many more were wrapping their palms around the bars in front of the windows and trying to pull them free, but the bars were holding strong. The rest of the zombies were flowing around the commotion like a river, content to explore other options. After all, after five years of pointless meandering they now had an entire populated town at their putrefying fingertips.

They were branching off in all directions. A horde of them rushed into the parking garage, but there were no personnel there at this time of night, Tyrell knew. Even more were assaulting the show windows in the plaza. One of the filthy skin-eaters found a brick and sent it through the window of the department store, and even before the glass finished crashing, zombies were spilling inside, knocking over precious, overpriced televisions.

Oh god, Tyrell remembered, *there might be a night watchman on duty—Bauer or Norton.*

"How in the *fuck* are we going to handle this, Ty?" Creyton asked, still wincing.

The zombies continued north, still rampaging, showing curiosity in the beauty salon Kendra operated, and then the clinic next door. They pounded against the walls.

Tyrell heard a multitude of screams coming from the hotel and he again threw his focus in that direction. It had not been breached, he saw—the screams were just from panic, not painful death.

Please keep your cool, people, he thought.

He knew there was plenty of food inside the hotel. Everyone could sustain themselves for days if necessary. But he didn't know how long it would take for him to figure this mess out.

Lightning crashed off in the distance and the murmur of thunder reached his ears two seconds later. After that the cries of the dead reclaimed the air.

"First thing's first," Tyrell said. He looked northward, to the station house. "We stock up. Then we go get our girls. We can hold out on the second floor."

"As long as you don't call it a *plan*," Creyton said.

"—Because a plan is just a list of things that don't happen," Tyrell finished. He kicked his stirrups and whipped the reins. "*Hee-ya!*"

They made straight for the office, dismounting their horses in the front lawn while they were still in motion. Tyrell parted his slicker and thrust his hand into his pocket, retrieving his keys. He fumbled for the correct one to unlock the door. Creyton stood out from under the protection of the awning, cradling his empty shotgun as he stared at the zombies in the distance, rain pounding off his slicker and his heels sinking in mud.

Tyrell found the correct key. As he made to shove it in the lock, the sirens above the Eastpointe Hotel finally kicked on, shaking him. It was much louder than he remembered, ominous and shrill and earsplitting, a long-winded whine. It would warn everyone who wasn't at the hotel or didn't already know the gate had been breached, but in that moment he wondered if it was a fair trade. The impression the noise gave him personally was one of impending death. The alarm was ill-suited as a warning—but as a doomsayer it was unparalleled.

I can solve this, he told himself. *But one thing at a time.*

He threw open the door.

In the cell in the far corner of the room, Danny Tasker was yanking up his jeans in mid-leap from the toilet. His face was flustered and frightened. "Oh holy Jesus, Marshal—what the hell's going on?!"

Tyrell made straight for the gun cabinet, sorting through his keys. Creyton stayed in the open doorway and studied the road.

"How close are they?!" Tyrell shouted.

"They're still down the road a stretch!" Creyton answered, anxiously shuffling his feet.

"What the—what the fuck's going on, Marshal?!" Danny Tasker interjected. He was cringing against the blaring siren. He looked like he might cry.

Tyrell fit the correct key in the lock, turned it, and pulled open the cabinet doors. He immediately grabbed a box of buckshot and tossed it at Creyton. All in one motion, Creyton caught the box in his free hand, knelt and placed the box on the floor, opened it, and started shoving shells into the Remington. He continued casting glances out the door.

Tyrell slid open one of the drawers to reveal several clips for his Glock, pre-loaded with 9x19mm parabellum rounds—*thank heavens for not scoffing at preparedness and caution.* Even though he still had shots left in his gun, he ejected the clip and loaded a completely fresh one. He stuffed more clips in his pockets anywhere he could find room.

"Is Mizuki with Kendra?" Tyrell asked.

"Yeah," Creyton replied, dumping shells for the shotgun into his own pockets. "At your place. We can grab them both at the same time."

"*Thank God for small fucking favors,*" Tyrell breathed.

"Hey! Hey! Hey!" Danny Tasker shouted, pressing himself against his bars and reaching through, pleading. "What's going on?!"

Tyrell finally turned to acknowledge him and his immediate thought was, *Dammit.*

He knew he couldn't leave him locked up. Christ, if something were to happen to him and Creyton, there'd be nobody to let Danny out of the cell. He'd starve to death in there.

Fucking goddammit.

Tyrell pounced to his feet and jogged to the cell, fumbling again with his keys. His foot crunched a plastic fork and kicked the empty milk bottle that Danny had responsibly placed outside his cell. He unlocked the cage door and allowed it to open. Danny watched him, his lips quivering.

"Town's been breached," Tyrell said. "Come here, Danny."

He grabbed Danny by the arm and marched him to the gun cabinet. His eyes swept across the combat shotguns before he realized he needed to keep it simple. He reached in and grabbed a Browning. He checked the clip, checked the safety, and cocked it. He handed it butt-first to Danny.

Danny didn't quite know how to react, his hand hanging open limply, so Tyrell forced the gun into his palm and made him close his fingers.

"We have to go get our wives," Tyrell said. "I want you to stand at that fucking door, and when you see us come back, I want you to open it up for us the second we're there. Do you understand?"

Danny gazed down at his own hand and at the cold metal gun he was holding. He looked back up at Tyrell, gulped, and nodded.

"Do you understand, Danny?" Tyrell repeated.

"Uh, yeah, man, I understand," Danny replied.

"Anything that's dead, shoot it in the head," Tyrell said. He didn't intend to sound condescending, but a nursery rhyme slipped out anyway. Still, hopefully it was simple enough to comprehend.

"Yeah, man. Sure," Danny said. "I've shot those things before."

"We're in this together now, Danny," Creyton growled from the doorway. "So don't fuck this up."

Tyrell swiped up the megaphone from his desk and dashed to the door, giving Creyton no reprimand for the disapproving stare he gave Danny. He threw himself on George's saddle and turned around to shout, "You'll be safe in there, Danny! All the first floor windows have bars! Just keep that door locked until you see us come back!"

From the doorway, Danny nodded. Then he hurriedly shut it.

Tyrell and Creyton cut directly in front of the approaching zombies and straight into the non-infested farmlands. They stuck close to the overflowing irrigation ditches. It was the straightest path. Tyrell felt the sense of impending doom—that while he was safe for now, soon zombies would be plowing their own paths through the fields. He felt like he was in a condemned structure scheduled for demolition and the timer was in its last few seconds of countdown.

As they rode past the old pro shop, caddy shack, and cart storage garage, Tyrell noticed the garage bay door was wide open and all the interior lights were turned on bright, shining out like a gaping maw. Inside sat the Superintendent's shiny red golf cart, abandoned. Tyrell knew the building had been converted to house farm equipment—tractors, gasoline, and diesel fuel—and the large flatbed truck was missing. Whoever had been driving the Superintendent's golf cart must have swapped vehicles. Fresh tracks in the mud leading back around the plaza revealed the direction the flatbed went.

Someone's trying to escape Eastpointe, Tyrell reasoned. *Figure they can smash their way over anything with the flatbed.*

But there was nothing he could do about it.

He and Creyton continued following the central irrigation ditch until they emerged on Roosevelt, the loud wailer only slightly fading in the distance. There were no lights on in any home, so Tyrell could only hope everyone was at the hotel. Nevertheless, he slowed his horse to a canter, brought out his megaphone, squawked it, and put it to his mouth.

He blared the message, "*THIS IS MARSHAL YOUNG. OUR TOWN HAS BEEN COMPROMISED. LOCK YOUR DOORS. IF YOU DO NOT WISH TO STAY IN YOUR HOME, COME OUTSIDE NOW. MY DEPUTY AND I WILL ESCORT YOU TO THE STATION.*"

He repeated the message all the way down Roosevelt Avenue, but no lights flicked on and no one was coming outside. The main housing district was a ghost town.

However, when they arrived at Tyrell's home, they saw the front door wide open and Kendra and Mizuki standing outside on the front porch, huddling under the protection of the small awning. Their wives were screaming at them before Tyrell and Creyton were even close enough to hear them.

Finally they heard, "Is it happening?! Is it finally happening?!"

"Yes, Kendra!" Tyrell shouted. "We have to go to the station! Come on!"

Creyton motioned to Mizuki with a wave of his hand and she obediently ran to him. He lowered his hand to grab hers, and lifted her up to share the saddle. Kendra took a couple of steps toward Tyrell, then stammered, "oh... oh..." and ran back into the house. Tyrell dismounted his horse and ran in after her.

He found her in their bedroom, fretfully gathering up miscellaneous family photos. He grabbed her wrists and shouted, "No, Kendra! Leave them! We can come back later!"

"No we can't and you know it!" she screamed. "I've had nightmares about this! It's happening!"

He didn't want to argue.

He wrapped his arms around her and physically carried her out of the house.

All Hell

"IT'S JUST A PRANK," Alexis said. "Or—or a short circuit. Lightning might've struck the fire whistle and set it off, you know?"

Courtney had a firm grip on her sleeve and was leading her across the boardwalk on the overlook plateau, heading for the staircase that zigzagged downward to match the slope of Cooper's Rock. The wooden planks beneath their feet were creaking with each step, and Courtney only then realized how rotted they were becoming, even sagging under her weight due to being waterlogged. Seemed nobody had bothered to apply sealant for over five years.

Alexis shrugged Courtney's hand from her sleeve. "Stop, Courtney," she said. "There's nothing wrong. You're totally overreacting."

Off in the distance, emanating from somewhere in the main housing district, Courtney heard someone—a man—speaking into a megaphone. His words were too garbled by the time they reached her ears, barely audible over the rain, the fire whistle, and the cries of the undead. It was just too much noise.

"What—what are they saying?" Alexis asked.

"I don't know," Courtney replied. "C'mon."

She again grabbed Alexis by the sleeve and started to guide her down the staircase.

Courtney's eyes had adjusted to the darkness as best they could, but she was relying mostly on the meager fragments of light reflecting on the puddles that accumulated along the handrails. They shimmered and sparkled almost beautifully. The further down the staircase she and Alexis went, however, the more shadowy the world became. She could barely make out the grass down below, and the forms of two golf carts parked by the side of the road. Nonetheless, descending into the shadows was her only option.

"It can't be real," Alexis said. Her matter-of-fact tone of voice made her sound like she was merely denying watercooler gossip, but there was an undeniable whimper in her breathing. "The fire whistle short-circuited, and the guy on the bullhorn is just telling everybody not to worry, you know? Not to panic? Like *we're* doing right now?!"

Courtney stepped off of the final stair and set foot on the soggy earth, releasing her grip on Alexis' sleeve. She sloshed toward her golf cart, holding her hands out in front of her so she wouldn't run into it headlong. Once she felt the shape of her cart in her nervous hands, she leaned inside and ran her palms over the dash, feeling for a particular switch. She found it and flicked it, and the headlights turned on with a flash, twin beams instantaneously cutting through the air and the rain like an all-powerful deity.

Shapes previously indiscernible in the darkness were now given almost perfect clarity, and the first one Courtney acknowledged was that of a naked man stiff-walking down South Street in her direction, his ribcage exposed, some internal organs laid bare. It was a disgusting sight if you weren't desensitized to it.

"Oh my god!" Alexis screamed, pointing at the thing with a jabbing finger as if it wasn't already blatantly obvious. "That's not real! That can't be real! They can't get over the wall! It's not possible!"

Courtney heard screaming elsewhere, though, and it wasn't just Alexis' echo. And Alexis was still screaming, becoming almost incomprehensible as Courtney turned and screamed back, "Alexis, be quiet!"

Alexis promptly covered her mouth with both hands, forcing the sounds to stay suspended in limbo. Her eyeballs were nearly bulging from their sockets from all the built-up pressure in her lungs.

Another girl's scream, oddly familiar, was crying, "*Heeeeeeelp! Oh help me! Oh please help me!*"

Courtney couldn't tell what direction it was coming from. It could have been north; it could have been west. It sounded faint, though, so it could even have been coming from inside a house. All Courtney knew was that those screams were from someone nearby, somewhere in the unforgiving darkness of night, lost in the storm.

"*Omigod*," Alexis breathed. "That sounds like Cindy Hayes!"

Courtney faced north, towards the main housing district. She screamed, "Where are you?!"

Then she listened.

The voice screamed back, "Hel—" and was cut short. Even after several seconds passed, no more screams were heard. The roar of rain seemed to swallow the cries in one big gulp.

"*Oh no*," Alexis uttered. "Do you think she's okay?"

"I don't know," Courtney replied. (A lie, and she knew it.)

She looked down South Street, locking her focus on the naked zombie. It was a good thirty yards away, but there were more behind it—lots more—spread out across the length of the road and meandering toward the golf cart's headlights. It seemed as good a beacon for them as any, Courtney figured.

"How did they get inside?" Alexis pressed, tugging on Courtney's shoulder. But she abandoned hope of getting an answer to this question and immediately fired a new one. "Somebody has this under control, right?"

"People are *dying*," Courtney said. "It's *not* under control."

"But—but my buddy Crey is the deputy here. He's really smart. Him and Ty will have a plan—a *contingency*, you know?"

"*Eastpointe* was the contingency."

Alexis huffed and stammered, "But—but you know what to do, right?"

Courtney hesitated before answering. She again studied the zombie up the road to check its progress. All she could think to say was, "I need a gun."

"*Oh my god this is freaking me out, Courtney! I'm so fucking scared!*"

And that was it for Alexis. She made the complete transition to blubbering baby, face cringing tight and tears flowing, shaking as if being electrocuted, the soles of her feet glued firmly to the ground.

Courtney grabbed her by the elbow. "Get in the cart. We have to go to the armory."

Alexis shook her head and put her palms up like she was rejecting foul food. She stuttered, "No, no—we need to go your house—it's just up the road, come on—we can lock the door and hide."

"And then what—*starve*? I don't keep food in the house. And I don't keep a goddamn *armory* in there either. We'd be stuck. And nobody's going to help us. We have to do this ourselves. Now come on."

Alexis shook her head again.

"Lexy, you've got to calm down and listen to me," Courtney said. "You have to listen to everything I say. Now, we have to keep moving, and we have to have guns. *Do you understand?*"

"I can't do this," Alexis stubbornly replied. "This was never supposed to happen."

"No kidding. Now, please, get in the cart."

Alexis wiped her forearm across her eyes to clear her vision, then timidly nodded, still crying. She fumbled her way around the golf cart and slid herself into the passenger seat, all the while staring off at the naked zombie. When she absently made to buckle her seatbelt, Courtney advised, "Better not."

She slid into the driver's seat beside Alexis. Once she was under the protective canvas hood, she realized just how thoroughly drenched she was. It made her feel like she was lugging a hundred pounds of clothes. Worse yet, she knew it made for easy gripping by undead hands.

She immediately pushed the button to engage the engine. It came on with a gentle hum.

She took a breath. She reminded herself that the roads were wet, and Eastpointe had poor drainage. The water would be deep in some places. Hydroplaning—or wrecking, no matter how severely—could mean death. So she had to be fast, but not too fast.

Guns were first on the list. Guns and ammunition.

She put some pressure on the accelerator and took the cart forward, turning the wheel to glide around the naked, gutless zombie. The thing wouldn't even get nourishment from eating somebody, Courtney knew, and that made it all the more senseless.

When the zombie lurched after the golf cart, Alexis screamed.

"Calm down!" Courtney shouted. "And keep your hands in!"

She weaved around two more ghouls venturing up the middle of South Street, the headlights sweeping across the visages of dozens more just ahead. They were spaced several car-lengths apart, so they must have been stragglers from the herd. The point of origin seemed to be Eastpointe's main gate. That meant the armory might already be swamped.

Courtney glanced to her right as she passed the old Worlds of Fun building. A section of it had been a church for the past five years, (serving the few people who still believed in that nonsense,) and now at least ten zombies were congregated just in front of the door. They were in a huddle on their bellies and their knees, soaked in what remained of their ragged clothing.

And they were feasting.

It must have been Cindy Hayes. It could have been where the screams had been coming from. Courtney quickly reasoned that after learning of her boyfriend's death, Cindy might have gone to church, alone, to ask why-God-why.

Alexis whimpered upon seeing a zombie shove a mouthful of meaty bone into its mouth.

"Oh God, they killed her," Alexis gasped. "That was Cindy! Oh my God they *ate* her!"

"Don't look at it!"

Alexis was getting almost violent in her manic, jerky movements, and it was having repercussions to the cart's balance. Courtney reached over and clasped her hand onto Alexis' arm, quite firmly, and shouted, "Calm down! There's nothing we can do for her! She's dead!"

Alexis turned and ferociously snarled, "You heartless bitch!"

"Fuck you! I'm keeping us alive!"

Alexis thrashed her legs again, giving just enough momentum on the right side of the golf cart for the tires to skip and lose traction, causing the whole cart to skim the surface of the road for several feet, screeching the whole way. Until then, Courtney had thought twenty miles an hour was a fairly safe speed.

The cart abruptly slammed sideways into one of the many zombies scattered across the length of South Street. The cart stopped all at once and the zombie's face smacked hard into Courtney's exposed left shoulder. The impact sent the zombie to the pavement spine first, its legs going up and over its head and sending the whole uncoordinated body rolling several times.

Courtney gasped in a panic. She slammed both feet on the brake as she craned her neck to get the best view of her shoulder, pulling at the fabric of her soaked designer shirt with shaking hands, breathing in rapid gulps of air. She looked for any tears or punctures.

Had that zombie had its mouth open? She tried to remember. She couldn't.

"Courtney, go!" Alexis screamed, turning sideways in her seat and cowering from another zombie lurching toward the parked golf cart.

Courtney released a relieved exhale. Though it smarted worse than getting hit by a brick, her shoulder wasn't bleeding. The fabric of her shirt hadn't been ruptured. She would live. There was no death sentence.

"Go!" Alexis screamed again.

Courtney let off the brake and applied the accelerator, easing up after the tires spun. Soon the cart was back in motion, weaving through the dead bodies. Alexis was still fidgeting in her seat.

Courtney concentrated solely on driving, finding holes in gatherings of zombies and maneuvering through them, trying to keep as far away as possible from outstretched arms. Zombies had completely overrun the old go-kart track and were starting to invade the bungalows on the other side. Some had even entered the farmlands. And very far up ahead, where the golf cart's headlights barely reached, Eastpointe's main gate was a swarming frenzy of walking dead.

This situation was most certainly *not* under control.

"*Dammit.*"

Courtney saw that her plan was snubbed. Too many zombies to count were already at the armory—*where all the damned precious guns were*—and were filtering shoulder-to-shoulder through the open door. The infiltration had already been well underway long before she arrived.

She heard the sound of automatic gunfire—an M-16, maybe—and the armory's open doorway lit up momentarily. The heads of two zombies burst open in several successive pops and they dropped on the spot. Many more bullets were missing entirely, pointlessly zinging out into the open air.

Somebody was inside, cornered, and too panicked to think straight.

Courtney decided then and there that the next best course of action would be to go to the hotel, where other people were. That's where Leon would be. He'd have evacuated the clinic and gone to the hotel, where his studly self would be motivating the men into action.

That's what Leon would do, right?

Courtney started to maneuver past the armory.

Alexis screamed, "Stop the cart! Stop the cart! I see Mister Bauer in there! He needs help! You have to help!"

"You wanna get shot!?"

Alexis gritted her teeth. "Just run over them!" She reached over with both hands and locked them on the steering wheel. She jerked it to the right, towards the mob assaulting the armory.

Courtney tried to keep control but it was no use. The cart was already skidding. She hit the brake—easing it, not slamming—but there was no stopping.

The cart did a complete spin, tires screeching louder than Alexis. Courtney held fast to the steering wheel with both hands so she wouldn't be ejected. But when she saw Alexis nearly slide out of her seat, she grabbed her shirt with one hand and held tight, planting her feet into the floorboard and stiffening up. The scenery swirled through her vision in a full circle.

Then there was impact.

One of the zombies turned away from the armory to greet the approaching cart, and it was promptly swallowed under the tires. The cart bounced and hit the rest of the ghouls as one solid mass.

The cart stopped, leaning slightly toward the passenger side. The zombie trapped under the rear-left tire flailed its arms and legs as it struggled to get free.

Courtney slammed on the accelerator. The cart wouldn't move. The zombie beneath the tire was acting as a mud puddle. The tire kept spinning across its torso, eventually breaching the surface of its dead skin, ripping deeper and deeper. Finely-ground guts and intestines churned upwards like debris from a wood chipper, painted an even more gruesome shade of red from the glow of the taillights.

Four undead hands reached in for Alexis as even more tried to crowd through. Alexis, still screaming bloody murder, turned to wildly kick at them. Few kicks connected, though one completely crushed a gaping jaw and another broke a rib.

One of the dead hands found a grip on her jeans, near her calf, and latched on tightly. It jerked her partway into the mob.

"Help me!"

Courtney was already in motion, locking her hands around Alexis' torso under her armpits and pulling with all her strength.

"Kick! Keep kicking!"

Alexis bent her knee and the zombie's grip slipped from her jeans, but found an even more secure handle on the shoestrings of her left sneaker. She used her right foot to pry the sneaker down her heel and then off of her foot entirely. The momentum sent the zombie recoiling backwards, still dumbly cradling the shoe.

Courtney dragged Alexis out of the cart across the driver's seat. They fell on the pavement.

The zombies were even thicker in this area. They were still coming through the main gate up ahead and were swarming across Eastpointe Lane, blotting out what few artificial lights the town had. And the fire whistle was incredibly loud at this short distance, the contraption now visible as a silhouette at the very top of the hotel.

Courtney screamed, "Are you bit?!"

Alexis had both her hands latched onto Courtney's forearm. Her eyes were crazed. *"I'm-sorry-I'm-sorry-please-don't-leave-me-alone-I-don't-want-to-die-oh-my-god-help-me-Courtney!"*

Courtney hurriedly stood, lifting Alexis up with her. She repeated, "Are you bit?!"

Alexis looked down to inspect herself. "N—no, but I lost my shoe."

"You're fine," Courtney said. "Come on."

She grabbed Alexis' hand and gave her a yank, forcing her to follow. A zombie that had been lunging at them fell face first on the pavement.

The automatic gunfire coming from the armory had long silenced, the shooter devoured. All the zombies previously assaulting the armory turned their attention to the two girls, shuffling around the golf cart in pursuit, interrupting the headlights and causing them to flicker against the shroud of darkness.

"I can't see anything!" Alexis cried.

"Just keep hold of my hand!" Courtney told her. "Move where I move! Just always keep moving!"

"Where are we going?!"

"The hotel!"

Courtney guided Alexis through the maze of walking corpses, gliding with learned precision. She needed to halt at one point to allow a dense cluster of zombies to lurch forward and break formation so she could scuttle past, but she never stopped moving for longer than a heartbeat.

Zombies were in the parking garage on her right and in the apartment building on her left. Up ahead, they were even in the plaza's show windows, trampling all over the dress she had been gawking at earlier.

Everything was screwed.

And then there was the thunderous explosion and the huge fireball that lit up everything in sight.

Courtney completely froze in place. It was instinct she couldn't control.

She watched, eyes open wide and her jaw hanging limp, as the entire face of the grand Eastpointe Hotel burst into flames.

The rear end of a large flatbed truck was sticking out of the main entrance. The front of the truck was buried deep in the hotel's lobby, glass and brick fragments strewn everywhere, some of it also flaming. Bales of hay resting on the truck's bed were ablaze, the blue tarps that had been keeping them as dry as kindling fluttering uselessly on the pavement. The fire reached with red fingers high into the sky, crackling and popping, fighting against the rain and holding its own. Damaged golf carts were knocked over on their sides all over the parking lot, showing the unstoppable path the truck had traveled. Zombies that had been assaulting the hotel were now cowering back and shielding their faces. Windows on the second floor imploded one by one.

Courtney breathed, "*Oh no.*"

Behind her, Alexis screamed.

They had lingered too long, and a zombie was pawing at Alexis' shirt. Courtney turned and struck the zombie in the forehead with her open palm. It reeled back and collapsed on its butt.

Courtney cried, "Come on!"

She pulled Alexis with her, her companion's almost incoherent blubbering mostly disregarded. Courtney knew it was only a matter of time now before she lost it, too. She could only take so much, and she was feeling despair seeping in already.

The zombies shuffled into a perimeter around the front of the hotel, giving a wide berth to the flames. There was at least fifty feet of unoccupied pavement. Courtney reasoned that it was the safest place to be, for now. She could think of nothing else.

She made her way to it, easily bumping zombies out of her way that hadn't noticed her and Alexis until then. She dove, yanking Alexis with her, and rolled awkwardly on the pavement. The heat from the nearby blaze was intense, but not unbearable.

It was the only oasis in Hell.

Laying back, breathing hard and supporting herself on her elbows, she studied the zombie onlookers to make certain they wouldn't risk the heat and lunge after her. It didn't seem like they would. They were too scared of the fire.

Courtney turned over onto her hands and knees. Still breathing hard, she lifted her gaze and looked at Alexis. She mouthed, "Are you okay?"

Alexis nodded.

Courtney lifted her gaze further, locking her eyes on a big five-gallon jug, colored bright red. As her focus cleared she saw more red jugs beyond, placed in what seemed to be intentional increments across the parking lot. It was very out of place for what passed as normal in Eastpointe on a normal day.

The fire whistle abruptly stopped blaring. It didn't even whine down—it just stopped altogether. The circuits must have melted, or its power line severed.

All at once screams filled Courtney's ears—those of the dead in front of her and those of the living trapped behind the hotel's barred windows.

"Courtney," Alexis muttered, barely loud enough to be heard. "What are we going to do?" Her voice sounded almost apathetic now.

Her despair was too contagious. Courtney couldn't shrug it off anymore. Screams—living screams of the dying—could be heard even over the din of the rest of the chaos. Pressure built in Courtney's eyes and tears gathered in the corners. She felt herself trembling.

"I don't know. I don't know what to do."

Fire could be seen on the second floor. It had to be spreading all through the interior, by now surely in the process of consuming Suds & Salutations. It was probably in the conference room, too. Maybe even the cafeteria. The fire was too sudden and too fierce for the paltry sprinkler system to handle—Courtney knew that much right away. And since it was raging from the inside out, the rain sure as hell wasn't going to stop it either.

"Why isn't anybody coming out?" Alexis asked.

Courtney stood, surprising herself at the strength she could still muster. She stared at the flames. "Because they barricaded the exits," she answered, realizing this only as she said it, and further realizing that they'd be stomping all over each other in there. She'd seen such things happen herself, a long time ago.

She thought of how those people didn't matter—only finding Leon mattered—that out of the whole lot of people only one of them was irreplaceable. For an instant she was ashamed for thinking this, but she felt she was the one who deserved to be happy. Everyone else had had their chance. These thoughts did not fade away.

She cringed. It reminded her why she hated herself.

Zombies from behind reached out for her and then immediately cowered back again, covering their faces. Then they'd reach out again, and cower back again, like the stupid automatons they were. More of the flock coming from the main gate filtered in beside them and behind them, unwittingly forcing the mass forward. The zombies in the forefront, howling against the heat, turned on those behind them.

Undead fighting broke out all across the perimeter. One of the ghouls sunk its fingers into another's mouth and pulled its face near, then bit off its upper lip. The other clawed at it with its hands, bellowing a primal, anger-filled shriek.

Alexis winced and scurried away. Courtney grabbed her by the arms and lifted her up, forcing her to stand on one sneaker and a socked foot.

"Be ready to—" she started to say, but then her attention was diverted to the southern edge of the hotel, where the structure met the apartment building next door and formed a wide alley. The fire had not yet spread there. But more importantly, there was someone there, fighting at the zombies with a very familiar aptitude.

It took Courtney only half a second to recognize Vaughn Winters, sans the top half of his uniform.

She shouted out, "Hey!"

Vaughn did not hear her. He was too busy punching at the zombies gushing out of the alleyway—*one handed*, Courtney noticed. His other hand held a big red axe. Vaughn was smart. He'd have a plan of some sort.

But can that axe cut through the bars in the windows, Courtney wondered. *And get everybody out of there?*

Courtney watched as Vaughn delivered the heel of his boot sideways into a zombie's kneecap. The bone immediately shattered, the knee bending a way it was not supposed to bend, and the zombie started to crumple. Before it could, however, Vaughn kicked it again, this time in the sternum, forcing it backwards and dominoing the crowd.

Courtney again shouted, "Hey!" but Vaughn did not hear. She grabbed Alexis' hand and said, "Come on." She started jogging in Vaughn's direction. She knew that between the two of them—if they worked together—they had a chance.

As she jogged she watched Vaughn's actions, uncertain what exactly was going on but certain she would figure it out and it would all make logical sense, but the more she saw the less sense it made.

Far from the fire, Vaughn positioned the head of his axe through the bars welded in front of a window. He gave the window a stiff poke and shattered the glass. He picked up one of the many red five-gallon jugs sitting nearby and screwed off the cap. He hefted up the jug and calmly aimed the nozzle through the bars, and soon clear liquid was being dispensed into one of the hotel rooms. His lips were pursed as if he was whistling a tune.

Courtney stopped jogging.

Alexis gasped, "What is he doing?"

Courtney screamed, "Vaughn?!"

A man's face whom Courtney only vaguely recognized as being seen during dinnertimes in the cafeteria—but definitely a man who had ties and friends and family in Eastpointe—appeared on the other side of the bars, screaming. He wrapped both of his hands around the bars and futilely started jerking on them. He shouted, "Help! Help me! Help me out of here!" He pressed his face between the bars as if he thought he could squeeze through.

In the next instant Vaughn planted the axe blade in the man's skull. Two lines of blood squirted out in opposite directions. The unknown man released one last gasp, almost like a cough. His eyes opened very wide from the shock, and stayed open.

It took a while before Courtney could accept what she saw. In that time Vaughn attempted to pry his axe loose from the man's head. It was stuck several inches deep.

"Vaughn you crazy bastard what did you do?!"

He heard her this time. He flicked his face in her direction, sneered, and went back to levering the axe handle up and down. The blade made sloshing noises in the dead man's skull.

"I, uh..." Vaughn said, still struggling with the axe, "I... *Fuck it.*" He gave up on retrieving the axe and turned his whole body around to face Courtney.

Courtney took a step back. Alexis ducked behind her and watched over her shoulder as if Courtney was an impenetrable shield from danger.

"Vaughn," Courtney said, much more quietly this time, "*what did you do?*"

"I, uh, lit a truck on fire and sent it into the hotel, and now I'm going on a killing spree," Vaughn replied. "Really—what does it fucking look like? That I'm planting daisies here? Spreading joy and goodwill?"

He took a step forward, and stopped. He looked down at Courtney's feet, staring at them for a few seconds, then gradually took his eyes higher, pausing to notice her knees, then her midsection, then finally her face. His expression did not change. Whatever he had assessed, he had done so inaudibly.

This was not the Vaughn she remembered. He had always been odd, sure, but not overtly cruel. Methodical maybe, but not evil. Now, his swagger was different. His eyes were different—and even the shadows below them. The Vaughn she knew seemed to have died on the cruiseliner, despite the fact that a man now stood here wearing his body. This was a stranger in front of her.

He raised his hand and pointed at the zombies surrounding the burning hotel, and stated with an almost uncanny politeness, "I'd like to see you devoured, if you don't mind."

He stepped forward.

"Stay away from me, you crazy bastard," Courtney gritted, stepping backwards, forcing Alexis to move with her. "I will rip your fucking eyes out if you come near me. I'm warning you." But her voice wavered at the end and she knew it, and she knew Vaughn noticed it.

He was smiling when he rushed her.

Alexis hit the pavement with a yelp.

Vaughn snatched Courtney up in a bearhug, securing her arms at her sides. He took two steps towards the zombies with her in tow. He was tall and her feet could not reach the ground to help her push against him. She flailed her legs.

"It'll be over quick," she could hear him saying. "You won't feel a thing."

Courtney turned in his grasp and arched her back. Vaughn's interlocked fingers slipped free. Before she could fall to the pavement she lifted her legs and locked his right arm between them. She held fast to his forearm with both hands and forced it close against her groin, keeping it trapped and immobile with the muscles of her inner thighs. And there she dangled from his arm, upside-down, the tips of her soaked hair brushing the pavement.

He attempted to shake her loose. He mumbled, *"You're just delaying the inevitable with this goddamn Jiu-Jitsu bullshit."*

Straining, she thrust with her hips, putting all her strength into it and applying as much pressure as she could. He tightened his arm, trying to defend.

All at once she felt his elbow dislocate, and heard it pop.

He screamed, "Ow, you bitch!"

He aggressively shook his arm, even jumping up and down twice for extra leverage. Courtney's hands slipped from his sweaty skin and she dropped. She tucked her head so it would be her shoulders that hit the pavement.

Vaughn remained standing. He held up his arm and quietly inspected it, tilting his head and crossing his eyebrows as if amazed at how awkward it looked to have a backwards elbow. He tucked his bicep close to his chest and gripped his forearm with his free hand.

He gave it a shove, followed by a twist.

His elbow popped back into place and he grimaced. Once the immediate surge of pain was over, he flexed his arm a few times to make sure it still worked.

He looked down at Courtney and growled.

Alexis screamed, "Fucker!"

Vaughn's head twitched.

Courtney could not see what exactly happened since Alexis was behind Vaughn, but she guessed Alexis had tried to punch him.

Vaughn, unfazed, turned to face her. Alexis did not even have time to flinch before Vaughn reeled back his fist and slung it into her nose with more force than even a punching bag could withstand.

Alexis' head lobbed backwards and two long, thick arcs of blood spurted from her nostrils. Her body was limp before it even hit the pavement.

Vaughn looked back to Courtney.

Courtney cowered away, scooting across the pavement on her butt, staring up at Vaughn's menacing form. A quick glance behind her revealed that their scuffle had brought them to within ten feet of the zombies in the perimeter, and they were snarling at her with reaching fingertips. She suddenly wished the hotel fire would get hotter. To hell with the people trapped inside—she needed the heat.

"Just keep moving like you are, Courtney. You're almost there," Vaughn said. "It'll be over in no time."

Courtney jumped quickly to her feet and sidestepped away from the ghouls.

Behind Vaughn, Alexis was moaning. She stirred, rolling over onto her stomach. She planted a palm on the ground and tried to push herself up. Thick streams of blood continued pouring from her nostrils.

"Alexis, get up!" Courtney screamed. "You have to get up! Just go! Just run!"

"*My doze iz broke,*" she mumbled. "*I cat breathe.*"

Vaughn was grinning, uninterested in the girl behind him. He was sidestepping with Courtney step-for-step, gradually closing the space between them and forcing her closer to the undead hands.

"Vaughn, stop this, please," Courtney said.

"You need to die now, Courtney," Vaughn hollowly replied. "It's time for you to go."

"Please, Vaughn..."

He suddenly lunged at her.

Courtney then saw his throat. It had a line of stitches across it and in that brief instant she decided to exploit that wound. She pictured herself thrusting her fingers into the unhealed cut and ripping the stitches apart and tearing the scary bastard's windpipe out. She pictured herself surviving this fight.

But Vaughn caught her hand with ease before it even got close.

"Krav Maga, bitch," he spat.

He twisted and lifted her arm in one sudden, violent jerk, and Courtney screamed long and loud as she witnessed her own elbow jut in an unnatural angle inside the sleeve of her last-of-its-kind thermal shirt.

She immediately went to the ground, cradling her arm and still screaming, as Vaughn planted his shin into her stomach. All her air evacuated her lungs all at once and her screams silenced. She fought to win it back.

Glancing up through the haze of pain, she saw frightened citizens of Eastpointe dropping out of the second and third floor windows of the formerly luxurious hotel like gassed wasps plummeting from a hive. Some did not move again after hitting the pavement, and some screamed in agony after suffering broken legs and ankles. Those uninjured suffered worse, as they got up and ran in a panic straight into the waiting arms of the hundreds of hungry walking corpses surrounding them.

And once Courtney got her air back, their screams easily drowned out her own.

Whimpering and crying freely, she took her focus to Vaughn one last time. He hovered over her with his foot raised, as if ready to deliver yet another stomp to a bug that refused to die. The flames cast him his shadow and the wails of the dying swirled around him. Rain seemed to batter everything except him.

Thin as a scythe he stood there.

And Courtney thought, *I'm getting what I deserve.*

Pariah

THEY TOOK THE LONG WAY BACK out of necessity, galloping their horses along North Street. Tyrell couldn't guarantee that the farmlands they had just traveled not five minutes ago were still free of teeth. There was no telling what number of creatures now lurked in the corn, rustling stealthily through the rows, ready to snatch someone and gobble them up. Better safe than sorry, even if it lost them a few precious minutes.

There were no lights on in the few bungalows that dotted the northern perimeter, so Tyrell had to assume there was no one else remaining to be warned. He rode by the houses, not bothering to pull out his bullhorn. Too much time had been lost already trying to get Kendra out of their own house and onto the horse. He couldn't slow down to give a message now.

He hoped he was doing the right thing. Furthermore, he *convinced* himself he was doing the right thing—the *wise* thing.

Surprisingly, it was around this time that he learned just how good Mizuki's English had become. Her Japanese accent barely lingered in her syllables. Every '*oh-shit!*' and '*what-the-fuck-is-happening?!*' that came from her mouth sounded very, very American. Creyton must have been proud.

Kendra was no better, though—probably worse. Riding on the back of Tyrell's saddle, she was constantly cursing into his ear about how all the family photos were now gone forever, about how all of their memories must not have been worth remembering since he had been willing to abandon them so quickly, about how ever since Terence's death all he wanted to do was forget all about him. Tyrell gritted his teeth and tried to tune her out. However, when she continued berating him, culminating in a lecture about how he was no different than the zombies now conquering their town—and that he hadn't been different than them for many years—he turned his head to tell her, "Kendra, this is really not the time for this."

He knew Creyton could hear every word being said, and he further knew that Creyton had been wanting to tell Kendra a thing or two for many years. If she had been a man, he probably would have. But as it stood, Kendra was Tyrell's wife—his best friend's wife—and Creyton could only listen and provide a supportive shoulder every time Tyrell's self-esteem took a hit. Tyrell appreciated that, even though he had to constantly keep Creyton at bay. He knew Creyton would verbally shred Kendra given half a chance. He was a sparkplug if left unchecked.

Finally, a distraction: A huge ball of fire blossoming up into the sky, and an explosion much different than the random bellow of thunder.

Creyton exclaimed, "Christ in fuck!"

Tyrell instinctively tugged the reins and slowed George's gallop. Creyton did the same for Lenny.

From their position on North Street, just east of the cemetery, the fire could be seen over top of the plaza annex. It lit up the dark clouds overhead, almost seeming to melt them away. It did not diminish in the slightest, even under assault by the inexorable downpour.

"That's my salon!" Kendra screamed. "I'm losing everything!"

"Yeah, it's all about you, Kendra," Creyton said from the side of his mouth, probably not actually intending for Kendra to hear. Mizuki cowered behind him, hiding her face in his back. Confrontation frightened her. Always had.

Tyrell ignored his friend's insult on his wife. Instead he bluntly said, "It's not the plaza. It's the hotel."

"*Christ in fuck,*" Creyton said again, this time in a breath.

"Oh my goodness!" Mizuki cried. "What happened?!"

The big wailer—*the doomsayer*—atop the Eastpointe Hotel silenced all at once. The town was immediately quiet.

Going out in a whisper, Tyrell thought.

But then the undead were heard, screeching and howling in the distance—but not too far in the distance. They were close and getting closer, spreading out and consuming all of Eastpointe as sure as cancer.

"Screw you, husband-killer!" Kendra screamed over at Creyton. She had heard him after all. Her eyes flicked to Mizuki. "You know he killed Hideko, Mizuki! That murdering bastard killed your husband! You're his war bride!"

"I didn't kill anybody, bitch! The only killer here is you, poisoning Tyrell one day at a fucking time!"

"All of you shut up!" Tyrell roared. Kendra dug her fingernails into his shoulder in retaliation for being reprimanded. He grabbed her hand in his own and yanked it away, squeezing tight, knowing it was hurting her and deep down relishing the sensation. He gritted, "*Stop it. Now.*"

Her lips turned into a pout, but her eyes were still fierce.

Silence. Everywhere. For as long as it lasted.

Creyton broke it by asking, "So is the office scrubbed?"

"No," Tyrell said. He took a deep breath, meditating, and exhaled slowly. "Plenty of guns and ammo on the second floor. And I have bottles of kerosene. We can make Molotovs. We can hole up and pick those dead bastards off one by one, for days if we have to. Plenty of food. Plenty of water. It's still the best choice. Agree or disagree?"

"I'm with you, man," Creyton said.

"Then let's roll while the rollin's good," Tyrell replied.

They kicked their stirrups and urged the horses into motion. Soon they were in another gallop, sprinting side-by-side into land already conquered by the undead.

George seemed to be handling the chaos well—or at least as well as a horse could. Lenny, on the other hand, was getting antsy. Looking over, Tyrell could see Creyton's horse bucking slightly, showing the first hints of rebellion.

"Do you have control?" Tyrell asked.

"I'm fine," Creyton replied. He was casting a mean look at the back of Lenny's head.

"Control?!" Mizuki exclaimed. "What does he mean by that?!"

"Our Lenny's just being a little obnoxious, sweetie," Creyton told her. "I can keep him in line. You just hang on tight to me, okay?"

"*Stupid horse*," Mizuki mumbled.

The horses rounded the bend onto Sunset Avenue and didn't slow down. As more and more zombies came into view, so did the blaze consuming the hotel. Tyrell cast his eyes back and forth, assessing the threat the zombies posed, then studying the fire, then repeating.

They rode until they were directly southeast of the office. There Tyrell stopped his horse. He could see no living person amidst the mob of undead. They had either been eaten or were simply nonexistent for the moment. He hoped for the latter.

He saw the burning remains of the flatbed that he had earlier noticed missing from the garage was now halfway into the hotel's lobby. Tightly-packed hay bales on the back were burning with unrelenting intensity. That meant even more hay bales were probably burning inside, and the hotel would soon be a husk, consumed from the inside out.

Oh no, he realized. *I told everybody to barricade the exits.*

He scrambled for the bullhorn in the saddlebag, found it, and attempted to turn the volume knob until he realized it could go no higher. He squeezed the trigger to squawk it once, then put the bullhorn to his lips.

He made his desperate announcement.

"ATTENTION EVERYONE. THIS IS MARSHAL YOUNG. YOU MUST EVACUATE THE HOTEL. MAKE YOUR WAY TO THE POLICE STATION. MY DEPUTY AND I WILL DO ALL WE CAN TO PROTECT YOU."

The bullhorn then dropped to his side, held loosely in his limp arm.

He wondered, *Oh Christ—am I stuttering again?* And he wondered, *Can they even hear me?* And he wondered, *Am I going to be responsible for the deaths of over five hundred human beings because I ordered them to barricade themselves in?*

It was too much to think about all at once.

"What the hell are you doing, Ty?" Creyton asked in a conspiratorial whisper. "You want to bring them to the office? The office can't hold them all."

"They all won't make it as it is," Tyrell grimly replied. "We need to at least give them a chance. I—"

Kendra screamed, "Ty!"

Tyrell looked down and saw that a zombie had snuck its way up from his blindside. It was ogling up at him and Kendra from behind wire-frame glasses that it had managed to keep intact and on its nose for the last five years, eyeballs appearing so big they could have been peering from behind a fishbowl. It opened its mouth and snarled, tilting its head sideways and leaning in for a bite.

Tyrell turned in his saddle and kicked up the toe of his boot. The zombie's jaw caved into the roof of its mouth and it stumbled backward as if suffering from vertigo.

Tyrell yanked the Glock from his holster, pointed it at the zombie's forehead, and pulled the trigger. A bloody hole suddenly appeared between the lenses perched on the zombie's nose and just as suddenly all the blood melted away under the rain. The zombie collapsed.

George lifted his hooves and uneasily sidestepped away from the corpse. He nickered his discomfort.

"Oh shit, Ty," Creyton said. "I'm sorry, man. I didn't see it—I didn't see the damn thing."

"It's all right. I'm fine," Tyrell replied. He turned his head around so he could see Kendra. He asked, "Are we fine?"

She nodded nervously, then lifted her arm and pointed across the way. "I love these people, Ty. You know I do," she said. "But there's nothing we can do for them. It's just us, babe. Get us out of here."

"For once in her fucking life she's right," Creyton added. "Let's get to the office and make our stand."

Tyrell swallowed hard. He made to lift up the bullhorn again but a slap from Kendra to the back of his wrist made him drop it. He wasn't sure if it was just the impact of the slap that made him lose his grip, or if he had been subconsciously willing and all he needed was the slightest catalyst. The bullhorn fell from the height of the horse and bounced three times off the pavement below. It looked pitiful way down there, all alone, rejected and neglected, getting pounded by the rain.

Tyrell somehow knew that that was the last he would see of it.

"We gotta go. Now," Creyton said.

Tyrell nodded.

He kicked the stirrups and sent George into motion for the last time, Kendra morosely wrapping her arms around him. Creyton followed immediately behind on Lenny. Mizuki was utterly quiet, her face still buried in Creyton's back.

"*These ugly fuckers,*" Creyton said. "We'll take 'em down—won't we, Ty?"

Tyrell didn't answer. He wasn't sure of anything at the moment.

"They'll regret this," Creyton went on. "I don't care if they *are* dead. I'll *make* them regret it. I'll find a way to make them feel pain and I'll make 'em feel it in fucking *spades*. They'll pay. They'll *all* pay."

Tyrell could only vaguely hear his friend ranting. His attention was too focused on their office up ahead. He counted thirty ghouls staggering around the front lawn before he stopped counting. They didn't seem to be attacking the door or any of the windows yet. They were unfocused. They must have been stragglers from the rest.

Birds away from the flock.

Children lost from their parents in the supermarket.

"Lay 'em to waste," Tyrell said. His authoritative tone was back and he felt somewhat relieved. "Clear a path for us and our ladies."

Creyton nodded. He lifted his Remington and shouldered it. He turned his head long enough to whisper to Mizuki, "Cover your ears, sweetie. It's going to be loud."

She nodded nervously and obeyed, preparing herself with a cringe frozen on her face.

Tyrell pointed his Glock pistol at the nearest zombie head. He held this position as he instructed, "I'll start from the left. You start from the right. Textbook holocaust. Whenever you're ready."

"I'm ready *now*," Creyton said.

The shooting began.

Heads popped left and right as round after round of parabellum and buckshot cracked through the air, retorts crying back at the thunder. Tyrell and Creyton had created their own storm within the storm, but theirs was even more furious, fueled by emotion.

The shooting paused as Tyrell and Creyton reloaded. Tyrell ejected his clip and loaded a new one taken from a pocket in his slicker. Creyton retrieved shells one at a time from his own pockets and shoved them—almost angrily—into his shotgun.

The shooting recommenced.

The front lawn turned into an orgy of carnage. Fallen bodies mingled in awkward piles. Legs were splayed over arms. Wide open, motionless eyes stared blankly in every direction. Tongues dangled from mouths.

By the time Tyrell and Creyton's aims met at the center, more walking corpses spilled into view from the outside. Tyrell hadn't cast a glance behind him for a while, (relying on the assumption that Kendra was watching their rear and would warn him of danger,) so he looked around.

Sure enough, zombies were approaching from every which way.

"We've got a path. It'll have to do," he said.

Then, for no apparent reason and from no apparent fault of its rider, Creyton's horse neighed and bucked, standing up straight on its hind legs and whinnying into the sky. Creyton and Mizuki were immediately shaken loose. A few feet further and they would have landed on softened earth, but they were heading for hard pavement instead.

Tyrell reached his hand out toward Lenny's reins, but Lenny was hopping away. Tyrell had never seen anything like it. Horses were unpredictable. He realized that now. Someone had had the bright idea of abandoning gas-powered vehicles in favor of grass-powered equines. What idiot thought of that?

Well, gee, that was my idea, Tyrell dourly mused as Creyton and Mizuki were falling in slow motion in front of him. *They're going to be injured because of my idea. I'm responsible for absolutely everything that's happening right now.*

Lenny returned himself to all four hooves only long enough to sprint away, kicking loosened chunks of asphalt violently backwards and whinnying left and right. It bucked into a wandering zombie and sent the thing careening away. The fucking animal had lost it.

It disappeared around a house up the street and wasn't seen again.

Thank God George isn't retarded.

"'Zuki, baby, are you okay?" Creyton was frantically asking.

Tyrell dismounted his horse and was quickly at Creyton's side. Kendra watched on from above, taking the occasional glance around at the walking corpses closing in. They were all over the place, everywhere. The town was theirs now.

"I—I am okay," Mizuki was saying, standing up. "Nothing broken. Stupid horse. *I told you it was stupid horse!*"

"I know, baby," Creyton said, wrapping his arms around her and kissing her. She looked squished in his embrace, but pacified. They were still in love, and Tyrell couldn't imagine himself holding Kendra that way. Not anymore. He was emotionally stale, and he knew it.

"We need to be indoors," he advised. "Pronto. Lickety-split and all that shit."

As if to add emphasis, he turned and shot a zombie in the head. It had been the closest one.

Creyton let go of Mizuki and scoured the ground with his eyes. He quickly located his shotgun where it had been tossed during the tussle. He snatched it up and started loading fresh shells.

Tyrell grabbed George's reins and started walking him toward the office with Kendra still on top. As unfortunate as it was, he knew he couldn't bring the animal inside with them. If it went nuts like Lenny had, the place would be torn apart. The people closest to him could die in the fracas. No, the best he could do was let George go once they reached the door. He wouldn't tie him up; he would just let him go and hope for the best. He needed to believe that in five years zombies hadn't changed—that they wouldn't attack animals.

George tamely and gingerly stepped over each and every zombie carcass littering the front lawn. Tyrell aided Kendra down from the saddle and pointed her to the office. He slapped George on the haunches and said, "Go, George."

George didn't go.

Tyrell slapped his haunches again and pushed. "Go, George."

George neighed and took off at a trot, still meticulously stepping over the formerly human bodies, then proceeded to gallop. He went north up Salisbury Lane. Even though new zombies were stepping off the pavement and onto the lawn, Tyrell couldn't take his eyes off his horse until it completely faded from view. It took only a matter of seconds, but those seconds were an invaluable commodity.

He aimed his Glock back and forth at the approaching ghouls, ready to shoot any who got too close. Beside him, Creyton was sheltering Mizuki as he too was studying which were the greatest threats.

"Watch your right, Marshal Young," he said.

"And watch your left, Deputy Hathaway," he replied.

Kendra was at the office door, shivering under the awning. She screamed, "Ty, it's locked! Gimme the keys!" Her voice was shrill when she raised it. He despised it.

Tyrell shouted over his shoulder, "Danny! We're back! Open it up!"

Stupidly enough, (he would later realize,) he expected the deadbolt to immediately unlatch and the door swing open, providing sanctuary. But even after a tense ten count, nothing was happening.

"Tasker, open the door!" Creyton shouted. His shotgun discharged and the closest zombie face disintegrated inwards. It collapsed to its knees and fell prone.

Tyrell fired his Glock three times, taking down three stumbling figures rounding the side of the building. It was difficult for just him and Creyton—two men—to cover a full one hundred and eighty-degree field of vision. He knew all it would take was just one jabberwock slipping through the cracks to ruin their party.

He yelled again, "Danny! The door!"

"The door, Danny!" Creyton added.

Tyrell glanced behind him. Nothing was happening. Kendra was still there, pacing left and right, waiting for either the door to open or Tyrell to toss the keys.

"*Oh, Christ,*" Tyrell muttered. He tucked his Glock under his armpit and parted his slicker. He thrust his hand into his pocket and grabbed his keys. He tossed them sideways at Kendra, who wasn't quick enough or dexterous enough to catch them. They clattered against the brick beside the door. She scrambled down to retrieve them.

Zombies were spaced only a few feet apart and all of them were diligently shuffling forward, centering their focus on the office. Those that had been in the forefront when the main gate was breached had already reached Eastpointe's northern border, and—finding no one there they could eat—were now turning on their heels and coming back. That was the direction Creyton was watching, his shotgun primed at their noses. However, the longest and thickest column of ghouls was oozing up from the east and from the south—Tyrell's direction. Most were likely trying to escape the heat of the burning hotel, though others were exiting from the nearby water station with pieces of the nightshift crew still between their teeth. Tyrell wanted to shoot them in particular.

"What the fuck is wrong with this thing?!" Kendra shouted.

"What?!" Tyrell shouted back.

"I unlocked it! I turned the thing! But it ain't opening!"

"Shit."

Tyrell backed his way up the two stairs and onto the small porch. Aiming his Glock at the approaching horde with his right hand, he reached out and grabbed the doorknob with his left. It turned freely in his grip, but when he pushed the door it wouldn't budge. He cast a glance at the deadbolt and saw it was unlocked—just as Kendra said—so that meant something was blocking the door from the other side.

He bent down and peeked in through one of the door's narrow, diagonal windows. He grunted when he saw the metal security bar propped up underneath the knob inside. He shouted, "Dammit!" He pounded on the door with the heel of his fist. "Open it, Danny! Open the door *now*!"

Creyton could hear the commotion. He cursed and fired a five shell barrage at the zombies walking across the lawn, going from left to right in quick succession, pumping and ejecting steaming, spent shell casings into the grass where the rain immediately cooled them. The spray effect from the barrage took down a few zombies, but not enough—not nearly enough.

Mizuki was panicked. She was screaming as Creyton grabbed her by the arm and led her up the stairs and onto the porch. He backed her against the bricks and stayed in front of her.

Tyrell glanced up and down the length of the office exterior. All the first floor windows were securely barred—again, another one of his ingenious ideas—and there was no way in.

He gritted his teeth and hammered on the door again. "Danny!"

Creyton was soon at his side, kneeling down to peer through the glass. That meant there was now no one covering their asses. Zombies were crossing the lawn unchecked.

Creyton exclaimed, "I see you in there, Tasker! Open this door you dirtbag motherfucker! You smelly slimeball shitsack! Open the fucking door!" A second passed. "I'm going to knock your teeth out you son of a bitch!"

Tyrell hurriedly hunched down beside Creyton so he could share the view. Sure enough, he saw Danny Tasker inside, backed up against the far wall and still trying to back up even further by planting his heels, putting himself as far from the front door as possible.

Tyrell shouted, "Danny, open the door!" He almost couldn't even hear himself over Kendra and Mizuki's panicked screams. "Danny!"

Danny was shaking his head side to side. He looked scared to death. He was as white as a ghost.

"Danny," Tyrell said, losing some of his gruffness, "You gotta suck it up now. Don't be a coward. Open this door."

Danny spoke something but Tyrell could not hear him through the thick door. However, he could read his lips easy enough. They said, '*No. You guys are all dead. Fuck you. Go away. This place is mine.*'

"Danny open the door!"

"Tasker you motherfucking dirtbag!"

"Shit!"

Tyrell backed away and spun around. A scattering of zombies was nearing the porch. He fired five rounds, dropping five ghouls, before his gun clicked. He ejected the clip and shoved a fresh one in. He started shooting again, bringing down the vanguard. There were now three-feet deep piles of carcasses in some places.

Kendra was screaming at him to do something, and Mizuki was likewise screaming the same thing at Creyton.

Tyrell hopped off the side of the porch and walked along the face of the building, gazing upwards, studying his options.

None of the second floor windows were barred. He had never thought it necessary to weld bars over them, and especially now he was extremely thankful that he wasn't as anal-retentive as everyone claimed. But even he never had the slightest inkling that one day he would have to scale the sheer face of his office building.

He decided on a window just over the porch awning. He lifted his Glock and aimed it at the glass. He emptied the last three bullets in the clip through the glass, shattering it. He hunched over and covered his head as some shards came plunging down, bouncing off the windowsill and coming right for him. One managed to cut a nice slice in his left ear.

He shook off the stinging pain.

He turned and shouted, "Kendra! Come on!"

She hesitated before comprehending what he was doing. She leapt off the porch and went to him.

Tyrell shoved the Glock into his holster and went down to one knee. He stretched out his arms and interlocked his fingers, palms up. He said, "Crey, help me."

Creyton was already bounding off the porch, holding Mizuki by the hand. He let go of her so he could take a knee opposite Tyrell. He cupped his hands in front of him.

"Come on, Kendra," Tyrell said. "Fast now."

She winced and whimpered nervously as she eased her foot onto Tyrell's hands. She grabbed the vertical bars in front of one of the first floor windows so she could help pull her own weight—which was a damn good thing, Tyrell knew, because she'd put on quite a bit of it over the last few years. She eased up her other foot and situated it on Creyton's hands.

They boosted her.

"Don't put too much weight on the awning," Tyrell said, not straining much at all. His adrenaline was making this a lot easier than he first thought it would be, but the awning was just thin aluminum. It wouldn't hold under pressure. "Keep your knees locked while we lift," he added. "And mind the glass up there."

She didn't reply, concentrating solely on not falling. Once Tyrell and Creyton had her as high up as they could take her, arms stretched straight up from their shoulders as if performing a cheerleading routine, Kendra lifted her left foot out of Creyton's hands and situated it on the edge of the awning. There were support beams there. The awning creaked in discomfort, but held. Tyrell tightened his lips for the brief time he had to bear all her weight on his own, but it turned out that the countless hours he spent in the gym served a legitimate purpose other than just the tree-trunk arms he could proudly show off, and he was especially happy he hadn't neglected his squats.

Gingerly and painfully slow at first, Kendra picked up pieces of glass off the windowsill between her thumb and forefinger and tossed them over her shoulder. Once Tyrell realized what she was doing, he grunted, "Come on, baby, you've got to move. If you cut yourself, I'll do the bandages. I promise. Just please get in there."

Kendra pushed the mostly hollow window frame upwards until it locked into place. With the bottom of the window even with the bottom of her belly, she leaned in, lifting her feet into the air and sticking them straight out. She slithered and flopped inside, motions reminiscent of a beached whale.

After a few seconds a light switched on, probably the one dangling from the ceiling with the pullstring. Tyrell then heard the sound of glass being swept away. Kendra was making herself useful, thank the Lord.

"Mizuki," Creyton said.

Standing over his shoulder, whimpering and undoubtedly uncertain she could accomplish this, Mizuki lifted her left foot and set it on Creyton's hands.

Creyton yelped, "Ty, behind you!"

Tyrell sprung up and turned around. A zombie—one of the especially ugly naked ones, only vaguely discernable as female—had crept along the edge of the building and he was now locking eyes with it from only an arm's reach away. As she snarled and leaned her face forward, Tyrell planted his hands on her shoulders and shoved the zombie bitch on her ass.

He drew the Glock from his holster and put a bullet in her brain, and gulped as he noticed how much progress the rest of the multitude of skin-eaters had made. They were encircling him and Creyton and Mizuki, some of them stumbling and falling down over the terminated carcasses on the lawn, but a lot had already negotiated the crude obstacle course. Two or three had even stepped up onto the porch Tyrell had abandoned only seconds ago.

The creatures in the front of the semicircle needed only take a few more lumbering steps and they could pile themselves on top of warm flesh.

Tyrell shot at them, making flustered jabbing gestures with his pistol. Some fell from bullet wounds in their temples and foreheads, but Tyrell found himself missing half of his shots. That wasn't good—not good at all.

Creyton turned and in one blast of his shotgun mowed down the three zombies traversing the porch. They staggered backwards and fell off like drunken sailors abandoning ship. Another shotgun blast sprayed buckshot in five faces at once, sending chunks of skin and skull bursting in every direction.

His shotgun clicked. He didn't have time to reload just yet.

"Mizuki," he said again.

Tyrell scrambled down to his knee across from Creyton, and Mizuki timidly attempted the process again. Grabbing tight to the bars in the first floor window, she placed one foot on Creyton's hands and one foot on Tyrell's.

They heaved her upwards, nearly pitching her completely, and her foot slipped from Creyton's hands. She shook it towards the awning, but missed. She scrambled with her hands to try to grab the bars in the first floor window again, but the rain had made them very slick. She fell backwards.

Tyrell reached up and caught her all by himself—somewhat clumsily—but good enough under the circumstances. His palm caught her posterior and his fingers quite unintentionally dug in between her cheeks as he sought to prevent her from falling further. She audibly groaned in discomfort. If the situation wasn't life or death, he figured Creyton would probably point and laugh and tease him about copping a feel off his (much hotter) wife. But the possible embarrassment of the situation was disregarded. Tyrell hoped they could talk about it later—talk about *anything* later—and have a good laugh. Hell, even reminiscing about filing income tax would be good enough for him.

But awkwardly enough, it occurred to him that he wished Kendra had kept as firm an ass, instead of letting herself go.

"Honey, be careful," Creyton said, dashing back in and grabbing her feet.

He heaved, and so did Tyrell, and soon Mizuki was up high again, grabbing onto the windowsill on the second floor and stretching out her leg so her foot could balance on the edge of the awning. Kendra leaned out the window and grabbed Mizuki's wrists. She pulled while Mizuki pushed, and soon she was getting yanked through the open window. All at once she disappeared inside, the button of her jeans catching a coarse brick and snapping off.

That had to hurt.

Tyrell chanced a quick glance over his shoulder. As he feared, there was no time for any more foul-ups.

"Come on," he said.

Creyton stayed on his knee. "No, you go," he said.

"Goddammit."

"No time to argue, man!" Creyton shouted. "You're stronger than me. You can pull me up next. I can't do the same for you. Now come on."

Tyrell mumbled, "Shit" but knew that—right or wrong—there was no time to argue. A decision had to be made—or *forced*, especially in this instance—and followed through.

He planted his foot in the cradle of Creyton's hands and grabbed the bars in the first floor window, squeezing them tight to avoid slippage.

Creyton roared as he lifted. His arms were shaking and his knees wobbled like they were ready to buckle. Furthermore, Tyrell knew his shoulder was weakened from repeated use of that Remington. Combined with the fatigue of everything else, adrenaline was the only thing preventing Creyton from completely crumpling.

Tyrell stretched out his leg and planted his foot on the awning. He reached up and grabbed the windowsill with both hands. He dangled there diagonally for a second or two before mustering his remaining strength and pulling himself up. His muscles burned. He now comprehended the importance of strength *and* stamina. He had the strength, but for the past five years he had neglected the stamina. Now he was paying for it.

In the same instant he thought it, he shouted, "Rope! Kendra, rope! There's rope in one of the cabinets! Get it ready for me! I have to haul up Crey!"

"What?! Where?!" she shouted.

"Just look, goddammit!"

He slipped through the window and fell to the floor, breathing hard and fast, heart thumping close to his chest. He grabbed the inside of the windowsill and used it to help himself to his feet. He stuck his head out the window.

Down below, Creyton lifted his shotgun toward the assaulting mob of skin-eaters and pulled the trigger. His gun clicked. He muttered, *Cheese and rice.* He backed up against the wall and frantically dug into his pockets for more shells. Ghouls were in reaching distance. One pawed at his slicker.

Tyrell stretched his arm out the window and pointed his Glock at the zombie's head. He pulled the trigger and the zombie's head split apart. Creyton pushed it backwards into the mob with a hard shove, knocking down two of them.

Tyrell picked off three of the closest ghouls, dropping them like flies, before his own gun clicked. He ejected the clip and shoved in a new one. Down below, Creyton put the point of his shotgun barrel into a zombie's chest and blew its intestines through its spine, spraying gore everywhere. He had fired before raising his aim up to the zombie's face, Tyrell knew, because he had run out of time and hadn't had a choice. The disfigured creature collapsed at his feet, writhing pathetically on the ground, severed nerve endings twitching.

A looped bundle of black rappelling rope suddenly appeared in Tyrell's view and he snatched it out of Kendra's hands. He pulled the knot and unwound it, tossing one end out the window and grabbing a firm grip on the other.

"Grab it!" he shouted. He didn't feel any weight being applied on the other end, or even a tug.

"I can't climb right now, man!" Creyton shouted. "They're all over me!"

Tyrell shoved his end of the rope toward Kendra and said, "Hold this." Thankfully she obliged without hesitation as he leaned back out the window with his Glock.

"What is he doing down there?!" Mizuki screamed, pressing hard against Tyrell's back, attempting to see for herself.

Creyton hadn't had time to load more than one shell into his Remington. He was swinging the empty gun like a medieval mace, the butt end caving a skull with a sickening crunch. A zombie snatched a firm grip on his slicker and drew close with its teeth.

Mizuki screamed, "Creyton, you will get up here this instant!"

Creyton grabbed the zombie by the throat and started forcing it back. Teeth clacked towards his forearm.

"Clear its head!" Tyrell shouted. He aimed straight down at the top of the zombie's skull. Creyton continued struggling with it.

Tyrell fired, but the shot only clipped the zombie's shoulder. It was moving too erratically, trying to find a way past Creyton's defenses. Tyrell steadied his shaking hand and fired again. The bullet penetrated the zombie's skull. It was motionless in Creyton's clutches as another ghoul latched onto his ready forearm and wrapped its teeth around it.

Creyton screamed. A mouthful of his slicker ripped away. Blood dribbled and squirted from his breached skin, tendons stretching and snapping as the zombie pulled its face away with meat between its teeth.

Tyrell shouted, "Fuck! No!"

He fired wildly into the crowd below. He aimed for skulls, but hesitated at those too close to Creyton. Only a couple of the ghouls fell. The rest were piling on. Creyton was becoming less and less visible in the midst of the mob, throwing frantic punches at attacking faces.

"Crey!"

Tyrell could only impotently watch as a soaked, dirty, filthy skin-eater planted its face into Creyton's neck and took a bite. Blood squirted all over its face.

Creyton shrieked loudly.

Tyrell cringed.

The skin-eaters forced Creyton down to his back. They clawed at his clothes. One of them managed a bite out of his hand.

Tyrell could watch no more. He searched for Creyton's screaming face amidst the sea of undead, hoping he could at least lock eyes with him, even if only for a fleeting moment.

He found Creyton's face, but Creyton had his eyes closed and wasn't able to look back. Wincing, Tyrell shot his gun repeatedly until one of the bullets finally took Creyton in the forehead.

He turned and brought himself out of the window, unable to acknowledge Mizuki screaming, "Creyton! My Creyton!" All he could hear was the smacking of lips and the gross tearing of skin from bone.

He slumped against the wall and sat down, feeling very faint.

Fire and Water

LEON WASN'T ENTIRELY DENSE. He wasn't going to be like a kidnapping victim told to keep their mouth shut or else—screw that. The very instant he heard Vaughn exit the clinic and slam the door shut behind him, Leon made as much of a ruckus as he could. He pounded on the door and the walls. He even opened the windows and yelled through the bars.

He knew he wasn't as analytical-minded as a female—Courtney, for example—but he considered himself a thinker nonetheless. He reasoned that since no one was coming to check on him, it must have meant they were all too busy partying. However, he knew murders in a small town couldn't go unchecked for long, especially the Superintendent's. People would be wondering where he was and come looking for him, especially with him not being present at the party. But would they know where he was?

Then again, Vaughn might have caused mayhem somewhere else, too, and maybe the cops were too busy dealing with it. He'd be in handcuffs soon enough, surely. But he might not tell them he'd locked Leon away. Maybe keeping this a secret would allow him to maintain his creepy grin all the way to prison. Or maybe Vaughn made a run for it, knowing there was nowhere in Eastpointe for him to hide.

Crikey, Leon thought, *I could be stuck in here all night.*

He decided not to analyze the situation anymore. He wasn't going to wait around, cowering in a corner and just waiting for someone to find him.

His male mind immediately thought in terms of destruction. If something didn't work, you kicked it. If it *still* didn't work, you broke it. This mentality worked well for him so far in life, so he rolled with it.

The cabinets were locked up, so he ripped off the cheap, flimsy doors and scoured through the insides. He rifled through the pockets of the two corpses in the room with him—praying they weren't going to get back up, (he never assumed any corpse wouldn't)—but didn't find anything helpful.

Poor Superintendent Wright... The old fellow had always been so nice.

And Dr. Mayfield... One less doctor in town couldn't be a good thing.

Leon wasn't entirely surprised that Vaughn had snapped. He had always expected the guy to go off on somebody at some point, but he *was* shocked as to the extent Vaughn had lost his marbles. Jesus, he never expected him to *kill* anybody.

When Leon was finished destroying things, he tried to break the security glass in the door the old fashioned way—with his elbow. He knew it was a mistake even before he tried it, and knew it was a mistake even through the pain while attempting it, but he kept on doing it anyway until he finally accepted that he needed to do something different.

Rubbing his bruised elbow and cursing under his breath, he looked around the room for other options.

He wondered, *what would Courtney do?*

And when he laid eyes on the metal bars in the frame of the hospital bed, he thought, *Well, I could break that, I guess.*

He heaved the bed over on its side and went to work.

The metal would not bend from his foot stomps, so he sighed and sat Indian-style on the floor, resigning himself to tediously unscrewing the bolts that kept them locked in place. He rubbed his fingertips raw, abrasive as sandpaper, before he accepted the bolts wouldn't turn with fingers alone. He retrieved a scalpel from one of the cabinets he had raided and tried to dig under the nuts beneath the bolt heads, scraping the rust away. He only needed to remove two, he realized, and he would have himself a weighty metal pole to swing around.

All the while he worked, Superintendent Ervin Wright's grotesque corpse was blankly staring at him from across the room. It didn't have a nose.

Leon mumbled, "*Oh, crikey,*" and tried to avoid looking at it. He pondered on other things—*anything* besides being locked in a room with dead bodies.

This was the first occasion he paid attention and actually heard his own voice. He suddenly realized that his New England accent was a lot thicker than he'd believed. Alexis had always thought it cute, he knew, but Courtney hated it, even teased him about it.

Oh well, can't please everybody, he thought.

No, think happy thoughts.

Just after finally removing the first nut and bolt, he heard the fire whistle turn on atop the hotel across the street. It was loud and easily penetrated the clinic's walls, overpowering the pitter-patter of rain and the booming of thunder. The whistle sounded just like the one he had heard on occasion back in his small town in Maine when the world was normal.

But the whistle wasn't shutting off. That meant it wasn't a mistake. It wasn't an accident, or else someone would have immediately shut it off. Leon knew this was bigger than just Vaughn murdering three people. Something was wrong out there. Really wrong.

A door slammed somewhere in the building—slammed *open*, it sounded like—and Leon jumped to his feet. He opened his mouth to yell for help but caught his voice in his throat before it escaped, and swallowed it back down. He realized that whoever had entered the clinic might not be somebody *wanting* to help.

Vaughn?

Leon walked on his tiptoes to the door, eased the curtain to the side an inch, and peeked through the security glass. He didn't see anybody. There was only a third corpse out there—Mr. Peters, head honcho of the Procurement Committee—lying on the lobby floor. He had bullet holes in him.

What did these people ever do to you, Vaughn?

Leon's eyes peered to the right, and lit up. From this angle he could see the other side of the receptionist's desk. Further, he saw that Courtney had abandoned her equipment there. Seemed the doll was giving up the zombie-killing profession. Her Socom was empty, clip ejected, but her wakizashi sat next to it, blade shimmering under the fluorescents. A sword didn't need ammo, but it wasn't doing Leon any good on the other side of a locked door. It was just a tease.

He jumped back when a glazed eyeball met his gaze on the other side of the glass. The curtain fluttered closed again.

"What the—how in the—!"

He heard streaking sounds as if somebody was wiping the glass down with Windex, but knew grimy hands made the same noise. There was a muffled moan, definitely undead.

He was convinced.

He dashed back to the bed and frantically started levering the metal rod up and down, casting nervous glances over at the door. He hoped the final bolt might be rusted enough that it would break if coerced and sweet-talked.

"Come on, baby, come on. You can do it."

Leon mentally assembled the facts. Firstly, there was a zombie in the lobby of the clinic. Secondly, a zombie in the lobby of the clinic meant it had first had to walk through town. That was probably what the fire whistle was all about. Hell, there were probably a *lot* of them out there. How could they have gotten in?

Vaughn could have...

No, surely not. He's not that crazy.

But then Leon admitted to himself that *yes*, Vaughn very well may be *that* crazy. If he was making a run for it, he wouldn't go on foot. He would take a vehicle. And then he might have just left the gate open, laughing with his middle finger raised behind him.

But there's always at least one watchman on duty—

The bolt snapped all at once and sprung across the room. Leon jerked the metal bar away as his prize. It was hollow, but it was four feet long and the casing was thick. It could do some damage. He put a firm grip on it.

As he stepped over Ervin and Mayfield's corpses, he said, "Christ, guys, I'm sorry." He had heard—a long time ago, probably off of *Discovery Channel*—that when someone dies they could still hear everything going on around them, at least for a little while. Even though it might be a little too late, he wanted to say something consoling. Under the circumstances, however, he wasn't able to come up with anything more appropriate than, "I think there's some really bad stuff going down out there, so... I'm sorry if I'm not showing the proper respect here, and all that."

A dead arm snaked through the bars on the far side of the room, probing the dry air with stiff fingers. The accompanying moan was easily louder than the one coming from the lobby. Leon watched and swallowed hard as more arms appeared beside it, until both windows were a vertical sea of grasping hands.

Zombies had surrounded the building.

He decided he needed to hurry.

He ripped away the curtain covering the window in the door, fully revealing the clinic's intruder. The skin-eater was waterlogged from head to toe, all swollen and moldy and funky, swaying dumbly side to side like a boat caught on a calm wave. Below the very uncomfortable-looking, nut-hugging shorts of its brown UPS uniform, lots of meat was missing from its legs, having been feasted on long ago. How it was able to walk now, Leon didn't know, and didn't care.

The window was composed of two panes of glass separated by wire mesh. The *3M Security* sticker in the lower left corner had never been peeled off. Leon could remember hauling the door out of a *Lowe's* near Providence a long time ago during one of the scavenger hunts. If he had known where the door was going to be mounted, he would have neglected it from the Procurement Committee's list and said it couldn't be found.

He poked at the glass with the metal bar to test its sturdiness—even though he had already given it a thorough inspection with his elbow—and realized that it was pretty damn solid even against the brunt of metal.

"This can be done," he said aloud, wanting the encouragement.

He took two steps back and then dashed forward, bearing the metal bar at his hip like a battering ram.

The noise wasn't nearly as loud as he thought it'd be; the crash was muffled because of the wireframe. His first stab broke roughly a quarter section of the first pane of glass, dented the wire, and sent shards of the second pane crashing to the lobby floor.

The former UPS driver didn't flinch. It had both its greasy palms on the glass, streaking gunky residue like fingerpaint. It eyed Leon, smitten.

Leon jabbed again. This poke pushed the wire back even further and sent more shards of the second pane crashing down.

Making noticeable progress, he held the bar over his head like a spear and jabbed downward. A six inch wide section of glass was broken away on both sides, and the wire mesh was peeling from its lining and bending outwards.

Once enough of the glass was gone and the wire mesh was pushed out of the way, Leon made to stick his hand through the hole so he could reach the doorknob on the other side. But the zombie saw the opening too quickly and reached its own hand through, disregarding the sharp glass digging into its skin.

"No, you dead prick," Leon said. "That's mine. Get your fucking hand out of there."

The zombie groaned defiantly.

Leon jabbed at its fingers with the tip of the metal bar, breaking three of them and slicing another off at the knuckle. The severed ring finger fell motionless to the floor on Leon's side of the door. Still the zombie did not remove its hand from the hole, instead reaching in even further, all the way up to its elbow. Leon broke its wrist with an overhand swing, but that didn't accomplish anything either.

He pressed the blunt edge of the bar squarely into the zombie's palm and manually maneuvered its arm back through the hole. Once it was out, Leon situated the bar against the zombie's sternum and gave it a hard push. Thankfully the bar didn't penetrate, and the sudden motion sent the zombie stumbling backwards. It was able to keep its feet coordinated for two steps before it was unable to keep pace and collapsed against the receptionist's desk.

Leon knew that would allow him a few seconds before the zombie could recuperate and stand up again.

He fit his hand through the opening in the glass, being very careful to steer clear of any sharp pieces that had already penetrated the zombie's skin. He was pretty sure the cure that had been shot into his heart the night before would not protect him from future infection, and he wasn't about to risk it.

Getting lucky twice in one lifetime is too much to hope for, he thought.

He gripped the doorknob on the other side and gave it a turn. It unlocked automatically. He carefully pulled his arm back through and placed it on the interior doorknob. He turned it and pushed the door open.

For some reason he expected an alarm to sound as if he had done something wrong, and when a peculiar noise gradually built up in his ears he figured it was the alarm he was expecting. The noise fought against the wail of the fire whistle for supremacy, and when it reached a crescendo, Leon recognized it as a whined-out diesel engine circling around the clinic. There was the sound of gears grinding, then catching, and the noise softened to a steady rhythm.

It's in third gear, whatever it is, Leon reasoned. *And picking up speed*.

Undead arms that had previously been assaulting the barred windows momentarily vanished. They had either been run over or taken a new interest in the vehicle passing by. But then the arms returned—whether new ones or old ones—and were just as relentless as before.

On the other side of the lobby in front of the receptionist's desk, the former UPS driver lifted itself to its feet and took two staggering steps in Leon's direction.

Leon dashed forward, gracefully swinging the pole upward in a perfect arc with all the momentum he could muster, bashing the ghoul on the underside of its chin. Its feet left the ground and its body went horizontal as it flew backwards like a pole vaulter at the apex of his jump, and hit the lobby floor all at once.

Leon bashed it in the skull as it lay there, finishing it off.

The entire clinic suddenly trembled. At the same time the main door shuddered against its frame, an ear-splitting crash made Leon wince. It sounded almost like an explosion, and it was too obnoxious for thunder. It had been *something else*—something bad—and Leon knew it.

The main door leading outside suddenly burst open again, rattling against its pneumatic closing system, kicking a knocked-over potted plant across the room and spewing black soil all over the pristine carpet.

A whole gush of skin-eaters shuffled inside, taking long strides, eyes wide, mouths agape, screaming incoherently, reaching out with waving arms. But they weren't immediately after food, Leon realized—they were taking shelter. They were scared of something— something that had them frenzied. Leon knew there was only one thing that really scared a dead person—*fire*—and peering over the zombies' heads and through the open doorway, he could see it raging in the hotel across the parking lot.

Situation: Officially FUBAR.

He hurled the metal pole like a javelin, but turned away before he could see what effect it had. He was already circling the receptionist's desk, going for the abandoned wakizashi—a much more practical weapon in close quarters.

He snatched it up and twirled it. He knew he needed to go for foreheads and no stroke could miss. He steadied himself. Sweat accumulating from his brow flowed around the bridge of his nose and into his eyes. He squinted it away.

And as the ghouls approached, it occurred to him how unprepared he was.

No shirt. Flimsy pajamas. In my bare feet...

—I am so screwed.

The first zombie to stagger close enough lost its scalp after a sharp slice of the wakizashi. A fluff of hair flew from its head like a toupee swept away in a breeze—chunks of skin and skull and brain matter dangling at the roots—and swirled round and round through the air until it came to rest on the carpet. When it finally settled, it looked like the road kill remains of a small animal. The zombie collapsed on top of it, freely leaking cerebrospinal fluid. It twitched a few times.

But there were more zombies—too many more—and the quarters were just too tight.

"Come on, puss-brains," Leon softly said. "I'll go out in a blaze of glory—will *you*?"

He reeled back the wakizashi and the remaining ghouls came at him all at once in one synchronized shuffle. Once he started swinging, however, cutting gooey slices in two undead foreheads, he realized that the zombies were attempting to shuffle around him instead of through him. They were still frenzied from the fire. Food wouldn't be on their minds until their simple instincts told them they were a safe enough distance from the flames.

This was the best chance he had to escape to whatever the hell chaos awaited him outside. He took it.

He rushed forward with the blade held horizontally in front of him, keeping one palm firmly planted around the hilt and the other palm flush against the flat side of the blade.

He cut a swath through the crowd. Zombies on his right were given sharp pokes in the temple with the wakizashi's pommel, stunning them at best, and zombies on the left had the blade carve through their skulls just above their ears. Most of these cuts were deep enough to cause termination. No more zombies were coming through the lobby entrance and the door was automatically closing on its own, its pneumatic system hissing rebelliously. Leon cleared the crowd and slipped sideways through the doorway before it closed completely.

He hadn't had room to maneuver inside the clinic, but outside he had all the room in the world, despite how many skin-eaters were there. He didn't know what to expect, but he was ready for anything. He glanced left, then right, wakizashi at the ready, waiting to be blindsided. Instead he was only soaked by the rain. The skin-eaters were too distracted by the fire across the street.

And once he gazed upwards, he was distracted, too.

His brain went numb. His fingers absently drummed the hilt of the wakizashi. All he could feel aside from his heart beating hard and fast in his chest was how cold his feet were.

The siren above the hotel was silent and probably had been for a while, and he was only now able to acknowledge how quiet the entire world was amidst the ringing in his ears. Even the torrential rain pounding the asphalt was softened almost to the point of tranquility, and all the screaming sounded like it was coming from underwater.

Out of sight, somewhere far up Sunset Avenue, he heard a voice behind a megaphone say, "ATTENTION EVERYONE. THIS IS MARSHAL YOUNG. YOU MUST EVACUATE THE HOTEL. MAKE YOUR WAY TO THE POLICE STATION. MY DEPUTY AND I WILL DO ALL WE CAN TO PROTECT YOU."

People are still in there?!

Leon had somehow assumed everyone was already in the process of evacuating. He didn't figure they'd wait around for an order telling to do so. But he now understood a lot, even though he had been locked in a recovery room in the clinic and unable to witness the disaster as it unfolded. It all registered to him in an instant.

No one had been ready for the skin-eaters. Not even the police. No one had been at the gate when the skin-eaters came through—and that was the only way they could have got in. If somebody had been standing there with a flamethrower, burning them down and driving them back as they came through the containment area, none of this would be happening right now.

Leon had expected *somebody*—somebody *else*, (not him, because he felt he had already done enough)—to take the situation seriously, and monitor it. That was all they needed to do. He wondered if he was the only one in all of Eastpointe who knew how dangerous the world still was. Sure, he lived within the walls too, but he had never allowed those walls to fool him. Never.

He rapidly shook his head to gather his senses. He had to go somewhere—do something—not stand in place. But where do you go—what do you do—when you arrive too late and nobody's there to tell you what's going on?

Across the street, he could see windows on the second and third floor—(except for the ones with fire and smoke billowing out of them)—lifting open and silhouetted human figures climbing out. Some immediately leaped. Others hung by their palms from the windowsills before letting go.

Leon couldn't bring himself to watch them fall. The scene in front of the hotel was a nightmare. He felt as if he had awoken to it instead of from it. It was a disaster—an old school disaster—and if the world had never gone to hell there would be news crews pulling up in their vans by now. The footage would have been on the ten o'clock broadcast.

Of the dozens of people that dropped from the windows, only a few were picking themselves up off the pavement. They were in shadows and Leon couldn't make out their faces. He didn't know if they were people he knew personally or not.

And for that, a part of him felt relieved.

The people were panicking, and instead of taking a moment to realize they were safe within the heat provided by the flames consuming the hotel, they were dashing headlong into the waiting arms of the surrounding skin-eaters. They were immediately gobbled up, swallowed under piles of clacking teeth and clawing hands. One man was running with his shirt caught on fire, frantically ripping it apart and tossing it away. Once the flaming shirt was gone, however, zombies closed in and tackled him.

It was the Fourth of July party, Leon knew. Everyone in town was at the hotel. That one building **held** everyone he had known for the last five years. Five years before that, he hadn't known any of them.

And they were all dying all at once.

Run, a voice inside him said. *Go back to Maine and find your old house. You could even plant a swell little garden outside, just like grandma had. Everything would be hunky-dory.*

The wakizashi slipped from his fingers and clattered to the pavement. The reverberating clanging noise it made was too loud.

Run and you'd be all alone. Snap to, goddammit.

He reached down and swiped up the wakizashi. He held the handle as tightly as he could with both of his trembling hands.

He winced and shuddered. The scent of death was in the air. It was similar to the smell he recalled when Delmas and Mike and Chris had their lives abruptly ended.

Do something. Come on. You've got nothing to lose now.

He remembered the voice over the bullhorn—the Marshal of Eastpointe telling everyone to evacuate to the police station. That meant there was still at least one person out there trying to salvage this situation. That meant there was still at least one person out there who hadn't given up hope.

Be part of the problem or part of the solution. Your choice.

He wondered if there was anything *worth* salvaging—or even enough to salvage anything at all.

Nonetheless, he forced his cold, bare feet to press forward. First his left foot, which he lifted up and placed in front of him. Then his right, which he placed in front of his left. He repeated this cycle even though he had no idea if, in the end, it would accomplish anything at all.

He had a path to follow, at least. There was a gap like a tunnel through the multitude of skin-eaters, stretching all the way from the plaza parking lot to the hotel parking lot across the street. The empty space was filled only with terminated corpses, some showing busted skulls from the impact of a collision with a fast-moving vehicle, others flattened or torn almost in half, tread marks easily apparent.

The path was the width of a large truck, maybe a semi or something like that, but Leon didn't put two and two together until he actually saw the truck—a flatbed for farm use—sticking halfway out of the hotel. Fire was erupting from all sides of it.

And Leon suddenly realized—*somehow just knew*—who was the cause of it all.

Vaughn.

Leon could picture him setting the truck in motion and jumping out at the last moment, grinning like a jackal and laughing like a mad bastard.

But why? Why would he do this?

Leon carefully stepped over the bodies scattered through the path, reminding himself he could not step on anything sharp. He couldn't allow his skin to be breached. It that happened, the slightest contact with anything undead might mean the end of him.

He was going to survive this. He was determined to.

Zombies were refilling the gap on both sides like sand pouring into an hourglass. They reached out for him, lurching forward, gaspless moans preceding each step. He probably looked like the easiest meal they ever laid eyes on.

Leon focused his eyes straight ahead. He crossed the road and placed his feet on the parking lot in front of the hotel. He stopped.

Golf carts that had been in the path of the flatbed were strewn all over, on their sides and on their tops. Little jagged pieces of them were everywhere. He stood up on his tip-toes and gingerly situated his feet around them, sidestepping almost in reach of the skin-eaters.

He focused forward again, looking past the zombies and even past the people running away from the hotel. Some were screaming. Others wore their terror on their faces as if they had been permanently molded from plaster. They would be inconsolable. Leon knew nothing he could say to them right now would slow them down. He would try to help the ones he felt he most likely could, and get them to the police station. He decided that was his plan. And strangely enough, it seemed the ones he could most likely help were those already injured by their fall from the windows. They weren't running around. They would listen.

Leon circled the perimeter of skin-eaters, and stopped. He raised his wakizashi. His hands weren't trembling from fear anymore—they trembled from an entirely different emotion altogether. He gritted his teeth.

He had located Vaughn.

He stood like a scarecrow not thirty yards away, hovering with one boot in the air, ready to bring it down on someone cowering on the ground below him. And when Leon narrowed his vision he saw that that cowering person was a female and she was injured. He recognized the shape of her easily enough.

—It was Courtney.

Not her, too, Leon thought. *Not her. You're not taking her.*

At the top of his lungs he cried, *"Vaughn!"*

Vaughn's body froze in the boot stomp position as he jerked his face in Leon's direction. The outline of his form wavered in the smoke, almost ethereal against the backdrop of flames. The rain had melted his stringy black hair flat in front of his eyes—and any other time those eyes might have intimidated Leon.

Courtney—*thank Christ*—had enough wits about her not to linger below Vaughn's presence. She used her elbow to drag herself weakly across the pavement, away from him and away from the skin-eaters.

Vaughn glanced down at where she had been, then shot his attention back to Leon. He lowered his boot and placed it on the ground. He slowly shifted his whole body in Leon's direction. He stood there, unmoving, for what seemed like an eternity.

Leon pointed the wakizashi at him and took a step forward. He shouted, "You and me, motherfucker!"

Vaughn didn't reply, but he might have grinned. Leon couldn't be certain.

Vaughn turned on his heels and slowly paced towards the hotel, seemingly in no big hurry. He walked with contempt by another female form cowering on the ground—Courtney was trying to lift her up with one arm, Leon noticed—and headed to one of the windows.

Alexis?! Alexis, too?!

The whites of Leon's eyes transformed red with rage. He stepped forward.

Zombies in the perimeter reached out for him. To Leon, they were just irrelevant scenery now, like the fake forest panoramas in family photos. They might as well have not even been there. He strode past any that weren't directly in his way, but those that stumbled too close were shoved to the ground with an almost indifferent attitude. They moaned—even *whined*, it sounded like—at having their instinct to eat be so blatantly disregarded.

Vaughn reached the window he had been heading to. There was a man propped up against the bars on the inside with the blade of an axe lodged in his skull that kept him upright. Vaughn placed his boot on the man's head, next to the blade, and yanked the axe free. Blood sprayed high into the air and the man's corpse slumped away from the window, disappearing inside. Leon couldn't recognize who it had been.

Vaughn, now carrying the shiny red axe, started walking towards Leon, more than willing to meet him face to face. Behind him the window inexplicably exploded, but Vaughn did not even wince. He continued walking forward at his own pace.

Accelerant, Leon realized.

There were big red jugs purposefully placed outside the window of every room that wasn't already on fire. They probably contained kerosene—or gasoline.

Vaughn's making sure he finishes the job.

Leon swallowed hard. He knew Vaughn was just too systematic, too logical and too methodical—and always had been. Quickly studying the heavy-duty fire axe Vaughn carried and comparing it to the thin blade of the wakizashi in his hands, he realized he could not stack up. There were just too many ways that Vaughn was better than him, including being smarter and tougher.

Leon accepted that he was scared. He stiffened up and proceeded forward, even against Vaughn's audible taunts.

"Yeah, you and me, Leon," he said. He motioned him to keep coming forward with a slight wave of his fingers. "Don't sing it—bring it."

"I'm going to end you, motherfucker," Leon replied, his voice almost crackling.

He continued closing the distance between them.

Vaughn chuckled. "And here I thought we were best pals. Isn't that what you said? Hell, I liked you so much I was going to ask you to prom."

Immediately after uttering the last syllable, Vaughn lunged forward, sweeping the blade of the axe in a wide arc.

Leon really hadn't been ready for it. He instinctually jumped backwards to stay clear of the blade, but his foot collided with a body lying prone on the ground. He wasn't sure if it had been a zombie or a human. He stumbled and fell.

Vaughn was grinning. There was no mistaking it now. There was no doubt about it.

Leon jumped back to his feet. He pointed the wakizashi straight at Vaughn and circled him. The blade provided some much-needed distance. When his fear left him, it left him empty. He wished he had his adrenaline back—or even his anger. He had nothing driving him now, keeping him focused. He would have to think his way through this on his own cognizance.

Vaughn swung again, showing no fatigue. The hefty blade of the axe met the paltry blade of the wakizashi with a loud clash and Leon nearly lost his grip on it. It vibrated violently in his hands. He quickly cast his eyes at the tip. It was dented, but it wasn't broken. He realized that if he didn't want to render the weapon completely useless he would have to deflect with the blunt side of the blade. Ninja movies had neglected that part.

Vaughn swung the axe the opposite direction, this time with the pick-shaped pointed poll screaming only inches from Leon's nose. Leon deflected the axe by bringing his wakizashi in on the backswing and adding more momentum. Vaughn stumbled two steps as he struggled to slow the axe's impetus.

Leon took the opportunity to jab with his wakizashi, using it like a rapier. It had occurred to him that he could do one thing Vaughn couldn't: *thrust.*

The tip of the blade cut into Vaughn's left shoulder, near the joint, and penetrated at least an inch. Leon placed his palm on the wakizashi's pommel and drove the blade several inches deeper. A large portion of it disappeared into Vaughn's skin as blood churned around it. Leon expected to soon see the tip shoot out the other side.

Vaughn stayed calm. He planted his boot in Leon's chest and kicked him away.

Leon lost his grip on the sword. It spiraled up into the air, spinning several times, reflecting flashing shades of red and orange from the nearby fire, and clattered on the asphalt. Sitting and leaning on his palms, Leon gasped and breathed deep to regain his air. He felt like he got hit with a sledgehammer, or received an electric shock.

Oh god that hurt.

Vaughn lowered his axe and used his free hand to study his shoulder, prying the wound apart with two fingers to see how much damage there was. He muttered, "*Fuck.*" Then, much louder, to Leon, "Fuck! For that I'm going to spill your insides!"

He went to lift the axe up high above his head and bring it down on Leon, but his shoulder gave out halfway up and the axe fell out of his hands. It hit the ground, kicking up a chunk of pavement. He stomped his foot and cupped his hand over his shoulder. He barked, "Arrgh!"

Leon tried getting to his feet, still sucking in air, when Vaughn appeared over him. Leon raised his left hand to try to defend whatever was coming. Vaughn grabbed all four fingers on his left hand all at once in a very tight grip, then twisted and turned and bent them backwards.

Leon felt all four of them break at the same time, near his knuckles. He opened his mouth to scream but couldn't, so instead his mouth hung open like a person ready to vomit but only able to produce dry heaves.

Vaughn pressed forward, putting Leon on his back, his lips curled in a sneer. Leon remembered enough of his judo training to continue rolling. He flipped Vaughn over and landed on top of him, straddling his torso.

They were very close to the hotel now. Leon could feel the heat from the flames warming his back. From the corners of his eyes he could see they were near the rear end of the flatbed truck. Clumps of the burning hay bales had spilled over the side and the rain was being ever harassing, trying its best to douse them, but the flames continued defiantly licking upwards.

On his back at the bottom of the brawl, Vaughn reached for Leon's eyeballs. Leon shoved the index finger of his uninjured hand into the gaping hole in Vaughn's shoulder and started digging.

Vaughn yelped and covered up.

At first Leon tried to alternate left and right fists to Vaughn's face, but yelped himself when he tried to curl up the fingers in his left hand. So he used only his right hand, keeping his fingers as tightly clenched as he could, aiming for Vaughn's right eye and putting all of his weight into each punch. He got in four solid shots before Vaughn bucked his hips and slid out from underneath.

Leon tried to stand, but as he turned Vaughn kicked him in the forehead with the metal heel of his boot.

Glistening sparkles appeared in his vision. His head felt light on his shoulders and started drifting backwards. He caught himself on his elbow. As the twinkles he was seeing gradually dissipated, they were replaced by blood. Leon gingerly touched two fingers to his forehead and realized Vaughn's boot had cut a deep gash over his eyebrow. He could even feel the bone. He cupped his hand over it to prevent more blood from getting in his eye.

Looking up at Vaughn, he saw that he had done some satisfactory damage. There was more than just a mouse below Vaughn's right eye. It was black and bleeding and had almost immediately swollen over much of his face. Leon guessed he had broken his orbital bone.

Then he heard splashing noises.

Vaughn heard them too, as they were being directed solely at him, and confusedly lifted his forearm to his face. He took a sniff and his eyes opened wide. He mumbled, *"What the—"* and turned around.

With him no longer blocking the view, Leon was able to see.

Courtney and Alexis were each on one side of a big red jug, sharing its bulky, unbalanced weight between them. When Vaughn turned around, they let go and allowed the container to bounce off the pavement. They stepped backwards, retreating away from him.

Vaughn growled, "You fucking cunts." He turned to step after them, but stopped and hunched over in pain, clutching his wounded shoulder with both hands.

Gasoline had gotten into the hole left by the wakizashi's blade. Leon knew it had to sting like a bitch.

"That's it, Vaughn," he said, lifting himself to his feet, blood dribbling from his brow. "It's over. You're done."

Vaughn turned away from the girls and faced Leon. He attempted to stand fully upright, but wasn't completely able. He still held his shoulder in both hands. He said, "It's over, huh? Checkmate? Is that what you're saying?"

"Yes," Leon said. "Come on, man. You know how this could end. Don't make it be that way." He paused, swallowed hard, and added, *"Please don't make it be that way."*

Vaughn managed a smile. "You know," he said, "my only regret is that I can't kill *everybody*. World's just too goddamn big for that."

"No, man, *don't*," Leon pleaded. "Don't make me do it."

"You win, you quintessential hero you," Vaughn said. "Good wins the day. Bravo. Fair maidens in every kingdom applaud you."

Leon blurted, *"No-Vaughn-don't!"* but Vaughn was already in motion.

Leon performed the finest Tae Kwon Do spinning thrust kick in his entire life—and he despised for what purpose, but he had to use the most powerful kick in his arsenal—catching Vaughn squarely in the sternum and sending him recoiling backwards with tremendous velocity.

Vaughn's spine collided with the edge of the flatbed and his boots trampled over the burning straw nearby. His entire body was covered in flames in less than a second, but he did not scream—not even once. His hair singed away to nothingness almost immediately, and soon after that his face melted to blackness. He flailed his arms before collapsing to the pavement in an unrecognizable heap. A moment after that, he was a motionless ball of fire.

Leon turned away. The smell of burning skin was so pungent he felt the tiny hairs in his nose wither. He had the urge to sneeze.

He staggered woozily. He inspected the cut above his eyebrow with his fingertips and when he brought his hand back down he saw it was covered in a thick layer of blood. He was losing too much, he realized.

He could vaguely discern Courtney at his side, asking him politely not to pass out.

He opened his eyes as wide as he could, and focused. Alexis was standing nearby, waiting to be told what to do. Her nose was shoved gruesomely out of whack, and bleeding. Courtney wasn't any better. Leon could tell by the way she was cradling her elbow that it was either dislocated or broken. Behind them, the hotel was now completely engulfed in flames. In front of them were hundreds of skin-eaters, and even those that had recently fed were wanting more. They were screaming and it was difficult to hear anything else.

But there were other survivors—ten or so, Leon saw—people who had not ventured too far from the burning hotel and snatched away by undead hands.

At least a few lives could still be saved.

"Everybody grab a gas can," Leon said. "We need to clear a path to the police station."

Remnants

THE SECOND FLOOR OF THE OFFICE wasn't much roomier than a standard attic. A person could stand up straight in most of it, but along the edges they would have to hunker down where the roof sloped in at a sharp angle. A long time ago the building was Eastpointe's billing office, where monthly invoices for electric, water and other expenses were calculated, and when Tyrell took it over for his own use he had had to empty the archives on the second floor. Mountains of boxes full of data processing forms and personnel files were hauled out in favor of cabinets chock-full of guns and ammo, pre-packaged MRE's, bottled water, bottles of kerosene and any other supplies he thought useful, either by whim or premonition.

But to Tyrell, at that very moment, it all seemed pointless. The room felt more like a coffin than anything else.

He averted his eyes from the window as far as he possibly could as he stood up and slid the clip from his Glock to check his bullet count. Some time ago—he wasn't sure when, exactly—he had tuned out the background noise of dissonant jabberwocks like the static of a poorly-tuned radio station, and he was hearing only the music— the rather monotonous music—of Mizuki sobbing in the corner, despondent and shaking so much she was likely in shock, (and therefore inconsolable until such time she was physically capable of snapping out of it,) and the quietness of Kendra as she held her in her arms. As he watched them he realized for the first time, with a fair amount of disgust, that Kendra and Mizuki's relationship was not one of best girlfriends, but rather a condescending parental liaison. Ever since Terence had died, Kendra treated everyone like a child. Tyrell couldn't imagine what manner of disdain people felt toward her as they sat below her scissors, getting their hair styled in her salon. And how had that disdain reflected itself upon *him*?

He figured it might be one of the reasons he felt like he was always paddling upstream.

He counted five bullets remaining in his clip. He realized he should have more—*always keep it full*—so he walked over to one of the supply cabinets, opened it, and retrieved a case of 9x19mm parabellum rounds. He spent the next minute quietly reloading. When he was finished, he slammed the clip into the butt of his gun.

The noise was abrupt enough to rouse Kendra from her coddling. She kept her arms around Mizuki and looked over at him as if he was just an annoying distraction—a stepchild, or something. She dryly asked, "Ty, what are you doing?"

Tyrell said nothing yet. Instead he laid his gun on top of the cabinet and removed his slicker from his shoulders. He folded it up as carefully as he would an article of clothing just taken from a dryer and put it away on an empty shelf. He took some time to tuck his shirt back into his belt and hoist his jeans comfortably around his waistline. He brushed off his shoulders, adjusted the cuffs of his very professional-looking, immaculately white button-up shirt, and checked his armpits for any sweat stains. He reached over to the adjacent cabinet, opened it, and unsnapped a rubber band from a bundle of road flares. He pulled back his ruined hair, braids unraveled and disheveled from the rain, and fastened it into a ponytail. He had always disliked ponytails, though. He didn't understand the point of having long hair if he just kept it slicked back like short hair anyway. But for now it was the best thing to do. Satisfied with his kempt appearance, he retrieved his fully-loaded Glock and held it at his side.

He faced Kendra, and just as casually as he would say he needed to take a quick restroom break, he told her, "You stay with Mizuki while I go kill Danny Tasker. I'll be right back."

Kendra stood up quick, absently letting her arms slip from around Mizuki. With no strength to support herself, Mizuki slumped sloppily to the floor, shivering and staring blankly in the general direction of the bundle of rappelling rope that likewise lay abandoned across the room.

"Don't you dare do that, Tyrell Young," Kendra said. "It's just us now. We need him."

"*Nobody* needs him," Tyrell replied.

"We need the extra gun hand. I can't shoot, and Mizuki sure as hell can't either."

"Yes she can. Creyton taught her," Tyrell said, immediately feeling awkward about talking about someone while they were in the room—like gossiping too loud, or something—and furthermore referring to someone who was departed. He had convinced himself years ago that the names of the dead no longer mattered, but he somehow knew that rule would never apply with Creyton. Besides, Creyton wasn't dead. He would never be dead. It wasn't his style.

"For now, please just do as I say," Tyrell finished.

He did not address Kendra again as he stepped over to the door that would take him downstairs, but he knew she was surely taken aback, maybe even cursing.

The overhead light flickered once, then twice, but came back on and stayed bright. It made Tyrell wonder how long electric would continue surging throughout town. He knew there was nothing stopping those walking corpses from crossing the bridge over the Saugatucket River, and further knew that the nightshift crew in the power plant didn't stand a chance. He hoped the power would last long enough, at least—long enough to do what needed to be done.

I hope the jabberwocks at least appreciate the mess they've made, he mused.

He stopped in front of the door, acknowledging that *preparedness and caution* was indeed his mantra, even in his subconscious—even in his sleep. Years ago he could easily have installed a one-way deadbolt, but he hadn't. It worked both ways. Whoever would have thought that he'd have to open the son of a bitch from the topside? But apparently *somebody* knew, even if that somebody was just Tyrell's ego, that inner voice everyone possessed—that inner voice that provided the occasional intellectual orgasm.

He turned the deadbolt and opened the door. He stood on the top step, concealed from view from below by the ceiling at the level of his feet. He could see most of the empty cell against the bare western wall, but nothing else. He waited and listened. He watched to see if the Browning pistol he had given Danny would appear in front of his eyes.

After a few seconds, Danny Tasker's voice nervously called out from below, "Marshal?! Um... that you?!"

"Yes, Danny, it's me," Tyrell called back. "I need you to come out where I can see you, hands in the air. You know the drill."

"Fuck that!" Danny shouted, still unseen. "You're makin' to kill me!"

Tyrell couldn't bring himself to lie, not even this time, and never could no matter what the consequences. He considered lying to be the most pointless gesture in the world. It never accomplished anything, in his opinion, except for the liar's own diminished respectability and self-worth. Nobody liked a liar; they ranked right up there with thieves.

"That's right, Danny," he said. "I do plan to kill you."

He aimed the Glock towards the bottom of the stairs, at about the height he estimated would be Danny's center-mass should he really oblige Tyrell and show himself. But then he heard frantic clanging and clanking and the sound of metal scraping, and had a pretty good idea what was causing it.

He jogged down the stairs, but froze once at the bottom as a bullet from a gunshot sizzled right in front of him and splintered into the wall. He took cover. On the second floor, Kendra had heard the gunshot and was screaming her demand to know if he was okay. He didn't answer.

"Those dead people would've followed you right in if I opened the door for you!" Danny was shouting, slurring his words like the unsophisticated dirtbag he was. "I—I'm sorry Deputy Hathaway died, but—but he was a dick, man! But you're cool, and you're okay, so that's all that matters, right?!"

Tyrell jumped from his cover with both hands steadying his gun and his elbows locked, his sights set on Danny Tasker's heart.

But it was too late. Danny had already moved the metal security bar from under the doorknob and flung the door open. He fired three shots from the Browning toward the ghouls assembled on the lawn and dashed outside.

Tyrell ran after him, but stopped once he reached the open doorway. Zombies were not attempting to come inside just yet; they had turned their attention to Danny Tasker as he was shoving his way through them.

Get him, Tyrell thought, gritting his teeth. *Eat that son of a bitch.*

But the zombies didn't get a grip on him, unfortunately, being as Danny had been well-rested and able to sprint at full speed and scream like a banshee at the same time. He shoved his way through the scattered mob and dashed through the junction of Salisbury Lane and Sunset Avenue. He started fading from Tyrell's sight roughly halfway down Joy Drive, heading for the farmlands. Tyrell knew that if Danny stuck close to the irrigation ditches and didn't venture into the fields, he just might get away. But—

"*That's not right*," Tyrell said aloud. "That's... that's..."

Then Danny Tasker was completely out of view, having passed the last of Eastpointe's few streetlamps, and Tyrell realized he was very vulnerable as he gaped from the open doorway.

Though he refused to look, he knew the remnants of Creyton's body were just a few feet off to his left. Zombies on the lawn—some with fresh blood on their faces—slowly turned away from the direction Danny Tasker was last seen and tilted their heads up at Tyrell. They did not blink away the rain getting in their eyes, nor did they wipe off their mouths, nor did they rub their full bellies. They were unaware and unappreciative of it all.

Tyrell growled.

One of the zombies moaned and stepped up onto the porch. Tyrell lifted his Glock and squeezed the trigger hard, blowing the zombie's brains out the back of its head. It silently collapsed. He shifted his aim a tad to the right and squeezed the trigger hard again. Another zombie collapsed.

What was I thinking, he wondered, as he continued shooting, taking his time, absently emptying every bullet in his clip into an undead skull. It occurred to him that there might be *just enough* ammunition stockpiled on the second floor to clear out all the zombies on Salisbury and Sunset, but even then every bullet would have to be rationed—each discharged only after a careful aim and a steadying breath—with frequent periods of rest, and the substantial amount of time it would take was incalculable. It would take days— weeks, maybe.

There was no salvaging Eastpointe. He was a fool to ever believe there was even a chance. He knew that now. If only he wasn't so prideful—so *responsible*—to know when enough was enough, like he did five years ago when he convinced Creyton they should abandon their posts at the failing rescue station in Canonsburg, Pennsylvania, and flee north.

He was just about ready to slam the door shut, lock it, and re-secure the metal bar under the handle when a streak of flames crossed the lawn in front of him, causing the ghouls to shriek and scamper away like injured bugs. The part of his mind that instigated his nightmares tried to convince him that a fire-breathing dragon had landed.

He stepped out onto the porch to investigate.

The liquid charging the flames poured onto the grass and spread out over the water, pooling outwards and being extinguished at the same time, constantly struggling in a tug of war. However, before each surge of flame dissipated under the pounding rain, it was enough for a few survivors from the hotel down the street to proceed several feet further. When they confronted more zombies, Tyrell saw, they flung more liquid from red jugs they carried. The path they created was crude and short-lived, but effective enough.

"Marshal!" one of them yelled, dashing up to the porch, out of breath and noticeably limping on a sprained ankle. "We made it. We... we lost a couple on the way over, but... we made it. Help us. *Please.*"

All in the same motion, Tyrell hurriedly shuffled to the edge of the porch and planted one palm on the man's shoulder—a man he only then recognized as Harless Henline—and shoved him into the office as he used his other hand—the hand holding the empty gun—to wave the others along. He shouted, "Move, move, move, people!"

He tried to make out who they were as they scurried past, but was only able to recognize two of them against the darkness, the rain, the dying flames, and the expressions of pain and panic on their faces. One was Doctor Connelly, looking the healthiest of the bunch. The other was Alexis Turner—Creyton's adopted sister—nursing a badly broken nose.

Tyrell muttered, "*Christ.*"

Alexis and another girl (who Tyrell only knew as the hermit of Eastpointe, by the name of Colvin) had the arms of a male form across their shoulders, grunting as they lugged his weight between them. There was a large gash above his eyebrow and he seemed unable to walk on his own, likely from the blood loss. His face was a crimson mask.

"Are there any more?" Tyrell asked.

The Colvin girl looked back at him and shook her head *no*.

Tyrell studied the ghouls congregated on the lawn for a couple of seconds, silently calculating their number and how many would be able to actually stand on top of the piles and piles of terminated carcasses at their feet.

You got as good as you gave, he thought.

He stepped into the office and closed the door behind him. He locked the knob and the deadbolt, then shoved the security bar firmly into place.

He turned, faced the crowd, and did a quick head count.

Eleven.

Kendra, guiding Mizuki, appeared at the bottom of the stairs.

Twelve, thirteen.

And himself.

Fourteen.

Fourteen survivors—*but don't get too hasty there, Marshal*, he reminded himself—fourteen survivors out of five hundred-some-odd people living in Eastpointe. Fourteen. That was all.

He wondered if chaos would ensue and if he would have to spend the next hour calming everyone down, but then he realized that everyone inside his office had seen so many horrible things over the last few minutes that they were either despondent or apathetic now. It made them all eerily quiet. He figured they were waiting for him to take charge. They trusted him, he knew. Maybe they felt everything would be okay now that they were in his care.

The pressure was on.

"Are any of you bit?" he asked.

Some in the group, only now realizing the certain death that might unknowingly be waiting for them, gave themselves a hurried once-over inspection. When they were satisfied their fate wasn't sealed, faces started turning to Tyrell and telling him, "No."

He breathed a relieved exhale and brushed his forearm across his brow, slinging the sweat away. Behind him, he could hear a zombie scratching at the outside of the office door. He knew he would have to get used to it.

He stepped away and hunkered down next to Alexis Turner, who had sat herself in the chair in front of his desk. She wasn't acknowledging him, so he gently lifted her chin with two fingers. She stared back up at him with teary, blackened eyes, but he paid more attention to her broken nose. He soothingly told her, "We can reset that. Don't you worry. Can you breathe okay?"

She nodded softly and replied, "I can breathe through my mouth, but I feel blood running down my throat." She snorted, as if for emphasis. "Is Crey—"

Tyrell quickly shook his head.

Alexis frowned and gazed at the floor.

The kid with the bloodied face—his name was Leon Wolfe, Tyrell remembered—had been laid out in front of Tyrell's desk. The knuckles on his left hand were grotesquely swollen and his eyes were barely open. The Colvin girl was kneeling over him, holding his head in the cradle of one arm and telling him, "Stay awake. You have to stay awake." She turned to the others in the room, probing their faces, and focused on Dr. Connelly. She said to him, nearly snarling, "*Help him.*"

Dr. Connelly took the girl by surprise, grabbing her triceps with one hand and her forearm with the other, and with a shove and a twist, forced the elbow she had been dragging around back into its socket. She yelped and hunched over—out of his way, conveniently enough. It was cold, but effective. Two birds in one stone.

Tyrell immediately admired the doc's take-charge attitude. He reasoned he must have worked the ER when the world was normal.

He studied the cut on the boy's brow and said, "I need a suture kit."

Tyrell looked over at his wife. "Kendra." She turned to him. "Upstairs. First aid cabinet. It'll be on your left. Go."

Thankfully she obliged right away.

Dr. Connelly turned to the girl, who was gripping her elbow tight to ward off the pain of having it so abruptly fixed, and whispered with a knowing nod, "He'll be fine."

Tyrell suddenly remembered that the girl was one of the specialists—one of the zombie killers. And so was Leon Wolfe, for that matter.

Things were starting to click into place.

Tyrell studied the rest of the faces.

Yes, things were starting to make sense.

First he acknowledged that his wife, Kendra, was safe—and that Rebecca Santoro, whom he had lusted over for far too long, was not among the survivors. Maybe someone was trying to tell him something. And when he looked around the room and acknowledged that Reverend Jeremy Hart was in the group—but not only that, he was also completely uninjured and still looking his usual spiffy self—Tyrell felt a chill.

There was hope yet. Hope of exactly *what*, though, he wasn't sure.

—Until he got an answer.

Sitting at Creyton's desk, grimacing at his sprained ankle, Harless Henline declared, "We need to evacuate Eastpointe. I, we—the Odd Fellows, I mean—had a contingency in place. We have two Greyhounds—loaded with plenty of supplies—and a tanker truck. They're in the parking garage. We just need to get there."

"And then what?" someone inevitably asked. "Where would we go?"

"Well," Harless Henline said, choosing his words, "there are places we can go."

Tyrell turned to face him, crossed his arms, and growled, "*Explain.*"

EPILOGUE

After Twilight

UPON FURTHER CONTEMPLATION, Tyrell realized he just needed to keep doing what he was doing. He had been a victim of circumstances out of his control, that was all. The fall of Eastpointe was not his fault.

His wife had survived. Creyton's widow and adopted sister had survived. Two zombie killing specialists had survived, and they could help him carry the slack. A doctor had survived and could tend to the wounded. One of the Odd Fellows, Harless Henline, had survived, and he could tell them where to go. Moreover, the goddamn *preacher* had survived.

Tyrell was convinced that if he stayed true to himself, everything would work out all right. He just needed to keep doing what he was doing, and as long as he did his best at whatever it was he was doing— just like he always did—everything would be okay in the end.

Further happenstances seemed to only verify this belief.

The storm was long gone by the time the evacuation plan was put in motion, revealing patches of encouraging blue sky between the breaking clouds, and the first thing Tyrell saw upon leading the survivors out of the office was his horse, George, standing at the edge of Salisbury Lane, waiting for him. It was then that Tyrell knew exactly what he had to do.

He told everyone he would meet them at the parking garage. He told them he would lead away some of the skin-eaters and provide a distraction. He told them to secure the Greyhounds and the tanker truck and wait for him. He told them he only needed ten minutes.

He took George for one last ride, whooping and hollering to attract as much attention as he could. Zombies were sloshing freely through the deep puddles that had formed in Eastpointe's streets, but now that they had eaten most everyone, they just moved aimlessly. They didn't appreciate what they had conquered; Eastpointe was just another landscape. It wasn't good enough for them—they needed more—so they lumbered after Tyrell with gaping mouths.

He went north, then east, riding past the cemetery on his left and the lake on his right, and entered the abandoned housing district. He dismounted his horse outside of a small bungalow where three zombies had gathered at one of the windows, trying to get inside. He calmly walked up behind them and shot all three in the back of the head.

With the window all to himself, Tyrell slid it to the side and hauled his muscular frame through the gap where iron bars used to be. It was easy—more than just a convenient happenstance. It was proof that the world had acclimated to him—to his style, to his way of doing things. It constantly provided him opportunities to keep things lawful and right.

He stood on the dirty carpet inside and brushed himself off. Sitting on the couch in front of him, partly lit up by the candle flickering on the coffee table, appearing not entirely surprised to see him, Danny Tasker said, softly, "I knew you'd show up."

Tyrell nodded. "That's right, Danny." He snuck a quick peek out the window to check how many zombies had seen him enter. They were scattered throughout the housing district, but not too thick. They wouldn't be a problem as long as he didn't linger.

Danny looked away and plucked the cherry off his joint, rubbing his fingers together in a *world's-smallest-violin* gesture, and placed the roach in one of the niches in the ashtray, for later. The marijuana smoke had already fogged up the entire living room.

"First off, I want to apologize for what happened at the station," Tyrell said, waving the air clear in front of his face. "I shouldn't have lost my temper with you. It was wrong of me. Besides, a Wild West gunfight would have been silly. Don't you agree?"

Danny raised his head and stared at him oddly. He was really, really stoned, and was probably struggling to mentally keep pace.

"We almost had one there, didn't we?" Tyrell said, chuckling a little. "An old-fashioned shoot-out. That's not the way things should be done."

Danny sniffled and retrieved the glass of water from the table next to him. He put it to his lips and continued swallowing in big gulps until there was nothing but ice cubes clinking around at the bottom. He said shakily, "Do you want a drink, Marshal? I'd be happy to pour you one. Power went off a couple hours ago, so if you want a cold one from the 'fridge, you'd best have it now."

"No thank you," Tyrell said, sliding the bundle of black rappelling rope from his shoulder. "No time for a drink—we're evacuating. I just found out there are other people in the world out there. People like us, hopefully. We're going to see if any of those people will take us in."

"But when you say *us*, you probably don't mean *us*, do you?" Danny asked. He chomped down noisily on an ice cube.

Tyrell nodded. He took a moment to look upwards and toss one end of the rappelling rope across an exposed beam in the attic. Then he went on, "Those people we're going to meet will be better off never knowing you, Danny. That's not me being insulting, it's just the truth. Bringing you along wouldn't be good for anyone at all. We're going to have our hands full as it is, you see, without having to worry about what kind of shenanigans you're going to pull. You're just... You're weight we can't afford to carry. Do you understand?"

Danny didn't answer.

Tyrell continued, "But leaving you here to starve to death—or get eaten alive if those things break in here—that wouldn't be right. So I have to consider what would be right. This isn't comeuppance, or capital punishment, or revenge. It's justice. It's the most logical thing to do. That's what justice is: *logical*."

He grinned inwardly as he began knotting one end of the rappelling rope. It occurred to him that this knot—the hangman's knot—had been taught to him in jest a long time ago when he and Creyton were toddlers at Cub Scout camp. It would be deemed irresponsible in a later day and age, but Tyrell knew the world had just gotten too damned uptight. Hell, he could remember how he and Creyton used to play lawn darts—and how only a few years later all the lawn darts started disappearing from store shelves, (being replaced by excruciatingly boring board games like *Tiddly-Winks*,) at around the time when overzealous parents realized they could start suing companies that manufactured anything that was even remotely dangerous.

Whatever happened to personal responsibility?

Whatever happened to personal *accountability*?

Yes, the world had just gotten too damned uptight.

Tyrell knew the rappelling rope he was using was very slick, so he fashioned thirteen coils to add ample friction. When he was finished he allowed the noose to hang freely, then scooted a nearby chair across the floor, screeching noisily the entire way, and situated it squarely below the noose.

Satisfied, he stepped back and said, "All right, Danny. It's ready."

Danny didn't move. "W-what?" he asked. "You're goddamn stupid if you think I'm really going to put my neck in that goddamn thing."

"Well, I ain't stupid, Danny, so that means one of us is wrong," Tyrell replied. He retrieved his Glock from its holster. "I won't kill you—you don't have to worry about that. But what I *will do* is shoot both your feet, then your kneecaps, then your hands—whatever it takes until you finally act like a man and get on this chair."

"You think I can't do it?" Danny said. "You think I can't be a man? That was always your problem, Marshal. Nobody ever gave me a chance here in this town. Not even you."

"You're wrong about that, Danny. But I don't have time to argue." Tyrell nodded toward the chair. "Suck it up. Don't think about it. Just do it. And remember you're the lucky one. Not all of us will have the opportunity to keep our dignity when we go."

Danny snarled, "You think I'm afraid? I'm not afraid." He all at once stepped up onto the chair. The legs creaked beneath him. "You see this?! You see?!" He yanked the noose open and stuck his head through. "You're not better than me, Marshal. I ain't afraid. I'll go out peaceful. You'll die slow. And I want you to remember how peaceful I went when those fucking zombies are tearing you apart."

Tyrell pointed and politely replied, "Place the knot behind your ear."

Danny grunted at his anger not being acknowledged or reciprocated. With a sneer, he situated the knot behind his ear.

Tyrell tried not to pay attention to the way Danny trembled. He wanted to give the man as somber of a send-off as he could. "Now, you'll need to hop off of that chair to give yourself a longer drop. You want to go peaceful, that's the way to do it."

Danny studied the floor. He allowed the toes of one foot to creep off the edge of the chair and poked them downward as if testing to see how deep a puddle of water was. He lifted his gaze to Tyrell for a moment, (and Tyrell pretended not to see his tears,) then looked at the floor again.

He defiantly hissed, "*See you in hell*" and stepped off the chair.

His neck did not break. He hadn't given himself enough of a drop. Instead he dangled, legs flailing as they attempted to find the chair again, his fingers trying to squeeze between his throat and the rope, his tongue sticking out of his mouth, gagging. His face and eyes turned red, going on purple.

Goddamn it, Danny, Tyrell thought.

He lifted his right hand and grabbed the waistband of Danny's filthy jeans, scrunching as much into his fist as he could, and all at once yanked downward.

He heard Danny's neck snap—like someone twisting a sheet of bubble wrap—and felt his body go limp. The smell of loosed bowels reached his nostrils. He turned away, holding his breath, keeping his nose pinched.

He exited Danny's house through the front door. A few zombies had found their way onto the lawn, so Tyrell lifted his Glock at any blocking the path between him and his horse.

With the last of his business in Eastpointe wrapped up, it was time to meet the other survivors at the parking garage. He wasn't sure where the road would take them, but one thing was for sure:

Today was the start of something new.

NEXT:

Twilight of the Dead

EXODUS

DYING TO LIVE
LIFE SENTENCE
by Kim Paffenroth

At the end of the world a handful of survivors banded together in a museum-turned-compound surrounded by the living dead. The community established rituals and rites of passage, customs to keep themselves sane, to help them integrate into their new existence. In a battle against a kingdom of savage prisoners, the survivors lost loved ones, they lost innocence, but still they coped and grew. They even found a strange peace with the undead.

Twelve years later the community has reclaimed more of the city and has settled into a fairly secure life in their compound. Zoey is a girl coming of age in this undead world, learning new roles—new sacrifices. But even bigger surprises lie in wait, for some of the walking dead are beginning to remember who they are, whom they've lost, and, even worse, what they've done.

As the dead struggle to reclaim their lives, as the survivors combat an intruding force, the two groups accelerate toward a collision that could drastically alter both of their worlds.

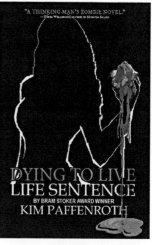

"A THINKING-MAN'S ZOMBIE NOVEL."
—DAVID WELLINGTON, AUTHOR OF MONSTER ISLAND

DYING TO LIVE
LIFE SENTENCE
BY BRAM STOKER AWARD WINNER
KIM PAFFENROTH

ISBN: 978-1934861110

Drop Dead Gorgeous
by Wayne Simmons

As tattoo artist Star begins to ink her first client on a spring Sunday morning, something goes horribly wrong with the world... Belfast's hungover lapse into a deeper sleep than normal, their sudden deaths causing an unholy mess of crashing cars, smoldering televisions and falling aircraft.

In the chaotic aftermath a group of post-apocalyptic survivors search for purpose in a devastated city. Ageing DJ Sean Magee and shifty-eyed Barry Rogan find drunken solace in a hotel bar. Ex-IRA operative Mairead Burns and RIR soldier Roy Beggs form an uneasy alliance to rebuild community life. Elsewhere, a mysterious Preacher Man lures shivering survivors out of the shadows with a promise of redemption.

Choked by the smell of death, Ireland's remaining few begin the journey toward a new life, fear and desperation giving rise to new tensions and dark old habits. But a new threat--as gorgeous as it is deadly--creeps slowly out of life's wreckage. Fueled by feral hunger and a thirst for chaos, the corpses of the beautiful are rising...

Drop Dead Gorgeous
by Wayne Simmons

ISBN: 978-1934861059

BY WILLIAM D. CARL

Beneath the dim light of a full moon, the population of Cincinnati mutates into huge, snarling monsters that devour everyone they see, acting upon their most base and bestial desires. Planes fall from the sky. Highways are clogged with abandoned cars, and buildings explode and topple. The city burns.

Only four people are immune to the metamorphosis—a smooth-talking thief who maintains the code of the Old West, an African-American bank teller who has struggled her entire life to emerge unscathed from the ghetto, a wealthy middle-aged housewife who finds everything she once believed to be a lie, and a teen-aged runaway turning tricks for food.

Somehow, these survivors must discover what caused this apocalypse and stop it from spreading. In their way is not only a city of beasts at night, but, in the daylight hours, the same monsters returned to human form, many driven insane by atrocities committed against friends and families.

Now another night is fast approaching. And once again the moon will be full.

ISBN: 978-1934861042

A ZOMBIE NOVEL BY TONY MONCHINSKI

Seemingly overnight the world transforms into a barren wasteland ravaged by plague and overrun by hordes of flesh-eating zombies. A small band of desperate men and women stand their ground in a fortified compound in what had been Queens, New York. They've named their sanctuary Eden.

Harris—the unusual honest man in this dead world—races against time to solve a murder while maintaining his own humanity. Because the danger posed by the dead and diseased mass clawing at Eden's walls pales in comparison to the deceit and treachery Harris faces within.

ISBN: 978-1934861172

Permuted Press
The formula has been changed...
Shifted... Altered... Twisted.™
www.permutedpress.com

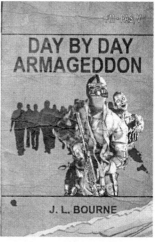

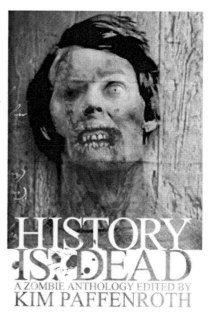
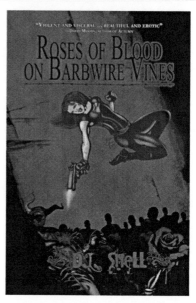

Breinigsville, PA USA
11 September 2009
223881BV00003B/1/P